D0019746

EARTH FLIGHT

Janet Edwards lives in England. As a child, she read everything she could get her hands on, including a huge amount of science fiction and fantasy. She studied Maths at Oxford, and went on to suffer years of writing unbearably complicated technical documents before deciding to write something that was fun for a change. She has a husband, a son, a lot of books, and an aversion to housework.

Visit Janet at her website: www.janetedwards.com
Or on Twitter: @janetedwardsSF

ALSO BY JANET EDWARDS

Earth Girl
Earth Star

JANET EDWARDS

Earth Flight

HARPER
Voyager

HarperVoyager
An Imprint of HarperCollins*Publishers*
77–85 Fulham Palace Road,
Hammersmith, London W6 8JB

www.harpercollins.co.uk

A Paperback Original 2014
1

Copyright © Janet Edwards 2014

Janet Edwards asserts the moral right to
be identified as the author of this work

A catalogue record for this book
is available from the British Library

ISBN: 978 0 00 744351 2

This novel is entirely a work of fiction.
The names, characters and incidents portrayed in it are
the work of the author's imagination. Any resemblance to
actual persons, living or dead, events or localities is
entirely coincidental.

Set in Meridien by Palimpsest Book Production Limited,
Falkirk, Stirlingshire

All rights reserved. No part of this publication may be
reproduced, stored in a retrieval system, or transmitted,
in any form or by any means, electronic, mechanical,
photocopying, recording or otherwise, without the prior
written permission of the publishers.

MIX
Paper from
responsible sources
FSC
www.fsc.org FSC™ C007454

FSC™ is a non-profit international organisation established to promote
the responsible management of the world's forests. Products carrying the
FSC label are independently certified to assure consumers that they come
from forests that are managed to meet the social, economic and
ecological needs of present and future generations,
and other controlled sources.

Find out more about HarperCollins and the environment at
www.harpercollins.co.uk/green

To Sal

PROLOGUE

This is the third book I've written. I wrote the first one for the norms, because I wanted to tell them what it's like to be born Handicapped. How it feels to be among the despised one in a thousand with an immune system that keeps you trapped on Earth, while everyone else can portal casually between the twelve hundred worlds of humanity.

I wrote about what happened at the start of 2789. How I lied my way into a class of off-world pre-history students, who were on Earth for their compulsory year working in the ruins of the ancient cities. I convinced them I was a norm, fell in love, got caught up in the rescue of a crashed Military spacecraft during a solar super storm, and was awarded the Artemis medal.

I thought that was the end of my story, but then an alien probe was detected approaching Earth, and the Alien Contact programme was activated. Its commanding officer needed someone like me, someone who knew Earth and was Handicapped, and I was the only one he'd ever met. He called in me and my boyfriend to help, and we ended up being the ones who sent a signal to the probe to trigger its communication sequence. The Military kept a lot of the details about that secret, so I wrote a second book about it in the hope that one day some future historians would read it and learn the full truth.

Those first two books are locked away in a highly restricted section of Military records, and now I only have one day to write my third book. This is about what happened after we sent the signal to the alien probe, and it isn't for the norms, or the historians, it's for me.

If I'm reading this, then I've already read the first two books, so I know Fian is a totally zan person. He'll tell me all about the things I didn't have time to write, or was too embarrassed to put into words. I hope I like him again. I hope I love him again. I hope we are very happy together.

But mostly I hope I'm not reading this, because if I am then my memory and everything that made me a person is gone, and this me is dead.

1

According to Earth Rolling News, Jarra Tell Morrath's favourite colour was green, she was a fan of the singer, Zen Arrath, and she was going to become a member of a Betan clan. My favourite colour was blue, and I didn't think much of Zen Arrath's legs, but they were right about the Betan clan.

'Oh chaos!'

There was the sound of a yawn from where two single beds had been wedged together. 'What is it this time?' asked Fian. 'Another interview with your ex?'

'No, I told Cathan he wouldn't just be my ex-boyfriend, but my *dead* ex-boyfriend, if he talked to the newzies again. Earth Rolling News has found out about me joining the Tell clan.'

The wall vid changed from showing a holo of me to showing one of Fian, and I shook my head. 'I still can't believe this. Only a few weeks ago, I could wake up in the morning and watch Earth Rolling News without seeing a single picture of either of us, but now . . .'

Fian sat up and brushed his long blond hair out of his eyes. 'We're famous now, Jarra. People on every world of humanity watched live vid coverage of us sending a signal to the alien probe in Earth orbit. Did you really think we could go back to join our pre-history class afterwards, and everyone would forget about us?'

'I didn't think we'd be going back to our pre-history class at all. I expected . . .'

I let my words trail off into a frustrated groan, remembering all the things I'd expected to happen. I'd thought everyone would be delighted Fian and I had sent the signal to the alien sphere. I'd assumed we'd stay with the Alien Contact programme, and be involved in all the exciting things they were doing.

I'd been a total idiot. Wherever I was, whatever I did, some people would never forget I was Handicapped. A week after we sent the signal, Joint Sector High Congress Committee ordered the Military to dump the throwback girl and her boyfriend.

'Colonel Torrek is furious about the way we've been treated,' said Fian. 'He's fighting to get us back in the Alien Contact programme.'

I'd been haunted by a secret fear for several days. I finally forced myself to put it into words. 'Colonel Torrek may be able to get *you* back, but not me. If High Congress make the Military move the base for Alien Contact to another world, like Adonis or Academy, then . . .'

Fian looked startled. 'That won't happen, Jarra. The alien sphere is in Earth orbit, so moving the base to another star system would make no sense.'

'It would make perfect sense to the prejudiced. They think the Handicapped are less evolved, subhuman, and hate the fact one of us helped send the signal to the alien sphere on behalf of humanity. They won't be satisfied with just throwing me out of Alien Contact, they'll want to get rid of the handful of other Handicapped who've been involved as well. Our faulty immune systems will kill us if we leave Earth, so they can neatly exclude all of us by moving Alien Contact to another planet.'

Fian shook his head. 'Colonel Torrek said only a few members of Joint Sector High Congress Committee are prejudiced against the Handicapped. The rest of the committee would never agree to move the base.'

'They agreed to order the two of us out of the Alien Contact programme, didn't they?'

'Yes, but there's a huge difference between getting rid of two people, and moving the entire base. You don't have to worry, Jarra. We just have to be patient and we'll both rejoin Alien Contact.'

I sighed. I wasn't a patient person, I hated waiting around in suspense like this, and all the newzie interest in us was making everyday life really difficult. It wasn't just that Fian and I daren't go out in public. We couldn't even get mail messages from friends, because our mail addresses were swamped with millions of messages from reporters. Military Command Support had tried giving us several secret mail addresses, but the newzies had somehow found out all of them within hours, so now everything was blocked except official Military mail.

The image on the wall vid changed to show the alien probe in Earth orbit, its central grey sphere almost invisible behind the thousands of constantly changing, multi-coloured strands of its glorious light sculpture. Hundreds of experts were trying to translate those light strands into words. I wondered how they . . .

A dreadful thought hit me. I shook off the spell of the mesmerizing light sculpture, and turned off the wall vid. 'Fian, you haven't told your parents about me joining my clan yet. You have to call them at once, before they see the story on the newzies.'

'I'm afraid it's already too late for that,' said Fian. 'Earth Rolling News have obviously been talking about that story all night, so the Delta sector newzies must be showing it too. It's morning here, but it's late evening on the inhabited continent of Hercules, and my father always watches the evening news on Delta Sector Vision.'

'I'm sorry.'

He shook his head. 'It's my own fault, Jarra. I should have told my parents weeks ago, but I kept delaying, waiting for a good moment. Stupid of me. There was never going to be a good moment to tell two prudish Deltans that their son's girlfriend was joining a clan from Zeus, capital planet of sexually permissive Beta sector.'

He sounded surprisingly calm about it, but I still felt horribly guilty. Fian had worked so hard to get his parents to accept me despite my Handicap, and now I was causing yet more trouble by joining a Betan clan. Fian's home planet, Hercules, was one of the strictest in conservative Delta sector. His parents were dubious about moral standards here on Earth, let alone those of notorious Beta sector.

'Changing my mind about joining my clan would be awkward now it's been reported on the newzies,' I said, 'but . . .'

'I'm not letting you change your mind just because my parents won't approve,' said Fian. 'You try and hide it, but I know you desperately want to have a family.'

I hated admitting it, even to myself, but that was perfectly true. I'd been portalled to Earth at birth to save my life, and my parents had handed me over to be raised as a ward of Hospital Earth. I'd grown up in their residences, hating the unknown parents who'd rejected me for being imperfect, but eventually I tried to contact them and was grazzed to find out they were Military. Moving to Earth would have meant abandoning their careers and wrecking the lives of my older brother and sister, so they had more excuse than most parents who abandoned their Handicapped babies, but . . .

Well, I still had a mess of conflicting powerful emotions about the parents who dumped me as a baby. The parents who I'd called months ago when I was on New York Dig Site and they were in far off Kappa sector. The parents who'd wanted to come to Earth to see me, but died before they could do it. I'd recorded my only call to them. One day, maybe, I'd be able to face replaying that conversation. One day, but not yet.

I thought I'd lost the chance of having a family forever when my parents died, but now their Betan clan was welcoming me as a member. I could never portal away from Earth, never visit the clan hall on Zeus, but I would still be part of one of the huge extended families of a Betan clan. I was staggeringly, unbelievably, bewilderingly lucky. Every kid in the residences run by Hospital Earth, whether they were in Nursery, Home or Next Step, dreamed of something amaz like this. It would have been incredibly hard to give up that dream, even for Fian.

'I'd better call my parents now.' Fian reached for his lookup.

By Deltan rules of behaviour, a couple of 18-year-olds on their second Twoing contract were barely allowed to hold hands, so Fian's parents mustn't see us together wearing only sleep suits. I pulled on a robe and headed for the door. 'I'll go and shower.'

Our pre-history class was spending the year excavating the ruins of the ancient cities of Earth, and staying in a series of basic dig site accommodation domes. That meant there were only three bathrooms for twenty-nine students, so I had to wait in a queue to shower. When I got back to our room, Fian was standing by the bed, his lookup discarded beside him. I didn't like the grim expression on his face.

'How bad was it?' I asked.

'Very bad.' Fian hesitated for a moment before continuing. 'My father ordered me to break our Twoing contract or he'll disown me.'

I had a sick, nervous feeling in my stomach. 'I could ask my clan to postpone the ceremony.'

'He isn't just angry about you joining the clan, Jarra,' said Fian. 'I've always been a bit . . . careful when talking to my parents about how we met. My parents thought I'd known you were Handicapped all along, but now my father's somehow found out what really happened.'

I stared down at my hands for a moment. I'd done the unthinkable at the start of this year, pretended I was a norm and lied my way into a pre-history course run by University Asgard in Gamma sector, instead of joining a course run by University Earth. I still felt guilty about the lies and . . .

'He's found out we're sharing a room as well,' Fian continued.

'Oh nuke!'

'He said a scheming ape girl had seduced me into a Twoing contract, and ordered me to dump the throwback right away.'

I fought to stay calm despite the insults. 'He was understandably angry when he said that.'

'I told my father that you'd apologized for lying, and I'd chosen to forgive you. I told him I was a very badly-behaved Deltan, and sharing a room was my idea not yours. Then I told him I'd no intention of breaking our Twoing contract and he could nuke off! He ended the call then.'

Well of course he had. Fian's father would never tolerate his son swearing at him. 'Fian, I don't want you falling out with your father because of me.'

'It's not just because of you; it's because of a whole list

of things.' Fian's face flushed with anger. 'He spent years mocking me for wanting to study history instead of science, and saying what a disappointment I was compared to my brilliant older sister. His method of subtly breaking the news to my mother that he didn't plan to renew their term marriage contract was to put their house up for sale. Then there was the way he reacted when he discovered an alien probe had arrived at Earth and I'd been drafted into the Military to help the Alien Contact programme.'

'That was a bit . . .'

Fian didn't give me the chance to finish my sentence. 'I actually thought he'd be impressed by that. His son playing a leading role in the first contact between humanity and an alien civilization! My mother was proud of me, but my father just started ranting on about how I should have nothing to do with the Military because of some ancient family grudge.'

Fian had been on bad terms with his father for years. The big question was . . . 'Did you talk to your mother too?'

Fian nodded. 'My father had already called her and told her everything. She said I should ignore him because he's too cold-blooded to understand people with real emotions. She said all that matters to her is that we're happy together.'

I had a dizzy moment of relief. I should have guessed Fian's mother would react that way. She wasn't just a born romantic, but determined to take the opposite side to his father in every argument these days. Fian's parents were at the end of one of the standard twenty-five year term marriages for people who planned to have children but didn't want to sign up to an unlimited full marriage. Fian's mother wanted to renew the term contract, his father didn't, and the final weeks of the relationship were descending into open warfare.

Fian was deeply upset by his parents breaking up, and I'd no idea how to help him. I'd only ever had a ProMum and a ProDad, paid by Hospital Earth to spend two hours a week with each of their ten ProChildren, and that was nothing like having real full-time parents. Candace was a wonderful ProMum to me, but I had to make appointments to meet her, and I'd hardly seen my ProDad since our big fight when I was 12 years old.

I sighed. 'When I first agreed to join my clan, I never thought anyone except the two of us would know or care about it.'

Fian hugged me. 'We're famous now, and that changes everything.'

2

By the time Fian and I arrived in the hall for breakfast, the rest of the class had already set out the flexiplas tables and chairs. The wall vid was on, showing Gamma Sector News since most of the class were from star systems in that sector. I recognized a horribly familiar vid sequence and groaned. With my worries about Fian's parents, I'd forgotten today was 1 June, the anniversary of Earth Flight.

Every Wallam-Crane day, all the vid channels showed the footage of the first portal experiment. Every Flight day, they ran a sequence about the first manned interstellar flight by drop portal. Thankfully, we'd missed most of the incomprehensible scientific bit about how the transmitting portal does all the work, and the instant when the drop portal dust ring simultaneously exists at both transmission and reception point, stabilizing its own incoming signal.

'. . . together with power issues mean this is limited to dust particles. When a link is established between two normal portals, it can be held open indefinitely, but a drop portal establishes for a maximum of 5.13 seconds before the ephemeral receiving dust ring dissipates,' said the commentator.

Fian and I went to join the queue at the food dispensers

and I frowned gloomily at the available menu. The panic over the alien probe had disrupted their regular service and restock, so we'd run out of most meal options. I settled for a glass of Fizzup, a plate of toasted wafers, and some reconstituted Karanth jelly. There was plenty of Karanth jelly left because of the rumour that eating it made your baby Handicapped.

No one understood what caused a baby to be Handicapped, so norms had a lot of these nardle superstitions about it. Researchers were always claiming to be on the verge of a major breakthrough, but they hadn't achieved anything since they first established the basic facts of the triple ten. There is a one in ten risk of a baby being born Handicapped if both parents are Handicapped themselves. One in a hundred if one parent is Handicapped. One in a thousand if neither parent is.

Fian and I carried our trays across to sit with the other three members of class dig team 1 at our regular table. Krath greeted us with an exaggerated weary sigh.

'It's not fair making us work on a holiday. Playdon's a slave driver.'

Lecturer Playdon turned his head to call across the room. 'I'm a slave driver with perfectly good hearing, and Flight day isn't a holiday on Earth.'

Krath gave an embarrassed groan and looked at me. 'I thought Flight day was a holiday everywhere.'

Amalie leant across to hit him on the back of the head. Krath was one of the big group of students from Asgard, who'd chosen a course run by their home university, while Amalie was from a planet in frontier Epsilon sector. I wasn't sure exactly what was going on between them. Krath was definitely chasing after Amalie, but she seemed more interested in teaching him common sense than having a romantic relationship with him.

Krath sighed. 'What did I do wrong this time?'

'Think about it, nardle brain,' said Amalie. 'Most of the population of Earth is Handicapped and can't portal to other planets.'

'Exactly,' I said. 'Wallam-Crane day is a holiday here, because he invented the portal and we can at least portal around Earth. We don't really celebrate it though, because that was the first step towards interstellar portals a century later. Flight day was the start of Exodus century, everyone pouring off world to new planets and leaving Earth to fall apart, so we just try to ignore it.'

I glanced over my shoulder at the vid. The commentator was talking about the S.T.A.R. – Simultaneous Transmission And Reception – series of automated probes, while the screen was showing an image of a curiously shaped ship in Earth orbit.

Dalmora gave me a sympathetic look. She was the only Alphan in the class, the daughter of the famous Ventrak Rostha who made the *History of Humanity* vid series, and I'd resented her at first sight. With her waist-long black hair adorned with flickering lights, and her lovely dark face delicately highlighted with makeup, I'd expected her to be a selfish, spoilt aristocrat. Instead, I'd discovered she was one of the kindest, most compassionate people I'd ever met.

'Would you like the vid turned off, Jarra?' she asked.

I shook my head. 'I've seen it dozens of times before so it doesn't bother me.'

I munched on my toasted wafers, keeping my back to the wall vid, but of course I could still hear it. They'd finally got to the interesting bit, so the odious commentator stopped talking over the ancient soundtrack. The calm female voice of the mission controller was calling for final confirmations from the various teams. I knew every word of this by heart, and the sound of all the different voices as they spoke the archaic accented version of Language from almost half a millennium ago.

'Countdown is holding at sixty seconds. Final checks. Drop portal focus?'

'Drop portal focusing confirmed at 98.73 per cent of optimal.'

'Telemetry?'

'Telemetry is green.'

'Power?'

'Power is green.'

'My board is showing clear greens,' said the mission controller. 'Mission Control to Earth Flight, are you ready for this?'

'Earth Flight to Mission Control,' responded Major Kerr. 'I've been ready for this all my life. Let's do it.'

'Prepare to pick up countdown at sixty seconds and initiate power build on my mark,' said the mission controller. 'Mark!'

As the countdown started, I gave in and turned to watch the wall vid. The image on the screen showed the view through the front window of the Earth Flight ship, the blackness of space contrasting with the blue and white curve of Earth below.

'Thirty-five. Committing to auto power spike sequence . . . Now!' The mission controller's voice and the background chatter stopped. They were on auto sequence now. Nothing could stop the power spike building and firing the primitive drop portal, so they could only count down the seconds and hope nothing went wrong. Of the thirty automated probes in the S.T.A.R. series, twenty-four had made it to their destinations, but six had exploded when the power spikes went unstable.

Everyone had stopped eating now, and was watching the wall vid in silence. There was something about this vid sequence that compelled you to watch it even though you already knew exactly what happened.

'Five seconds,' said the voice of the mission controller. 'Four. Three. Earth Flight, take us to the stars!'

The image went totally black as the drop portal fired. There was an agonizing delay, with the sound of increasingly tense voices as Mission Control waited for contact from the tiny comms portal on board Earth Flight. Finally, there was a white flash that broke up into multi-coloured jagged lines. Those formed together for an instant, dissolved again into randomness, then stabilized.

It was a grainy picture now, from the days before they'd invented two-way comms portal twinning or message streaming. The scene it showed was almost identical to the earlier one, but the continents on the blue and white planet were a different shape.

'Earth Flight to Mission Control,' said the breathless voice of Major Kerr. 'Drop portal from Earth successfully completed. The comms portal established after only three mill of fine-tuning. I hope you're getting visual as well as audio feeds, because this is the most beautiful sight I've ever seen.'

There was an audible sigh from around the hall, as everyone released the breath they'd been holding, and the class started eating and talking again. The vid sequence still had a few minutes to run, but no one was interested in Major Kerr's spacewalk to detach the portal sections attached to the outside of his ship and assemble them. No one cared about how that created the first standard portal link between Earth and another star system, or the other ships that portalled in through it. No one wanted to hear how Major Kerr's first description of the new world led to it being named Adonis. They only cared about the symbolic moment when Earth Flight took humanity to the stars.

I bit my lip, remembering the Flight day when I was 4

years old. I'd sat on the floor with the other kids in Nursery, watched the vid coverage, and asked a nurse when I could portal to Adonis. She'd shaken her head and gently explained I couldn't do that because I'd die. It had taken me a few minutes to understand what she was saying. I already knew the people I saw in the vids had families, while my friends and I didn't. I couldn't believe I'd been cheated out of the stars as well.

I could still feel my shocked outrage at the monstrous unfairness of it. A feeling that was repeated again and again as I grew older. When I was 5 years old, laughing at a joke on the vids about stupid, ugly apes, and an older kid slapped my face and told me to stop laughing because the joke was about people like us. When I was 7, and there was a lesson at school about how Earth was run by the off-worlders on the main board of Hospital Earth. Other people, *real* people, got to vote about how their own world was run, but the Handicapped had no say in what happened on Earth.

The final insult was when I was 9, and discovered Earth was physically in the centre of Alpha sector but not legally part of it. The off-worlders hadn't just rejected me and everyone like me, they'd rejected Earth itself because we lived there!

Fian gave me a worried look. 'Are you all right, Jarra?'

My psychologist at Next Step kept telling me it was pointless making myself unhappy by brooding over things I couldn't change. I didn't have much faith in psychologists, but he was probably right about that. I forced away the old bitterness. 'I'm fine.'

The Earth Flight vid sequence ended. Krath went over to the wall vid just as a Gamma Sector News presenter started talking. 'Now the news headlines for today. Major Jarra Tell Morrath is to join one of the Betan Military clans.'

16

The entire class stopped talking and stared at me as if I'd grown an extra head.

'Talks between the two political factions on Hestia have failed to reach an agreement,' continued the presenter. 'The . . .'

Krath turned off the wall vid and gave me a grazzed look. 'Jarra, that story's a nardle mistake, isn't it? You aren't Betan.'

This was chaos embarrassing. Like most of the class, I'd grown up with prejudices about Beta sector. Only months ago, I'd been joining in their jokes about Betan sex vids, giggling at the scanty clothes Betans wore, and saying Beta sector couldn't be trusted because it had been on the verge of war with the rest of humanity during its Second Roman Empire period.

Then I discovered I'd been born into a Betan clan, and they actually wanted contact with me. Anyone who'd grown up in Hospital Earth's residences would understand exactly why I'd promptly rethought my attitudes, but I was in a class of norms. They wouldn't know how rejected kids longed to have a family, and I didn't want to explain that sort of private emotional stuff, so I kept my response simple and matter of fact.

'It's perfectly true. I was raised on Earth, but my birth family were Betan. You should have realized that. The newzies have been talking for weeks about me being descended from Tellon Blaze, and he was Betan.'

'Tellon Blaze was Betan!' Krath waved his hands in disbelief. 'I didn't know that.'

'Of course you wouldn't,' said Lolmack, open contempt in his voice.

Lolmack and Lolia were the only two Betans in our class. They were older than the rest of us, married, and had a Handicapped baby. At the start of this course, Krath had made some remarks about the Handicapped being subhuman apes. He'd changed his opinions now, but Lolmack still held a grudge against him.

'The other sectors never mention Tellon Blaze, the hero who saved humanity from the chimera of Thetis, was from Beta sector,' continued Lolmack. 'They never admit it was Beta sector that saved civilization from total collapse after Exodus century. They never tell our side of the Second Roman Empire, or try to understand our culture, or . . .'

'That doesn't matter now,' Lolia interrupted in an oddly tense voice. 'Jarra, is it true what Earth Rolling News is saying? The Tell clan are making you a clan member?'

Lolmack made a horizontal, air-slicing movement with his left hand; a classic Betan gesture of rejection. 'That's just an outlander news channel making a mistake.'

'It's not a mistake,' I said.

Lolmack stood up and hurried over to me. 'You're sure, Jarra?' he demanded. 'The Tell clan aren't just acknowledging your birth, but offering clan membership?'

I didn't understand the urgency in his face, but I nodded. 'The presentation ceremony is in three days time.'

'A presentation ceremony!' Lolmack turned to his wife. 'That would . . .'

'One of the Handicapped being formally presented to a clan of the *gentes maiores*!' Lolia put her hands to her face. 'If that happens . . .'

I was shocked to see she was crying. 'I don't understand why this is so . . .?'

'Jarra,' she said, 'a handful of clans have acknowledged a Handicapped birth, but none has ever offered clan membership. The Tell clan are of the *gentes maiores*, the aristocracy of Zeus. If they do this, it could change our lives!'

I stared at her, totally bewildered by her dramatic words.

'There's a lot of prejudice against the Handicapped on Betan worlds,' said Lolmack.

'It's like that in all the sectors,' I said. 'I've grown up watching off-world vids, and they all use the same insults. The only difference between Handicapped and norms is a fault in our immune system, but they call us throwbacks, Neanderthals, and ugly, smelly apes.'

'It's a bigger problem in Beta than the other sectors though, because of the clan system,' said Lolmack. 'The shame of a Handicapped birth doesn't just affect the parents, but the whole clan.'

Lolia nodded. 'When our baby was born Handicapped, the other partner in our triad marriage instantly divorced us. Lolette wasn't genetically his child, but . . .'

Lolmack went to put his arm round her. 'By saying that, he proved himself lower than the clanless. If things had been reversed, I would still count Lolette as my daughter, and still be here with you on Earth.'

Lolia smiled up at him. 'I know that. He was more of a loss to you than to me.' She looked back at me. 'Hospital Earth rules meant Lolmack and I had to choose between making our daughter their ward and never seeing her again, or moving to Earth to be with her. Clan council ordered us to give up our ape child or be disowned. To have our own clan calling our daughter an ape and threatening us . . .'

'Clan council had no choice,' said Lolmack. 'Alliance council had ruled the alliance could not afford the loss of status of a Handicapped birth, and threatened to remove our clan from the alliance if our child's birth became known.'

He pulled a face. 'So we joined this course to have an excuse for being on Earth. All this time, we've lived with the fact that if Lolette's existence becomes known, our clan cluster must disown us to save their position in the alliance, but if the Tell clan welcome you as a clan member . . .'

'It would change everything,' said Lolia. 'Just seeing you on the newzies has already made a difference to the way Betans speak of the Handicapped. Every clan was watching the vid coverage when you and Fian sent the signal to the alien sphere. Every clan saw how you looked and spoke and acted like any normal human. Every clan heard you named as a descendant of the great Tellon Blaze.'

Her words tumbled out eagerly now. 'Jarra, if a clan of the *gentes maiores* make you a clan member, alliance council may agree to acknowledge Lolette's birth, perhaps even permit her to be formally presented.'

Lolmack shook his head. 'Don't build your hopes impossibly high, Lolia. The vital thing is to have Lolette openly acknowledged, so we can stop living in fear of being made clanless. We must contact clan council at once.'

I was startled to hear Lecturer Playdon join in the conversation. 'I'll excuse both Lolia and Lolmack from this morning's dig site work so they can discuss this development with their clan. Tomorrow, we'll still be working on the Eden ruins in the morning, but in the afternoon we'll be packing and moving to London Main Dig Site.'

'But the General Marshal's making a statement about the Alien Contact programme tomorrow afternoon,' said Krath. 'We can't miss seeing that.'

'The announcement is at 17:00 hours Earth Africa time,' said Playdon. 'We'll stay here to watch it, but I want everyone to be packed ready to leave directly after it finishes. Fortunately, Earth Africa is on Green Time plus two hours, while Earth Europe is on Green time, so we'll gain two hours in the move.'

He paused and pointedly glanced towards Fian and me. 'I'll do a last inspection of the dome just before we leave.

Students aren't allowed to move dome walls, so I'm sure I won't discover any of them are missing.'

Fian and I exchanged embarrassed glances, while the rest of the class laughed at us. Everyone knew we'd illegally moved the wall between our two single rooms to make a double.

'How many days holiday do we get before starting work on London Main?' asked Krath.

Playdon gave him one of his evil smiles that meant bad news. 'None.'

There was a collective groan from the class. We all knew Playdon's smile meant there was absolutely no point in arguing, but Krath tried it anyway.

'None? We're supposed to get at least three days break when we move dig sites!'

'You all missed an entire week of work due to the alien probe,' said Playdon, 'so you've got some catching up to do. Clear away breakfast now.'

I started piling plates on to a tray, picked it up, and looked at Fian. 'Do you believe me becoming a clan member will really help Lolia and Lolmack?'

'They obviously think so. It's much bigger than just those two and their baby though, isn't it? 92 per cent of Handicapped babies are handed over to be wards of Hospital Earth. The older sectors have the highest populations, so at least a quarter of those babies must be being born to Betan clans. If the clan attitudes change so it's easier for Betan parents to come to Earth with their baby, it could mean thousands of children each year have a chance to grow up with their family.'

Fian was right and my psychologist had been totally wrong. It wasn't pointless making myself unhappy over the unfairness of things, because there was something I could do to change them for the better.

21

When we sent the signal to the alien probe, it had been a significant moment for humanity. When the Tell clan of Zeus welcomed me as a clan member, it would be just as significant a moment for the Handicapped children of Beta sector.

3

At exactly 16:59 hours the next day, Fian and I sprinted into the hall and found the rest of the class sitting on neat rows of chairs facing the wall vid. We collapsed on to the two empty chairs next to Krath.

'What took you so long?' Krath shook his head at us. 'It was only one wall. You could have built a whole dome by now.'

'The wall didn't want to go back,' said Fian. 'We won in the end, but . . .'

Amalie sighed. 'Please don't tell me you fixed the bottom corners first.'

Fian and I exchanged glances. 'We did . . .' I said.

Amalie shook her head sadly at our incompetence. She'd been born only a few years after her world came out of Colony Ten phase and was opened up for full colonization, and had spent her childhood helping to assemble buildings from flexi-plas sections. 'It's much easier if you start with the top.'

'Why aren't you two in uniform?' asked Dalmora.

'We'll be going through Earth Africa Transit,' said Fian. 'Playdon suggested we'd be less conspicuous in civilian clothes.'

'It's starting!' Krath shouted.

Everyone went quiet and listened to the presenter on the wall vid. 'Earth Rolling News now joins the cross-sector live link from Academy in Alpha sector for an announcement by General Marshal Renton Mai, commander-in-chief of the Military.'

The image changed to show a man in a pure white uniform, standing at a podium with the flag of humanity behind him. He began speaking in a relaxed voice. 'The light-based communication from the alien probe clearly has a huge amount of data content. Deciphering that content and locating the alien planet of origin is likely to take a considerable period of time. Alien Contact is therefore moving from initial response phase into a longer term commitment and there will be a number of changes.'

I held my breath as the General Marshal went on.

'Military Base 79 Zulu on Earth will be upgraded and become the permanent base for the Alien Contact programme. It will also house two research groups. One investigating the alien technology discovered in Earth Africa, and the other concentrating on the light signals from the sphere.'

I started breathing again. Alien Contact was staying on Earth!

'The guard on the alien sphere will be maintained but downgraded in scale,' continued the General Marshal. 'A search for the alien planet of origin has already commenced in Alpha sector, and will be extended into other sectors.'

He paused for a moment. 'There are corresponding adjustments to the command structure. The command of the Alien Contact programme will become a General Staff position reporting directly to me. Colonel Riak Torrek is promoted to the rank of General and will remain in overall command of Alien Contact, and in direct command of the search efforts. Commander Nia Stone is promoted to Colonel and takes command of Military Base 79 Zulu and the guard on the alien sphere. Commander Mason Leveque is promoted to Colonel and takes command of the twin research efforts as well as threat assessment. Commander Elith Shirinkin is promoted to Colonel and takes command of the five Earth solar arrays.'

The vid image panned out to include the audience, and the General Marshal started taking questions from eager newzie reporters. I was startled by the first question.

'Delta Sector Vision here. What about Fian Eklund and Jarra Tell Morrath?'

'Captain Fian Eklund is promoted to Major, and Major Jarra Tell Morrath to Commander,' said the General Marshal.

I gasped, totally grazzed by my promotion. It was nardle enough being a Major, but . . .

'Commander Tell Morrath and Major Eklund will be reporting to Colonel Leveque while continuing with their specialist pre-history training,' continued the General Marshal.

'The rumours that High Congress ordered their removal from the Alien Contact programme have now been confirmed by several discontented committee members,' said the Deltan reporter. 'What's your opinion of this controversial interference in Military staffing?'

'The Military Charter states the Military should remain politically neutral,' said the General Marshal. 'I can't comment on the decisions of Joint Sector High Congress Committee, however a few hours ago I was sent extra clarification of that particular order for the public record.'

He glanced at the Military forearm lookup attached to his sleeve. 'High Congress state that Commander Tell Morrath and Major Eklund were removed because they do not have the appropriate skills to assist Alien Contact at this point. This is a purely temporary measure to enable them to continue their studies. They will return to the Alien Contact programme as soon as either the sphere's message is translated or the alien planet of origin is found.'

I sighed with relief. Fian and I would return to Alien Contact!

The General Marshal pointed to another of the forest of raised hands, and a woman spoke. 'Beta Sector Daily. What about Commander Tell Dramis and Major Weldon?'

'Commander Tell Dramis takes command of the search teams in Zeta sector, with Major Weldon as his deputy,' said the General Marshal.

My frustration returned. My cousin Drago was already out in distant Zeta sector searching for the aliens, and my old friend from Next Step, Keon, was helping with the research into the light sculpture. Fian and I would return to the Alien Contact programme, but not until some unknown time in the future.

A blatantly hostile voice asked the next question. 'Beta Veritas. Why promote Jarra Morrath, but not Drago Tell Dramis?'

'Bigot!' Lolmack and Lolia chorused the word before I'd worked out the significance of the man missing out the clan prefix in my name.

The tone of the General Marshal's voice made it clear he'd also realized he was dealing with someone prejudiced against me. 'I've promoted every officer who played a significant part in establishing contact with the alien sphere, including Commander *Tell* Morrath. Commander Tell Dramis and Major Weldon had already received their promotions, and Commander Tell Dramis was strongly opposed to the suggestion of a further promotion to Colonel. His exact words were that he'd rather be locked in a prison cell with a Zeus sewer rat.'

There was a burst of laughter from both the audience on the vid screen and my classmates. Drago had done a lot of talking on the newzies – his jet-black hair and devastatingly handsome face made him incredibly popular with their viewers – and everyone could picture him saying those words.

'Alpha Spectrum,' said the next questioner. 'How long will it take to find the alien home world?'

'That depends how far away it is,' said the General Marshal. 'Humanity currently has well-established inhabited worlds in Alpha, Beta, Gamma, and Delta sectors, fledgling colony worlds in Epsilon and Kappa sectors, and has just begun Planet First assessment of possible colony worlds in Zeta sector. A complete search of that area of space will take between five months and a year, depending on how we divide manpower and resources between Alien Contact and Planet First efforts.'

'A year!' The Alpha Spectrum reporter's words were echoed by Krath sitting next to me. 'But each sector only has 200 star systems. How can it possibly take that long to search them?'

'Each sector only has 200 *inhabited* star systems,' said the General Marshal. 'Portalling between inhabited worlds gives the illusion they're packed closely together, when they're actually scattered widely across space. We're extremely selective when we choose our colony worlds. For every star system with a planet satisfying the criteria of Planet First, there are a hundred with a planet where human beings could survive with some difficulty, and many thousands with planets completely unsuitable for human life but with their own alien plant and animal life in abundance. Far more star systems exist without any sign of life at all.'

The next questioner sounded aggressive. 'Gamma Sector News. You believe the alien home world is within humanity's space? How could Planet First Stellar Survey have missed a planet with an advanced alien civilization?'

27

The General Marshal shook his head. 'On the contrary, we believe the alien home world is probably further away than that. Tactical considerations, however, mean our first priority is to eliminate any possibility of it being within humanity's space. Expansion was extremely rapid during Exodus century. Humanity was too impatient to spend enough time checking its colony worlds, let alone waste effort on uninhabitable star systems.'

He paused for a moment. 'That reckless overexpansion led to the near collapse of our civilization. It may also have led to signs of an alien civilization being missed in Alpha, Beta or Gamma sectors. After a century of colony worlds struggling to deal with issues overlooked by those first rushed Planet First checks, there was a new attempt to expand and the nightmare of Thetis. A single lethal alien animal species was overlooked, portal quarantine procedures failed, and the chimera infested other worlds, threatening the survival of the human race.'

There was a moment of grim silence before the General Marshal continued. 'After the lesson of the Thetis chaos year, humanity finally realized it was vital to allow Planet First teams the time and budget to do a meticulous job, but financial and logistical realities mean we still can't make an exhaustive search of uninhabitable star systems. I'd be extremely surprised if we'd missed a planet with technology sufficiently advanced to construct the alien probe in Delta, Epsilon or Kappa, but those sectors will be rechecked anyway.'

The Gamma Sector News reporter wasn't giving way to anyone else. 'The newly formed Isolationist Party feel searching for the alien home world is a mistake because humanity would be better off *not* encountering aliens.'

'I fail to understand the logic of trying to pretend an alien civilization doesn't exist when they've already got a probe orbiting our home world,' said the General Marshal. 'We urgently need to know if any of our inhabited worlds are dangerously near alien territory. I'll take a question from someone else now.'

The next questioner went back to the subject of Fian and me. 'Alpha and Omega. Our viewers want to know when Commander Tell Morrath and Major Eklund will be available for interviews. They've made no public appearances since the signal was sent.'

The General Marshal smiled. 'I'm fully aware of the ferocious levels of public interest in Commander Tell Morrath and Major Eklund. Fortunately, the remote location of their class protects them from continual invasion of privacy by the vid channels of every sector. No Military officer should have to suffer merciless interrogation by the newzies.' His smile widened. 'Except for myself of course.'

'But Commander Tell Dramis and Major Weldon appeared on Earth Rolling News for extensive periods,' said the Alpha and Omega representative.

'Only to provide public information on behalf of the Military.' The General Marshal paused for a second. 'That's all for now. If you want my answers to any questions that weren't asked, then I'm sure Gamma Sector News will be happy to invent some for you just the way they did after my last newzie conference.'

The General Marshal left the podium while everyone was still laughing at that comment, the vid coverage switched back to the Earth Rolling News studios, and Lecturer Playdon went up to the wall vid and turned it off.

'A year!' Krath sounded as frustrated as I felt.

'If the alien home world is near to Earth, then it may only take a couple of months to find it.' Playdon turned to look at me and Fian. 'Congratulations on your promotions, Commander Tell Morrath and Major Eklund.'

I was startled by my classmates applauding. Not all of

them of course. When they found out about my lies and my Handicap, some had accepted me, but others tried to drive me away with insults. Eventually, I'd won grudging tolerance from most of the ape haters, and now I was famous a couple of them were fawning over me in a way that made me want to vomit, but there was one person pointedly folding her arms and refusing to give even a token hand clap. Petra would never stop hating me. Not after Joth's death.

There was the usual stab of pain as I thought of Joth. I blamed Petra for his death, because he was killed doing something stupidly dangerous after an argument with her. She blamed me, because the argument was about her making him insult me. We could both be right, or both wrong. It really didn't matter. Nothing could bring Joth back, and Petra and I would always be enemies.

'Put the chairs away and fetch your luggage,' said Playdon.

A few minutes later, the hall was crowded with people and bobbing hover bags, as the class waited for Playdon to do his final tour of inspection.

'It's unusual for High Congress to clarify an order like that,' said Dalmora. 'They're obviously very embarrassed by all the comments on the newzies.'

I sighed. 'But not embarrassed enough to order Fian and me back to Alien Contact right away.'

She tactfully changed the subject. 'I'm looking forward to seeing a new city. I hope we'll spend some time at Jaipur or Chennai later in the year. It would be totally zan to be excavating one of the cities where my ancestors lived.'

'I've started working on my family tree,' said Amalie, 'but I've only got as far back as 2640. My ancestors were all on planets in Gamma sector then.'

Fian sighed. 'I'll never know about mine. My great-grandparents were all on Freya in Alpha sector during the conflict there, and its planetary records were deliberately destroyed. All I know is Freya was originally settled from Earth Europe. What about your ancestors, Jarra?'

I shrugged. 'They'll have been from everywhere. The Betan planets all had open colonization, and members of a Military clan marry people from lots of different worlds anyway.'

I was dodging the question. The truth was the Tell clan had a complete family tree on record, but I hadn't dared to look at it. Fate had robbed me of a family twice already. Once at birth, and again when my parents were killed. If I looked at the Tell family tree before I was actually a clan member, I might tempt fate into making something go wrong a third time.

'My aunt worked out our family tree all the way back to Exodus century,' said Krath. 'I've got ancestors from all five of Earth's continents, so I don't care what cities we go to. I just hope there's no more rainforest, or sabre cats, or dire wolves. I've had enough of those here at Eden.'

'I still can't believe people deliberately genetically salvaged dangerous creatures,' said Fian.

'Earth isn't civilized,' said Krath, for about the thousandth time. 'The ruins. The animals. The insects. The solar storms bringing down the portal network.'

Playdon returned just in time to hear him. 'As I keep saying, the Military Planet First teams carefully select every colony world and make it safe for humans. Earth is our only world that never went through that process, and the vast abandoned areas are dangerous.'

He glanced round the class. 'We'll be portalling inter-continent to get to London Main. If we keep close together, with Jarra and Fian in the middle, people may not notice them going through the Transit areas. If we get split up, then I'll stay with Jarra and Fian. You've all got the new dome portal code, so we'll be able to meet up there.'

Playdon led the way to the portal room and we hurried after him, clicking our key fobs to make our hover bags chase us. Fian and I stayed in the centre of the crowd as we trooped through the portal and gathered under a location board saying 'Africa Transit 3'. Once the whole class and their luggage had arrived, we headed on past the flashing signs about inter-continental portal charges, and joined the queue for a portal that was already active and locked open to Earth Europe. The queue had been moving rapidly forwards but suddenly stopped.

Amalie groaned. 'The portal's cut out. It's flashing a congestion warning.'

I sighed. 'Some idiot with more hover bags than brain cells must have stopped in the arrival zone on the other side of the portal to count his luggage.'

'There's only a few people ahead of us in the queue,' said Amalie. 'I hope it doesn't . . . Oh chaos, you've been spotted!'

I turned to look behind us. Transits were usually full of purposefully hurrying figures, but now everyone was standing still, staring at Fian and me. A rhythmic sound started, I realized people were clapping, and felt myself grow hot with embarrassment.

'If we're stuck here for long we'll get mobbed,' muttered Amalie.

She was right. People were constantly arriving through portals but no one was leaving, so the watching crowd was growing larger at frightening speed. Lots of people were holding up lookups to make vids of us, and someone was bound to have called Earth Rolling News by now.

'The portal's open again,' called Playdon. 'Jarra, Fian, go first!'

The rest of the class moved aside to let us reach the portal, and the sound of applause instantly cut out as Fian and I stepped through it to Earth Europe. Playdon arrived a moment later, and we hurried on past a sign that said 'Normal Portal Charges Now Apply'. I glanced over my shoulder and saw some of the class running to catch us up. There was a lot of hover luggage chasing us as well. I hoped some of it was mine.

We reached a local portal and Playdon rapidly dialled. 'Warning,' said the portal, 'your destination is a restricted access area. If your scanned genetic code is not listed . . .'

I didn't hear the rest of it, because Fian hustled me through the portal with him. We stepped out into the standard grey portal room of a dig site dome, and automatically headed out of the door to allow space for other people to arrive. I paused in the corridor to count the number of hover bags following us. 'Zan! All the luggage is . . .'

'Throwbacks have no place in a noble clan of Beta sector!' said a strange voice.

I turned, shocked by the words, and something wet splattered across my face. I dropped the key fob I was holding, and lifted my hands to protect myself, but it was too late. My eyes and mouth were burning and I couldn't see or breathe.

4

I was blind and helpless, battling against pain to get air into my lungs. There were sounds of a fight somewhere very close, fists hitting flesh and agonized gasps. What was happening? Was someone attacking Fian? How could someone have been here, in what should have been an empty dome, lying in wait for us?

'Playdon, get her to hospital!'

That harsh, angry voice was definitely Fian. Arms grabbed me from behind, half carrying me. There was the siren of a portal medical emergency alarm, which abruptly cut out to be replaced by the sound of voices. We'd portalled. We must be in a Hospital Earth Europe casualty unit now.

'Code ten!' Playdon's voice yelled next to my right ear. 'Code ten! Chemical contamination!'

I was dragged sharply sideways and liquid sprayed over me. I whimpered in panic before I realized this wasn't another attack. I was in a decontamination shower.

'Jarra, open your eyes and your mouth!'

I forced them open, and the pain eased as the decontamination fluid did its job. Playdon's blurred face was inches from my own, his dripping hair a startling contrast to his usual neat appearance.

'Does it still hurt? Can you see?'

I managed to speak. 'Just a faint stinging now, and I can see.'

'Good. Can you stand by yourself?'

'Yes.'

Playdon cautiously let me go, and moved back the short distance the shower allowed. 'It's totally inappropriate for me to shower with my students, but in the circumstances I think we'd both better stay in here a while.'

My nose was working again now, and even the strong odour of decontaminant couldn't drown out something more powerful. 'Oh no! He threw skunk juice at me?'

'Yes.'

My attacker had shouted about Beta sector, and thrown Cassandrian skunk juice in my face. This was about me joining the Tell clan. Lolia and Lolmack thought it was wonderful, but the people like Petra, the ones who hated apes . . .

The shower door opened, and a woman in doctor's uniform looked in at us. 'Undiluted skunk juice is extremely dangerous.' Her head turned away for a second as she gulped in some clean air. 'Fortunately, our scans show you got into the decontaminant quickly enough to avoid serious burns. Please remain here for a few more minutes.'

The shower door closed, leaving me alone again with Playdon in what suddenly seemed embarrassingly close quarters. 'I'm really sorry about this.'

Playdon brushed his wet hair out of his face. 'It's not your fault, Jarra. I don't know how that man got into the dome, but . . .'

The doctor opened the door again. She was wearing a mask now. 'Please step outside, but try not to touch anything.'

I followed Playdon out of the shower, nearly gagging on my own stench as I left the decontaminant. My eyes wouldn't focus properly, but I could make out the shapes of a reception desk and rows of empty seats. This place had probably been full of people when I arrived, but they'd all fled when they caught the first whiff of skunk juice, all except the unlucky doctor who had to treat me.

The doctor handed a mask to Playdon, and then tipped some tablets from a bottle into two tiny cups. 'These are meds for shock.'

Playdon gulped his down, but I shook my head. I didn't like things that messed with my mind.

The doctor was obviously suffering badly from the smell despite her mask, but she bravely started waving a scanner at us. 'Skunk juice comes from a Cassandrian fruit and is completely odourless until activated by binding to the skin. The creature called the Cassandrian skunk deliberately rolls in fallen fruit to make itself smell as a defence against predators.'

I could tell by the way she recited it, that she'd just looked up skunk juice on the Earth data net. 'I'm sorry about this,' I said.

'Please don't apologize, Commander. Whoever did this to you should . . .' Her sentence was interrupted by a series of musical chimes from the portal, and she looked startled. 'This unit's in lockdown. Why is someone portalling in?'

I tensed, preparing to face another attack and determined to handle it better than last time, but the person stepping out of the portal was Fian. He hurried towards us, and I hastily stepped backwards. 'No! Don't touch me!'

He frowned, but obediently stopped with a short distance between us, accepted a mask the doctor helpfully waved at him, and put it on. 'I've been worried sick, but I couldn't come until I had the situation under control.'

Playdon made an odd choking noise. 'Perhaps you could tell me what's been happening back at the dome, Major Eklund. You ordered me out of there so fast that I barely even saw the intruder.'

Fian blushed. 'I apologize, sir. I knew I could trust you to get the right medical help for Jarra, so . . . The prisoner's been taken to Zulu base for medical treatment and questioning, and the class are waiting in the dome hall while Military Security check the area. I handed command over to Major Sand of Military Security before I came here.'

'You handed command over . . .' Playdon gave way to laughter behind his mask. 'Fian, didn't it occur to you for a single moment that you were a student, I was your lecturer, and I should be the one dealing with the intruder?'

Fian had a totally grazzed expression on his face. 'No, I . . . We were under attack, it's the job of the Military to defend civilians, and . . .' He shook his head in complete bewilderment. 'Why did I react like that? I'm just a history student thrust into uniform.'

Playdon shook his head. 'I think you've successfully made the transition from civilian to Military, Major Eklund.'

The hovering doctor was studying her scanner. 'Commander Tell Morrath, the skunk juice has bonded to the skin of your face, hands and scalp. You also have minor eye damage that should respond to regeneration fluid treatment within a few hours. Your companion,' she nodded at Playdon, 'fortunately didn't have direct skin contact with the juice.'

Playdon wasn't skunked. I sighed with relief.

The doctor put on some gloves, sprayed my eyes with something that made my vision even blurrier, then produced a jar of something blue. 'This gel will neutralize the remaining unbonded juice, Commander, making it safe for people to touch you. It will also reduce the smell to a certain extent, and accelerate the degradation process from several weeks to two or three days.'

Stinking for a couple of days was a lot better than stinking for weeks, but . . .

The doctor started plastering gel on my hands and face. 'You'll notice some discolouration of your skin where the skunk juice has bonded. That will return to normal within a few days.'

Fian watched with a frown. 'Is this the best treatment you've got?'

'The only other treatment is to surgically remove the skin layer and put the patient in a regrowth tank,' said the doctor. 'We prefer to avoid unnecessary major surgery.'

My mind conjured up hideous images of being skinned alive. 'I'll stick with the gel.'

The doctor finished work on my face and hands, and moved on to my scalp and hair. 'We'll give you some gel to take with you. Apply it three times daily, covering hair and affected skin areas but avoiding the eyes, until the discolouration has completely vanished. Be careful not to wash or shower during that time, because water may re-activate the skunk juice.'

My hair felt like cold, slimy strands of seaweed now. I fought the urge to shudder. 'Why did the prisoner need medical treatment, Fian? Did he accidentally skunk himself?'

'No. Lolmack realized the man wasn't just attacking you, but his daughter's future as well, and hit him harder than a runaway transport sled. He broke his nose, arm, and three ribs. Lolmack says being a member of a low status clan involved in the sex vid industry means you have to be able to take care of yourself in a fight.'

'I'd noticed that . . .' I broke off as the doctor applied gel to my nose and mouth. The stench of skunk juice was replaced by an overpowering odour of flowers.

'The gel is scented with Osiris lilies, to mask the remaining aroma of skunk juice,' said the doctor.

Fian took off his mask and sniffed. 'That's a lot better. Very, very flowery though. I see what you mean about the skin discolouration.'

'That's absolutely nothing to worry about.' The doctor started updating my medical records.

I looked down at my hands and saw blotches of green and dark purple. Nothing to worry about? What the chaos did my face look like? I was ugly and I stank. I was like something out of the worst jokes the norms made about the Handicapped. 'I can't go back to the dome.'

'It's perfectly safe now, Jarra,' said Fian. 'Military Security are there.'

'It isn't fair to make everyone suffer this smell.'

Playdon took off his mask. 'It's not that bad now, Jarra. You can hardly smell the skunk juice for the Osiris lilies. That's a very overpowering odour, but not unpleasant.'

'But . . .'

Playdon held up a hand to stop my protest. 'You're coming back to the dome, Jarra. It's bad enough having one of my students attacked while under my care. I absolutely refuse to exclude you from my course because of your injuries.'

5

We stepped through the portal into the dome at London Main, and I saw the hazy figures of four Military Security officers saluting me.

'I must find my hover bags and change into dry clothes,' said Playdon.

Fian nodded. 'We'll find a room so Jarra can lie down and rest.'

I wanted to hide away in a room, but . . . 'If the class have to see me looking like this, I'd rather get it over with right away.'

Fian sighed. 'We'll go to the hall then.'

The four Military Security officers stayed guarding the portal, but we passed several more in the corridor. This was insane. Someone had thrown skunk juice at me, and Military Security was reacting as if they'd tried to assassinate a head of sector.

Fian took my arm and guided me round a couple of white humming shapes that must be air-purifying units. I hoped the Military would let us keep those for a few days to make life more bearable for everyone.

Yet more Military Security officers stood on guard inside

the hall, while our classmates sat huddled around tables. When we walked in, the Military saluted, and there was a scraping of chairs as people turned towards us.

'Jarra,' said Dalmora in a shocked voice. 'You look . . . You look dreadful.'

I felt that said everything. Even Dalmora, with her deeply ingrained tact and diplomacy, couldn't think of a kinder word than dreadful to describe my appearance.

An officer came up and saluted me. 'I'm Major Sand, sir. We've just completed full scans, both inside and outside the dome, and found no further threats.'

I stared at him blankly for a moment, before working out I was the senior officer present. Major Sand had given me a situation report and was awaiting orders. I wasn't in uniform, I'd never met this man, but he knew who I was. The whole of humanity did. Even a random doctor in a Hospital Earth casualty unit recognized me and addressed me as Commander.

I ran my fingers through the greasy lank ribbons of my hair. I couldn't cope with this now. I looked like a monster, I stank, and I was groping my way through a frighteningly hazy world. Was the regen fluid helping my eyes or making them worse?

'Please, keep . . .' I tried to think of the right Military words to use and completely failed. 'Keep dealing with it.'

Another officer hurried into the room. 'Sirs, Zulu base warns the General is incoming.'

The Major gave a single heartfelt groan, turned, and headed for the door. I suddenly felt shaky and dreadfully tired, so I sat down on a chair by the wall and let my head sag forward into my hands. I was vaguely aware of Fian positioning a couple of the air purifiers nearby, and then tugging another chair over to sit next to me. I couldn't tell if the air purifiers were having any effect, because the cloying scent of Osiris lilies had overwhelmed my nose. I'd probably never be able to smell anything else ever again.

There were a couple of minutes of silence before Playdon came into the hall and said something to the class. I heard the words but couldn't make sense of them. I really was like an ape in an off-world joke. I was ugly, I stank, and I was stupid as well.

More people arrived, a figure in a white jacket in the lead, followed by two others in standard Military uniforms. It took my sluggish brain a moment to work out the white jacket must be Riak Torrek in his new General's uniform. I blinked my eyes, got them to focus long enough to recognize his face and those of Colonel Leveque and Major Sand behind him, struggled to my feet and saluted.

'I shouldn't need to say this is unacceptable,' said General Torrek in an angry voice.

Riak Torrek had been a close friend of my grandmother. I was the first child born into the family after her death in action, so in Military tradition I was her Honour child and carried her name. I'd known Colonel Torrek took a special interest in me because of it, and felt pretty relaxed around him, but General Torrek seemed far more intimidating, a grimly disapproving stranger.

I realized I was still wearing the wreckage of my civilian clothes. I hadn't thought to ask Dalmora where my hover bags were and change into uniform. I was a dumb, dumb ape. 'I apologize for the state of my clothes, sir.'

The General's voice lost the harsh note. 'I should be the one apologizing to you, Jarra. The Military failed in our duty to protect you. Please sit down before you fall over.'

He turned to Major Sand and now his voice was icily cold. 'Major, please explain how an intruder gained entry to this dome.'

I thought I heard a faint gulp from Major Sand, before

he answered in an impressively steady voice. 'Portal access was secure, sir, and we were monitoring all aerial traffic. Unfortunately, London Main Dig Site is in far less hostile terrain than Eden. The intruder gained entry to the nearby London Fringe Dig Site and walked here.'

'You let him walk in!' General Torrek gave a despairing groan, and turned to Colonel Leveque. 'Why did this happen? We were expecting intrusive reporters, not violent attacks.'

'When Gaius Devon tried to force us to make an unnecessary attack on the alien sphere, we used the tactic of deliberately focussing public attention on Commander Tell Morrath,' said Leveque. 'That succeeded in its objective of making Devon betray his uncontrolled prejudice against both the Handicapped and the aliens to the public, thereby discrediting him, but has also had unforeseen consequences.'

General Torrek frowned. 'You mean one of my command decisions caused this?'

'Indirectly, sir,' said Leveque. 'For the first time, people on all of humanity's worlds have seen one of the Handicapped appear on their vid channels. Many of them are rethinking their old prejudices in the face of reality. The severely bigoted deeply resent this shift in the attitudes of society. The news that Commander Tell Morrath was to join an aristocratic Betan clan escalated that resentment into violence.'

He paused. 'This particular assailant intended to intimidate Commander Tell Morrath into returning to the obscurity he considers proper for her. It's quite possible that others will attempt to permanently eliminate what they see as a threat to the proper social order. We must assume that Major Eklund is also a potential target as a result of his relationship with Commander Tell Morrath.'

My head wasn't working too well, and I found Colonel Leveque's sentences confusing at the best of times, but it sounded like he was saying . . .

'I'm not having my officers murdered by bigots,' said General Torrek. 'I'll authorize whatever protective measures you want.'

Colonel Leveque nodded. 'I'll flag them both with automatic pre-empt status so they can bypass the queues at Transits, assign them a bodyguard, and issue guns for them.'

I'd been right then, I thought numbly. Colonel Leveque really was suggesting that people might try to kill Fian and me.

'They've been instructed to continue their pre-history training while they're waiting to rejoin the Alien Contact programme,' said Leveque, 'but if it proves impossible to adequately secure this location then . . .'

'If I can interrupt you there,' said Playdon, 'several other dig sites are as inaccessible as Eden. I could arrange to swap dig site assignments with another team.'

'That would be an excellent solution,' said Leveque. 'I'll also be urgently investigating how this attacker knew exactly when your class would arrive here.'

'I've repeatedly warned my students not to give information about Jarra or Fian to anyone,' said Playdon.

The class had been a silent audience to all this, but now Steen stood up. 'That scum knew we were coming here because Petra told him!'

Leveque raised his eyebrows. 'Do you have any evidence for this accusation?'

'I don't need evidence,' said Steen. 'Petra started running a hate campaign against Jarra the minute she found out she was Handicapped, insulting her and making her life a misery. Petra was always calling Jarra a stinking ape, so I bet the skunk juice was her idea.'

There was a brief pause, followed by Fian, Playdon and General Torrek all saying almost exactly the same words. 'Why didn't I know about this?'

I didn't need to reply. Fian was already answering the question. In fact, he was having an entire angry conversation with himself.

'I knew Petra was prejudiced against Jarra, but I'd no idea she was actively insulting her. It's always the same. We're on our second Twoing contract, but does Jarra tell me when she has a problem? No. Does she ask anyone for help? No. Does she even hint someone's been persecuting her for months? No, she doesn't. I swear, one day I'll strangle her!'

'Please don't strangle Jarra today, Fian,' said Leveque. 'When Military Security officers are guarding two people, and one of them tries to strangle the other, they get confused about the appropriate course of action. Besides, Jarra's clearly suffering from shock.'

'I'm perfectly fine,' I said.

'I disagree,' said General Torrek. 'I'd ask why the doctors didn't treat you for shock, but after my years serving with your grandmother I can guess the answer. She hated taking meds as well.'

'Were any other class members involved in this abuse?' asked Colonel Leveque.

Steen hesitated for a second. 'Petra tried to drag some of the rest of us into the name calling, but we wouldn't get involved.'

I was grazzed to hear this. My own memory of events was that Steen had spent two months calling me a throwback and pointedly holding his nose when he passed me in the corridor. I opened my mouth to speak, but Petra was ahead of me.

'It's not true! I called Jarra some names, but you were just as bad. You're only crawling to her now because she's famous.'

Steen shook his head. 'If the rest of us ever said anything

45

rude, it was only because you kept nagging us, just like you nagged poor Joth. You wanted to drive Jarra away so you could get your claws into Fian. When words weren't enough to get rid of her, you tried skunk juice!'

'What?' Fian's voice interrupted the pair of them. 'What's been going on here?'

I urgently blinked my eyes. The regen fluid must have worked because this time the world came into focus and stayed that way. Fian was on his feet now, his face and stance showing his fury.

'This is because of me?' He advanced on Petra. 'You helped that man throw skunk juice at Jarra because you wanted to split us up?'

Petra scrambled to her feet and tried to back away, but only succeeded in knocking over her chair. 'I didn't have anything to do with the skunk juice!'

Playdon moved to stand between them. 'Stop this, all of you!'

Fian looked past him at Petra. 'Jarra and I are together. Nothing and nobody is coming between us.'

He turned, came back to sit next to me, and took my hand. His unblemished skin against the mottled green and purple of mine.

'I'm arresting Petra and taking her in for questioning,' said Leveque.

Petra's eyes widened in shock. 'You can't arrest me. You aren't a police officer.'

'Incorrect,' said Leveque. 'Legally any member of the Military is also a police officer empowered to deal with interplanetary crimes.'

'I may have called Jarra a rude name once or twice,' said Petra. 'That might get me warnings from Lecturer Playdon under the Gamma sector moral code governing our course, but it isn't an interplanetary crime. I didn't have anything to do with the attack on Jarra, but that wasn't an interplanetary crime either.'

I admired Petra's courage, but I knew she was making a big mistake arguing with Leveque. I watched him give one of his relaxed smiles, and held my breath waiting for him to pounce on his prey.

'Your last point is debatable, since the attacker came to Earth from Atalanta in Beta sector specifically to harm Commander Tell Morrath,' said Leveque, 'but I'm happy to abandon any action against you under interplanetary law.'

Petra looked surprised to have won so easily. Steen started to protest, but Fian urgently shook his head at him.

Leveque's smile widened. 'I now arrest you for crimes against humanity under the powers of the Alien Contact programme.'

Petra gasped. 'You can't do that! I have rights.'

Leveque shook his head. 'Contact with an alien civilization potentially threatens the survival of the human race. Everyone studies the Alien Contact programme in school, so you should know its emergency powers override everything. I'm not even restricted by the protection of humanity laws, let alone your personal human rights.'

He paused to give Petra the chance to speak, but she'd sense enough to keep quiet this time. 'Both Commander Tell Morrath and Major Eklund have made multiple valuable contributions to the Alien Contact programme, and I consider it highly probable they will do so again in future. Mere suspicion you were involved in harming irreplaceable personnel is enough for me to perfectly legally pick up a gun and kill you. I can also use any methods, however extreme, to interrogate you before execution.'

He glanced at one of the guards. 'Take the girl to Military Base 79 Zulu.'

The guard took Petra by the arm and led her off. The rest

of the class watched her go with stunned faces, but Playdon moved to face Leveque.

'I have a duty of care to my students. I'll insist on regularly visiting Petra to satisfy myself she isn't being mistreated.'

Leveque seemed amused. 'I'll authorize your visits, but I assure you I've no intention of torturing the girl. I just wanted to frighten her so she'd stop wasting my time with childish defiance and lies. Now let's discuss possible new locations for your class.'

6

I stood on a stage, looking out at a sea of faces, and heard Petra's hugely magnified voice speaking. 'But the funniest thing is Jarra thought the skunk juice would wear off. She didn't know she'd be stuck like this forever.'

There was a deafening roar of laughter, and I saw Petra standing in the middle of the audience. I jumped off the stage, intent on reaching her and murdering her, but I couldn't get through. There was a solid wall of faces. No bodies, not even heads, just faces hovering all around me.

'Jarra, it's time to get ready for breakfast.'

I woke up with a gasp. In the dim light of the room glows at their lowest setting, I saw Fian looking at me.

'Another nightmare?' he asked. 'The attack again?'

'No, this one was weird. Lots of floating faces.'

'I'm sure you'd have had less nightmares if you'd taken your meds.'

I groaned.

'And why the chaos didn't you tell me or Playdon about Petra calling you names? We could have dealt with her for you.'

I groaned again. 'That's exactly why I didn't tell you.'

'What do you mean?'

'Remember after the Solar 5 rescue, when I was in a hospital regrowth tank having my leg fixed. You went and told the class I was Handicapped.'

Fian frowned. 'Well, someone had to tell them.'

'Yes, but that someone was me, not you. I was the one who was Handicapped. I was the one who'd lied to them.'

'It would have been very unpleasant. The class were shocked and people said a few things that . . .'

'I realize that. I should still have faced them myself.'

'That's a . . .' He broke off. 'No, I see what you mean. I hated standing by watching Lolmack fighting that man with the skunk juice. He was doing my job for me, fighting my battle, and I felt so . . .'

He shook his head. 'Never mind that now. I understand what you're saying. I should have waited until you were out of the tank and let you talk to the class yourself.'

'Exactly,' I said. 'You meant well, but it actually made things far worse. Petra kept jeering at me for being a coward and hiding behind you, so . . .'

Fian finished the sentence for me. 'So you couldn't tell me or Playdon what was going on, because that would prove Petra was right.' He paused. 'I promise I won't fight your battles *for* you again, but I'd like to fight your battles beside you. There's a big difference.'

I grinned with relief. 'Fighting battles together is fine.'

He grinned back at me. 'You're still a nardle for not taking your meds though.'

'You're a nardle too. Did you see the look on Playdon's face when you insisted on moving the wall?'

Fian laughed. 'It didn't take long with Amalie organizing the whole class to help.'

'It wasn't the time it took, or the fact everyone was totally exhausted by then, it was the sheer idiocy of wanting to share a room with me when I smell like this.'

I paused to pick my words carefully. 'Fian, it's not just the perfume, it's . . . Well, it might be sensible for you to keep a distance from me for a while. Leveque said our relationship was making you a target too.'

'I've been waiting for you to suggest that idea, so I could tell you to forget it.'

'But . . .'

'No!' Even in near darkness, I could recognize the determined angle of Fian's jaw. 'I meant what I said to Petra. I'm not letting anyone split us up. I'm definitely not allowing some exo and his skunk juice to put a physical wall between us. With three air purifiers in here the smell really isn't a problem.'

He'd used the 'exo' word; the insult the Handicapped use for off-worlders. I smiled to myself. We were fighting this battle together.

Fian rolled away from me, turned up the glows to full brightness, and got out of bed. I'd suggested we should leave a gap between our beds until the skunk juice wore off, but he'd insisted on having them wedged against each other as usual. Fian was wonderfully, madly stubborn, and I loved him for it.

'Time for me to shower and get ready for breakfast,' he said.

I watched enviously as Fian headed out of the door. I was desperate to wash the greasy gel out of my hair and be properly clean again, but I couldn't. Water would make the skunk juice start burning my skin again.

I picked up the hateful jar of gel and went across to the mirror. The regen fluid had finished healing my eyes, so the reflection of my face was a perfectly focused, lurid green and purple mess.

51

I sighed and carefully rubbed gel into my skin, choking at the overwhelming scent of Osiris lilies. I'd spent my life wistfully dreaming of the hundreds of worlds I could only see on the vids, never visit in real life, but I was glad I'd never go to Osiris and see its famous fields of luminous white flowers opening at sunset, flooding the air with their fragrance. I'd smelt enough nuking Osiris lilies to last me to my hundredth.

I'd just finished putting on my uniform, when Fian came back into the room. I giggled at the look on his face. 'Wait outside for a few minutes while the gel dries and the air purifiers catch up with the smell.'

'No, I can cope.'

He heroically shut the door behind him and started changing from his sleep suit into his uniform. On a normal day, I'd have said something about his excellent legs, or even made him blush by using the butt word that was regarded as shocking outside Beta sector, but today I just turned away and attached my curved Military forearm lookup to my left sleeve where it clung neatly in position. The exo with the skunk juice hadn't managed to put a physical wall between us, but certain things wouldn't be happening for a few days.

'I've just realized I didn't take my gun with me to the shower,' said Fian. 'I mustn't leave it lying about like that or Playdon will throw a fit.'

'No one else could fire it, and all Military guns and lookups have tracking devices and can be disabled remotely if they get lost or stolen.' I went over to the bed and reached under the pillow for my own gun.

'Tell Morrath confirmed,' said the gun. 'Active power 3. Single target. Safety engaged.'

I remembered the training Fian and I had been given. We were to keep the guns on power 3, which meant anyone we shot would be paralysed for hours. We were to use single target except in extreme circumstances. Scatterfire would hit multiple targets at once, so you had to be really careful using it.

I stared down at my gun. Physically, it felt perfectly natural to be holding it, the grip had been moulded to fit the scanned medical records of my hand, but mentally . . .

Although I was Military now, I'd still never expected to hold a gun intended for use against another human being. I wasn't living in the days of pre-history when humanity fought wars. I wasn't a Military Security agent. I wasn't on a hostage rescue squad.

Fian picked up his gun, and it chattered away at him. 'Eklund confirmed. Active power 3. Single target. Safety engaged.'

'Wearing protective impact suits all day is impossible,' said Fian, 'but I'm surprised Leveque hasn't given us some sort of body armour.'

'He doesn't need to. All Military uniforms are made of special material that's highly resistant to fire, acid, knife attack, and projectile weapons.'

'That's good. So, where do we put the guns?'

'You're right handed, so the holsters will be on the right hip and left side of your uniform.'

'They are?' Fian ran his hands over his uniform. 'Oh, this little pocket thing. I hadn't noticed it before.'

I was still standing there like a nardle, looking at my gun. 'Fian, do you think you could actually shoot someone?'

He put his gun in the holster on his right hip. 'Yesterday morning, I would have said no, but now . . . If someone tries to hurt you again, then yes, Jarra, I'll shoot them.'

The lookup on my sleeve chimed with a message and I frowned. 'Major Rayne Tar Cameron of Command Support says the Tell clan council have been notified of the attack. They've postponed the presentation ceremony and will contact me when they've made new arrangements.'

Fian nodded. 'It's sensible to give you time to recover.'

I was still frowning as I followed Fian out of the door and down the corridor. Delaying the ceremony might be sensible, but it meant more days of suspense for Lolia and Lolmack. For me too.

Most of the class were already in the hall, sitting at tables and watching Earth Rolling News on the wall vid. A couple of presenters were talking in angry voices about two images on the screen. One was a girl with her face radiating pure delight. The other was a beaten wreck, with slimy hair, mottled skin, and lifeless eyes. They were both me.

Playdon stood up. 'The story is on all the sector newzies as well. The Military made a statement three hours ago. I bookmarked it for you.'

He went over to the wall vid controls. One of the Earth Rolling News presenters was cut off in mid-sentence, and the image changed to show Colonel Leveque. If this statement went out three hours ago, Leveque had probably been up all night, but he appeared as pristine and relaxed as ever.

'The Military regret to confirm there has been an attack on Commander Tell Morrath and Major Eklund. The perpetrator has been arrested and charged. Three further individuals are being questioned in connection with the incident.'

He paused for a moment before continuing. 'This attack was organized by parties with extreme personal prejudices against the Handicapped. I warn anyone contemplating further such action that although Commander Tell Morrath and Major Eklund are temporarily assigned elsewhere, they remain key personnel of the Alien Contact programme. The Military will not hesitate to use deadly force in their defence.'

The recording ended and the screen went blank. I stared at it for a few seconds before speaking. 'They're questioning three more people. Petra and . . .?'

'Two people on Atalanta in Beta sector,' said Playdon. 'I suggest you eat now. I want to start the mandatory dig site introductory and safety lectures straight after breakfast.'

Fian and I obediently headed for the food dispensers and picked up trays. 'I wasn't taking much notice of things when we portalled out of London Main,' I said. 'I know we're in Earth America, because Leveque wanted us in the same time zone as Military Base 79 Zulu at White Sands, but which dig site are we at?'

'California Rift Dig Site,' said Fian.

'What? But . . . Foundation classes aren't allowed there.'

He shrugged. 'Playdon must have special permission from Dig Site Command California.'

We loaded up our trays and went across to join Dalmora, Amalie and Krath at their table. Fian tugged a couple of air purifiers closer to us.

'Sorry about the smell,' I said.

'The flower scent is quite pleasant,' said Dalmora.

Krath's lookup chimed. He checked it and groaned. 'My nuking dad wants me to tell the Military I was involved in the attack so I get arrested.'

We all stared at him in disbelief. 'Why does your dad want you arrested?' asked Fian. 'I'm not totally against the idea, but . . .'

'He says it would be a great exclusive story for his nardle conspiracy vid channel, *Truth Against Oppression*.'

'I hadn't thought it possible,' said Amalie, 'but your dad has even less sense than you, Krath.'

I had a terrible thought. 'Oh chaos! My ProMum and my friends must have seen reports of the attack on Earth Rolling News. They'll be worried sick, but they won't have been able to call me because my mail is blocking everything except Military calls. Major Tar Cameron's working on a filtering system to relay recorded messages from my personal contacts, but . . .'

I tapped frantically at my Military lookup, and saw Candace's face appear.

'One moment,' she said, and her image froze as she put the call on hold. That meant Candace was with one of her other nine ProChildren. I felt a stab of guilt at stealing part of someone else's precious two hours with her.

About a minute later, she was back. 'Sorry about that, Jarra. My other ProChildren mustn't find out I'm your ProMum. It would be very psychologically harmful for them to feel I'm comparing them to the famous Commander Tell Morrath.'

I was too grazzed to speak. Hospital Earth rules forbade Candace from discussing her own family or her other ProChildren with me, so she'd never mentioned them before, and her calling me famous felt . . .

'Hospital Earth has a standing injunction preventing newzies breaching ProParent confidentiality,' Candace continued with an anxious air, 'so it shouldn't get public as long as you don't mention me in any interviews.'

I wasn't stunned any longer, just hurt. I'd thought Candace would be worried about me, but she hadn't even asked how I was. I fought to keep my voice maturely calm and untroubled. 'If we ever do interviews, I'll be careful not to mention you.'

'Good.' She smiled. 'I'm relieved to see you're already looking better. The picture on Earth Rolling News frightened me, but Colonel Leveque explained about the medical gel and said the skin discolouration would be gone within a few days.'

My selfish feeling of hurt vanished. I should have realized the Military would contact my ProMum as well as my clan council, and that was why Candace wasn't as worried as I'd expected.

'I'm afraid I was a little rude to him at first,' said Candace.

'I was angry about the Military letting someone attack you.'

I think I groaned at this point, because she looked apologetic. 'I'm sorry. It's been such a short time since you were getting into trouble at your Next Step. It's hard to adjust to you being not just an adult, but a high-ranking Military officer. Fortunately, Colonel Leveque was very understanding and we had a nice long chat about you.'

My ProMum had had a nice long chat to Colonel Leveque about me! I held back a scream of embarrassment. 'What exactly did you say?'

'Oh, we discussed your childhood. He seemed very interested.'

I remembered all the times I'd made a total nardle of myself, imagined Candace telling Leveque about them, and held back a shudder. 'I'm taking up someone else's time with you, so I'd better go now.'

When I ended the call, Fian laughed. 'I'm just picturing Candace scolding Leveque for not taking proper care of you.'

I gave a whimper of heartfelt despair. 'And then boring him by chatting about my childhood!'

Fian shook his head. 'Leveque's quite capable of reassuring Candace and getting rid of her at high speed. I'm betting the conversation was his idea. He likes collecting information.'

'But why would Leveque want information about me?'

'No idea. I'd better call my mother. My father too I suppose.' Fian stood up and gestured at my untouched plate. 'Please eat something, Jarra.'

I watched with a frown as Fian backed off a discreet distance and tapped his lookup. Fian's mother would be worried about his safety. She might join in his father's attempts to split us up.

'Jarra,' said Dalmora.

I turned to look at her. 'Yes?'

'Eat!' Dalmora, Amalie, and Krath chorused the word in unison.

I sighed, picked up a toasted wafer and took a bite. It tasted of Osiris lilies. 'There's no need to nag.'

'You always stop eating when you get hurt or upset,' said Dalmora. 'It's bad for you and it worries Fian.'

Fian's call to his mother seemed to end amicably, so I relaxed and dutifully munched more scented breakfast, then recorded a quick message about how I was fine but hated stinking of perfume. I sent that to all my friends from Next Step, and then wrinkled my nose as I considered my ProDad. I'd always felt he cared about the money he got from Hospital Earth, not about me, but he might be worried. I'd just sent him the message too when Fian shouted a single word.

'No!'

The background chatter of the class abruptly stopped, and everyone turned to look at him. A Major standing in a characteristically Military pose, his left arm raised in front of him as he gazed at the lookup on his left sleeve with a grim expression. I felt a stab of shock, remembering the Deltan boy I'd met at the start of this year, and realizing how the last few months had changed him, had changed both of us. My Deltan wasn't a boy any longer.

'I told you, the answer is no.' Fian's voice was only slightly quieter than before. 'I'm not coming back to Hercules, I'm not studying science, I'm not quitting the Military, and I'm not leaving Jarra for some drearily dutiful Deltan girl. Goodbye, sir!'

Fian gave his lookup an aggressive stab to end the call, and lifted his head. All around the room, people hastily faked an intense interest in eating. Fian marched back to our table and sat down, his simmering anger obvious enough that even Krath wasn't fool enough to say anything.

The awkward silence continued until Playdon stood up and walked to the front of the hall, indicating he wanted to start his lectures. The class automatically responded by dumping the remains of meals into the waste disposal, putting dirty dishes into the cleanser, and moving furniture. Within three minutes, the tables were stacked at the side of the hall, the chairs were lined up in rows, and we all took our seats.

'Half of human knowledge was lost in the Earth data net crash in 2409,' said Playdon. 'Science, technology, history, literature, medicine, all obliterated in a mass of data corruption. There are no surviving detailed records of the history of this area between 2100 and 2250, but at some point in that period there were either one or two massive earthquakes.'

Playdon tapped his lookup, and a weird image appeared on the wall vid. 'Records from 2250 show that several old cities had been replaced by a single new city, San Angeles. Humanity had defied nature by building this new city directly across the earthquake fault line, on the vast artificial platform we call the California Land Raft.'

He turned and gestured at the wall vid. 'This platform consisted of four hundred independent islands, connected together by flexible bridges. You're seeing the view from the ground of one of the eight huge, automatically adjusting legs of one of these islands. The city of San Angeles was abandoned by 2380, but even now, over four centuries later, most of these legs are still fully functional and compensating for the ground movements resulting from earthquake activity in this area.'

Playdon tapped his lookup again, and the image changed to show something with eight long spiky legs, and a flat shell-like back. 'This is a side view of one of the islands.'

Krath summed up the reaction of the whole class, including me. 'It looks like a weird, creepy, mechanical spider.'

Playdon changed the image again to show a whole army

of spiders. 'Here we can see a view of the full Land Raft. Virtually all of the flexible bridges between the islands have collapsed, and the few remaining ones are far too hazardous to use. Twenty-three islands nearest the fault line have exceeded the adjustment capability of their supporting legs and also collapsed. A further thirty islands are highly unstable and too hazardous for further exploration.'

His next image was a patchwork of coloured squares. 'These are the hazard colour coded islands of the Land Raft. Black islands have fallen or been abandoned. Red islands have an estimated survival time of less than fifty years, and amber between fifty and one hundred. Green islands have experienced relatively little movement and may still be standing for many centuries. Current archaeological efforts are concentrated on salvaging what we can from the red islands. Since these sections are nearing their safety limits, any earthquake activity is very dangerous and . . .'

Playdon broke off his sentence, stood for a moment in silence, and then strode straight past us and out of the hall.

7

'What the chaos?' Krath twisted round in his seat to watch the hall door close. 'Did Playdon get a message on his lookup?'

'I didn't hear it chime.' Dalmora stood up for a moment, gave the door a worried look, then sat down again. 'I expect he'll be back in a minute.'

A few people got drinks, while others started checking their mail on their lookups. After five minutes, Dalmora turned to me. 'You should go and see if Lecturer Playdon is all right, Jarra.'

I replied without thinking. 'Me? Why not you?'

Dalmora looked embarrassed. 'He might not like it.'

I could have slapped myself. The whole class knew Dalmora had a crush on Playdon and he was carefully avoiding being alone with her. I'd been as tactless as Krath at his worst. 'Sorry.'

Amazingly, it was Krath who saved the awkward situation by speaking in a chattily cheerful voice. 'The highest ranked officer present has to take command, sir.'

I giggled from pure relief. 'We aren't under attack, nardle brain!'

I stood up and went out of the hall to look for Playdon. He wasn't in the corridor, but I could hear the sound of voices coming from the portal room. The rest of the class were all back in the hall, so who the chaos . . .?

Remembering the ambush the previous day, I drew my gun before peeking cautiously into the doorway of the portal room, but relaxed as I recognized the two men with Playdon. They were his friends, Rono and Keren of Cassandra 2 research team. Playdon and Keren had their backs to me, but Rono's eyebrows shot up as he saw my gun. I pulled a face of silent apology and put it away.

Rono patted Playdon on the shoulder, and gave Keren a nod, before coming over to me. He touched his lips with one finger, then gave a beckoning gesture and led me back into the hall. Most of the class didn't know Rono, so they stared at him in total bewilderment as he went to stand in front of the wall vid.

'I'm Professor Rono Kipkibor, senior team leader of University Cassandra Archaeological Research Team 2. Some of you've already met me, and the rest of you will remember helping rescue my team from under a collapsed skyscraper at the New York Dig Site. I'll be giving you the rest of your introduction to the California Rift Dig Site.'

I went back to my seat and Dalmora gave me an anxious look. I shook my head at her to show I didn't know what was going on either.

Rono glanced at the image on the wall vid. 'I see Lecturer Playdon's already talked about the island structure of the Land Raft. The giant supporting legs of these islands are made out of diamene, and the island platforms are formed of connected diamene strips.'

There was some furtive whispering behind me, as a couple of the class puzzled over the scar tissue that marred Rono's dark forehead, making him look like someone in a history vid of the days before fluid patch treatments. The scar was the result of the solemn Keren losing his temper and punching Rono on newly regrown skin, and Rono was deliberately keeping it to tease him. I didn't understand how two such contrasting personalities had ever got into a relationship with each other.

'The strips are designed to move independently during earthquakes, so buildings are laid out in wide blocks along each strip.' Rono tapped his lookup to show a new image on the wall vid. 'The islands all have identical layouts. This is an aerial view of one of them, showing the central park surrounded by regimented blocks of buildings with wide gaps between them where the strips meet. Guess what we call the gaps between the buildings.'

'The gaps?' asked Krath.

'Correct,' said Rono. 'I'm glad someone's awake out there. As you can see, there are twenty gaps running the length of each island from north to south. They're connected by one gap running east to west through the centre of the island. Like the bridges, that gap was used for emergency access when the portal network had to be shut down during solar storms.'

He paused. 'The buildings on the islands have structural frames bonded to the diamene platform, so they're held firmly in place when the platform angle tilts during an earthquake. All the walls have imbedded reinforcement mesh running through them, but they're still riddled with cracks and liable to drop lumps of concraz on your head. Every gap has twin red safety lines painted on it. Between those two lines is safe, but you never put a foot across a red line without your impact suit hoods up and sealed. Understand?'

We all nodded.

'Understand?' repeated Rono. 'I want to hear you say it.'

'We understand.' We chorused the words like a bunch of little kids in Nursery.

'Due to the small size of Land Raft islands, there are no emergency evac portals on the dig site,' said Rono, 'but there are twin accommodation domes on each island. Teams are assigned in pairs, and co-ordinate their excavation work so they can help each other in case of accidents.'

He grinned. 'Less experienced teams are always paired with research teams. Cassandra 2 were supposed to be nursemaiding Cassandra 11 pre-history degree course, but we were fool enough to agree to them trading dig site allocations with you lot. I'm sure we'll regret it.'

There was a nervous ripple of laughter from the class. After months of Playdon's formal teaching style, we found Rono a bit of a shock.

He waited for everyone to quieten down before turning serious again. 'The main danger here is earthquakes. If the quake warning sirens shriek, then you evacuate as fast as possible. We're working on red risk islands, and even a minor quake may push one of the supporting legs past its limit or break the strip connections, so you get the chaos out of here. Understand?'

We responded in ritual chorus. 'We understand.'

'One final thing,' said Rono. 'Four years ago, Dannel Playdon's wife was killed at the California Rift. This is the first time he's been back here since then. You don't mention that to him, you pretend you don't notice if he looks upset, and you call me at once if you think he needs help. I warn you that if anybody causes him any trouble, I'll personally take them to the edge of this island and throw them off. It's a very, very long way down, so even if they're wearing an impact suit they won't repeat the mistake. Understand?'

We all stared at him in shock. I hadn't even known Playdon

had been married, let alone that his wife . . . No wonder Playdon was so paranoid about dig site safety.

'Understand?' repeated Rono.

'We understand,' we said.

'Good.' He turned off the wall vid. 'Our domes are in the central park, and that's perfectly safe without impact suits. Let's go outside and escape the sickly smell of Osiris lilies.'

He led the way towards the dome exit, and everyone pulled frantic faces at each other before trailing after him. This was the first time the class had ever left a dome without wearing protective impact suits. We'd started the year in bleak winter at New York Main Dig Site, where wolves were roaming outside our dome. We'd moved to Eden, in the heart of a rainforest holding scimitar cats and a whole range of nasty insects. Now we found ourselves in bright sunshine in . . .

Well, this might once have been a park, but now there were no flowers, only patchy grass and a scattering of stunted trees. Next to our accommodation dome was the usual sled storage dome, and facing us were two matching domes that must belong to Cassandra 2. A pathway ran off into the trees to the right, and over to the left was a curved blue shape.

'We've got a swimming pool!' Krath shouted joyously.

Rono laughed. 'The park swimming pools are the best thing about the Land Raft islands. They only needed re-lining with flexiplas to make them functional again. Now pay attention to three safety rules.'

He raised one finger. 'Number one is obvious. Don't wander out of the park into the ruins. If you aren't wearing an impact suit, they're utterly lethal.'

He raised a second finger. 'Number two. Birds of prey nest on these islands. Don't disturb them, because they'll attack you to defend their young.'

He raised a third finger. 'Number three. The sun here is

stronger than most of you will have experienced on your home worlds. If your skin is liable to sunburn badly, there's protective sun block in the store room.' He glanced pointedly at a couple of the class, including Fian. 'Don't come crying to me if you forget to use it. Understand?'

He'd got us trained now, so we chanted the words in unison. 'We understand.'

'Good.' He clapped his hands. 'That's it. Take a break.'

Everyone else sprinted back into the dome, but I went over to Rono. 'I'm causing far too much trouble staying with the class. I'll call my commanding officer and ask to go somewhere else.'

Rono looked apologetic. 'I was joking about the Osiris lily smell, Jarra. I really wanted to get outside because I love the sunshine at the California Rift. It's just like back home on Cassandra.'

'I didn't mean the joke.' I struggled to keep my voice under control. 'Lecturer Playdon shouldn't be forced to come here and face painful memories to keep me safe.'

Rono shook his head. 'Playdon wasn't forced to do this. He had plenty of teams offering to trade dig site assignments, and he deliberately chose this one so he could try facing the past in the company of his friends.'

'Oh.' I felt a total nardle.

Rono grinned and patted my shoulder. 'I'm very glad Dannel Playdon's students appreciate him.'

The rest of the class started reappearing and heading for the pool. Most people, including Fian, were wearing the skintights they normally wore under impact suits, but a few had proper swimming costumes. Rono ran to the pool himself, pulled off his clothes to show a swimming costume that barely covered the legally private areas, and dived into the water.

Fian came over to join me, and I gave an envious sigh.

66

'I can't go in the water until the skunk juice wears off, but you enjoy a swim.'

He shook his head. 'I'll wait until we can both go swimming.'

'Don't be ridiculous,' I said. 'You will go swimming, Major Eklund, that's an order.'

He shook his head again. 'One slight problem, sir. I can't swim.'

'What? Everyone learns to swim at school.'

'Not on Hercules. Deltans feel school time should be spent studying science. When you recover from the skunk juice, you can teach me to swim. Until then, we'll just watch the others having fun.'

We walked towards the pool, and found the ten members of Cassandra 2 research team had taken over one end of it, while our class were milling round in the water at the other. I saw Krath go over to the diving area and start climbing the ladder to the highest diving board.

Fian frowned. 'Do you think the idiot's safe going up there?'

'I don't know,' I said. 'Krath's usually good at practical things, but . . .'

Krath reached the diving board, waved his arms, and yelled. 'Look at me, Amalie!'

Our class all looked up, but Rono ignored him. I wished Playdon was here to make sure Krath didn't break his stupid . . .

Krath did a perfect dive that included a forward somersault. I relaxed and laughed at Fian. 'I'm sure Krath would teach you to swim if you ask him nicely.'

Fian made a disgusted noise, and we watched Krath climb the ladder to do an even fancier dive that started with a handstand. A dozen dives later, Playdon appeared next to me and frowned at the crowd in the pool.

'Why aren't my class working?'

Rono swam to the side of the pool, and heaved himself out in one swift movement. 'They *are* working. They're acclimatizing to the sunshine.'

Playdon shook his head and shouted. 'Asgard 6, out of the pool now!'

Rono winked at me and whispered. 'I knew this would get him back to normal. Playdon hates seeing his classes lazing around when they should be doing something educational.'

The mob in the pool groaned but obediently climbed out and gathered round us in a dripping group. I backed away nervously to stay clear of water droplets.

'I want to complete the introductory lectures today, so we can start work on the dig site in the morning,' said Playdon. 'Jarra obviously won't be able to wear an impact suit for a couple of days, so Amalie will substitute as tag leader for our dig team 1.'

Amalie looked worried. 'I'm not sure . . .'

'You'll do brilliantly,' I said.

'It will be good experience for you, Amalie,' said Playdon. 'While we're working on the dig site, Jarra can stay in the dome and do that remedial work I set her on the mathematical theorems of historical analysis. I won't accept trivial excuses like alien spheres for her delaying it any longer.'

'Nooo!' I wailed, while the rest of the class laughed at me.

'Everyone get dressed now and . . .' Playdon broke off as his lookup chimed to signal emergency mail. He tapped it, read the message, and looked startled.

'Colonel Leveque informs me Jarra and Fian's bodyguard will be arriving within the next few minutes. Apparently, the bodyguard is . . .' Playdon paused to double check the mail message as if he was still having trouble believing it. 'His Excellency Captain Draven Fedorov Seti Raven, Knight of Adonis.'

There was a moment of stunned silence, before Krath spoke. 'It must be a joke.'

I couldn't believe it either. The Adonis Knights were descendants of the first colonists on Adonis. Humanity learned a lot from that first colony. Mostly about all the things that could go wrong when people tried to live on an alien world with its own abundant life and intricate ecology and the portal link failed. After that, the Military Charter was written to establish what later became the cross-sector Military. Their first job was to clean up Adonis and make it safe, then their fledgling Planet First teams moved on to open up other colony worlds.

Playdon shook his head. 'I can't imagine Colonel Leveque would . . .'

He broke off because a man in a Captain's uniform had just come out of our dome. The new arrival couldn't be much more than twenty years old. He was slim, with short, dark hair, and had what would have been a very ordinary face if it wasn't for the thin, horizontal, black and white stripes on his right cheek.

I frantically counted the stripes and made it ten. Chaos take it, I wasn't just looking at an Adonis Knight. This man had completed the legendary set of ordeals based on the first colonists' struggle to survive, including a desert trek, fighting predatory animals, a week without food, and two days without water.

The title of an Adonis Knight only meant you were a rich aristocrat with heroic ancestors, but completing all ten trials of Adonis . . . Respect!

8

I had my eyes closed and my face lifted, glorying in the sensation of warm water cascading over my skin. I ran my fingers through strands of squeaky-clean hair and inhaled the faint fragrance of shower spray. This was blizz. Utter ecstatic blizz!

Someone hammered on the bathroom door, and I heard Amalie shouting. 'Jarra, there's a queue out here. For chaos sake, come out of there before you dissolve!'

I groaned and reluctantly switched the shower to dry mode. Amalie must have heard the shower change note, because the hammering stopped. A couple of minutes later, I stepped out of the shower and stood gloating at the sight of my wonderfully unblemished face in the mirror. The hammering on the door started again.

'I'm coming!' I tugged on my robe, picked up my gun and my lookup from the shelf, opened the door, and faced a queue of three impatient people.

'Sorry,' I said. 'I wanted to make sure I got rid of all the Osiris lily smell.'

Amalie groaned. 'You had an hour-long shower yesterday afternoon. We all told you the smell was gone afterwards.

You still insisted on having two more showers and a swim in the pool. The. Smell. Has. Gone.'

'I could still smell it this morning.' I sniffed. 'I think it's gone now. I'm not sure.'

Amalie sighed and went into the bathroom. His Excellency Captain Draven Fedorov Seti Raven had been leaning casually against the corridor wall waiting for me. Now he escorted me to my room, checking for threats with the tiny sensor in his left hand, while his right hand hovered close to his gun.

I went into the room, found Fian already dressed in his uniform, and got dressed myself. When we went back out into the corridor, we discovered our bodyguard was talking to himself.

'. . . understand that but I'm not happy. She's a potential threat!'

'I'm afraid you're stuck with it, Birdy,' said a disembodied male voice.

I frowned. 'Where's that voice coming from, Raven? It's not your lookup.'

'It's coming from the implant bonded to my skull,' said Raven. 'It's SECOP talking.'

'SECOP? Does that stand for Security Operations?' I asked.

'It does, Commander,' said the voice of SECOP.

I was startled. 'You can hear me?'

'In emergency mode, they can see and hear everything I can,' said Raven. 'In normal mode, my implant selectively relays statements prefixed with SECOP. Everything else remains private, but my implant has rolling two-hour recordings of everything I see and hear. In the event of my death, or traumatic injury, that data is automatically dumped to SECOP.'

'It is?' Fian pulled a face. 'Next time you stick your nose into something private, I'll have to remember not to kill you for two hours.'

'Sorry again,' said Raven. 'It sounded like an intruder was attacking you.'

I smothered a giggle. The previous night, Fian and I had celebrated my recovery from the skunk juice by watching a new episode of Fian's favourite vid series, *Stalea of the Jungle*. It ended with Stalea throwing her boyfriend across a jungle clearing, pinning him to the ground, and forcibly kissing him. Fian and I were happily re-enacting this scene for our personal entertainment, when an Adonis Knight heroically charged into the room to save us from being murdered.

In the interests of peace, I tried a random change of conversation. 'Don't the protection of humanity laws apply to implants?'

'Implants aren't banned like robots or clones,' said Raven, 'just restricted by the same rules as gene therapy. You can use them to treat medical and cosmetic problems as long as they don't enhance someone's abilities beyond the normal human range.'

'You're claiming an internal comms system is normal for humans?' asked Fian.

'No,' said Raven, 'but when Military Security agents are undercover on assignment, a visible external comms unit can get them killed. I'm claiming that's a cosmetic problem that justifies using implants instead.'

Fian frowned. 'You're bending rules that exist for very good reasons. I've been arguing with my father for years about this, because my great-grandfather was a member of Cioni's Apprentices. A huge amount of scientific knowledge was lost in the Earth data net crash. We're still blindly accepting many things as facts because records state they were once proved. Cioni's Apprentices were trying to recreate the lost science and proofs, find out what was true or not for themselves.'

He shrugged. 'I agree with my father that's a good thing to do, and totally support other scientists working on it, but

72

Cioni's Apprentices went to inhuman extremes. They didn't just cause the Freya conflict, and the Persephone incident, but the horror of what happened on Gymir. We need the protection of humanity laws to stop that sort of thing happening again.'

Raven gave Fian a startled look. 'Your great-grandfather was an Apprentice? Well, yes, I agree the Apprentices took things too far, but plenty of things bend the rules a little. Look at the dome cleaning system. The autovacs break the rules on both robots and artificial intelligence.'

'No they don't,' said Fian. 'They can't create another robot, they fail the Owusu intelligence ratings, and they have no digits capable of manipulating . . .'

I knew the real disagreement here was still about *Stalea of the Jungle* and privacy, so I gave a pointed cough. 'I'm starving to death.'

The other two abandoned their argument and we headed to the hall. Raven stopped just inside the doorway, following his regular morning routine of tensely surveying the room for a few minutes, presumably checking to see if any of the class showed signs of having turned into psychotic killers overnight. Fian and I carried on walking to the food dispensers, collected our breakfasts, and went to join Dalmora, Amalie, and Krath at our usual table.

Krath shook his head at us. 'I still don't understand why you've got an Adonis Knight as a bodyguard.'

I shrugged. 'Colonel Leveque said he picked Raven because it would be impossible for anyone to bribe him.'

Krath sighed. 'Yes, the families of the first Adonis colonists all got land grants in perpetuity, so Raven must be stinking rich. I wish I was. All the girls would throw themselves at me.'

Dalmora, Amalie, and I gave him matching glares. Krath hastily changed the subject.

'Draven Fedorov Seti Raven.' He started counting on his fingers. 'Draven is the randomly generated gender specific. Fedorov is the historic reference. Seti . . .' He broke off. 'I've forgotten again.'

Dalmora had already explained the Adonis Knight naming system three times, but she patiently did it again. 'Seti is the month of the fourteen-month-long Adonis year when he was born, and Raven is the Earth nature reference.'

'It's too complicated,' said Krath, 'and randomly generating a name is a nardle idea.'

'The Adonis colonists were selected from every region of Earth, and created new traditions to symbolize the fresh start for humanity,' said Dalmora.

'Well people obviously didn't like the new traditions,' said Krath. 'Nobody else randomly generates names.'

'The colonists for other planets in Alpha sector weren't chosen in the same way,' said Dalmora. 'Many of the planets were settled from specific regions of Earth and brought their old customs with them. Other sectors just had open colonization, but you still see major differences between the planets of Alpha sector even today.'

I stopped eating for a moment to join in the conversation. 'Hospital Earth Administration staff pick what they consider appropriate names for its wards from an approved list. They gave me a different surname as a child, but they let me keep my original first name because Jarra is an old enough name to be on the approved list. They haven't updated that list for about a century. My best friend from Next Step, Issette, is always complaining about having such an old-fashioned name.'

'My great-grandmother was called Issette,' said Amalie. 'I think it's a sweetly quaint name.'

I giggled. 'Please, never say that to my Issette. She'd scream.'

'Anyway,' said Krath, 'I'm glad Raven doesn't make us use his title or . . .'

'Shut up, Krath,' hissed Amalie. 'He's coming.'

Raven put his breakfast tray on the table and sat down in his regular seat, chosen so he'd have his back to the wall and a clear view of everyone in the room. 'Good morning.'

I heard the wall vid go on, and a presenter say my name. I turned and saw the Beta Sector Daily banner streaming across the top of the vid image.

'. . . Commander Tell Morrath as a clan member. The scale of demonstrations, both in support and opposition, increased after the skunk juice attack. The situation escalated further last night, with violent clashes between rival demonstrators outside the Parthenon. We're now getting reports of demonstrations on other Betan worlds, including Janus, Romulus, Aether and Artemis.'

The image behind the presenter showed a night-time view of the famous Beta Sector Parliament building, with its rows of statues of former First Speakers of Beta sector. The figures of fighting people were silhouetted against the floodlights.

'The demonstrators are acting as individuals,' continued the presenter, 'with clans still awaiting indications from alliances of their official stance on this unprecedented move by a clan of the *gentes maiores*. The August clan have still made no comment, leaving their alliance and the entire reactionary faction in confusion, though there are allegations that either the August or the Fabian clan are secretly orchestrating the protests against the Tell clan ceremony.'

Lolmack made a noise of disgust and turned off the wall vid. 'The demonstrations prove we've strong public support, but the alliances still don't have the courage to declare themselves.'

I sat there, totally grazzed. I'd been huddled in my own

75

self-absorbed little world for the last few days, carefully avoiding watching the newzies because they kept showing those two horribly contrasting images of me. I'd had no idea there was a political storm raging in Beta sector, with demonstrators fighting outside the Parthenon itself.

'I don't understand Betan politics,' said Krath. 'What's the *gentes maiores*?'

'Betan society was inspired by ancient Rome, basing its clan structure on it, and naming the Parthenon after one of its famous buildings,' said Lolmack.

I blinked, opened my mouth to object, but shut it again because Lolmack was still talking.

'The highest ranked Betan clans are the *gentes maiores*, the clans of the Founding Families of Zeus,' he said. 'Some official positions, like the First Speaker of Beta sector, are traditionally held by a member of those clans.'

He glanced in my direction. 'The Tell clan is the one exception among the clans of the *gentes maiores*. Tellon Blaze was born into a clan of the middle rank, but after the Thetis crisis a grateful Beta sector honoured him by granting him the right to found a new clan of the rank of the *gentes maiores*.'

'So how do the alliances work?' asked Amalie.

Lolmack looked round, saw he had the whole class listening to him now, and settled into lecture mode. 'Clan alliances are based around political or business interests, and bridge the social divides. The Military clans are all of the middle and first rank, and belong to the Military clan alliance headed by the Tell clan. Lolia and I belong to a plebeian clan of the lowest rank, a mere clan cluster without the right to a true clan name. We make sex vids so . . .'

He gave a shrug of resignation. 'Our clan is in an alliance headed by the Breck clan of the middle rank. Being in an alliance is the first step towards getting our clan officially recognized, but we've little status and no influence in alliance council decisions.'

'That's why your clan has to accept whatever the alliance decides about Lolette?' I asked.

'Exactly,' said Lolmack. 'If we caused trouble, the alliance would discard us, and we'd have to begin again from nothing. It should have been so different. Our clan has no status but we're wealthy. We'd arranged to buy adoption for our child.'

I frowned. Lolette wasn't an unwanted baby. Lolmack and Lolia had made great sacrifices to keep her. 'I don't understand what you mean by buying adoption.'

'A clan may adopt someone as part of marriage negotiations, because they're impressed by someone's talent, or if they're given a large financial incentive,' said Lolmack. 'Lolette should have been adopted into the Breck clan as a baby. She'd have remained our daughter, but she'd have been elevated to the middle rank and . . .'

He pulled a pained face. 'Lolette was born Handicapped, so now we'll be grateful if she's even acknowledged by our clan cluster.'

The silence after that was broken by Playdon's voice coming from near the door. 'Since this is a pre-history course, I'd like to point out the original Parthenon was not a Roman building but a Greek temple.'

Lolmack shrugged. 'There's no real difference. Ancient Rome and Greece were both on Earth and far back in pre-history.'

I smothered a giggle as I saw the expression on Playdon's face.

'There is a very significant difference,' said Playdon. 'Although Beta sector claims to be inspired by ancient Rome, there were many initial misconceptions, and of course Betan society has evolved over the centuries.'

He paused for a second. 'Now I've important news for you. Military Security have released Petra. I've spoken to

77

her about the issue of insulting Jarra, and she knows I won't tolerate any further breaches of the Gamman moral code.'

Steen stood up. 'You can't let Petra rejoin the class!'

'I can and I will,' said Playdon. 'Military Security arrested her, interrogated her, and decided she's innocent. Anyone with access to the dig team assignment schedule would know when this class was moving to London Main. Whoever passed on that information, it wasn't Petra. I'm moving her from our class dig team 4 to team 5 because ill feeling between team members can be dangerous, but I'm not throwing a student off this course for a crime she didn't commit. Please sit down, Steen.'

Steen didn't move.

'I asked you to sit down.'

There was another moment of suspense before Steen flung himself down in his chair. Playdon nodded, turned, and went out of the door.

'Why is Steen so angry, Jarra?' Raven asked in an urgent whisper.

I sighed. 'Steen hates Petra. One of the students in our class, Joth, was Twoing with Petra. They had an argument and Joth got himself killed doing something stupid. Steen was a friend of Joth. He blamed Petra for what happened, so . . .'

'I was Joth's friend too,' said Krath, 'and Steen's right. We should all insist that . . .'

He broke off because Playdon was back, with Petra standing next to him. There was an awkward silence and I realized some of the class were looking at me. I took a deep breath, forced myself to stand up, and walked across to Petra.

'I hope we can make a fresh start.'

She stared at me, her expression changing from defiance to shock. I waited a second, but Petra seemed far too grazzed to say anything, so I just went back to my seat.

'Krath frowned at me. 'Why didn't you tell Petra to nuke off?'

'Because Playdon's done a huge amount to help me since I joined this class. I'm not rewarding him by stirring up trouble when he's grieving for his dead wife.'

'Jarra's right,' said Dalmora. 'We must respect Playdon's decision.'

Krath glanced at Amalie and then Fian, but they both nodded agreement.

'Fine,' muttered Krath. 'Have it your way, but I'm not happy about Petra being back with us.'

'Neither am I,' said Raven.

9

A crowd of figures in impact suits were gathering by our sled storage dome. Impact suits are wonderful things. When a ruined building collapses on your head, or something explodes and sends debris flying at you, the special fabric triggers and goes solid to protect you. The only problem is they're chaos difficult to put on. I'd been proud that I could suit up in the Military standard time of two minutes, but I'd just seen Raven casually beat my best ever time by ten seconds.

'I can't believe how fast you suited up,' I said.

Raven laughed. 'I've had special training, Jarra.'

The last few stragglers arrived, and Playdon started talking. 'Now Jarra is able to come with us, we'll drive to the edge of the island. You can all admire the view from the Land Raft before we start our excavation work.'

A few minutes later, our line of hover sleds was heading along Gap 15. There was an unbroken wall of buildings on either side of us, towering up to about twenty storeys high. In ancient vid images of San Angeles, these buildings were dazzling white, and their long uniform lines had a regal elegance, but time had aged the concraz to a grubby pale grey and scarred it with cracks and holes.

Our sleds kept carefully to the safe zone between the two red lines, so we had the luxury of keeping our hoods down for the trip, instead of breathing the musty, filtered air inside our suits. I was sitting on the bench seat of a transport sled, between Fian and Raven, our three Military impact suits conspicuous among the standard black suits worn by the other students.

There was an excited yelp from opposite us. 'Alien Contact have announced they've finished searching Alpha sector!' said Krath.

Everyone madly checked their lookups. 'So the alien home world definitely isn't in Alpha sector,' said Dalmora. 'I must admit I'm relieved. It would have been worrying to think of it being near my family on Danae.'

'And the General Marshal's speech was only a few days ago,' Krath said joyfully. 'If they can search Alpha sector that quickly, then it won't take long to find the aliens after all.'

'Alien Contact started searching Alpha sector the moment the alien probe arrived at Earth,' said Fian.

'Oh,' said Krath. 'That's months so . . . Why don't they borrow more people from the Planet First teams, or even stop working on the new colony worlds entirely for a while? The Isolationist Party would whine about it of course, because they don't want us to find the alien home world, but nobody else would care.'

'My brother would care,' said Amalie in acid tones. 'His Colony Ten group are on standby waiting for Planet First to declare the next Kappa world safe for first stage colonization.'

'Oh.' Krath shut up.

Raven hastily changed the subject. 'Why did people go to all the effort of building this Land Raft? Wouldn't it have been much easier to build San Angeles somewhere else?'

'They wanted to prove nature couldn't beat them.' I sighed. 'Imagine what it was like living back then, with their incredible cities and fantastic technology.'

'It wasn't a paradise back in 2250,' said Fian. 'They had some huge environmental problems to . . .'

He broke off as a block of concraz suddenly tumbled from one of the buildings and crashed to the ground, underlining the reason for the red danger lines. Raven frowned at it for a second before continuing the conversation.

'Their technology wasn't as advanced as ours in some areas. They could portal around Earth, but not to other worlds.'

'Some of us still can't,' I snapped. 'Back in 2250, no one would have sneered at me for being Handicapped. They didn't even know the Handicap existed.'

'Sorry,' said Raven. 'I was tactless.'

There was an uncomfortable silence for a couple of minutes, while I indulged myself with bitter thoughts about selfishly smug people who weren't just born norms, but rich Alphan aristocrats as well. Then I calmed down and felt guilty.

'Sorry, Raven. I'm frustrated and angry at fate for trapping me on Earth, and at the bigots on Joint Sector High Congress Committee for ordering me and Fian out of the Alien Contact programme, but it isn't fair to take that anger out on you.'

'If it's any consolation, Jarra, I think most of the committee members regret that decision,' said Raven. 'They were heavily criticized for it, especially after the skunk juice attack. Some people said they were partly to blame for that, because they sent you away from the safety of Zulu base.'

I pulled a face. 'The committee members obviously don't regret it that much, because they haven't ordered us back.'

Raven shrugged. 'They've already backed down once, issuing that clarified order about your removal only being temporary. They'd have to be desperate to totally reverse their decision.'

'I've been as bad tempered as Jarra,' said Fian. 'It's not just the frustration of having to wait to rejoin the Alien Contact programme, but the strain of having someone following us round all day and sleeping outside our door at night. I know you're doing it to protect us, Raven, but it sometimes feels like I'm Threeing instead of Twoing.'

I frowned. 'Raven, if you're sleeping in the corridor, aren't the autovacs a problem?'

'They were annoying the first night, trying to sweep me up, but they've classified me as a permanent obstacle now,' said Raven.

I pictured Raven stubbornly holding his ground in the corridor against the autovacs. It was funny, but it also emphasized how hard and how patiently this Alphan aristocrat was working to keep Fian and me safe. Fian was obviously thinking the same thing, because he groaned.

'I surrender. I'll try to stop complaining about privacy, but remember I draw the line at a triad marriage.'

I giggled. 'Since I'm Betan, I suppose I . . .'

Fian waved a finger at me. 'No, Jarra! No triad marriage!'

We'd reached the edge of the island now. Ahead of us, we could see two other islands of the Land Raft, each supported on massive legs that went down, and down, and . . . The sleds stopped and everyone got off and slowly walked towards the low wall that guarded the sheer drop.

'Don't get too close to the edge,' said Playdon, 'that wall's badly cracked.'

We stopped at a safe distance from the edge, and stood there in awed silence for a few minutes. The view was stunning but also terrifying. It wasn't just the height; the two nearest islands looked like giant alien spiders, and beyond them were dozens, hundreds more, set out in neat lines. It gave me the unnerving impression I was watching an invading force marching across the ground to conquer Earth.

With an alien sphere up in orbit, and the Military busily searching for the alien home world, I daren't say that aloud. 'Amaz,' I said instead. 'We must be as high up as the top of one of the old skyscrapers on New York Main Dig Site.'

'I don't believe it.' Raven's voice cracked with emotion. 'I really don't believe it. This can't be real.'

I heard harsh birdcalls, and turned to see a flock of what looked like crows swooping over a nearby building. A much larger bird launched itself from the top of the building, and soared out over the edge of the Land Raft. Wings spread wide and rigidly unmoving except for the feathers at its wingtips, it circled to ride a thermal upwards. A second huge bird appeared through a jagged hole that must have once been a window, and followed it. I tipped my head back to watch them flying, and saw other birds circling even higher in the sky.

I pointed up at them. 'Look!'

'A variety of birds, particularly birds of prey, use the Land Raft as a nesting site,' said Playdon. 'They treat the islands as their private artificial mountain tops, and will fly out for large distances to hunt prey on the ground below. If they start swooping at you, get your suit hoods up and sealed quickly to protect your faces.'

'Is that likely to happen?' asked Amalie.

'Only if you disturb a nest,' said Playdon. 'Another day, we'll portal down to explore the California Rift area at ground level. We'll see the Land Raft from below, visit the wreckage of one of the toppled islands, and take a look at the earthquake fault line itself.'

Raven shook his head. 'I'm being seriously unprofessional here. I should be watching for trouble, not staring at impressive views.'

Fian glanced across at where Krath was standing with

Amalie, and then leaned towards Raven and whispered. 'Raven, could you give me some combat lessons?'

Raven looked startled. 'I could, but why? It's my job to do any fighting.'

'After the attack on Jarra . . . Well, I'd feel happier knowing I could deal with a situation like that without Lolmack's help. We'll have to find somewhere quiet in the park to practise though, because I don't want Krath watching and making fun of me.'

Raven opened his mouth to speak, but closed it again, frowning at something. I saw Petra was walking towards me. She stopped when she was still a few paces away.

'What does she want?' asked Fian.

'No idea,' I said. 'It's probably best if I talk to her alone.'

I went forward to meet Petra. She looked round warily at the watching class and Playdon, before speaking in a low voice intended only for me.

'So you want a fresh start? Well I don't. Even when I thought you were human, I didn't like the way you constantly showed off. Once I found out you were really a lying, throwback ape . . .'

I'd been angry at her insults before, but I wasn't this time. Petra had been through a nightmare of questioning by Military Security, but she was still forcing herself to defy me so she could hang on to some shreds of her pride. I respected that.

I suddenly realized the two of us were very alike. Looking at Petra now was like seeing my own mirror image. If she hated all Handicapped, I'd had an equally indiscriminate hatred of norms before I joined this class. If she used words like ape, I'd used the word exo often enough in the past.

'I think you began with an unfair prejudice against the Handicapped in general,' I said, 'but I agree you've got perfectly valid reasons to dislike me now. The lies I told. The way I used my knowledge of Earth and the dig sites to try and prove I was better than the rest of you. It was Steen that accused you, got you arrested for something you hadn't done, but it certainly wouldn't have happened if I wasn't in the class, so . . .'

Petra gave me a puzzled frown, hesitated, and then spoke in a rush of words. 'I wasn't involved in the skunk juice attack, but I did send a message to Fian's father. I told him exactly how you met his son, and said you were sharing a room.'

I was too startled to speak. Fian's father had found out the truth from Petra! Did I tell Fian or not? It would only make the situation worse, so . . .

No, I couldn't hide this from Fian. I wanted him to let me make my own decisions and fight my own battles, and I had to let him do the same. Petra had sent a poisonous message to his father, and it was up to Fian to decide what to do about it.

Petra was still talking, a hint of apology mingled with the self-justification in her voice. 'Everyone had forgiven you for the lies. The newzies were all talking about you. Fian was adoring you and you didn't deserve him. It wasn't fair! Not after . . .'

She didn't finish the sentence. She didn't need to. The raw, painful subject of Joth's death was overshadowing this whole conversation. I could understand that every time Petra saw Fian and me together, laughing, talking, hugging, or arguing, it would rub in the fact that Joth was dead and she was alone.

'No it wasn't fair,' I said. 'I don't deserve someone as totally zan as Fian, but he isn't letting anyone split us up. Not you, not his father, and not the people throwing skunk juice at us.' I paused. 'Petra, you've had your revenge by setting Fian's father against us. Let it end there.'

I turned and went back to rejoin the others. Raven's tense

face relaxed, and his right hand moved away from where it had been hovering over his gun. I grinned at him.

'Were you expecting Petra to try and throw me off the Land Raft?'

I meant it as a joke, but he didn't laugh. 'I was prepared for that, as well as several other possibilities. You've already been hit in the face by skunk juice, Jarra. Next time, someone may try to kill you. You don't seem to be taking that seriously, but I must. I'm your bodyguard and it's my job to stop them.'

10

I was grazzed to discover Krath and an Adonis Knight shared a passion. For horror vids!

'This has the best holo effects of any of the vids set in the Thetis chaos year.' Krath adjusted the settings on the huge wall vid in the hall. 'It's a pity we have to watch it right after dinner though. Horror vid parties should be late at night.'

'I'm not allowing late night parties when everyone has to work on the dig site next morning,' said Playdon.

Krath sighed. 'Can we at least dim the lights?'

Playdon went and dimmed the lights, then sat on a chair in the corner. The class settled themselves on cushions on the floor, and I saw Fian glare across at Petra.

'I'd like to murder that girl,' he muttered.

'Military officers aren't allowed to murder civilians,' I whispered. 'At least give her credit for confessing she sent that message to your father.'

'I don't know why you're defending Petra. Steen's told me all about how she insulted you.'

'Steen's blaming everything on her, but he called me a lot of names too and . . .'

I sighed. I couldn't explain my muddled thoughts about how I'd started all this by lying my way into this class, and how the old me might have done the same as Petra if the situation had been reversed. If a norm had lied her way into a class of Handicapped, rubbed my nose in the fact she was better than me at history, and started Twoing with a boy I loved, I'd have been the one throwing insults around. It wouldn't have been the exact reverse, Petra would still have been the privileged one who had a real family and could portal to other worlds, but . . .

'I can understand her side of things.'

Fian shook his head. 'Well, I can't. The only reason I'm not making a formal complaint to Playdon is because I don't want to worry him right now.'

The vid credits started with an image of a heroic young man wearing a Military cadet's uniform.

'Tellon Blaze doesn't look much like Jarra,' said Krath.

'There are two good reasons for that,' I said. 'Firstly, there are a lot of generations between me and Tellon Blaze. Secondly, that isn't the real Tellon Blaze, just a vid actor.'

Raven passed me a bowl of something. 'It's an Adonis tradition to eat popcorn at vid parties.'

I'd never heard of popcorn. I peered at it suspiciously, before munching a lump of the peculiar stuff. There were startled squeaks around me, as holos of black spiky creatures shot out from the screen and started creeping round the hall, hissing at us.

'Dalmora, is your father going to make a history vid about Thetis?' asked Amalie.

'He intended to,' said Dalmora, 'but he's changed his mind. He feels it would be irresponsible to remind people of the chimera of Thetis when we're about to contact an intelligent alien species.'

Raven gave a guilty look at the holo chimera that were

now retreating, snarling, to the wall vid. 'He's right. I really shouldn't have . . . I hope everyone here understands the difference between the chimera and intelligent aliens with their own civilization. Every world we colonize has already evolved its own indigenous plant and animal life. The chimera were just a lethal animal species that were missed by the Planet First checks. Chimera had some incredible natural abilities that let them sneak through our portals and infest other worlds, but they weren't intelligent.'

I wasn't sure he was helping by saying that. I felt it just emphasized the point that humanity had barely coped with the chimera, an animal species that had no weapons and operated purely on instinct, and an alien civilization could be a vastly bigger threat.

'Don't worry, Raven,' I said. 'Everyone in this room must have already watched a dozen horror vids about the chimera. One more won't make any difference.'

The credits finished and the vid itself started. There were screams when the winged form of the chimera started flying round the room, and someone dropped the popcorn bowl.

After thirty minutes, we reached the point where Tellon Blaze made his legendary call to the General Marshal on Academy in Alpha sector. 'The Planet First team thought there were thousands of different animal species on Thetis, and they'd eliminated all the dangerous ones, sir,' he said. 'They were wrong. There's only one species on Thetis. Everything is different forms of the chimera!'

My lookup chimed, I read the message, and blinked with surprise. 'My cousin, Commander Drago Tell Dramis, is on his way to visit us.'

Fian and I stood up and headed for the door, and Raven gave a last regretful look at the wall vid before following us. We'd only just arrived in the portal room, when the portal flared to life and Drago stepped out of it.

I was about to ask why Drago was here, when I realized the answer. I'd been impatiently waiting for clan council to send me details of the rearranged presentation ceremony, but Drago had come to tell me there wasn't going to be one. I fought to keep my voice calm. 'We'd better go to our room.'

I led the way, and Raven took up position on guard duty in the corridor, while Fian, Drago and I went inside and closed the door.

'I'm pleased to see you're looking your lovely self again, Jarra,' said Drago.

I was in no mood for his flirting. 'I've seen the demonstrations on the newzies, Drago. I'd no idea making me a clan member would cause so much trouble.'

He nodded. 'The clan knew it would be controversial, but didn't expect things to get quite so dramatic. That's why I'm here.'

'If the Tell clan don't want me as a member now, please just tell me and . . .'

I broke off and bit my lip. It was stupid to feel so wounded by this. I'd coped perfectly well without a family for my whole life, so why should I care if some nuking Betan clan had thought better of having a throwback as a member? It was actually a good thing, because I'd always had reservations about Beta sector. The only reason I wasn't totally delighted about being dumped, was because Lolia and Lolmack would be devastated.

'Of course we still want you, Jarra,' said Drago. 'We're a small clan, so you were our first Handicapped birth. Clan council always planned to make you a clan member one day, and they aren't changing their minds now just because . . .'

He broke off for a moment to laugh. 'The Tell clan are proud of their heritage as the descendants of Tellon Blaze. Can you imagine what the hero of Thetis, the man who fought the chimera, would think of his heirs retreating from a few demonstrators waving placards? He'd disown the lot of us!'

There was an odd, dizzy feeling of relief.

'Please sit down, Jarra.' Drago glanced round, obviously looking for a chair, failed to find one and gestured at the bed.

I still stood there like a nardle until Fian put his arm round me and guided me to sit down next to him on the edge of the bed. 'Jarra has been under a lot of stress recently.'

'I appreciate that,' said Drago. 'It's why I've portalled back from Zeta sector to talk to you in person rather than just call you.'

I forced my brain to start working again. 'How could you do that when you're commanding the search of Zeta sector?'

Drago grabbed a cushion from the corner of the room, tossed it on the floor, and sat on it facing us. 'I'll only be away from Zeta sector for an hour or so. I'm travelling on a Military pre-empt, with my portal signal relayed straight through the system, so I don't have to wait in queues at all the Off-worlds and Sector Interchanges.'

I suffered a moment of pure jealousy. Drago could step into a portal in this dome and instantly reappear in a Military base in distant frontier Zeta sector. I couldn't even travel to Adonis. I thrust my envy aside, because Drago was still talking.

'I'm here to consult both of you about the arrangements for the ceremony, but first I need to explain what's been happening in Beta sector. The prejudiced are scared that Jarra joining our clan will set a precedent for others.'

I nodded. 'Our classmates, Lolia and Lolmack, have a Handicapped baby. Their alliance council say if there's enough public acceptance of me joining the Tell clan, they'll acknowledge Lolette's birth. Lolia and Lolmack are glued to every news report. One minute full of hope that Lolette may even be made a clan member, and the next in total despair.'

'We believe a lot of clans and alliances are secretly on our side,' said Drago, 'but only the Military alliance clans are openly supporting us. We have to fight and win this battle before the rest will risk their clan status by taking a public stand.'

He smiled. 'Well, we're good at fighting battles, and if no alliances are committing themselves to supporting us, none are saying they're against either. In the past, any clan considering granting clan membership to a Handicapped child has been subjected to huge social and political pressure. In the end, they've all backed down, so only a few have even acknowledged a Handicapped birth.'

His smile widened. 'The usual tactics couldn't really harm us, but the fact nobody is even trying them is highly significant. This isn't about an unknown Handicapped baby. The whole of Beta sector has seen you on the vids, Jarra, and knows you're descended from their hero, Tellon Blaze. People are rethinking their old assumptions.'

I shook my head. 'If public opinion was really on our side, there wouldn't be demonstrations against us.'

'The people with deeply ingrained prejudice don't want things to change,' said Drago. 'They're a minority of sad people who can't feel good about themselves unless they can smugly look down on someone else. The skunk juice attack didn't just delay our ceremony, it started furious debates on all the newzie channels. One side calling it a cowardly and shameful attack. The other saying everyone was over-reacting to a harmless joke.'

'Harmless joke?' Fian spat out the words. 'What's harmless about pure skunk juice burning someone's eyes and skin? If we hadn't instantly portalled Jarra to hospital . . .'

Drago raised a hand to stop him. 'I totally agree, and so do a lot of other people. Let me show you something.'

He tapped the Military lookup on his arm, and projected an image on the room wall. It was the same picture I'd seen on Earth Rolling News, showing the two contrasting versions of me. One happy, the other a beaten wreck. Beneath it was a line of text. 'Has Beta sector abandoned Fidelis?' I stared at it blankly. What was Fidelis?

'The day after the attack, this image started appearing on Betan shopping centre publicity boards,' said Drago. 'A few hours later, all the major Betan vid channels started showing a vid clip in their promo slots.'

He tapped his lookup again, and the image on the wall changed to a picture of Tellon Blaze. A voice started talking.

'We gave Tellon Blaze a hero's welcome. We gave him the right to found a clan of the *gentes maiores*. We gave him a majestic clan hall on Zeus.'

The image abruptly changed to the one of me with lank hair, and my face blotched lurid green and purple. The voice spoke again. 'We gave his daughter a face full of skunk juice.'

Drago tapped his wrist and the vid clip stopped, with that image of me still projected on the wall.

I shook my head. 'That's nardle. I'm not Tellon Blaze's daughter.'

Drago's left hand made the horizontal, air-slicing, Betan gesture of rejection. 'In Beta sector, the terms son and daughter have a wider meaning. Both the image and the vid clip were hammering home the same point. The attack on Jarra was a disgrace to the honour of Beta sector, breaking Fidelis by rewarding faithful service with a violent assault. The people behind this are throwing vast amounts of credits at their campaign, but they're staying carefully anonymous. Clan council know it isn't the Military, they know it isn't our alliance, and they can't work out who the chaos else it could be.'

Drago shrugged. 'Whoever it is, they're getting their message across and bringing more and more people on to our side. The prejudiced responded last night by sending a mob to paint insults on the walls of our clan hall. They knew they were asking for trouble attacking a Military clan hall, so the cowards ran for it seconds later. The newzies arrived suspiciously rapidly after that, and took vids of the hall before we could clean it up. All the newzie channels showed the coverage, and there was a full blooded fight between two rival parties of demonstrators outside our clan hall at dawn this morning.'

He laughed. 'Officially, the clan all stayed quietly indoors during that, but I'm betting some of the younger clan members sneaked out to practise their unarmed combat on the enemy. Now the newzies are asking clan council for a public statement about the ceremony, which is why I'm here to discuss plans with you.'

I'd no idea what there was to discuss, so I waited for Drago to explain.

'Clan council are furious about pathetic bigots throwing skunk juice at you and painting insults on our clan hall. Normally, a presentation ceremony is a private clan affair, but council want to invite all the clans of the Military alliance to witness this one. Their idea is to make a spectacular vid of the ceremony, with all the Military banners flying, and hand it over to the newzies so everyone can watch how we made you a clan member.'

Drago paused for a moment. 'That's what clan council would like, Jarra, but they understand you may not want to invite further attacks by making yourself the centre of a political storm. We can have the quiet ceremony we originally planned, or even hold it in total secrecy and not tell anyone it happened. The decision is entirely yours.'

I thought of those terrifying moments when I was blind

and helpless from the skunk juice. I didn't want to go through anything like that ever again, but . . . 'Having this ceremony in secret, as if it's wrong and shameful, wouldn't help people like Lolia, Lolmack, and their baby. Let's invite the Military alliance, and put it on the newzies!'

Drago grinned. 'When I saw the image of you after the attack, I was worried by the defeated look in your eyes, but that's the real Jarra talking. The Military can't get involved in Beta sector politics, but we've got permission to hold the ceremony at Military Base 79 Zulu because you're under Military Security protection.'

His eyes flickered towards Fian and back to me. 'We need to discuss some other details now. Our opponents know they're losing their real argument, so they're resorting to personal attacks. If they can discredit you, Jarra, they'll make the presentation ceremony a hollow victory because no other clans would follow our example.'

Fian frowned. 'What sort of personal attacks?'

Drago's face had an oddly wary expression. 'Please remember neither I, nor the clan, are criticizing Jarra. I'm just explaining the enemy tactics.'

If people had found out about some of the stupid things I'd done as a kid . . . 'Tell us.'

'They're attacking Jarra's moral standards because of the relationship between you two,' said Drago.

'What?' Fian was suddenly on his feet.

Drago raised both hands in surrender. 'Never hit a superior officer, Fian, especially when he's on your side.'

Fian slowly sat down again. 'But . . . how can they possibly criticize us? We're sharing a room, but everyone knows Beta sector is permissive. Their sex vids and . . .'

Drago sighed. 'People make ridiculous assumptions about Beta sector because of those vids. When other sectors brought in prudish rules about showing certain body areas, the sex vid industry naturally moved to Beta sector, but only nameless gutter clans and outlanders have anything to do with it.'

He paused. 'The truth is that Beta sector is just as strict, or even stricter than other sectors, it just follows a different set of rules. In Beta sector you're perfectly free to have whatever casual sexual relationships you wish, but you give up that freedom when you make a commitment to a partner or partners. Since Exodus century, Betan culture has been based around the extended family groups of its clans, with Fidelis as its central principle. Fidelis is about mutual obligations and keeping faith, about love and loyalty to your partner or partners, to your family, to your clan, to your planet, and to Beta sector.'

He paused. 'Let me give you an example. Clan council was told your classmate, Lolmack, helped defend Jarra during the attack. Now Lolmack's clan cluster have a clan of the *gentes maiores* willing to speak in support of them being officially recognized and granted a true clan name. That is Fidelis.'

I was grazzed. I knew how desperately Lolmack and Lolia's clan cluster wanted official recognition as a clan.

'Other sectors are suspicious of Beta sector because it's different from them,' continued Drago, 'but that feeling goes both ways. Jarra is being criticized because she has a Twoing contract with a non-Betan. Since she was abandoned to be raised on Earth, it's unfair to blame her for following Earth customs, but . . .'

I was the one angrily standing up this time. 'I'm not splitting up with Fian!'

'Clan council aren't suggesting that,' said Drago.

Fian frowned. 'So what are they suggesting?'

'There are two possibilities. One option is you stay together but cancel your Twoing contract. Jarra is perfectly free to have any casual relationship she wants.'

I shook my head. 'I don't understand what's wrong with having a Twoing contract.'

'Twoing contracts are made without including your clan, which is considered furtive and dishonourable, an insult to both your clan and your partner. They're also only for a limited time, and that's . . .' Drago waved his hands. 'Betans don't approve of term relationships, especially term marriages. A marriage may fail and the partners decide to end it, but we feel it's wrong to begin one by cold bloodedly setting what's effectively a future divorce date.'

'I totally agree,' said Fian. 'I don't like end dates even in Twoing contracts, and I'd never accept a term marriage after seeing the effect of one on my mother.'

'I suppose we . . .' I let the words trail off. I wanted to join my clan, set a precedent for other Handicapped kids, but this would still be very difficult.

'Jarra's a nice contract girl,' said Fian. 'She wouldn't be happy if we were together without a Twoing contract. What's the other option?'

'A Betan betrothal,' said Drago.

I sat down again. 'What's the difference between a betrothal and a Twoing contract?'

'A Betan betrothal is where the partners declare their intention to marry in the future, and their clans give their consent to the formal contract,' said Drago. 'The betrothal continues until you marry or petition your clan councils to break it. When Beta rejoined the other sectors at the end of the Second Roman Empire, the recognition of all Betan betrothal contracts and marriages, whether for duo or triad partnerships, was a key condition in the reunification treaty. Earth Registry, like every Registry outside Beta sector, just ignores the clan contract side. They treat betrothals as a continuous series of three month Twoing contracts, automatically renewing them until the partners tell them to stop.'

I didn't have any problem with a continuous series of Twoing contracts. I looked at Fian and he nodded his agreement, so I spoke for both of us. 'Yes, we could do that.'

'There's just one small complication,' said Drago. 'It's not socially acceptable for a member of a clan of the *gentes maiores* to be betrothed to a non-Betan, because they're effectively clanless and have no social status.'

Fian looked puzzled. 'But you married Marlise, and she isn't Betan.'

'Yes. We're a Military clan, so we regularly have marriages with non-Betans. There's a standard way of dealing with this situation.' Drago paused. 'Fian, how would you feel about being adopted?'

11

Our line of sleds drove along Gap 19. I was sitting with the rest of team 1 and Raven at the back of a transport sled. We had our impact suit hoods down to enjoy the sunshine, while Krath checked newzie channels on his lookup and babbled at us.

'Still no news from Alien Contact. I suppose the Isolationists are happy about that, but all this waiting is really frustrating me.'

'Think how Fian and I feel about it,' I said bitterly.

'My nardle dad has joined the Isolationist Party,' added Krath. 'He keeps messaging me, ranting on about how human culture shouldn't be polluted by alien influences. Oh and he wants me to talk you two into appearing on his stupid vid channel.'

'The answer's no,' said Fian.

'I told him that and . . .' Krath broke off and stared at his lookup. 'Totally amaz!'

I frowned. 'What's happened now?'

Krath grinned and used his lookup to project a holo image in midair. I watched in horror as miniature figures of Fian and I madly kissed each other.

'It's practically Betan sex vid standard,' said Krath in a gloating voice.

'Oh nuke!' I buried my face in my hands.

'That's a vid of us kissing after we sent the message to the alien sphere.' Fian's voice was impressively calm. 'We were at the Military quarantine post. It's not surprising a Military vid bee recorded us, but how the chaos did the newzies get hold of the vid?'

'I don't know and I don't care,' I moaned. 'What will your father think when he sees it?'

'Nuke my father,' said Fian.

The vid clip ended, but Krath promptly started replaying it.

'Krath,' said Dalmora, 'turn off that vid clip.'

'But I'm studying Fian's kissing technique,' said Krath.

'Turn it off!' said Amalie.

Krath sighed and turned off his lookup. 'I wish we could all go to the Tell clan ceremony instead of just watching it on the newzies afterwards. What's a Betan betrothal like, Jarra?'

I groaned. 'I don't know yet. I haven't dared to ask, but it's bound to be horribly embarrassing.'

'The clan said I could invite my family and Jarra could invite her ProParents,' said Fian. 'My mother's coming, my sister said she's too busy, and my father said I was out of my mind.'

'Candace is coming,' I said, 'but I didn't invite my ProDad. Technically, he isn't my ProDad right now anyway. After the Military found out he'd sold our secret mail addresses to the newzies, Hospital Earth suspended his ProParent status pending a hearing.'

'Your ProDad can think himself lucky you talked Colonel Leveque out of pressing charges against him,' said Fian.

Raven grinned. 'SECOP tell me Rayne Tar Cameron's still complaining about that. She wanted him locked up for life, or preferably executed, for creating extra work for her team.'

'Was your ProDad involved in the skunk juice attack as well?' asked Krath.

I shook my head. 'No, thank chaos. I've always known he cared more about getting paid than about me, but it would be horrible to think my own ProDad helped someone attack me.'

Dalmora tactfully changed the subject. 'As clan members, you'll automatically become Betan citizens. Will Fian's name change to Fian Tell Eklund?'

Fian shook his head. 'Clan custom is that only descendants of Tellon Blaze use the clan prefix.'

'When do you have to actually get married?' asked Krath.

'No fixed date,' said Fian, 'but if we haven't got married by the time we're thirty, we have to appear before clan council every year for a social responsibility lecture.'

I laughed. 'Drago says his father gives him that lecture every few weeks anyway.'

Krath shook his head. 'But what if you hate each other and want to split up?'

Amalie hit him.

'Ouch,' said Krath. 'Raven should stop Amalie hitting me.'

'I'd stop her hitting Jarra or Fian,' said Raven, 'but she can hit you all she likes.'

'We can petition clan council if we want to break the betrothal,' said Fian. 'If I've been a clan member for a year and a day, I'd still keep my dual Deltan and Betan citizenship afterwards, but I'd be thrown out of the clan because my adoption depends on my relationship with Jarra.'

I was grazzed. 'I didn't know that.'

'It's in clause 8 of the betrothal contract,' said Fian.

'I gave up trying to understand that after clause 3,' I said. 'I hadn't realized Betan betrothal contracts had so much legal stuff. Drago said ours was simple compared to the ones linked with clan business mergers and property transfers, but . . .'

I broke off my sentence because our sleds had stopped moving. Playdon jumped down from the lead sled, and spoke over our suit communications units so everyone could hear him. 'We're excavating two residential buildings today. Team 1 will work on this one.' He pointed at the closest building. 'They'll use the team circuit for their communications, and team 4 will be their relief. Team 2 will work a little further along the gap. They'll use channel 1, and team 3 will be their relief. Team 5 will just be watching.'

There were enthusiastic cheers from the members of team 5, who hated excavation work and planned careers as theoretical historians rather than archaeologists.

Working teams started shuffling sleds, while everyone else arranged themselves on transport sleds to watch. Since team 4 would be working shifts with us, they sat on the nearest transport with some of team 5. I noticed Steen and Petra glaring at each other.

Dalmora went to her enclosed sensor sled, Amalie and Krath to their bulky heavy lift sleds, and Fian to the slightly smaller tag support sled. I stood on the safe side of the red line and stared up at the building, planning my tactics. It was over twenty storeys high, with flexible joints connecting it to the neighbouring buildings on either side. A network of cracks ran through the front concraz wall, but the imbedded reinforcement mesh still held it together. I sighed, pulled up the hood of my impact suit and sealed the front, sentencing myself to the faint mustiness of the suit air system.

My team had their sleds in position now. I headed across to Fian's tag support sled, put on a hover belt, and waited for a moment while he attached the lifeline beam to the tag point on the back of my impact suit. Beyond the red line, the perfectly smooth surface of the gap was littered with fragments of concraz. I used my hover belt to skim over them, and set up two special directional sensors next to the wall of the building.

'Sensor net is active and green,' said Dalmora on the team circuit.

I went across to join her on the sensor sled. The six peripheral hazard displays were all completely clear, so I concentrated on the central display. Dalmora played with the sensor controls, expanding the image upwards and rotating it.

'You've got two intact floors right at the top of the building,' she said. 'The rest have collapsed.'

Playdon arrived to check the display himself. 'Those two top floors will be highly unstable. You'll have to work from outside the building and cut your way through the wall, Jarra.'

I nodded. Impact suits are amaz at protecting you, but I didn't want to test mine by having a mass of concraz fall twenty floors and land on my head.

Playdon handed me a laser gun. 'I'll stay here while you do the cutting. I know I don't need to tell you to be careful with the laser.'

'No, sir. Lasers scare me to death.' I checked the safety catch was on the evil thing, then headed towards the building. The front wall had a central gap where the door had been, so I just needed to extend the hole sideways in both directions to give us good access.

I carefully positioned myself to one side of the doorway, and turned off my hover belt so I could stand perfectly still. A large piece of concraz fell from somewhere high above, narrowly missing me.

'Errr, you're using laser cutters today?' Raven asked on the team circuit.

'Only the smaller laser guns,' said Playdon.

'Laser guns are just as lethal as full size cutters,' said Raven. 'They can cut through impact suits as easily as they cut through walls.'

'I believe I've mentioned that to my class several times,' said Playdon.

There was smothered laughter on the team circuit. Playdon reminded us of the safety issues every single time anyone used a laser.

'It's just . . . I didn't realize your excavation work was so dangerous. Civilians shouldn't be taking such risks.'

A chorus of voices instantly responded with the proud joke that had started when the dig teams at New York Main Dig Site rescued the Military from the wreck of Solar 5. 'We aren't civilians, we're archaeologists!'

Raven's resigned sigh was perfectly audible over the team circuit. 'All right, but please be careful, Jarra.'

'Don't worry,' I said. 'Fian is taking care of me. He's an amaz tag support.'

I waited a moment to make sure the building wasn't going to shed more concraz on me, then switched the safety off the laser gun.

'Laser on.' I triggered the deceptively innocent looking, glittering beam.

'Laser on,' echoed Fian's voice on the team circuit.

I cut horizontally across from the top of the doorway, and then vertically downwards, the beam of the laser slicing smoothly through the concraz wall and its reinforcing mesh. As the section of wall started toppling forward, I cut the laser and set the safety on.

'Safety on,' I said.

'Safety on,' echoed Fian's voice.

As he spoke, the lifeline beam tugged at my back, pulling me upwards and away from the building. I dangled in midair as rubble cascaded through the newly widened hole. When things calmed down, Fian landed me gently on the ground again.

I cut out three more sections of wall, then started extending the hole on the other side of the original doorway. As I was making the first vertical cut, a whole area of wall broke under the weight of rubble behind it. Rocks tumbled towards me as I set the laser gun to safety and shouted the vital words. 'Safety on!'

Fian's lifeline beam snatched me upwards, but one large block of concraz hit my side. My impact suit instantly triggered, the material locking around me, knocking the breath out of me and freezing me rigid, right arm still outstretched with my hand gripping the laser gun. I hovered on the edge of impact suit blackout, dimly hearing voices over the team circuit. One of them was Fian.

'Jarra, are you hurt? Jarra?'

I came back to full consciousness, breathless and still unable to move. 'I'm fine.'

'I hate having to wait to pull you out,' said Fian.

'Safety rules forbid moving someone holding an active laser for very good reasons,' said Playdon. 'The laser only has to waver to shear off an arm or worse. Everyone should understand that by now.'

Voices chorused on the team circuit. 'We understand.'

Playdon groaned. 'I wish you'd all stop parroting that like 2-year-olds. I should never have let Professor Kipkibor near one of my classes. Jarra, stop giggling!'

I couldn't pretend it wasn't me because everyone said I had a very distinctive giggle. 'Sorry, sir. I'm unfrozen now, Fian, so you can put me down.'

Fian landed me on the ground near the building. The hole in the front wall was much bigger than I'd planned, but that would just make my job easier. I took the laser gun back to Playdon.

'Thank you,' said Playdon. 'I'll go and supervise team 2 doing their laser cutting now. Call me at once if you have any problems.'

'I aged about fifty years in the last five minutes,' said Raven in a plaintive voice. 'Is it really worth taking all these risks just to find out about history?'

'We find more than history,' I said. 'Just before Exodus century, human civilization was at its peak, building incredible places like Ark, Eden, and New Tokyo. Then everyone rushed off to new worlds, the Earth data net crashed, and we lost half of human knowledge. These ruins are full of clues to lost science, either preserved by pure chance or protected inside a stasis box.'

'Lots of everyday items use ancient technology rediscovered by dig teams,' added Fian. 'Food dispensers, impact suits, even hover luggage.'

'I'd no idea,' said Raven.

I inspected the huge heap of rubble in front of the building. A small statue was glowing blue amongst the white and grey of concraz. I picked it up, admired the still perfect, glowplas figure of a dancing girl, then took out my tag gun and spent a couple of minutes firing electronic tags at the larger chunks of concraz.

'Amalie, Krath, please shift that lot over to the left.'

The beams of the two heavy lift sleds came to life, swinging across to lock on to the electronic tags and lift the concraz out of the way. I left them working and headed back to the transport sled with the statue.

'Raven, look at the fine detail on this. That means it was carved by hand, not manufactured in a mould. Back in the days before humanity reached Adonis, some artist spent ages lovingly creating this.'

'Fascinate!' Raven cradled it reverently in his hands for a moment, before handing it over to be packed away in a container.

As the heavy lifts moved away the larger debris, more came tumbling out of the front of the building. When it was stable, I searched through it, but found nothing except shards of glass. I tagged another batch of rubble for the heavy lifts, they shifted it, and the next rubbish cascade gave us the dented flexiplas case of some electrical item. Its contents were probably destroyed by time or already familiar to us, but we'd pack it and send it for examination by experts just in case.

'Drag net, please,' I said.

Amalie and Krath widened their heavy lift beams and used them to drag the smaller rubbish out of the way, while I indulged myself with a five-minute rest on the bench at the back of the tag support sled. When I stood up again, there was a nagging pain in my left side where the impact suit material had triggered to protect me from the block of rubble. I ignored it and headed back to the building. As a tag leader, I constantly suffered impact suit bruising from falling rubble and ricocheting tags, but my team always overreacted and blamed themselves when I got hurt.

We'd been working our way through rubble for at least another hour, when I saw a strange, fuzzy black object among a jumble of concraz lumps. 'Hoo eee! We've got a stasis box!' I yelled.

There was a chorus of cheers. Playdon must have been listening to us on the team circuit, because he came over to check the stasis box before we loaded it on to the transport sled.

'What's inside?' asked Raven.

'We won't know until Lecturer Playdon opens it,' I said. 'It looks like a standard memorial stasis box. People were leaving Earth, never to return, and they left stasis boxes in their abandoned houses, preserving farewell messages and sentimental items like wedding dresses. If you're lucky, the data chips include recordings of old newzie programmes and other precious data.'

'If you find lost technology, you can get a small fortune in rewards,' added Krath. 'When we were working at Eden dig site, we found an ancient research lab and . . .'

Playdon interrupted him, speaking on the team circuit. 'Team 1 will rest now. Team 4 continue the excavation.'

I groaned. Steen, tag leader of team 4, was already heading towards me. I went to meet him, and reluctantly handed over my hover belt and tag gun. The background hum of my comms changed note as Playdon spoke to me on a private channel.

'Jarra, I can tell from the way you're moving that you're in pain.'

I set my comms to reply on the private channel. 'Just impact suit bruising, sir.'

'You're quite sure you haven't cracked a rib?'

'I'm sure, sir.'

The rest of team 1 handed over their sleds to members of team 4, and we all went to sit with Raven on the transport sled. I set my comms to listen only, then unsealed my impact suit hood and opened it, savouring the moment when the fresh air hit my sweaty face. Blizz, pure blizz.

I watched Fian yank down his hood and struggle to sort out a tangle in his long blond hair using clumsy, fabric-enclosed fingers. I'd grown used to accepting the oddities of twenty different planets. Fian wouldn't carry a comb around with him. Krath was scared of butterflies. Dalmora was horrified if she was late for something. Amalie held her shoes upside down and shook them before putting them on.

'Fian, are those spots on your face?' asked Krath.

Fian glared at him. 'No! It's a rash from the sun block irritating my skin. The doctors at Zulu base have sent me some better quality stuff that should fix the problem.'

'It's nice the Military worry about your spots,' said Krath.

I heroically held back a giggle, used my Military lookup to send a message to my friend Issette, then displayed a holo image of a graph in midair.

'I thought you'd finished that work on historical analysis theorems for Playdon,' said Krath.

I sighed. 'I have, but when Playdon saw it he said it showed I had deeper underlying problems. He's started me on a remedial maths course.'

'Can't you get Fian to do it for you?' asked Krath. 'Playdon couldn't tell the difference.'

'I bet he could,' said Fian.

'Playdon's right,' I said. 'I can't spend my whole life dodging everything mathematical. The whole thing is my bullying school science teacher's fault. She kept telling everyone I was stupid, and the maths teacher joined in because he didn't like me.'

'I'm sure you weren't the easiest of pupils, Jarra,' said Fian, 'but those teachers sound very unprofessional.'

I shrugged. 'Most Handicapped babies are abandoned at birth, so Hospital Earth has huge problems finding enough staff in all areas of childcare. The Nursery units must be properly staffed, because babies can't feed themselves, so other residences and schools have to take anyone they can get. My history teacher was brilliant, he loved his subject, but my science teacher just wanted victims to bully.'

'I'd always assumed Hospital Earth hired people from other worlds,' said Raven. 'I'm an idiot. If people won't go to Earth to care for their *own* Handicapped babies . . .'

'We were constantly lectured about it in the residences,' I said. 'We had to be mature and self-sufficient and help care for the younger ones. We should choose careers in childcare because it was our responsibility to raise the next generation of abandoned babies from other worlds.'

'It surely isn't all left to the people who grew up in residences themselves,' said Raven. 'Don't some of the children of the Handicapped . . .?'

I shook my head. 'Nine out of ten of the children of Handicapped couples are born norms and head off to live on other worlds when they grow up. Hospital Earth keep talking about solving the problem by passing a law to force all the Handicapped to work in childcare for five years after leaving school.'

'Hospital Earth couldn't force a law like that on people,' said Fian.

'The main board of Hospital Earth run this planet and they can do anything they like,' I said. 'They aren't elected by us, they're off-worlders appointed by the sectors.'

Raven frowned. 'You can't mean the citizens of Earth have no say in its laws.'

'That's exactly what I mean,' I said. 'The only thing stopping the board members passing that law is they're worried forcing people to work with children would increase the child abuse numbers. They don't want to mess up their performance statistics and lose their precious Year End bonuses.'

The sensor sled alarm wailed, and we all turned to look at where team 4 were working. I saw the lifeline beam snatch Steen up into the air, and there was a crash of falling masonry from inside the building.

'What the chaos was that?' asked Raven.

'The two remaining upper floors must have collapsed,' I said. 'That's good. It'll be safe to work inside the building now.'

Steen was lowered to the ground and went back to work. For the rest of the morning, I battled to make sense of mind-numbingly boring maths problems, occasionally asking Fian to explain something. Eventually, Playdon's voice came over the team circuit and put an end to my suffering.

'Cassandra 2 tell me they're stopping work now, so we'll

pack up as well and head back to the domes with them. After we've eaten lunch, I'll open the stasis box, and then we'll start the afternoon lectures.'

A few minutes later, the sleds of Cassandra 2 drove past us, and our sleds started moving to follow them. By the time we reached the dome, I was wondering if I should put a fluid patch on my side. I didn't usually bother to treat impact suit bruising, but this was especially painful.

We all hurried into the dome, hoods down, eager to strip off the rest of our burdensome impact suits and shower. Team 1 all had rooms close together near the store room, so we headed down the corridor as a group. Raven was in the lead, followed by me and Fian, then Krath, Amalie and Dalmora. We'd nearly reached our rooms when I heard a sudden shrill sound I didn't recognize.

'Down!' Raven screamed the word.

I stared at him like an idiot for a split second, and he threw himself at me, knocking me to the floor. Another weight landed on top of me, which meant Fian was playing hero and protecting me too. The shrill sound must be coming from the tiny sensor Raven habitually carried. Fian and I had joked about the way he constantly scanned and rescanned the dome for threats but . . .

There was a deafening sound, and the flexiplas wall of the corridor flew straight at me.

I must have been unconscious for a few seconds after that. I woke to the sickening sight of Amalie lying on the floor next to me, her face slashed open to the bone and pouring blood. Krath was bending over her, seemingly unaware of the shard of metal that had stabbed right through his impact suit into his left arm.

Playdon's voice shouted from somewhere close by. 'Outside! Everyone, get back outside!'

112

I tried to sit up, but my head hurt like chaos. Arms grabbed me from either side, and Fian and Raven carried me back down the corridor, Fian's voice softly cursing in my ear. 'Nuke it, nuke it. Chaos typical that something would miss both of us and hit Jarra. She attracts trouble like . . .'

'I'm all right,' I said. 'Help Amalie.'

'Playdon and Krath are bringing Amalie,' said Fian.

There was the sudden warmth of sunlight as we went outside, and I saw the shocked figures of my classmates, Dalmora at the front with tears streaming down her face. Members of the Cassandra 2 team were running towards us, with the unmistakable purple and silver impact suit of Rono in the lead.

'What the chaos happened here?' he asked. 'Something lethal in your stasis box?'

'No,' said Raven. 'It was a small-scale, proximity activated, explosive device. A Military Security team are already portalling in to secure this dome. We'll use the portal in your dome to evacuate casualties to Zulu base for treatment.'

'Explosive device,' repeated Rono. 'Someone planted a bomb?'

'Petra,' said Steen's voice in instant accusation.

'Not Petra,' said Raven. 'The bomb was brought here while we were working on the dig site.'

'You can't be sure of that,' said Steen.

'I *am* sure of it!' snapped Raven. 'I'm not completely incompetent. I run constant sensor checks for threats, and this dome was totally clean when we left it.'

'But I . . .'

Playdon interrupted the argument. 'Rono, I'm going to Zulu base with my injured students. Can you take charge here?'

'Of course,' said Rono.

'But I still think . . .' Steen tried to speak again.

Rono turned to face him. 'Steen, if you don't shut up, I'll throw you in the pool to demonstrate that people wearing impact suits sink like rocks!'

Ten minutes later, I was lying on a bed in the Medical Centre at Military Base 79 Zulu, while the Medical team leader waved a scanner at me.

'I'm perfectly all right!' I wailed at her. 'You should be taking care of Amalie and Krath, not wasting time on me. There's a piece of metal stuck in Krath's arm, and Amalie's face . . .'

I broke off my sentence because the memory of Amalie's face made me feel queasy and horribly, dreadfully guilty. I'd known that agreeing to my clan's plan, defying the prejudiced, would make me a target. I hadn't thought an attack could injure not just me and Fian, but my other friends as well. People could be dead right now and it would be my fault. I'd been stupid, stupid, stupid!

'They're receiving treatment, Commander,' said the Medical team leader. 'Your own injury is potentially far more dangerous. You were hit on the head by a metal bolt and knocked unconscious.'

'I'm fine now.'

She sighed. 'Possible brain injury must be taken extremely seriously. Even massive injuries to the rest of the body can be successfully treated in full body regrowth tanks, but there are strict legal controls on the regrowth of brain tissue since it can result in loss of memory and personality.'

She frowned at her scanner, turned round to reach for something, and I felt the distinctive chill of something being sprayed into my neck.

'What was that?' I asked.

'Medication to prevent concussion. You can sit up now, Commander.'

114

I hastily sat up, swung my legs over the side of the bed, and stood up.

The Medical team leader sighed again. 'Please avoid exercise for the next twenty-four hours, and report any symptoms of nausea.'

I opened my mouth to say that my only symptoms of nausea were when I thought about Amalie's face, but thought better of it. Any mention of feeling sick would probably get me imprisoned in the Medical Centre for days.

I hurried out of the room into the adjoining waiting area, and nearly collided with Playdon. 'Where are . . .?'

I let the words trail off into nothing, as I saw Krath and Amalie sitting in the corner of the room. They were wearing sleeveless hospital robes over their skintights, and Krath had his right arm protectively around Amalie. He had a grey regrowth unit wrapped round his left upper arm, while Amalie had a red regrowth unit covering one side of her face, like some peculiarly lop-sided insect carapace.

'I'm so sorry,' I said. 'This is all my fault.'

'It's the nuking bomber's fault, not yours,' said Krath.

'But the bomb was aimed at me. Civilians shouldn't have to cope with things like this. Amalie's face . . .'

Amalie spoke in a slow, slurred, but determined voice. 'My face will be perfectly healed by tomorrow. Anyway, we aren't civilians, Jarra, we're archaeologists!'

I was torn between tears and laughter at her words. Before I could give way to either, three more people entered the room. Fian, Raven, and Colonel Leveque.

'Jarra, how is your head?' asked Fian.

I ignored him, turning to Colonel Leveque instead. 'Sir, we can't stay with our class any longer. We're putting their lives at risk!'

'I've already had this conversation with Major Eklund,' said Colonel Leveque. 'For security reasons you will both remain at Military Base 79 Zulu until after the Tell clan ceremony is safely over.'

I relaxed. Zulu base held the Alien Contact programme and was running on code black security protocols. No enemies could reach us here.

12

Fian ate his last mouthful of breakfast, and sat back in his chair to watch me stuffing myself with cheese fluffle on toasted wafer. He sighed. 'I still can't believe the Supplies team added cheese fluffle to this apartment food dispenser especially for Jarra.'

Raven left the table for a moment to get himself another glass of frujit. 'The whole base knows Jarra's addicted to cheese fluffle, so of course Supplies added it to her food dispenser. She's a Commander and that's only one step down from full Colonel.'

I paused between joyous mouthfuls. 'How does everyone know about me and cheese fluffle?'

'The Military work together and live together,' said Raven. 'Everyone knows everything about everybody.'

I finished eating, checked the time, and groaned.

'What's wrong?' asked Fian.

'I have to call Rayne Tar Cameron,' I said, 'and she scares me to death.'

Fian laughed. 'Order Raven to do it.'

'That would be cowardly.'

I took a deep breath and tapped at my lookup. Major Tar

Cameron's face appeared on the screen, with an expression that was several degrees less icy than I expected. 'Command Support. How can I help you, Commander?'

'I'm afraid Major Eklund and I need some new uniforms. Military Security salvaged what they could of our belongings, but as you can see our uniforms got a bit battered in the explosion.' I gestured at the jacket I was wearing.

'We'll send uniforms to you immediately, Commander,' she said in a briskly efficient voice. 'Does your bodyguard require replacement uniforms too?'

'No, Raven's things were stored in a room outside the blast area.'

'If any other items need replacing, then just give us details. We can order any non-Military items from civilian sources for you.'

I pictured the frosty Rayne ordering sleep suits and under-wear for me, and held back a shudder. I'd do my own shopping.

'Allow me to wish you and Major Eklund every happiness on your betrothal,' she added.

'Uh, thank you.' I ended the call and shook my head. 'That's odd. Rayne Tar Cameron has always reminded me of my school science teacher, but this time she didn't complain about anything, or even give me the disapproving look that makes me feel like an Adonis slime worm.'

'Is this the first time you've spoken to her since your promotion, Jarra?' asked Raven.

'Yes. She's just been sending me recorded messages, not . . . I suppose the promotion does make a difference. It was chaos ridiculous though, promoting me to Commander.'

Raven grinned. 'The whole of humanity watched you two contact the alien sphere. Even High Congress accepted the Military had to promote you after that.'

'Well, I'm not complaining about Jarra's rank, since it gets us this huge apartment,' said Fian. 'You could have a proper bedroom for yourself, Raven, instead of sleeping on the living room floor.'

'I prefer to guard the apartment door. It's . . .' Raven broke off as his lookup chimed. He studied it anxiously for several minutes while Fian and I waited in suspense. I finally gave in and asked.

'Something wrong?'

He looked up at me. 'No, it's just the preliminary report on the bombing. The analysis of my hand sensor's records confirms I scanned that area immediately before we left the dome and it was totally clear.'

He leaned back in his chair and ran his fingers through his hair with a sigh.

Fian frowned. 'Why are you looking so relieved? You knew you'd done that.'

'I knew it was part of my automatic routine,' said Raven, 'but I couldn't specifically remember doing it yesterday, any more than I could specifically remember breathing. I spent half the night worrying that I'd somehow forgotten, missed detecting that explosive device, and it was my fault people were injured.'

I was grazzed. I'd been so busy blaming myself that I hadn't realized poor Raven was feeling guilty too.

'You did everything perfectly,' said Fian. 'You probably saved our lives, because if we'd carried on walking into the blast zone with our impact suit hoods down . . .' He pulled a pained face.

'You were right about Petra then,' I said. 'She couldn't have planted the bomb. Everyone in both our class and Cassandra 2 were working on the dig site.'

'Given the civilian injuries, it's impractical to attempt to keep news of the bombing secret,' said Raven. 'An official statement is being released to the news channels. You are advised that any details not included in that statement should be regarded as completely confidential.'

Fian laughed. 'That doesn't sound like you, Raven. You're quoting Leveque.'

Raven nodded. 'This report came from him. One of the maintenance staff carried out the regular service and restock of the food dispensers yesterday morning. The explosive device was hidden in a box of food cartons that she delivered to the store room next to your rooms. Military Security believe she was completely ignorant of the contents of the box, so someone else must have tampered with it.'

I suddenly felt a lot more cheerful. For some nardle reason, it was comforting to know that no enemy had reached our dome, or entered the room I shared with Fian. There'd just been someone innocently delivering a box to the store room.

Raven suddenly laughed. 'Well, this explains why Rayne Tar Cameron was so eager to please you, Jarra.'

'It does?' I frowned. 'Why?'

'Because her Command Support team were supposed to make sure everything delivered to your dome was checked by Military Security, but they somehow overlooked the items being brought by maintenance people. It was Rayne's deputy, Captain Lorin, who made the mistake, not her, but her whole team will have had a withering lecture from Colonel Leveque. She probably thought you were calling to complain as well.'

Only minutes later, there was a chime from the apartment door. Raven jumped up, used the door controls to check who was outside, then opened the door to show a man with a rack of uniforms.

'I'm Captain Marston, sirs,' he said. 'Major Tar Cameron sent me with your replacement uniforms.'

Raven used a hand sensor to check the uniforms before he allowed them inside the apartment. Two days ago, Fian and I would have been amused by his paranoia. After yesterday's explosion, we didn't find it funny.

After Marston had gone, Raven closed the door, and stood there looking at it for a moment.

'Something wrong?' I asked.

Raven blushed. 'No. I was interested to see Qwin Marston. He's just been transferred here after getting betrothed to Rayne Tar Cameron, so the whole base is gossiping about him.'

'Rayne Tar Cameron is betrothed?' Fian grinned. 'I always thought she was an illegal robot, not a real human being with emotions.'

'I should have asked Marston what Betan betrothals are like,' I said.

Fian and I took the uniform rack into our bedroom and changed clothes, then went back to the living room to call Dalmora and check how Amalie and Krath were recovering. I was hugely relieved to find all three of them together, and Amalie's face perfectly healed.

'My face looked dreadful because it was bleeding so much, but it was just a straightforward cut,' said Amalie. 'The bone in Krath's arm was chipped, so he needs to keep the regrowth unit on for a few more hours.'

Krath pulled a face that was probably supposed to look stoic and brave, but looked more like he had indigestion.

'We'll be camping in the Cassandra 2 dome hall for a couple of days, while Military Security repair our own dome,' said Dalmora. 'Lecturer Playdon says he'll be sending you vids of the lectures you miss.'

I laughed and ended the call, feeling bouncy with relief at seeing my friends looking themselves again.

'If the Military are going to make a statement about the

121

bombing, we'd better send messages to everyone telling them we're all right,' said Fian.

I nodded. 'Good idea. I don't want Candace getting worried again.'

Fian and I recorded brief messages and sent them out, then I turned to Raven. 'I was wondering . . . You know we had to answer some tests before we could send the signal to the alien sphere?'

'Of course,' he said. 'I watched the vid coverage.'

'A friend of mine from Next Step, Keon, solved the last test when no one else could.'

Raven nodded.

'The Military have called him in as a civilian adviser to help decode the light signals from the alien sphere.'

'I'm aware of this.'

There seemed something odd about Raven's voice. He was probably puzzled by me telling him all this, so I hurried on with my explanation. 'Keon's Twoing with my best friend, Issette, and she's moved to live with him at Zulu base. During the day, Keon will be working and Issette will have classes for her Medical Foundation course, but I wondered if we could go and see them this evening.'

'I don't see any reason why not,' said Raven in that odd voice.

We spent the morning on the painful task of sorting through the crates of our mangled possessions, watched vids of Playdon's lectures in the afternoon, then went to visit Issette and Keon. Colonel Leveque was obviously being extra cautious after the bombing, because he sent a team of four Military Security officers to escort us.

We went down the corridor to the nearest base internal portal, two of the Military Security officers went through the portal ahead of us, followed by Raven, then Fian and me, and finally the other two Military Security officers. I was embarrassed that a simple visit to my friends was causing so much trouble.

Last time I'd been at Military Base 79 Zulu, it was just an array of huge domes set up at lightning speed on a suitable area of flat grassland. Now I was looking at houses in what could have been a standard Earth settlement. 'What are the big buildings over there?'

'That's the Military school,' said Raven, 'with a residence next to it for children whose parents are away on assignment. Base gossip says Colonel Leveque and Colonel Stone's children are arriving from Kappa sector tomorrow.'

'I didn't know they had children,' said Fian.

'A 14-year-old girl, and 10-year-old twin boys,' said Raven. 'Everyone's placing bets on whether they keep reciting percentages like their father.'

I laughed, not just at the joke about Colonel Leveque, but at Raven being an expert on base gossip. Presumably it was part of a bodyguard's job to be aware of everything that was going on.

Issette and Keon's house was a short distance down road 6. I was startled to see it had square walls instead of being the standard dome shape. Issette had sent me a long recorded message about how wonderful their house was, but I still hadn't expected anything quite this luxurious. I touched the doorplate, and a moment later the door opened.

'Jarra, Jarra, Jarra!' Issette beamed at me, then her expression changed to a glare as she saw Raven. 'What's that exo doing here?'

'Raven's our bodyguard,' I said. 'What's the problem?'

'He arrested Keon!' said Issette.

I stared at Raven. 'You arrested Keon? When? Why?'

Raven took a nervous step backwards. 'Before I was

assigned as your bodyguard, and because Colonel Leveque ordered me to.'

I waved my arms in despair. 'It made sense for Leveque to arrest Petra and my ProDad, but why arrest Keon? We'd never have contacted the sphere without him.'

'Exactly,' said Raven. 'Colonel Leveque naturally recruited Keon to assist in the research effort. Keon said it sounded like too much effort and refused, so Leveque ordered me to arrest him.'

I groaned. 'Keon was always refusing to do things at school. It drove the teachers crazy.'

'Surely even the legendarily lazy Keon Tanaka knew he'd never get away with that approach with the Military,' said Fian. 'He isn't still locked in a cell, is he?'

'Of course not.' Keon appeared from inside the house and grinned at us. 'Leveque proved he could make me extremely uncomfortable, I proved he couldn't make me think up answers for him, then we started to negotiate.'

I frowned at him. 'How could you be so stupid?'

Keon shook his head. 'I helped solve a single test, and I'm now a highly paid senior grade civilian adviser, with a luxurious house, my own lab, and a team of research assistants. You and Fian actually contacted the alien sphere, but you're not just still studying history and living in primitive accommodation on a dig site, you've got people throwing skunk juice at you and trying to blow you up. Consider which of us is stupid.'

Fian laughed. 'Keon's got a point there.'

I ignored him. 'For chaos sake, Keon. Contacting an alien civilization is a pivotal point in human history that could affect the future survival of our species. You should be doing everything you can to help, not demanding fancy houses.'

Keon's grin grew wider. 'I see no reason why I can't help

and have a fancy house for me and Issette. The Alien Contact programme has an unlimited budget.'

'Can we please go inside before we attract attention?' Raven waved his hand sensor at the house.

'I'm not having *him* in our house,' said Issette.

'Fian and I would have been killed in that explosion if it wasn't for Raven,' I said.

'Oh.' Issette thought about that for a moment, and her glare changed to grudging acceptance. 'Well, in that case . . .'

The four Military Security officers stayed on guard outside, while the rest of us went into the house. Issette insisted on immediately giving us a tour, so we trailed round after her, dutifully making admiring noises at each room. When we arrived in a room dedicated to Issette's old fluffy toys, including the deeply treasured, purple object called Whoopiz the Zen, I asked a question that had been worrying me.

'Issette, when you moved here to join Keon, you transferred from your Medical Foundation course in Europe to one in America. Isn't transferring courses bad for your studies?'

She shook her head. 'Things were getting really difficult in my old class. Everyone goes a bit wild when they escape from all the rules in Next Step, but some of the class were taking things too far. You can't expect lecturers to keep teaching when the students are throwing things at them.'

I blinked, imagining how fast Playdon would deal with students like that.

We moved on to the last room in the house. At first, I thought it was totally empty except for a black cube, but then I saw creepy, dimly glowing holo caterpillars crawling round the walls and ceiling. I backed nervously towards the doorway. 'What the chaos?'

'It's a test I'm running to analyse the light signals from the alien sphere.' Keon sighed. 'It's not supposed to be doing that.'

125

We retreated to a room with lots of cushform chairs and a huge wall vid. Issette handed round glasses of frujit, and then started telling us about the regrowth tank work she was doing on her new course. Given Fian and I had both spent time in full body regrowth tanks recently, I could have done without some of the more gruesome medical details. I was relieved when she started chattering about the house again.

Being here with Issette and Keon should have been just like the old days when we lived in Next Step, but Fian was sharing a cushform chair with me, and an Adonis Knight was sitting, quietly watchful, in the corner. I was oddly aware of the division between Military uniforms and casual civilian clothes, grouping me with the off-worlders rather than the Handicapped friends of my childhood.

Keon gave Issette an indulgent look. 'Issette's dreamed of a proper house of her own ever since Nursery.'

Fian grinned. 'Jarra never seems to care about where we live.'

'Jarra cares about family not houses,' said Keon. 'All through Nursery, Home and Next Step, she claimed she didn't care that her parents had abandoned her, but it obviously bothered her more than any of us.'

I glared at him. 'You're talking rubbish.'

'Really? You don't want to have a family? Given what you're putting yourself through to join this Betan clan . . .'

'Stop playing psychologist, Keon!'

Fian laughed. 'Why does Jarra have such a huge problem with psychologists?'

'Because she was test group,' said Keon. 'All of us in test group were left hating psychologists. Issette thinks they're wonderful, but she was in control group and they just had to do some standard behaviour and development tests.'

Fian frowned. 'What do you mean by test group and control group?'

'When we were 8-year-olds in Home, some off-world researchers used us in their psychology experiment,' said Keon. 'There were three Homes in our settlement and all the kids were split between test group and control group.'

I groaned. 'I'd really rather forget about . . .'

Fian interrupted me in a sharp voice. 'Why were they experimenting on you?'

'Researchers always use Handicapped kids in their experiments,' said Keon.

'But that's outrageous.' Raven suddenly joined in the conversation. 'The protection of humanity laws strictly regulate experiments on children.'

Keon shrugged. 'Some people would argue Handicapped kids aren't human so those laws don't apply, but it doesn't matter anyway because Hospital Earth has guardian authority over its wards. Researchers just have to ask them to get permission to use a group of us.'

Raven shook his head. 'Hospital Earth are supposed to care for their wards, not let people experiment on them!'

'They don't let them do anything too drastic to us of course.' Keon gave a cynical laugh. 'If a researcher accidentally killed a whole batch of ape kids, the board members might miss out on their vast Year End performance bonuses. This particular lot of researchers were studying our reactions to insects. Maeth's still got a phobia about them.'

I didn't have a phobia about insects, but I had highly unpleasant memories of those tests, so I changed the subject. 'Maeth's last message to me was really peculiar. Is anything wrong?'

'She's just jealous,' said Issette. 'We're all jealous about you joining your clan of course, but Maeth's really envious of all the fuss on the newzies about your betrothal as well.'

She turned to Raven. 'Our friends, Maeth and Ross, have been planning their wedding for years, but under Earth law

127

they couldn't even have a Twoing contract until they were 18 and legally adult. They still can't get married until they've completed three Twoing contracts adding up to at least a year.'

'Cathan's sulking too, Jarra,' said Keon. 'He keeps sending us all whining messages about how you're really his girl-friend, so he should be the one joining your clan, be in the Military, and have an Adonis Knight guarding him.'

I shook my head in despair. 'I dumped Cathan over a year ago!'

'His ego still won't accept you really meant it.' Keon laughed. 'I can sympathize with him a little. I can't help thinking that if I'd handled things differently, I could be Twoing with you myself.'

He winked at Issette. 'When I imagine the life I could be leading now, it gives me nightmares. Wearing a hideously uncomfortable impact suit. Working on a dig site with ruins collapsing on my head. Having skunk juice thrown at me, and people trying to blow me up. Worst of all, being constantly ordered around by Jarra.'

'I don't order Fian around!' I turned to Fian for support. 'Do I?'

'No, sir!' said Fian, cowering theatrically.

I groaned. Sometimes Fian can be quite impossible.

Keon laughed. 'Of course, you're a *Stalea of the Jungle* fan, Fian, so presumably you like dominant women.'

Fian grinned. 'Growing up in Delta sector was pretty frustrating. The rules on behaviour are incredibly strict, and girls won't give clues about whether they want you to push the boundaries because they're scared of being labelled shameless. I briefly had a girlfriend once, until I misread the situation and shocked her by trying to hold her hand. She was righteously horrified and instantly dumped me.'

He shrugged. 'Anyway, *Stalea of the Jungle* is very popular

128

with boys in Delta sector, because Stalea is a girl who . . . makes it extremely clear what she does and doesn't want from her boyfriend. I like that about Jarra too.'

'I can see your point,' said Keon, 'but I remember Jarra throwing Cathan across the room last Year Day. I'd be scared of a girlfriend who could do that.'

Keon was enjoying himself teasing me and Fian, and Issette was giggling, but I could see Raven had a look of frozen embarrassment on his face. I tried to move the conversation away from *Stalea of the Jungle*.

'Fian's no need to be scared of me, because he can throw people across the room too.'

'Really?' Keon gave Fian a disbelieving look.

Fian nodded. 'Raven's been giving us lessons in both armed and unarmed combat.' He stood up. 'Let me demonstrate by throwing you across the room.'

Keon hastily raised both hands in surrender. 'No need for that! I believe you, but I still think Jarra must be terrible to live with.'

'Oh she is,' said Fian in a martyred voice. 'Especially since Playdon forced her to start a remedial maths course . . .'

'Nooo!' shrieked Issette. 'Not Jarra doing maths! When we were at school . . .'

She was interrupted by three Military lookups chiming in unison. I glanced down at the message that had just arrived and gasped.

'Joint Sector High Congress Committee has ordered Fian and me to rejoin the Alien Contact programme!' I turned to Raven. 'I thought you said they'd only do that if they were desperate?'

He grinned. 'High Congress *are* desperate, Jarra. They ordered the Military to send you two away from the safety of Zulu base. Even after the skunk juice attack, they ignored repeated Military recommendations they should send you back. Now you've been injured in a bombing and the newzies are calling for resignations. The members aren't just worried about losing their seats on the committee to some of the rising stars in Parliament of Planets, many of them are feeling personally guilty about what's happened.'

'Are they feeling guilty because Jarra was injured, or because *norms* were hurt?' asked Keon in a cynical voice.

'I can assure you that my uncle is feeling equally guilty about everyone who was injured,' said Raven.

I blinked. 'Your uncle is a member of Joint Sector High Congress Committee! I'd no idea. I'm sorry if I've been a bit . . . rude about them.'

'You had good reason to resent their actions,' said Raven. 'I was unhappy about them myself.'

My lookup chimed again with another message. Fian and I weren't just back in the Alien Contact programme, we'd be attending a command meeting tomorrow morning!

13

Raven and the same group of four Military Security officers escorted us to the command meeting. Raven paused outside the door to talk to himself for a second.

'SECOP, we're outside the meeting room. Is it clear inside?'

'Guaranteed squeaky clean, Birdy,' said a disembodied female voice. 'We've got more than your two to worry about. The man himself is coming.'

Raven remained on guard outside the door, while Fian and I entered a small room with a round table surrounded by seven chairs. Three of them were already occupied. Colonel Mason Leveque sat between his wife, Colonel Nia Stone, and, unbelievably, Keon Tanaka.

I gave Keon a confused look, wondering what the chaos he was doing in a command meeting, before belatedly remembering to salute. I aimed the salute at Colonel Stone, since she and her husband were the same rank but she was the senior officer in the chain of command, commanding officer of the base and General Torrek's deputy. Out of the corner of my eye, I could see Fian carefully copying me.

Stone waved at the two seats next to her. 'Welcome back, both of you.'

Fian and I sat down, and there was a moment or two of silence before the door opened again. Everyone stood up as two figures entered the room. I stared at them, totally grazzed. SECOP had said the man himself was coming. I'd assumed that meant General Torrek, but it hadn't. One of those two figures was General Torrek, but the other wore a pure white uniform. Oh chaos! General Marshal Renton Mai, commander-in-chief of the Military, was here in person!

I stood rigidly at attention, facing the General Marshal while desperately watching Colonel Leveque out of the corner of my eye. I saw his arm move and matched his salute. Stomach churning, I held not just the salute, but my breath as well, until the General Marshal gave a nod. Everyone relaxed and waited until General Torrek and the General Marshal had sat down before sitting down themselves. I finally dared to breathe again.

The next few minutes passed in a blur. General Torrek said something that I instantly forgot, and then Colonel Leveque took over.

'The sphere's signal began repeating itself after a period of 493 hours and 11 minutes. We believe each light strand is a separate message, and we're estimating the number of light strands as in the region of 20,000, but the situation may be even more complex than that.'

He turned to Keon, who put a black cube on the table in front of him and started talking in a relaxed voice. 'The final test before the signal was sent to the sphere was about a technique used in laser light. I happen to know it really well, because I used it in a laser light sculpture called Phoenix Rising. I'll use that to demonstrate it for you.'

Keon activated his cube and a light sculpture sprang to life, a mass of whirling colour that periodically fused together for a moment to form a bird with outstretched wings.

'What's happening here is the light strands are set up in

132

groups of three,' said Keon. 'They're constantly moving and at intervals the three strands in each group line up and use the technique I'm demonstrating to become a single combined light strand. Those combined strands form the bird in this sculpture.'

He turned off his light sculpture. 'My analysis of the light strands coming from the alien probe shows it's doing the same thing, but it's keeping the light strands permanently in the combined state. If I did the same thing in my light sculpture, you'd only see the bird phase.'

'You're saying we haven't got 20,000 messages to untangle and translate, but 60,000,' said the General Marshal. 'Why did the aliens combine them like that?'

'To condense the data,' said Keon. 'Actually though, it's far more than 60,000 messages. I played around with the idea of extending what I did with Phoenix Rising to another level, so the combined light strands are grouped in threes and can combine again to make another image. I couldn't manage two successive combinations, but the aliens have.'

'That gets us up to 180,000 messages,' said General Torrek.

'Exactly,' said Keon, 'but my latest test suggests it's possible they combined at least one level further, taking it up to 540,000 messages.'

Colonel Stone frowned. 'Over half a million messages, each lasting for almost 500 hours. What can they possibly be saying to us that takes that long?'

'They must have sent us huge amounts of information on their culture, history and science,' said Leveque. 'Our problem is deciphering it. Just separating the data streams will be extremely complex, and then we have the translation problem.'

I thought of the obvious example from pre-history and winced. Leveque must have noticed my expression because he turned to me.

'You have something to contribute, Commander Tell Morrath?'

Oh nuke, I was going to have to speak in front of the General Marshal! I thought for a second, trying to work out the best way to explain this to non-historians.

'Language has been the official common tongue of humanity since 2280, but before then there were an unbelievable number of different written and spoken languages. There was a classic example way back in pre-history, when people spent hundreds of years trying to decipher a forgotten written language. They only managed it when they discovered the Rosetta stone, which had the same text in multiple languages. With the alien messages, we have no Rosetta stone, and we don't even have the common reference points of being the same race, so we'll . . .'

I broke off for a second. 'Wait!' I hammered my forehead with the palm of my right hand, trying to grasp a fleeting thread of thought. 'I'm an idiot. Of course we have a Rosetta stone. The aliens must have known we'd have this problem, so they've given us some reference points!'

'I think we need a further explanation,' said Leveque.

'Sorry, sir. I just . . .' I took a deep breath. 'Before we could signal the alien sphere, we had to answer some test sequences, but I think those were more than just tests. They were our Rosetta stone. When we separate out the messages from the alien sphere, one of them will be saying those sequences. That's probably all it will be saying, repeating it over and over. The other messages will be packed full of different data, but we look for one that keeps repeating.'

'Excellent,' said Colonel Leveque. 'That . . .'

He was interrupted by the distinctive sound of a lookup playing the first few notes of the latest song from Issette's favourite singer, Zen Arrath. I looked in horror at Keon, then realized it was coming from the General Marshal's

134

lookup. The commander-in-chief of the Military was a Zen Arrath fan!

General Marshal Mai glanced down at his mail message and sighed. 'The conflict between the two factions on Hestia is escalating, so Parliament of Planets has called an emergency session to authorize sending in peacekeeping forces to evacuate refugees. I'll have to return to Academy to deal with that, so we'd better move on from the translation problem to the more urgent issue.'

I blinked. What was more urgent than communicating with an alien race?

Colonel Leveque looked pointedly at Keon. 'Thank you for your contribution.'

Keon tucked his light sculpture cube under his arm, stood up, and ambled out of the room. Colonel Leveque waited until the door was closed behind him before speaking.

'The Military have been approached by a group of Hospital Earth researchers working on a cure for the Handicapped immune system problem.'

For a second, I was just bewildered by the sheer unexpectedness of his words, but then I was hit by pure fury. Hospital Earth's researchers had been claiming to be on the verge of a breakthrough for centuries. Generations of the Handicapped had been born, lived their lives hearing empty promises of a nuking cure, reached their hundredth and died. The researchers would never achieve anything other than tormenting us with false hope. I was still struggling to think of a way to say this without swearing when Fian spoke.

'Sirs, if Hospital Earth are suggesting Commander Tell Morrath should volunteer to test some cure then I wish to protest in the strongest possible terms. Hospital Earth's research into this problem has already killed at least six of their test subjects.'

'I assure you, Major, I'd never consider any such suggestion,' said General Torrek. 'Please listen to Colonel Leveque.'

'You two were recently involved in the discovery of an ancient research facility in the ruins of the city of Eden,' said Leveque. 'Its research results had been lost in the Earth data net crash, but copies were found on data chips stored in a stasis box. Some of that research involved the Handicapped immune system problem.'

I gasped. I didn't believe Hospital Earth's researchers would ever find a way to help the Handicapped, but the magicians who built Eden, Ark, and the California Land Raft could do anything. 'They'd found a cure?'

Leveque shook his head. 'Unfortunately, they'd proved a cure was effectively impossible.'

For a split second, I'd imagined myself free to travel to Adonis, to Zeus, to any of the worlds of humanity, but it would never happen. I would never leave Earth. I stared down at the table and fought to keep my face under control.

'The only potential cure was to override the Handicapped immune system with an artificial whole body control system,' said Leveque. 'That isn't a realistic option. An individually tailored control system would have to be developed for each person, and installed through major surgery with a suicidal risk of fatal consequences.'

Leveque was a specialist in threat assessment. When he said something was suicidally dangerous, I believed him. A few months ago, I might have thrown away my life in a desperate attempt to become human whatever the risks, but now I wouldn't. Whatever the prejudiced thought, I didn't need to *become* human. I already *was* human.

'There is, however, a different answer,' continued Leveque. 'The Eden data shows the Handicapped immune system is only adversely affected by conditions on a small percentage of worlds. Unfortunately, the Planet First teams have been deliberately selecting colony worlds of this specific type, because they're also worlds that experience low levels of solar storms.'

I stared at him, utterly stunned. The interference from solar storms messed up portal transmissions, so humanity chose colony worlds where solar storms were rare events, but that meant they'd been deliberately choosing worlds that would kill people like me. Nuke that!

'The Military wish to request a modification to Planet First selection criteria,' said Leveque. 'This would allow us to select some colony worlds that would suffer regular portal outages due to solar storms, but would also be compatible with the Handicapped immune system.'

My grazzed brain fought to understand his ornate words. Humanity lived on twelve hundred worlds scattered across six sectors of space, and I could never go to any of them, but if they found new worlds for the Handicapped . . .

'This issue is now my highest priority,' said the General Marshal. 'I've just suffered endless weeks of knowing there was a potentially hostile alien probe orbiting Earth and we had no way to evacuate the civilian population off world to safety. The aliens could still prove to be hostile, so I consider it strategically vital to have another planet where we could evacuate the Handicapped. Given Earth is our third highest populated world, I'd prefer several such planets, ideally at least one in each sector.'

A planet for the Handicapped in each sector! That wouldn't just be good strategically, it could change everything for us. 92 per cent of parents abandoned their Handicapped babies rather than face the stigma and culture shock of moving to Earth, but if parents could just move to another world in their home sector . . .

'Changing the Planet First selection criteria requires a vote of full Parliament of Planets,' added the General Marshal, 'so we'll need public opinion on our side to achieve it.'

There was a sick feeling in my stomach. 'Sir, the prejudiced will fight against this. They claim the Handicapped are less evolved than normal human beings because we can only survive on Earth. All the insults they use for us are based on that. Apes, Neanderthals, throwbacks. The moment one of the Handicapped steps on to another world and doesn't die, it'll prove they're wrong. We just need worlds chosen to have the right conditions for us, exactly the same way that norms do.'

The General Marshal nodded. 'After my recent interactions with certain members of Joint Sector High Congress Committee, I'm fully aware that we'll face bitter opposition from those with entrenched prejudice. That's why I came here today to meet you and Major Eklund.'

Fian and I exchanged startled glances.

'The vast majority of people have never visited Earth,' continued the General Marshal, 'so they've never met one of the Handicapped in person. They'd never even seen one of the Handicapped on the vids until General Torrek and I decided to put you into the public spotlight. Now the whole of humanity has not only seen one of the Handicapped on the newzies, but is taking a personal interest in her relationship with a normal born human.'

The General Marshal paused for a moment. 'The incident with the skunk juice was obviously deeply regrettable, but it generated a huge wave of public sympathy for what the newzies have been describing as two star-crossed lovers. Psych Division felt we could build on this situation to generate the public support needed to get the Planet First changes approved. They released a vid clip of you two kissing so they could study the public reaction.'

I gasped. 'So that was how the newzies got that clip!'

'You are on record as having said you'd do anything to help Earth, anything at all, Commander,' said Colonel Stone. 'Psych Division assumed that statement was still valid.'

'Well, it's valid for me, sir, but . . .' I glanced at Fian.

'It's valid for me too, sir,' said Fian. 'I have a recurring nightmare where I'm forcibly dragged through a portal to safety, while Jarra is left on an Earth being attacked by aliens. We must get these new worlds for the Handicapped.'

'Excellent,' said the General Marshal. 'Psych Division report the vid of you kissing heightened hostility in a small minority of people, but increased sympathy in the rest. The news of the bombing strengthened that sympathy, especially when we released vid images of the blast scene. Psych Division feel a romantic betrothal will bring public support for the Handicapped to a peak, so I'm preparing to approach Parliament of Planets immediately after your betrothal ceremony. If the vote fails, but there's sufficient support in one particular sector, we would still have a chance of getting that sector to request a planet under the specialist world rules.'

'The specialist world rules,' I repeated. 'You mean like Winter in Gamma sector, sir? They requested a planet much colder than Planet First rules normally allow, to be used for some manufacturing work.'

'Exactly,' said the General Marshal. 'Any sector has the right to request specialist planets within its own territory.'

I felt there was just one flaw in this plan, and that was me. 'Sir, I've never been good at being romantic, especially in public.'

I heard a smothered laugh from Fian, but the General Marshal's expression was perfectly serious as he replied. 'You now have the perfect opportunity to work on that, Commander. I've been advised that you have a childhood history of impulsive actions and emotional outbursts, beginning as a 2-year-old when you locked a nurse in a store room, so it would be unwise to allow you to give any live interviews.'

The General Marshal knew about me locking evil Nurse Cass in the linen store room! How the chaos could . . .? I remembered Candace innocently chatting to Leveque and cringed.

'There is, however, no risk with pre-recorded vid statements,' continued the General Marshal. 'Commander Tell Dramis is returning from Zeta sector to assist in making a vid statement from your clan, where you and Major Eklund will talk about your impending betrothal and how much you love each other. I'm pleased to see that Major Eklund's skin condition has been completely cured. Psych Division felt that spots would spoil the romantic effect.'

At another time, I would have giggled at the appalled expression on Fian's face as the General Marshal mentioned his spots, but I was too busy with my own worries.

'But . . . I won't know what to say.'

'That's not a problem,' said the General Marshal. 'Psych Division are writing you a script.'

14

'You'll be pleased to hear the vid is being shown on newzie channels in every sector,' said Drago.

I groaned. The previous day had been a ghastly ordeal, with vid bees mercilessly recording my struggles to say romantic lines about my enduring heartfelt love for Fian. To make matters worse, Fian seemed to be hugely enjoying the whole thing, and the vid technicians kept telling him he was a natural vid star.

'I was dreadful,' I said.

'Psych Division felt you looked endearingly shy,' said Drago.

I groaned again. I'm not the sort of person who wants to look endearingly shy.

'My father's seen it,' said Fian happily. 'He's sent me three furious messages.'

'Things aren't getting any better between you two then?' asked Drago.

Fian shook his head. 'My father thinks he can just order me to do whatever he wants.'

'My father thinks that about me too.' Drago laughed. 'Mind you, he's not just on clan council, but a General as well, so most of the time he's right.'

'I bet your father doesn't make the sort of remarks about Marlise that mine makes about Jarra,' said Fian.

'Mother would never allow father to be rude about Marlise,' said Drago. 'Mother thinks Marlise is a good influence on me.'

'Your mother is a General too?' I asked.

Drago shook his head. 'Mother's a civilian, so she outranks all of us.'

The three of us were standing in the middle of the base's newly added Flight Simulation area, facing two of the bulky grey simulators. Raven was on guard duty over by the door, being unnervingly silent and respectful because Drago was here.

'Jarra seemed to find yesterday very stressful,' said Drago, 'so I thought we'd take a break before the ceremony rehearsals tomorrow and have fun with some flight simulation programmes. I know you've only handled an aircraft in midair, Fian, so I'll help you try some take-offs and landings.'

Fian shook his head. 'I'd rather not. They scare the chaos out of me.'

Drago laughed. 'I'm not surprised. I've seen Jarra taking off in a survey plane, and the way she hammered the thrusters terrified me.'

I blushed. 'I know I don't need to hit them so hard, but . . .'

Drago pulled a sympathetic face. 'I understand, Jarra. You were dreaming of launching yourself to the stars, like the rockets of the ancient space programme.'

His words gave me an idea. 'Leveque said the Handicapped need worlds that have solar storms like Earth. Maybe that means what's important for us isn't to do with the planet at all but the star it orbits.'

Drago shrugged. 'Possibly.'

'In which case, Drago, it could be perfectly safe for you to give me a ride in your fighter up into orbit.'

'I've told you before that rides in my fighter are totally out of the question.' Drago shuddered. 'General Torrek wouldn't just demote me if anything happened to you; he'd make me spend the rest of my life as a supply clerk.'

Drago set the controls on both flight simulators, then he and Fian vanished inside one of them. I sighed and climbed into the other. When I sat in one of the two front seats, holos immediately appeared, and I stared round in confusion. Behind me were rows of holo-generated seats filled with figures in Military impact suits. What the chaos sort of Military ship was this supposed to be? It looked huge, much bigger than the real flight simulator, and surely too big to fit through any portal.

A voice spoke from my control panel. 'Solar 1, you are clear to launch when ready.'

Solar 1! Now I understood what the holos were showing. This was a solar array transport ship, which would be sent through a portal in pieces and assembled in space at its destination. They were normally used to move sections of solar array into position, but this one had been converted to carry passengers.

This simulation was recreating what happened months ago, when the crews of Earth's five solar arrays were trapped in space by a solar super storm bringing down the portal network. They'd had to convert ships only designed to operate in space, to attempt to enter Earth's atmosphere and land.

I faced forward again and saw the inside of a vast hangar. This ship had no hovers, so I cautiously used thrusters on minimum to manoeuvre out of the open doors, and gasped at the view outside. Bright dots of stars were scattered across the blackness of space, and Earth startled me by hanging overhead rather than below me, apparently on fire with the lurid bright green flames of the aurora caused by the super storm.

I used the mix of real and holo controls in front of me to project the white line of my optimal course on my main display screen, then spoke. 'Solar 1 is launching.'

'Deity aid you, Solar 1.' The voice from my control panel was distorted by static and heavy with emotion. The recorded voice of an officer on far away Adonis, who was agonizingly aware the seventy people aboard Solar 1 were probably going to die.

I hit my thrusters and chased a flashing dot on my main display that showed my ideal speed and position. The burning green planet Earth gradually drifted, so it was first to my side and then below me. I couldn't see any landmarks as I skimmed above the glowing emerald aurora, or even tell if it was night or day down there.

The dot vanished, replaced by a white image of a ship with lines running across it. Words flashed an urgent red. 'Correct entry angle! Correct entry angle!'

I played with the thrusters, and brought the nose of my ship down. The flashing words changed to amber before vanishing. I was at the correct angle for atmospheric entry, my shields were set to maximum, so now I could only hold my breath and hope.

As I entered Earth's atmosphere, a crazy juddering started. I fought with the controls, trying to keep my ship at the correct angle, aware of flashing red warnings about shield temperatures. Those suddenly vanished, meaning we'd survived re-entry, but I had a new problem. My thrusters were hiccupping madly, either affected by the solar super storm or just struggling with being in atmosphere and a gravity well. I was dropping like a rock.

I instinctively hammered the thrusters to maximum, and

checked the white guideline on my screen. Chaos take it, I was too low, much too low. There was green and pink fire overhead, and dark ground below me. Off to the right, was something bright that looked more like the lights of a settlement than a random fire started by the super storm. I mustn't crash on a settlement and kill civilians.

I wasn't gaining height, but I was losing it less rapidly than the flashing dot on the white line. In a few more seconds, I'd have matched it, but the ground was too close now. I instinctively lifted my knees, hugging them with my arms to make myself into a ball. There was a single vicious jerk and the simulation cut out.

'80 per cent,' said an automated voice. 'You have landed with nine passenger injuries and no deaths.'

I sat up straight and tried to calm my breathing. I hadn't expected a simulation to feel so real. I'd scored 20 per cent less than the real landing, but I'd never flown anything like . . . On the other hand, the original pilot wouldn't have flown anything like this either. Ships never went through atmospheric re-entry, they just portalled directly into a planet's atmosphere.

I was startled by the holos starting up again and a voice speaking. 'Solar 2, you are clear to launch when ready.'

Drago must have set the simulator to throw all five of the flights at me. Nuke him! I pulled myself together and prepared for my second launch. I knew what I was doing this time, so I did pretty well with the Solar 2 flight, but then came Solar 3. I knew its thrusters had been affected by the solar super storm, cutting out entirely just as it was about to land. Two people, including the pilot, had died.

All through the flight, I tried to plan for the landing, but it was useless. The ship was tumbling helplessly as it hit the ground, and the holo images around me flashed red before cutting out. That meant I'd died in the crash.

145

'71 per cent,' said the automated voice. 'You have landed with fifty-seven passenger injuries and four deaths.'

Solar 4 seemed easy in comparison, and I actually scored 2 per cent higher than the real landing, but then came Solar 5. My launch had been delayed because they hadn't finished converting the ship in time, and I came through the atmosphere far out of position for my intended landing site. I saw the black mass of the New York ruins ahead, just the way it had happened on the real Solar 5 landing. My best options were to land on the flatter area of the New York Fringe Dig Site, or try to reach the river or the coast.

I couldn't manage any of those. I was too high to hit New York Fringe, too low to reach the coast, and there were too many skyscrapers between me and the river. I managed to swerve and miss one jagged, skeletal giant of the past, but three more loomed directly ahead. I could only aim for the ground between two of them.

'93 per cent,' said the automated voice. 'You have landed with twenty-six passenger injuries and no deaths, but your ship is buried in rubble.'

'I tried to reach the river and failed as well,' said General Torrek's voice.

I turned, startled, and saw him standing at the entrance to the flight simulator. General Torrek had been the original pilot of Solar 5. I wondered what he thought of my amateur efforts to copy his landing.

'Can you come out please, Commander?' he said.

'Yes, sir.' I went across to the entrance, jumped down, and frowned as I saw the look on General Torrek's face. Something was obviously wrong. Fian and Drago were standing waiting next to Colonel Leveque and Colonel Stone. Fian's puzzled expression told me he didn't know what was going on either.

'Major Eklund,' said Colonel Leveque, 'are you aware your great-grandfather was a member of an organization sometimes referred to as Cioni's Apprentices, which was involved in several breaches of the protection of humanity laws?'

Fian stared at him. 'This is about my great-grandfather? Yes, I knew he was a member, sir. You knew it too. We had a conversation about him the day Jarra and I joined the Alien Contact programme.'

Leveque nodded. 'Have you had any involvement with this organization yourself?'

Fian gave a bewildered shake of his head. 'No. How could I? It doesn't exist any longer.'

Leveque glanced down at a small object in his hand. 'There is a 98 per cent probability that Major Eklund is telling the truth.'

'Of course I'm telling the truth,' said Fian. 'Why are you asking these questions?'

'Because an Interplanetary Crime Unit in Beta sector has reopened your great-grandfather's case, and ordered your arrest for formal questioning,' said Colonel Stone in a grimly angry voice. 'They claim it's purely coincidental they're doing this just before the Tell clan ceremony.'

'I hardly need to say the probability of that being true is vanishingly small,' added Leveque.

'They're arresting Fian to stop the ceremony!' I looked anxiously at General Torrek. 'You can't let that happen, sir. People have already tried to kill us, so there's no knowing what they'd do to Fian!'

'I'm not handing one of my officers over to suffer purely coincidental injury or death,' said General Torrek. 'What are our options here, Mason?'

General Torrek's use of Leveque's first name signalled he was shifting the conversation from formal to relaxed style. Leveque automatically responded by using first names himself, but his sentences stayed as complex as ever.

'We can use Alien Contact powers to protect the safety of one of our key personnel, but refusing to allow Fian to be questioned could be viewed as an admission of his guilt.'

'I have to go then,' said Fian.

'I'm not letting you do this,' I said.

'If I don't, this crime unit will claim I'm guilty of crimes against humanity. They'll say you knew about it, Jarra. After that, they just have to remind everyone about Gymir to destroy any chance of the Military getting new planets for the Handicapped.'

General Torrek frowned. 'If I must send one of my officers into the chimera's den, then he's not going unprotected. Mason, I want you and a Military Security team to go with Fian.'

'Unfortunately, that may be exactly what our enemies want us to do,' said Leveque. 'Jarra obviously can't go with us to Beta sector, and we can't adequately protect both her and Fian at two different locations without involving new personnel.'

'Why is that a problem?' asked Fian.

Leveque sighed. 'Analysis of the explosive device at your dig site dome indicates some components came from Military sources, and a 96 per cent probability they came from Military Base 79 Zulu itself.'

'What he means,' said Stone bitterly, 'is there's an enemy in Zulu base. In *my* base! Your bodyguard and the four other Military Security officers assigned to protect you can't be involved, or you'd already be dead, but everyone else is suspect.'

It took me a moment to absorb that, and work out what it meant. I wanted the people we trusted to concentrate on protecting Fian. He'd want them to concentrate on protecting me. We needed another answer here, because our enemies would just attack whichever of us was most vulnerable.

'This crime unit will drag out their questioning to make sure Fian isn't back for the ceremony,' said Drago. 'I'd better warn clan council.'

He moved away and started talking rapidly into his lookup. I buried my face in my hands, thinking frantically. Fian had to go to Beta sector, which meant I had to get everyone to go with him, but they'd never leave me alone and unprotected unless . . .

'Which officers are least likely to be a threat?' asked General Torrek.

'Drago's team have had extensive contact with Jarra without any problems and should be trustworthy,' said Leveque. 'However, fighter pilots would be an inadequate substitute for trained bodyguards.'

I lifted my head. 'There's a much better answer. Everyone protects Fian. Earth is my planet and I know more about it than any off-worlder. I'll go and hide. If the enemy can't find me then they can't hurt me.'

'You have a specific place in mind?' asked Leveque.

I didn't but . . . Yes, I did! 'There's a place no one else knows exists. No one at all. It's not mentioned in any records, I discovered it totally by accident, and I never told anyone.'

Nia Stone looked thoughtfully at me. 'Jarra's right that no one can harm her if they can't find her, and she's demonstrated her specialist knowledge of Earth before.'

Fian stared at her. 'You surely aren't considering Jarra's plan?'

'Our existing tactics for protecting you two haven't worked that well,' said Stone.

'But it's suicidal!' said Fian.

'No it isn't,' I said. 'You walking into an enemy trap is suicidal.'

Fian turned to General Torrek. 'You can't let Jarra go off alone!'

General Torrek frowned. 'I don't like the idea, but . . . Do we have any other options, Mason?'

'This course of action does have a degree of risk,' said Leveque, 'but a substantially lower one than either inadequately guarding two targets at locations known to the enemy, or including suspect personnel.'

He paused for a moment. 'Regarded purely tactically, our best option would be to protect Jarra and send Fian for questioning without any defence. I estimate an 89 per cent probability he would suffer fatal injuries, generating a massive wave of public sympathy that would allow us to achieve the changes to the Planet First selection criteria.'

My face must have shown him exactly what I was thinking, because he smiled at me. 'Please don't attempt to murder me, Jarra. It's my job to point out all viable courses of action, even those I would personally regret taking.'

'I don't sacrifice my officers like pieces in a game of chess.' General Torrek swapped back to Military formal manner for a moment. 'We'll follow your plan, Commander Tell Morrath.'

'I strongly object, sir,' said Fian.

'Your objection is noted, Major,' said General Torrek, 'but I've made a command decision and you must accept it.'

Fian gave me a deeply frustrated look. 'At least take Raven with you.'

'No. I can't vanish if I'm dragging round an Adonis Knight.'

Drago came back to join us. 'Clan council just hit orbital levels of fury. Skunk juice thrown at a daughter of our house, insults painted on our clan hall, and now this! Clan council

150

want me to accompany Fian. Under Beta sector law, he has the right to have a representative of his clan present to advise him during questioning.'

'I'm not actually a clan member yet,' said Fian.

Drago laughed. 'Our clan has publicly declared it intends to adopt you, Fian. Betan law recognizes your right to our protection under Fidelis.'

'Has clan council decided on a new date for the ceremony, Drago?' asked General Torrek.

'They want to keep the delay to a minimum,' said Drago. 'Will another week be enough time?'

General Torrek nodded. 'If the crime unit haven't finished their questioning by then, I can call a halt on the grounds they're disrupting the Alien Contact programme. Nobody will believe it takes more than a few days to prove innocence or guilt.'

'Good,' said Drago. 'Clan council said to warn you they're changing the arrangements so we'll need a bigger hall for the ceremony.'

'Bigger?' I asked. 'Why?'

Drago grinned at me. 'I told you clan council were furious. We aren't just making a vid now. We're going to have a live link of the ceremony for the newzies, and we're inviting the Fifty!'

Leveque smiled. 'Excellent tactics. I was concerned about a possible attack on the actual ceremony, but there's minimal risk of anyone resorting to violence when the banners of Beta sector are present.'

I didn't understand a word of this. 'The Fifty? Banners?'

'It's traditional to invite representatives of the fifty alliances headed by the clans of the *gentes maiores* to witness major events such as alliance mergers,' said Drago. 'They can also be invited to witness private clan ceremonies in exceptional circumstances, and clan council have decided this is exceptional. Custom dictates the Fifty can't refuse the invitation of a fellow clan of the *gentes maiores*, so they'll all send representatives.'

He laughed. 'There'll be a lot of urgent conferences about who they pick to represent them, whether to flatter us by sending a member of the head clan, or insult us by sending someone from the lowliest ranked clan in the alliance. I expect most will play safe and choose a representative from the middle ranks, but whoever they send will be bearing the banner of their alliance.'

I was still trying to understand this. 'And that means no one will attack the ceremony?'

Drago nodded. 'Even another attempt to delay the ceremony would show disrespect to the Fifty and make the alliances declare support for us, but an actual physical attack when the banner bearers were present . . . It would be an act of war against every clan in Beta sector, because they're all either a member of one of those alliances or in one of their factions.'

I was grazzed. I'd thought joining my clan would be simple, but the situation kept spiralling further and further out of control.

'Are we allowed to know details of your planned hiding place, Jarra?' asked Colonel Leveque.

'It's best if nobody knows, sir.' I took off my Military lookup and my gun, and handed them to him. 'I can't take these with me. I won't take any supplies with me either. That way the enemy can't possibly get any clues about my plans, or plant any tracking devices on me.'

General Torrek frowned. 'I'm not happy about you being unarmed and out of contact.'

'Military lookups and guns have built-in tracking devices and remote disabling as an anti-theft measure,' I said. 'If there's a spy in this base, they could locate me, send people

152

after me, and deactivate my gun remotely so I was a helpless target.'

'Only Command Support or Military Security officers would have the necessary authorizations for that,' said Leveque, 'but that's still a significant number of people.'

General Torrek sighed. 'Very well.'

'I want to portal out of the base to a random civilian portal,' I said, 'and use that to portal on to an unknown destination. I'm already flagged as having automatic Military pre-empt status, so I'll be able to portal anywhere on Earth.'

'What about the billing system, Jarra?' asked Fian. 'Civilian portals automatically send updates to Portal Network Administration for billing and traffic monitoring. If someone accesses the records for your genetic code . . .'

'We can get those records deleted,' said Colonel Leveque.

Fian shook his head. 'If someone's continually monitoring the system for Jarra's genetic code, watching for her movements, they'd see them before they're deleted.'

'What happens when a portal stays open for multiple travellers?' asked Drago. 'Does it send information for each person?'

'The more people travelling together to a destination, the cheaper the portal rate,' said Fian, 'so the portal sends information on everyone when it deactivates.'

Drago grinned. 'Easy then. We set the portal for multiple travellers, Jarra goes through, and then we destroy the portal while it's still active.'

'Destroy a portal?' I gulped. 'Portals are expensive.'

'Portal Network Administration can bill the Alien Contact programme for a new one,' said General Torrek.

'We'll make a statement on Earth Rolling News when it's safe for you to return, Jarra,' said Leveque, 'and I'll set up a special portal code to bring you directly to where we're protecting Fian. We can use the standard base portal code with some extra characters. What would you find easy to remember?'

I thought for a second. 'Apollo.'

'I'm surprised a planet in Alpha sector has significance for you,' said Leveque.

I laughed. 'I wasn't thinking of the planet, but the ancient space programme.'

15

We stood by a civilian portal on a deserted beach. I dialled my destination code, the portal established, and I carefully locked it open for multiple traffic.

'Be careful,' said Fian. 'If you get yourself killed, I'm going to strangle you!'

I laughed. I wanted to say something hopelessly soppy, but I was too aware of Drago and Raven standing next to us, holding guns set to maximum heat setting. 'You be careful too.'

I stepped through the portal, and turned to look back at it. For thirty seconds it glimmered steadily, then abruptly flickered and cut out. Drago and Raven had turned the transmitting portal into molten metal. I was on my own now.

Over to my left was a large dome, with a faded sign that brought back an avalanche of old memories. 'Home E161/8822.' I'd lived here as a little kid with Issette, Keon, Maeth, Ross, and the others. Beyond it were the domes of Homes E161/8823 and E161/8824, our traditional friends and rivals.

According to the rigid Home schedule, the kids and staff should be inside for dance class, but I couldn't risk standing around in plain sight. I ran towards the bushes growing against the dome wall, found the tunnel shaped path through them was still there, and crawled along it on my hands and knees. I'd grown since my days in Home, so it was a tight squeeze and twigs caught in my hair.

The spy at Zulu base would soon discover I was missing, and my enemies would start hunting for me. My Nursery, Home and Next Step were listed on my public record, so I had to move on quickly. I daren't use a portal again, but there were older ways to travel.

When I reached the hollow in the middle of the rhododendrons, I found what I was looking for. Every Home had its rebels who would hide out in places like this to dodge scheduled activities. Two kids of about eight years old glared at me from the shadows, instinctively aggressive at the sight of an adult intruder, then their faces changed to be utterly grazzed.

'Jarra Tell Morrath!' They chorused in unison.

The boy and girl were dressed in familiar dark brown tops and trousers, almost identical to the ones I'd worn myself years ago. I'd hated the way we were all dressed alike, and poor Issette had pined for the colourful and frivolous clothes the children in vids wore, counting down the days until she'd reach Next Step and have an allowance to buy her own outfits.

I fought off the moment of nostalgia, and concentrated on the present. 'I need your help. You know some people want to hurt me?'

'We saw it on Earth Rolling News.' The girl's voice was fierce. 'The stinking exos want to stop you joining your clan. They threw skunk juice at you and blew you up. Now they've arrested Fian!'

I nodded. 'I'm hiding until Fian gets back. You mustn't tell anyone you've seen me until after that, not even the other kids.'

'You can trust us,' said the boy. 'Everyone knows you're a 22. The newzies came and made vids of us, not just Earth Rolling News but Beta Sector Daily too! The 23s and 24s were so sick about it.'

I gave a startled giggle, picturing the 22s showing off in front of the vid bees. It would become part of Home E161/8822 legend, told to every new arrival, how Jarra Tell Morrath had lived here and the newzies had come to make vids.

The girl nodded eagerly. 'We'd never give you away. We're not just 22s, we're Betan as well.'

There was a longing note in her voice that was painfully revealing. Kids in Home spent a lot of time daydreaming about their unknown parents, and declaring they were from one sector or another. In my day, no one ever claimed to be Betan, but this girl had been watching the reports about me on Earth Rolling News. When I was presented to my Betan clan, how many Earth kids would be watching the vid coverage and dreaming it would happen to them? For some of them at least, that dream might one day become reality.

'True to 22,' the two of them said in ritual unison.

'True to 22,' I repeated the childhood oath in a nardle emotional voice. It was a promise that I wouldn't let them down. Nothing would stop me getting to that ceremony and changing their future for the better.

If I was going to keep that promise, I needed to be practical now. 'What are your names?'

'I'm Keon,' said the boy.

'I'm Sadia,' said the girl.

Another Keon, I thought, his name chosen from Hospital Earth's approved list. 'Keon, Sadia, is flicker beacon 46 still wired?'

Sadia shook her head. 'They found that when some nardle

157

forgot to put the mesh back and rabbits got in. We've wired 48 now.'

'Wonderful. I'll need to get to 48 without being seen. A lookup would be useful too. Do they still have a pile of old ones in stores?'

'Yes,' said Sadia. 'Follow us.'

I crawled through the bushes after the two of them, feeling like I was eight years old again myself.

'You wait here!' ordered Sadia as we reached the edge of the bushes. 'Keon will check flicker beacon 48 is clear, and I'll steal a lookup.'

I obediently waited. It seemed like fifteen minutes, but was probably only five, before the two of them arrived back. Sadia handed me a battered lookup.

'I checked it works,' she said.

'Thanks, this is absolutely perfect.'

'Flicker beacon 48 looks clear,' said Keon, 'and no one's at the brook, but if someone does show up don't frizz. Even the 23s and 24s know better than to give you away.'

Frizz was a new word to me, but the kids in Home were always lightning fast at copying the latest slang used by children in off-world vids. 'Sadia, Keon, thanks again. When this is over, I'll tell the newzies how you helped me.'

I stood up, sprinted across an area of open lawn, and dropped to my knees next to flicker beacon 48. The smooth metal column curved high up into the air, with the settlement force fence glittering on either side. This was a small settlement with only a few hundred houses, a shopping square, a Nursery unit, and a cluster of Home domes foolishly located right next to the force fence. Naturally, the kids had added a discreet circle of wire to create a hole in the field.

I lifted aside the sheet of wire mesh that covered the hole, wriggled through, and carefully pulled the mesh back into place again before running on into the woods ahead. Some parts of Earth, like the rainforest around Eden, were lethally dangerous, but most settlements were in special safe zones protected by animal control barriers from creatures like wolves and sabre cats. I was in Earth Europe safe zone now.

I slowed to a walk as I followed the track made by many small feet to where a brook scurried over smooth stones. This was our old playground. Issette had squealed at how cold the water was. Cathan had sulked when we pretended we were going to play hide and seek and then ran off without looking for him. Maeth and Ross had played house in the hollow of an old dead tree.

We'd been happy to share the brook with the rabbits, foxes and deer who came to drink, but we'd back away nervously, ready to run, when the wild boar came snuffling their way out of the trees. All the new kids were sternly warned to be especially careful if they had babies with them.

The other warning was never to stray into the trees beyond the brook. The year before I arrived from Nursery, one of the youngest boys had wandered into the woods and got lost. The kids from all three Homes searched desperately for hours, finding him only just before sunset. The lot of them arrived back after bedtime roll call and found all the Homes in uproar, with frantic ProParents searching the settlement.

After that, everyone kept within strict self-imposed boundaries. Everyone except me. I did what no one else seemed to have thought of doing, and looked up some maps so I wouldn't get lost. They were ancient ones of course – maps weren't important now every settlement was just one step away on the other side of a portal – but I could find some of the old landmarks. The brook still ran along the same route. The road had become a wide, flat, grassy path. A village was just heaps of crumbled stones.

I'd scavenged among those stones and found tarnished

coins, a broken china cat, and a silver bracelet that I gave to Issette as a Year Day present. Those childish excavations had shown me the living past was all around us and started my love of history.

I crossed the brook on stepping-stones carefully placed by the massed efforts of children, and went on through the trees to the old road. That led me to another that was staggeringly wide, its route lined with jagged metal and concrete stumps. I walked along the colossal ancient highway for hours, skirting sections that had once been held up on pillars and now lay fallen and broken.

It was dusk by the time I reached a wide river. The gap in the centre of the bridge was bigger than the last time I'd walked this way, but I didn't need to get across. I turned to my right instead, following the riverbank until I saw the glow of a settlement ahead, and the closer, brighter lights of a huddle of four very unusual houses. Ones built long before Exodus century, and painstakingly repaired by enthusiasts who'd relearned old skills of working with stone and wood.

I'd helped work on them myself, and was left wondering how people put roofs on houses in the days before lift beams and hover belts. I suppose experts did the job centuries ago, while we were a bunch of bumbling amateurs and needed all the modern help we could get.

These were real homes, not museum exhibits. The people living in them had picked houses close to a settlement, they had modern sanitation and heating, a portal, and a couple of hover sleds for emergencies.

There was a force fence surrounding the houses to keep the deer and rabbits out of the gardens. I walked up to the keypad controls and entered the security code. The date the Earth data net crashed.

The glitter of the section of fence in front of me abruptly

died. I walked inside, restarted the fence behind me, and went to knock at the door of the nearest house. The metal knocker, shaped like a lion, was a genuine relic from the days of pre-history.

After a minute, the door opened, and I saw the familiar figure of a man in his forties. He was wearing reproduction nineteenth century clothes, so he must have just got back from helping out with some historical re-enactment event.

He looked totally grazzed to see me. 'Jarra! What are you doing here?'

I smiled at the man who was far more than just a school history teacher. He'd given up endless weekends and holidays to take the school history club to work on the Fringe dig sites of ruined cities. He'd taught me how to wear an impact suit, run a heavy lift sled, and fire a tag gun. He'd helped make me who I was today. When I left school, I tried to tell him how much I appreciated everything he'd done, but I'm chaos bad at emotional stuff and probably didn't make much sense.

'I'm hoping to borrow some camping equipment, sir,' I said.

16

The insistent chime of my lookup dragged me out of a dream where Colonel Leveque sat in a field of Osiris lilies, training a class of rabbits to calculate probabilities. I opened my eyes to a sight that was even weirder than the dream. I was in a vast cavern, its walls lined with glowplas that shone gently in response to a shaft of sunlight coming through a hole in the roof. The effect would have been incredibly lovely if it wasn't for the carvings.

I'd no idea how the artist had managed it, but he'd carved figures actually within the glowplas rather than on the surface, their hands pressing forwards, giving the creepy impression that real people had been trapped inside and were struggling to escape. To make things worse, their faces had mouths stretched inhumanly wide in manic smiles.

I didn't know whether the carvings were intended as adverts, or as warnings, to the customers who'd come here to get powered on blizz. I found them disturbing, but I had to put up with them because this was the perfect place to hide. Even when it was in use back in the twenty-third century, there'd have been no record of it on the Earth data net, because supplying blizz was illegal. Its customers would only have known its portal code, not its location.

Then came Exodus century, people streamed away from Earth, and the details of blizz were lost in the Earth data net crash. Nowadays, only historians like me knew the origin of the word blizz, and that you usually said pure blizz because impure blizz killed its users.

With the people and the blizz gone, this cavern had been left abandoned and forgotten for centuries, until the day I'd been walking by and literally stumbled across the hole in the cavern roof. I'd been somewhere I shouldn't have been, on my way home after doing something I shouldn't have done, so I'd never told anyone about my discovery.

I crawled out of my sleep sack, grabbed a carton of food from my hover bag, and walked past the broken remains of an archaic portal to where a rope ladder dangled from the hole in the roof. I climbed up it and took a cautious look above ground. The people searching for me would probably have guessed I was somewhere in Earth Europe. I didn't think anyone would ask questions at Home E161/8822, they wouldn't expect to learn anything from kids who'd arrived after I'd moved on to Next Step, but I'd talked my history teacher into taking his friends to visit some old students of his at Berlin Main Dig Site. I might be over-reacting, but I wasn't risking anyone being hit with mind-bending drugs to make them betray me.

Things were just as peaceful outside as they'd been for days. The usual moa was there, pecking the grass by the edge of a tangle of bushes and brambles. I knew moa weren't dangerous, they were one of the few genetically salvaged species allowed to pass freely through animal control barriers, but I was still wary of a bird that size. Fortunately, it seemed equally nervous of me.

I sat on the grass, took out the lookup Sadia had given

me, and started checking newzie channels. The lookup was one of hundreds of thousands supplied to Hospital Earth, and would have done ten years' service with multiple owners at some Next Step, before being replaced with a newer model and passed on to Home E161/8822. So long as I only used it to watch vid channels, there was no reason for anyone to link its identity code to me.

I had an alert set so the lookup chimed when major news stories broke in Beta sector. It had woken me twice during the night. Once because a famous vid star had died, and later with some political story about clan Marius withdrawing from the August alliance.

I skipped through the main newzie channels for sectors Alpha through Epsilon. Several were replaying the Tell clan vid statement. They seemed especially fond of the bit where I broke down in embarrassment while saying a cringingly romantic scripted line. If I heard one more vid presenter say I was endearingly shy and vulnerable behind my Military facade, I would vomit.

The alert chimed and the lookup changed channel to Beta Sector Daily. The Betan alliances were still staying safely neutral on the issue of me joining my clan, but the newzie channels had started taking sides, and Beta Sector Daily was our strongest supporter. I saw a smiling Drago announce that the Interplanetary Crime Unit had found no evidence against Fian and would soon be releasing him.

'Hoo eee!' I yelled in delight, startling the poor moa so it ran away into the bushes.

Beta Sector Daily went back to their studio and a presenter started talking. 'There are calls for an official enquiry into the conduct of . . .'

I changed channel to Beta Veritas, which was the leading voice of the opposition. '. . . failed to establish active involvement himself, but his undesirable ancestry is still . . .'

'Bigots!' I shouted.

I swapped channel again to Delta Sector Vision, who were interviewing a blonde girl. I was about to change channel yet again, when I heard her say she'd been boy and girling with Fian before he went away to university.

This was Fian's ex-girlfriend! I studied her critically. She would have been pretty if it wasn't for the big nose.

Well, maybe the nose wasn't really *that* big, but she was obviously doing the same as Cathan, exaggerating things to get on the newzies. The interviewer seemed to realize that too. I indulged myself by watching him poke fun at her for a little longer, then washed in a nearby stream and reluctantly opened my carton of food.

My history teacher stored some of the history club equipment at his home. He'd been able to lend me one of the club's few precious hover belts, as well as an impact suit, skintight, and other oddments, but food was a problem. He'd only had two crates of cartons of Osiris mash, which the club were given free after New York Main supplies department accidentally ordered a hundred times more than they actually wanted.

After living on Osiris mash for days, I'd grown to hate it, but my only other option was to try fishing in the stream. People really did catch and eat fish back in the days of prehistory, but I was a twenty-eighth century girl, used to meat and fish tissue grown in vats. Even if I could make myself kill an innocent fish that was happily swimming around in front of me, how would I cook it? I'd cooked potatoes and saus on a camp fire, but genuine fish had bones and heads and . . .

I was glumly munching my way through my carton of Osiris mash, when my lookup chimed for another alert. A male presenter was talking.

'. . . reactions to Major Fian Eklund being attacked on Hercules in Delta sector.'

'Nuke it!' The lookup was showing Beta Sector Daily. I checked their text news feed, but it hadn't updated yet. Their idiot presenter was babbling about Betan clan alliances now. I didn't care about nuking alliances, or joining Betan clans! I should never have let Fian get involved in this. I'd been stupid, stupid, stupid!

I madly changed channels. Surely one of them would tell me . . . I recognized the angry woman talking on Delta Sector Vision. Fian's mother!

'. . . beaten up for having a Handicapped girlfriend. These people should . . .'

Beaten up implied Fian wasn't dead or seriously injured, didn't it? I checked Delta Sector Vision's text news feed and finally found the details I needed. Minor injuries. Thought to be receiving medical treatment at a Military base in Delta sector.

I suddenly felt giddy, so I dropped the lookup into my lap and rested my head on my hands for a moment. Fian wasn't badly hurt then, but why had he done something as totally nardle as going home to Hercules instead of coming straight back to Earth, and why had the Military let this happen? Raven and Drago were supposed to be protecting Fian. When I saw them, I would . . .

I would do what? Try and pin the blame on them? Fian had been beaten up for having an ape girlfriend who dared to challenge the traditions of Beta sector. This was all my fault. I'd started this whole crazy chain of events by applying to University Asgard instead of University Earth.

My instinct was to head straight back to Military Base 79 Zulu, but that would be criminally stupid. Fian was still in Delta sector so I mustn't give our enemies the chance to attack me as well. I had to keep my head, follow our plan, wait until Fian was back on Earth before leaving my hiding place and portalling to join him.

I went back down into the cavern to shovel my belongings into my hover bag, then dragged the bag up the rope ladder to the surface and sat on the grass, impatiently watching Earth Rolling News until I finally saw General Torrek appear. He said the words I needed to hear. Fian was back on Earth!

It was going to take me several hours to travel to the nearest portal. I wanted to save time by calling Zulu base and asking for an aircraft to pick me up, but it was too big a risk. The spy at Zulu base might eavesdrop on that call and learn my location. If I was right about enemies searching for me in Earth Europe, they might reach me before the Military aircraft.

I sighed, put on my hover belt, clicked the key fob to make my bag start chasing me, and hovered off along the valley. When I reached a river, I skimmed along above it at the maximum speed of my hover belt. Heading downstream, the flowing water added to my speed, so I was moving perhaps three times as fast as someone on foot.

I knew it was time to leave the river when the current suddenly increased. My map showed a waterfall somewhere ahead, and I didn't want to go over it. I aimed for the bank, steadied myself on an overhanging tree branch, and snagged my hover bag before the current could steal it from me. There was a brief struggle to pull myself up on to the bank, and then I was safe on dry land.

Progress was much slower now because I was going uphill. When I reached the high point, I got a clear view of the surrounding countryside. Far away to my left was another hill with two stylized human figures on top of it. One male and one female, their hands holding a planet above their heads. The unmistakable Spirit of Man monument.

I wrinkled my nose in disgust. Off-worlders had built this vast monument, to mark the site of Earth's first true interstellar portal, and commemorate the historic moment when the first colonists portalled from Earth to Adonis. It had always felt like a deliberate insult to me. Two of those colonists died within minutes of setting foot on the new world. That was when they discovered some people were Handicapped. That was the moment humanity was divided into the norms who had the ticket to the universe, and the people like me, the apes and the throwbacks, who could look up at the stars but never reach them.

I turned away from the monument, and looked in the direction I was going. There was the distinctive glittering line of an animal control barrier running through the valley ahead, and a huge forest covering the slopes of the low hills beyond.

I sat down for a moment to study my map. The forest hadn't been here when this map was made, but somewhere among those trees was an old road that would lead me straight to where an archaeological research team was excavating an ancient underground storage facility. I could use their portal to get to Zulu base.

A herd of deer appeared from the forest. I watched the barrier flash brightly, its sensors checking the deer as they walked through it. During the chaos after Exodus century, many of the new colony worlds had problems with dangerous species reaching their inhabited continent. Now they all had barriers like this, selective force fences that allowed through all but restricted species, dividing the inhabited continent into about a dozen sections. Their barriers were just a safety precaution, but Earth's barriers were constantly working to defend the safe zones from dangerous creatures.

The restricted species list varied from planet to planet of course, but one creature was on all of them. The nightmare of Thetis ended with the extinction of the chimera over a quarter of a millennium ago, but the Military still followed the standing orders of the legendary Tellon Blaze. Every Military ship and sled had chimera detectors. Every animal control barrier checked for them. It was strange to think the glittering force field ahead of me was still blindly following the orders of my long dead ancestor, checking for a dreadful threat that no longer existed.

I didn't want any problems with the wolves on the other side of the barrier, so I changed into my borrowed skintight and impact suit before heading on into the valley. I held my breath as I went through the barrier, feeling my skin tingling and my hair standing on end as the force field flared brightly around me.

I'd just reached the outskirts of the forest when I saw a dark speck in the sky. That was an aircraft, and it was coming straight towards me! I told myself not to panic. Aircraft were rare, very rare, but people did use them sometimes. This one looked too small to be delivering a portal to a new location, and a dig site survey plane wouldn't normally fly across country, but there were emergency rescue flights sometimes. The plane could be flying to the coast to help a pleasure boat in trouble.

I shouldn't panic, but I shouldn't take chances either. I pulled up my impact suit hood and sealed it, then hovered at top speed into the forest with my hover bag chasing after me. As I dodged my way between tree trunks, I could hear the aircraft getting closer. The massed leaves overhead meant the pilot wouldn't be able to see me, but almost all aircraft carried some sort of sensor equipment.

I heard the aircraft getting closer and then circling overhead. It was definitely hunting me then, but how had my enemies found me? How could . . .?

The animal control barrier! The barriers must send reports on what crossed them, and my enemies had been watching that data. Nuke it!

I headed on through the trees as fast as I could. The aircraft definitely had sensors; the big question was if it had weapons as well. In theory, the Military controlled all the weapons of humanity, because every legally constructed gun included a device to let it be remotely disabled if it fell into the wrong hands. In reality, no system was perfect, and the people hunting me might have illegal weapons.

I heard a strange hissing sound, and glanced behind me in time to see trees explode into balls of flame. 'Oh nuke, nuke, nuke!'

I skimmed onwards, setting my hover belt to maximum height to clear a fallen tree, and frantically thinking. The people in the aircraft were using a Planet First incendiary weapon. They'd probably got it from the spy at Zulu base. I was wearing a standard dig site impact suit, which would protect me from fire, but only for a short time.

I had to get to water. A stream wouldn't help me; I needed a river or a lake. There was no lake nearby, but I could cut across to meet the river again. I tried to picture the map from memory. The river was somewhere to my right.

I swerved right, and the trees ahead of me burst into flame. I dodged left to avoid them, then went right again. The sound of the aircraft faded, and then grew louder again as it circled for the next attack. How far was that nuking river? It should be close but . . .

The world turned red, and I was burning, burning, burning, then the impact suit temperature controls brought things down to merely scorching hot and my feet landed on the ground. The heat had killed my hover belt, so I had to do my own running now.

I forced my feet to start moving and stumbled on, blinded by flames and smoke. I made it out of the fire, looked up like a nardle at the aircraft directly overhead, and slipped. I tumbled over and over, falling helplessly, hands grabbing for ground that had totally vanished. I caught a glimpse of what was below me just before the fabric of my suit triggered, sending me into impact suit blackout.

17

When I drifted back to consciousness, I thought I'd had an accident on the dig site, and wondered why things were so strangely quiet. My suit comms should be squawking Mayday codes, Playdon and Fian should be yelling at me on team circuit, and Dig Site Command talking to me on auto distress channel, but the only sound was my own breathing.

Then the memories came flooding back. I'd removed the comms unit from my suit so it couldn't be used to locate me. I'd been running through fire with an aircraft chasing me. I'd found the river I was looking for, but it was deep down in a ravine and I'd slipped over the edge.

I opened my eyes and saw only confusing bright mist. As I was falling, I'd seen a waterfall and a rocky cauldron of churning water. I must be underwater now.

I heard myself whimper in fear. Dig site sensor sleds constantly checked for the six major hazards. Fire, electrical, chemical, water, radiation and magnetic. Underground waterways on a dig site could be lethal, sweeping someone away where no help could reach them. Their suit would keep recycling their air, but it would slowly grow more and more toxic until . . .

'Don't be a nardle,' I yelled at myself. 'You're not going to suffocate. You aren't in an underground river. You're just at the bottom of a pool of water, you idiot, so get yourself out.'

Impact suits are heavy. I couldn't swim to the surface wearing mine, and if I tried taking it off then I'd probably drown before I could get free of the tightly fitting fabric. My only option was to get on my hands and knees and crawl along.

I could see the hazy outlines of boulders through the mist of water and bubbles. They were slippery with algae, so it was a struggle to get over them. When I finally reached what must be the edge of the pool, I found only sheer vertical rock. I groped my way along it, panic rising as I found more and more cliff edge. I must have done a complete circuit of the pool by now. I was trapped!

An accident a couple of months ago had left me with a fear of impact suits. I thought I'd defeated it, but now the old terror hit me again. I had to get out of my suit. I had to . . .

I felt the shapes of small pebbles under my hands, and a much gentler slope. A minute later, I was sitting on a boulder at the edge of the water, yanking down my impact suit hood. After the Solar 5 rescue, the Military had awarded me the Artemis medal, their highest honour. Thank chaos there was no one here to see a holder of the Artemis medal shaking with fear about falling into a little pool of water.

I put my hands over my face for a few minutes, until my breathing calmed and my nerves stopped jangling, then belatedly remembered the aircraft and looked hastily up. The steep sides of the ravine limited my view of the sky, and there was a lot of noise from the waterfall, but the aircraft seemed to have gone.

Of course it had gone. The people aboard it would have

been watching me on sensors, and seen my life sign suddenly vanish as I fell into the ravine and went deep underwater. They'd think I was dead, and they'd get away fast in case someone had seen them firing that weapon, reported it, and the Military came to investigate.

Unfortunately, that wouldn't happen. I was in one of Earth's huge wilderness areas. I knew the archaeological research team were the only people near here, and their camp was on the other side of the hills so they wouldn't have seen anything.

I looked round for my hover bag, but it wasn't in the pool. I picked my way across jumbled rocks to where the river rushed further on down the ravine, but still couldn't see the bag. It probably hadn't made it through the fire.

No hover bag meant no lookup. No lookup meant I couldn't call for help. I'd have to climb out of this ravine, either wearing the cumbersome impact suit, or barefoot in only my skintight.

I looked up again and saw the smoke in the sky was getting thicker. A lot thicker. Trees had spread across Europe in the four hundred years since Exodus century, and there were forest fires every summer. The incendiary weapon must have started one, which was just about the last thing I needed right now.

I had to think of a plan. No one would come to fight a forest fire out here in the wilderness. It would be left to burn itself out, and that could take days or even weeks. I couldn't stay down here for days without food. Besides, the clan ceremony was tomorrow morning America time. I had to reach a portal by mid-afternoon tomorrow Europe time.

Judging from what was happening to the smoke above me, the wind was driving the fire on through the forest towards the hills. I'd never make it through the burning forest to reach the archaeological research team. I had to get out of the trees by the shortest route possible, and head back towards the animal control barrier, but what would I do when I reached it?

If I went through the animal control barrier again, my enemies would know I wasn't dead and come straight back here. I'd have to stay between the forest and the barrier, which meant a choice between heading north or south. I tried to remember the map, think of somewhere this side of the barrier that might have a portal, but couldn't.

Well, I'd worry about that when I reached the barrier. I studied the rocky walls around me. The area near the waterfall was wet and slimy, climbing the ravine on the opposite side of the pool would leave me on the wrong side of the river, and there was a nasty overhang near the top of the cliff on this side.

I started moving downstream, heading for where the side of the ravine sloped rather than being a sheer drop. When I reached the narrowest part of the ravine, I had to wade through the river itself. I stayed in the shallows, but still had to work my way from one jutting rock to another, clinging to them to stop myself from being swept away by the current.

The ravine widened again, and I could get out of the water and stand on a miniature shingle beach. I had a much better view upwards now. This slope was definitely climbable, but there was acrid smoke and ash drifting in the air, and I could see a burning tree hanging over the edge of the ravine.

I hesitated. Climbing back up into a forest fire was a totally crazy idea. I had no food, but there was plenty of water here. I could wait things out for a day or two at least. Fian would be worried sick, but . . .

No, I couldn't do that. The Fifty were going to be at the ceremony. If I didn't show up, it would be disrespectful to them and offend every clan in Beta sector.

I sealed my hood and started climbing the slope. My suit hampered my movements, but I needed its protection because I was being showered with debris from above. Mostly just fragments of soil and rock, but once a whole burning branch hit me, triggering one side of my suit so I had to wait for the impact suit material to relax before I could move on.

I slipped back down twice, but on the third attempt I finally reached the top and pulled myself cautiously over the edge. The ground was blackened and smouldering, and the trees around me were on fire. The suit air filters saved me from having to breathe the billows of filthy black smoke, but the heat would soon overload the cooling system.

I started running, feeling my suit temperature rising, and hoping like chaos that I was going the right way. There was a flash of bright blue among the ash on the ground. The blue of my hover bag! I risked a swerve sideways to grab it, hugged it to my chest, and staggered on into the blessed normality of green trees and then out into dazzlingly bright sunlight. I'd made it!

I'd made it out of the fire, but my suit temperature was still at burning point. I ripped the front open and yanked the hood down, gasping with relief as the smoke-scented breeze hit me. The air was still warm from either the sun or the fire, but far cooler than my suit.

I slowed to a walk, felt my suit temperature drop towards a more bearable level, and was just starting to relax when there was a blur of movement to my left. Something feline with massive muscles sped past so close that I could have reached out my hand to touch it. Sabre cat!

I gave a squeak of alarm. With my suit hood down, the cat could rip my face apart with one casual sweep of a paw. Fortunately, it was intent on putting as much distance as possible between it and the forest fire, streaking off southwards along the line of the animal control barrier.

'Idiot!' I yelled the word at myself, and pulled my hood back up with shaky fingers before sealing my suit again. I should never have opened it, but if I hadn't then I'd have had burns, so . . .

I walked closer to the barrier and knelt to examine my bag. The hovers were obviously dead, and the bag wouldn't open, but its material had been burnt completely through at one end so it was only held together by the wire reinforcements. I started yanking my belongings out of the hole. The melted cartons of Osiris mash had welded themselves to the charred remains of the sleep sack, but they hadn't reached my uniform and shoes.

I put the singed but intact uniform and shoes aside, and burrowed further into the bag, hunting for one vital thing. The lookup. I was just thinking it had fallen out of the hole in the bag and been lost somewhere back in the forest, when I found it in one piece and unmelted.

'Thank chaos!'

I tapped at it, eager to call Colonel Leveque for help, but it didn't respond. I tried again and again, but still nothing. A Military lookup would have survived the heat of the fire, but it had been too much for an elderly civilian model.

'Nuke it!'

I made one final attempt at coaxing the lookup back to life before giving up. Now what? I looked at the glittering animal control barrier in frustration. I had virtually no chance of finding a portal on this side of it, but crossing it would be suicidal.

I'd have to head either north or south. North seemed the sensible choice, since the sabre cat had gone south. I turned back to my heap of belongings. The sleep sack was utterly disgusting, but I'd better take my uniform. It wasn't worth burdening myself with any of the rest, or the bag with its wire reinforcements hanging . . .

Wire! I glanced from the wrecked bag to the animal control barrier. I knew how to wire a settlement force fence. This barrier was much fancier but the same principles surely applied. If I could make a gap in the force field, the barrier wouldn't detect me passing through, and wouldn't betray me to my enemies.

I picked up the bag and my uniform, and followed the animal control barrier until I reached the nearest giant flicker beacon. Then I sat on the ground and started the slow job of removing stubborn shreds of material from the precious wire reinforcements.

18

Wiring the animal control barrier had been a brilliant idea, but it would have been even more brilliant if I'd thought of it the first time I went through. Then there'd have been no enemy aircraft, no fire, no falling into the ravine. I could have simply hovered my way through the forest for an hour or so, introduced myself to the archaeological team, and used their portal to rejoin Fian.

Instead, I had to trudge across country on foot to reach the Spirit of Man monument. I wore my impact suit for the first hour in case the enemy came back, then changed into my uniform so I could walk faster. I'd hoped to get there before sunset, but those colossal statues were much further away than they looked.

I had to rest for the night and start moving again at dawn. When I finally reached my goal, the sun was directly overhead, which surely meant I'd made it in time. There were swarms of people gazing upwards at the statues, while a guide told them exactly how tall they were, but all I cared about was the stunningly beautiful sight of a group of portals.

I hurried towards them, vaguely aware of the guide's voice faltering and stopping. I reached the nearest portal, was about to dial, then saw the refreshments dispenser next to it and hesitated. I'd been able to drink all I wanted from streams, but I was starving hungry.

There was cheese fluffle on the menu! I gave in to temptation, entered my credit code, and grabbed my carton. I ripped it open, seized the spoon, and was madly eating ecstatic mouthfuls of cheese fluffle when I realized about five hundred people were standing watching me in stunned silence.

'Commander Tell Morrath, are you hurt?' asked the guide, his eyes on my singed uniform.

I guiltily stopped eating. 'I'm fine. Had a bit of trouble. Got to go now.'

When I entered my special code, the portal started talking to me. 'Warning, your destination is a restricted access area, and . . .'

I gave a farewell wave to my bewildered audience and stepped through the portal, arriving in a large hall filled with people.

'Thank chaos for that,' said a toga-clad figure.

I blinked as I recognized him. 'Drago, where's . . .'

I didn't need to finish the sentence, because Fian came out of the crowd and started ranting at me. 'Jarra, where the nuke have you been? We just got a credit alert saying you'd bought a carton of cheese fluffle at the Spirit of Man monument. I've been going crazy with worry, and you're sightseeing and buying cheese fluffle!'

I glanced down at the carton in my hand, and gave a guilty giggle. 'Sorry, I was starving hungry.'

Colonel Leveque and General Torrek appeared, both conventionally dressed in Military uniform. 'We were concerned for your safety, Commander,' said Leveque. 'A sudden silence from the opposition indicated a significant possibility you were dead.'

'They probably thought I was.'

General Torrek frowned at my uniform. 'You've been in a fire, Jarra. Are you injured?'

'There was an aircraft with a Planet First incendiary weapon but that's not important now. I'm not hurt.' My eyes were back on Fian. He was wearing a sleeveless white tunic, leggings, and some strange boots with archaic lacings.

'I would argue it's extremely important, Commander,' said Leveque. 'If they had a Planet First incendiary weapon then there is a high probability it was obtained from this base. Details of this attack could assist my attempts to identify the enemy agent.'

I was still studying Fian. There were colourful bruises on his right forehead and his left cheek. 'I'll tell you about the attack later. There isn't time now.'

'Very well,' said Leveque, 'but I'll want a detailed report immediately after the ceremony.'

I turned to glare at Drago. 'You let Fian get hurt and you haven't even got him medical treatment!'

Drago cowered and raised his hands in surrender. 'We did! We did! We just kept a couple of bruises for the newzies. We kept some for me and Raven too. Look!' He pointed at a dramatic bruise on his own face.

I finally noticed Raven standing next to Fian, and saw he had a spectacular black eye. 'Raven, did you arrest the people who attacked Fian, or just shoot them?'

'We let them off with a warning,' said Raven.

'What?' I stared at him in pure disbelief.

He gave me a pleading look. 'It was a tricky situation, Jarra. We couldn't shoot people when Fian was the one who started the fight, but we joined in on his side.'

Fian started the fight? My mind had an odd, blank moment. Fian wasn't the type to start a fight.

Colonel Leveque had been talking into his lookup in a

181

low voice, but now he rejoined the conversation. 'I should put all three of them on report. The Military strongly disapproves of officers brawling with civilians.'

'I was the senior officer present,' said Drago. 'It was my responsibility. You should demote me.'

General Torrek shook his head. 'There's no point in trying to dodge promotion any longer, Drago. The General Marshal has said you have great potential.'

Drago looked horrified. 'Oh no!'

'By the way,' added General Torrek, 'your parents dined with me last night. I mentioned the incident when you appeared unsuitably dressed in a dining hall, and your father wants to discuss it with you immediately after the ceremony.'

Drago turned to bang his head against the wall. 'Please, someone have mercy and shoot me.'

'That's a very tempting offer.' Drago's wife, Major Marlise Weldon, arrived, dressed in a toga like her husband. 'Welcome back, Jarra.'

'Thank you.' I frowned at Fian. 'What were you doing on Hercules, and why were you starting fights?'

Fian sighed. 'My father asked me to visit him. He claimed he was having second thoughts about leaving my mother, but he actually wanted to talk me into dumping you. He'd invited a crowd of my school classmates over to help him do it. Naturally, he chose the ones he approved of, the ones who'd jeered at me all through school because I was interested in history instead of science. When they started calling you names, I lost my temper and . . .'

'I apologize for interrupting,' said Dalmora's voice from behind me, 'but we must get Jarra ready for the ceremony.'

Dalmora was an Alphan aristocrat and just asked politely, but Amalie and Issette were with her and believed in direct action. The pair of them grabbed my arms and dragged me away. We went past a group of people that included Colonel Stone, Lecturer Playdon, Candace, and Fian's mother. I tried to stop and talk to them, but Issette yanked me into a side room, stole my cheese fluffle carton, and thrust me through a door into a bathroom.

'Shower!'

I obediently peeled off my blackened uniform, and stepped into the warm fragrant water of the shower. Blizz, pure blizz! I could have stayed in there for hours, but Amalie was shouting at me through the bathroom door.

'Hurry up, Jarra! Your first lot of clothes are by the door.'

First lot of clothes? I reluctantly switched the shower to dry cycle, stepped out while my hair was still damp, and found the clothes were very similar to Fian's outfit. I dressed, worked out how to lace the boots, went out of the bathroom, and was instantly shoved into a chair.

'Does anyone know what's going to happen in this ceremony?' I asked.

'Drago will explain,' said Dalmora. 'Quiet now!'

She started dabbing makeup on my face and lips, and a total stranger came into the room and started doing things to my hair. I wanted to say hello to her, but daren't open my mouth.

Dalmora, Amalie and Issette were wearing matching sleeveless dresses that hung to the floor in long flowing folds of silver and palest eggshell blue, and their hair was ornately arranged. Whatever was going to happen in this ceremony, they were obviously part of it. I compared their outfits to my simple tunic and leggings, and started worrying about what I'd be wearing later. If I had to wear a dress as long as theirs, I'd probably trip and fall flat on my face.

Several centuries went by before Dalmora allowed me to escape from the chair and go back into the main hall. A man in Captain's uniform instantly came up and offered me a tray of food and drink.

I shook my head. 'No thanks. I've already had cheese fluffle and now I'm too nervous to . . . Oh, you're Captain Marston. You're betrothed to Major Tar Cameron, aren't you?'

He disconcerted me by giving me an angry look. 'Yes, sir.'

'Can you tell me what happens in Betan betrothal ceremonies? I missed the rehearsals so . . .'

Rayne Tar Cameron hurried up, snatched the tray from Marston, and glared at him. 'I need you to help me in hall 2. Now!'

The pair of them went off, and I heard laughter from behind me. I turned to see Drago and Marlise. 'What the chaos was that about?' I asked.

'Rayne and Qwin seem to be having a few relationship problems,' said Marlise. 'They had a big argument at breakfast this morning, and Rayne threw a bowl of cereal at Qwin right in front of Colonel Stone.'

'Really?' I laughed. 'I'd no idea Rayne could be so . . .'

'Human?' Drago grinned. 'It was a bit of a surprise to everyone. At any other time, Nia Stone would probably have ignored it, but the dining hall was full of special guests here for the ceremony, including the terrifying General Hiraga herself! Rayne's on report for the first time in her impeccable career, and in a filthy mood.'

'Oh, I see.' I moved on to a far more important subject. 'Drago, I don't have a clue what I'm supposed to do in this ceremony.'

'Don't worry, Jarra. There'll be four parts to the ceremony. Your presentation, Fian's adoption, the contract approval, and the betrothal. You don't need to say anything during the presentation because it's normally done when

184

you're a baby, you aren't involved in the adoption ceremony, and you'll be away changing clothes during the contract approval.'

'It's the betrothal that's worrying me.'

Drago grinned. 'We'll talk you through everything you have to do and say in that. You're already wearing the comms devices.'

'I am?'

He tapped the side of his face, and I heard his voice talking in my ear. 'The jewelled pins in your hair. I'll give you instructions, you just follow them.'

'Oh,' I said. 'Yes, that works.'

'Given the complications of Military assignments, it's never easy to get many of the clan physically in one place, but we've managed enough to look respectable, and . . .' He tugged back the sleeve of his toga to reveal his forearm lookup, and tapped it. 'How are we doing on the banners of the Fifty, Caius?'

'All fifty banner bearers have arrived now,' said an unfamiliar voice. 'The Fabian alliance naturally sent their lowest ranked clan member, but the August alliance sent someone surprisingly respectable and . . . Oh chaos!'

Drago frowned. 'What's wrong?'

'You won't believe this, but Lucius Augustus Gordianus just portalled in. Look!'

A holo image appeared in midair, showing two people standing near a portal. A man who might be anywhere between sixty and eighty, and a much younger woman. They were wearing ornate formal togas, and the woman carried a baby in her arms.

'What the nuking hell does Lucius want?' Drago heard my gasp and pulled an apologetic face at me. 'Sorry, Jarra. That phrase isn't as rude in Beta as in other sectors, but . . . I don't understand why the head of the August clan council is here. Our clans haven't exactly been on good terms since Thetis.'

Caius spoke from the lookup. 'What do we do, Drago? Turning him away would be a huge insult, but if he's here to cause trouble . . .'

Drago buried his face in his hands for a second. 'The woman with Lucius is his daughter, Juliana Augusta Helena. Clan August would never involve their closeted womenfolk in anything violent, and disrupting the ceremony would be disrespectful to the Fifty, so . . .'

I took a step closer to the holo image. 'Drago, look at the bracelet on the baby's arm. That's a Hospital Earth Nursery identity band!'

'Nuk . . .' Drago shook his head. 'I mean, chaos take it. The grandchild of Lucius Augustus Gordianus has been born Handicapped, which explains everything that's been confusing us. The August clan keeping so quiet. Who was running that expensive publicity campaign. Even the shock news about clan Marius withdrawing from the August alliance.'

He ran his fingers through his hair. 'Lucius must have been fighting some major battles within both clan and alliance. I have to give the man credit for courage, because he's gambled his whole political career for that baby. Clan Marius obviously wouldn't stomach getting involved, but if Lucius has imposed his will on the rest of the August alliance then . . .'

Drago started rattling instructions into his lookup. 'Caius, Lucius has come here as a public display of support from clan August. Give him and his daughter the most fulsome welcome you can, and take them into a room by themselves. Don't, whatever you do, mention the baby unless they do. I'm betting some more heads of clans in the August alliance will show up as well, so put them in with Lucius and his daughter.'

186

Drago ended the call and turned to his wife. 'Marlise, can you tell General Torrek what's happening? I'll warn my father. I saw him talking to Jaxon earlier. Come along and meet them, Jarra.'

My brother, Jaxon. Oh chaos! With everything else that had been happening, I hadn't thought about the possibility of meeting my brother or sister. I trailed reluctantly after Drago, to where two men in togas were talking.

'Jarra, this is my father, General Dragon Tell Dramis, and your brother, Commander Jaxon Tell Galad,' said Drago.

I was startled to recognize the older man's face. This was the General who'd called me to break the news that my parents had been killed.

'I'm delighted to meet you at last, Jarra,' he said.

'Thank you, sir.'

'We're not in uniform, Jarra. You should address me as cousin.' He gave me a relaxed smile.

Drago started telling his father about the surprise guests, and I was left facing my brother. We'd only exchanged impersonally polite recorded messages before now, so I didn't know what to say. Jaxon finally broke the awkward silence.

'Our sister, Gemelle, sends her apologies that her assignment doesn't allow her to be here. She wishes you every happiness.'

'Thank you,' I muttered. 'I mean, thank her for me.'

There was another painful silence. I knew I wasn't helping much, but I felt it was up to Jaxon to make the effort here. He'd grown up with our clan and our parents, while I'd been abandoned on Earth. He could have said he was sorry about what had happened, instead of trying to avoid looking at me. What was wrong with him? Was he another of the bigots who didn't think I was really human? Had he been forced into being here to present me to the clan?

Drago finished his explanation, and his father nodded. 'I'll go and welcome Lucius Augustus Gordianus myself.'

He vanished off, which left Drago free to check how my brother and I were getting along. It must have been obvious our first meeting was a disaster, because he spoke with artificial cheerfulness.

'We'd better start getting ready for the ceremony.'

I gulped. I still didn't know what would happen during the betrothal, but it was bound to involve me saying something romantic and I was incredibly bad at that sort of thing. I was about to make a complete nardle of myself in front of a vast audience.

19

I was in a strange room that had three walls entirely covered with vid screens and equipment, and a fourth wall that was a massive glass window. I looked through the window at a huge hall below, with banks of seating and a wide central aisle leading to a raised platform. 'Can the people down there see us?'

'No,' said my cousin, Caius. 'The glass is one way. It looks just like the wall from the other side.'

The front two rows of seats down in the hall were empty, presumably reserved for those actually taking part in the ceremony, but the rest were filled with people. Fian's mother was easy to spot because of the shiny clothes that were fashionable in Delta sector. Candace was sitting next to her.

'You could sit down.' Caius gestured at where Drago and Jaxon were sitting.

I shook my head. I was far too tense to sit still, so I paced round the room, watching several Military officers working at the banks of equipment that controlled the security system, vid bees, lighting and sound in the hall below.

'Shouldn't we be starting?' I asked.

'We're about to open the live link for the newzies.' Drago nodded at the glass wall. 'The lights are already dimming.'

I realized he was right. The lights in this room were staying at full brightness, but the hall below was gradually getting darker.

'Opening live link now,' said one of the Military officers. 'We have three Beta sector newzie channels connecting. Make that five, ten . . . Military links to Kappa and Zeta are open. Alpha channels joining now. Delta. Gamma. Here comes Epsilon. We've over a hundred channels open already and more still joining. You've got one of the biggest live audiences in history for this.'

Great, I thought. No pressure, no pressure at all!

Drago tapped the side of his face, and I heard his voice through the jewelled pins in my hair. 'All right, everyone. Other sectors have been getting their ideas of us from the gutter sex vids for far too long. Let's show them the real Beta sector. Let's show them Fidelis!'

Those words ended on an inspiring note, then there was a short pause before he continued in a more business-like voice. 'Music cue clan in three, two, one. Now!'

I heard the sound of drumbeats in the ominous rhythm that was the start of the Thetis March. I should have guessed the clan of Tellon Blaze would use that music. I moved closer to the window, and looked down at the almost total blackness in the hall.

'Positions for entry of the clan,' said Drago. 'Torches in three, two, one. Now!'

There was a dramatic flash of light by the entrance to the hall. Flaming torches hovered in midair around a column of perhaps thirty men and women wearing togas. The first two held the poles of banners that fluttered out in a nonexistent wind. The banners of Beta sector and of the Tell clan.

The music grew louder as the column of people moved slowly down the central aisle, and climbed the steps to the platform. They formed into a semi-circle facing the audience, with the flaming torches around them and a banner at each side. Drago's father, Dragon Tell Dramis, was in the centre, a step or two ahead of the others. The Thetis March reached a dramatic peak and then there was sudden silence.

'The Tell clan welcomes the clans of the Military alliance,' said Dragon Tell Dramis.

'Music cue alliance,' said Drago. 'Clans enter in three, two, one. Now!'

This time the music was the hymn of humanity, and there were no flaming torches, just spotlights on groups of figures, each led by someone carrying their clan banner.

'The Ray clan,' said Dragon Tell Dramis. 'The Tar clan. The . . .'

I glanced at the wall vids and saw they were showing close-ups of the banners. If I hadn't been a mass of nerves, I would have been fascinated by their history.

Dragon Tell Dramis ended the roll call of the Military clans. Their members placed the banners in holders along the wall at the left side of the platform, forming a vibrant mass of colours, and went to sit down in the reserved seats.

'The Tell clan welcomes the fifty banners of Beta sector,' said Dragon Tell Dramis.

'Music cue Beta sector,' said Drago. 'The Fifty enter in three, two, one. Now!'

The music changed to the Beta sector anthem, and a line of fifty elderly men and women entered, all dressed in identical white togas trimmed with imperial purple. They carried their banners down the aisle in solemn procession, then placed them at the right side of the platform and sat down in the front row of seats.

'If anyone hasn't heard the news yet,' said Drago, 'we've

some unexpected guests. Try not to look too shocked, because the Beta sector newzies will be replaying this moment for days.'

'The Tell clan welcomes the August clan,' said Dragon Tell Dramis.

I could see heads turning in the audience below, some people even standing up to get a better view of the man carrying the August clan banner, and the young woman beside him with the baby in her arms. I had to admire the way the man and woman appeared calmly unaware of everyone staring at them.

Drago tapped me on the shoulder, and pointed a finger at the portal in the corner of the room. I gulped. There would be some more clans of the August alliance, and then me!

Jaxon joined me at the portal, and we stepped through into a dimly lit room. A young man in a toga began rapidly gabbling instructions.

'You go through the door opposite, and stand in the centre aisle. Nobody will see you in the darkness. When the torches either side of you come on, you start moving towards the platform. Don't touch the torches, they're being controlled remotely.'

We went through the door into blackness, and Jaxon startled me by speaking in a harsh, emotional voice.

'I'm sorry. I was a selfish kid back then. I threw tantrums about how moving to Earth would affect my schooling, my future career, my . . . It was all about me. I never stopped to think about you.'

I didn't know what to say, and there wasn't time to say anything anyway because Drago's voice was giving us instructions again. 'We're back on script now. Music cue Thetis march. Jarra, Jaxon, you're on in three, two, one. Now!'

Torches flared either side of us, and I saw vid bees

skulking around in the shadows sending images out to the newzies. We paced slowly past the rows of seats packed with people, reached the platform, and stood facing Dragon Tell Dramis.

'Who comes to the clan?' he asked.

'Jaxon Tellonus Galad, son of Marack Tellonus Galad, son of Jarra Tellona Morrath of the line of Tellon Blaze,' said Jaxon.

'Why do you come to the clan?' asked Dragon Tell Dramis.

'I come to present my youngest sister to the knowledge and kindred of the clan of her birth,' said Jaxon. 'Let it be heard . . .'

There was a pause, a long pause, and then Drago's voice spoke in my ear. 'Let it be heard in the halls.' He waited before speaking again in an urgent, pleading voice. 'Come on, Jaxon. This is no time for one of your guilt trips. You were no more to blame than all the rest of us. The clan broke faith with one of its own, the clan shares the shame, but we're making things right for Jarra now.'

I glanced sideways at Jaxon, and saw the years of pain in his face. I hadn't realized . . . I'd had to live with the fact I'd been abandoned at birth, but my clan had had to live with the fact they'd abandoned me.

I'd been gradually learning about Fidelis, and what it meant to Betans. My clan had broken Fidelis when they handed over one of their children to Hospital Earth. Other clans might be able to cope with the guilt and dishonour of that, but it was much harder for the proud descendants of the legendary hero Tellon Blaze. That was why they'd defied all the opposition to hold this ceremony. That was why they'd decided to have vid bees sending coverage out to the newzies. That was why they'd invited the banners of Beta sector as witnesses.

This ceremony wasn't just about giving me the family I'd

never had, or about gaining sympathy for the Handicapped so the Military could find us new worlds. It was also about restoring the honour of my clan.

Jaxon was still mutely standing there. Nothing Drago could say would get through to him. Only I could do this.

I took my brother's hand. 'It's time to forget the past and concentrate on the future. We're making this right for all of us.'

'Let it be heard in the halls,' Drago's voice prompted again.

'Let it be heard in the halls.' Jaxon's voice was shaking and there were random pauses between his words. 'I present the noble born Jarra Tellona Feren, daughter to Gemena Raya Feren and Marack Tellonus Galad, who was son of Jarra Tellona Morrath of the line of Tellon Blaze.'

The blur of names confused me for a moment. Tellona and Tellonus were the full female and male versions of our clan prefix, that a Military clan would only use on formal occasions, but why the surname Feren? Had Jaxon messed up or . . .

No, he was right. That would have been my original birth name by Betan naming conventions. I belonged to the Tell clan because it was higher ranked than the Ray clan, but a female child took her mother's surname.

Jaxon had his voice back under control now. 'Let it be heard in the halls that the noble born Jarra Tellona Feren is Honour Child to the noble born Jarra Tellona Morrath and in custom bears her name.'

Dragon Tell Dramis spoke now, with a hint of relief in his voice. 'Let it be heard in the halls that the Tell clan acknowledges the noble born Jarra Tellona Morrath and welcomes her to the kindred of her clan.'

A flurry of drumbeats followed his words, and a woman stepped forward to put a toga round my shoulders and tug its folds into place. Someone else was putting a delicate wreath of green laurel leaves on my head, carefully adjusting its position.

I was part of the clan of my birth now. I had a family, and Lolia and Lolmack would be celebrating back at the dig site dome. One of the Handicapped had been welcomed into a clan of the *gentes maiores* of Beta sector. That meant their daughter, and all the children like her, would have the chance of a family too.

20

I became aware of a tugging at my arm, and Drago's voice speaking in my ear. 'Jarra, wake up! Turn to face the audience. Face the Fifty.'

Jaxon's hand tugged at my arm again, and we both turned to face the audience. The Fifty, in their white and purple togas, were standing in front of us.

'Let it be heard in the halls that this is the noble born Jarra Tellona Morrath of the clan of Tellon Blaze,' said Dragon Tell Dramis.

Drumbeats sounded.

'Let it be heard in the halls that this is the noble born Jarra Tellona Morrath of the clan of Tellon Blaze,' he repeated.

Drumbeats sounded again.

He said the same words a third time, and I remembered Drago telling me about his marriage to Marlise. You said things three times to bind them under clan law.

'I'll count you down, and then you both bow to the Fifty,' said Drago. 'Three, two, one. Bow!'

We bowed, and the men and women of the Fifty bowed formally in return. Drumbeats sounded a final time, and the Fifty sat down again.

'Now turn and join the clan,' said Drago.

I saw the gap in the ranks where Jaxon and I were to stand, went to my place, and people came to hug me and murmured words in my ear. I was lost in a nardle haze of emotion, but then Dragon Tell Dramis came to hug me, and being hugged by a General shocked me back to sanity.

The clan formed their semi-circle again, and the anthem of Delta sector, with all the fancy rippling notes, started playing. I hadn't heard Drago giving a music cue, so presumably he'd taken me out of the comms circuit. A spotlight focused on a lone figure walking down the centre aisle.

Fian looked perfectly calm and composed, his long blond hair reflecting the light, and his simple tunic and leggings a stark contrast to the ornate togas of the clan. I'd been scared stiff when all I had to do was stand silently at Jaxon's side, but Fian would have to do his own talking. He wasn't even doing this for himself; he was doing it for me. He was totally zan!

He reached the platform and glanced towards me. I had a breathless moment as I saw him smile before he faced forward again. A woman was in the centre of the clan semi-circle now.

'Who comes to the clan?' she asked.

'I am Fian Andrej Eklund.'

'What is your clan?'

'I have no clan,' said Fian. 'I am of Hercules in Delta sector.'

'What do you beg of us, outlander?' She said the last word in a harsh, unwelcoming voice.

'I beg from no one,' said Fian.

'What do you gift us, outlander?'

'I bring no gift.'

'What service do you pledge us, outlander?' This was the

third time she'd used the word 'outlander', and the way she said it made it clear it was an insult.

'I serve no one,' said Fian.

'If you neither beg, nor gift, nor pledge service, then you trespass among us, outlander!'

The woman's arm swept up. I heard myself gasp as I saw she held a sword levelled at Fian's throat. In different circumstances, I'd have been wondering if it was genuinely ancient or a reproduction, but right now I was only worried about how sharp it was.

'I do not trespass among you,' said Fian. 'I was summoned as Paul was summoned by Kairos.'

The woman kept the sword aimed at his throat. 'Who summoned the outlander?'

Drago's father stepped forward to stand on Fian's right. 'I am Dragon Tellonus Dramis and I summoned him. A daughter of our house was lost, as Helena was lost, and he stood with her as Paul stood with Helena.'

'You would offer welcome to an outlander?' asked the woman.

'This is no outlander,' said Dragon Tell Dramis. 'This is my son under Fidelis and I challenge for him.'

'This is no outlander.' Jaxon moved to stand on Fian's left. 'This is my brother under Fidelis and I challenge for him.'

'Who stands against?' asked the woman. There was a long silence, and she repeated the question. 'Who stands against?' Another wait, and she repeated it again. 'Who stands against?'

'None stand against him but you,' said Dragon Tell Dramis.

The woman finally lowered her sword. 'Then I accept the precedent of Paul summoned by Kairos, and do not stand against him.'

There were drumbeats again. This time I saw where the

sound was coming from. A man at the side of the platform was playing a genuine drum, hanging in a harness from his shoulder like something from far back in the days of pre-history, but I couldn't spare more than a single glance for him. Fian was being wrapped in a toga, and crowned with a green laurel wreath. He turned to face the audience, and Dragon Tell Dramis stood next to him.

'Let it be heard in the halls that this is the noble Fian Andrej Eklund, adopted son presumptive of the clan of Tellon Blaze under the precedent of Paul and Kairos.'

This time I was ready for the sound of the drum and for him to repeat the words twice more to bind the adoption under clan law. As before, the Fifty stood, and there were formal bows before the clan started hugging Fian. I went forward to hug him myself, but Dragon Tell Dramis blocked my way.

'Oh no you don't.' He gave me an amused smile. 'Hugging each other before the betrothal would be scandalously improper, and besides you both have to go and change now.'

He ushered me off through a side door. I stepped into what seemed like darkness compared to the glaring lights of the platform, and gave a startled squeak as someone grabbed my arm.

'Jarra, Jarra, Jarra, come on!'

'Issette! You scared me to death.'

She pulled a buggy-eyed, incredulous face. 'You're never scared of anything. Come on!' She dragged me down a corridor. 'They've started approving the betrothal contract, so we don't have any time to spare.'

I was thrust into a room where Dalmora and Amalie were waiting. Issette pushed me straight past them and behind a screen. 'Change quickly!'

I gave a single horrified glance at the dress hanging on

the wall. The skirt was so long it would trail on the floor behind me, and the top . . . 'I can't wear that!'

'Yes you can,' said Dalmora's voice. 'You'll look beautiful, Jarra.'

'But it's indecent!' I shrugged off my toga and yanked my tunic over my head, losing my laurel wreath in the process. 'People will see my fronts!'

'That's a perfectly respectable dress for both Alpha and Beta sectors,' said Dalmora. 'A bit low cut for Gamma, Delta, and Epsilon, but . . .'

'My point is that it's a bit low cut for Earth!' I tugged off my boots and leggings.

'It's an exact reproduction of the dress Helena wore at her betrothal to Paul,' said Dalmora. 'The newzie channels have been constantly giving sexual content warnings because they're showing live vid feed of a Betan betrothal. Half the audience will feel cheated that you're wearing clothes at all, so a slightly revealing dress isn't going to worry anyone.'

'But . . .'

'Jarra, this is chaos important for all the Handicapped,' said Issette, 'so shut up and put your dress on!'

I gave a moan, reluctantly pulled on the dress, thrust my feet into some delicate silver strappy objects, and turned to look at my reflection in a nearby mirror. The dress was a lovely thing in shimmering white and silver. I was showing more of my body than I would in my skintight, but it wasn't quite as bad as I'd expected. The back was terrifyingly low, but showing my back wasn't as bad as . . .

I stepped out from behind the screen, and submitted to being preened by Dalmora and having a garland of flowers put on my head. 'People keep talking about Helena, Paul and Kairos,' I said. 'Who the chaos were they?'

'You don't know?' Dalmora's eyes had the tearful look that always meant she was thinking of something romantic.

200

'All the newzies have been showing vids about them for the last day. The greatest love story in Betan history!'

I blinked. We were re-enacting the greatest love story in Betan history for the newzies! Had my clan thought of this, or was it Psych Division's idea?

'Helena was the daughter of Kairos,' continued Dalmora. 'She was lost as a baby when . . .'

'We haven't got time to tell stories now,' said Amalie, 'or we'll miss our cue.'

Dalmora made a final adjustment to my flowers. 'Yes, we'd better get moving.'

We went out of the door and turned right. I heard a voice speak in my ear.

'This is Caius. Drago is leading the betrothal ceremony, so I'm taking over on cues and words. The Fifty are witnessing the betrothal contract now, so we need Jarra in position in three minutes. For chaos sake, warn me if she's running late and I'll get Drago to do some random talking.'

Dalmora tapped one of her hair slides. 'We're nearly there, Caius.'

'Excellent,' said Caius.

We took another right turn, went through a door, and arrived back in the dimly lit room I'd been in at the start of the ceremony. The same young man was there.

'They were having trouble with the snow in rehearsal,' he said, 'but they think they've fixed the problem.'

Snow? I didn't have time to ask why we had snow, because Caius was speaking in my ear.

'Cue Jarra's entry music.'

There was a soft piping music that I didn't recognize. I took a deep breath, and the four of us went out into the darkness and stood on the centre aisle. Dalmora tugged me a little further to the right, and adjusted the folds of my dress. I still had absolutely no idea what was going to happen during this betrothal ceremony, and it was much too late to ask questions now.

I stared ahead at the brightly lit platform. The clan were at the back, while Fian was at the front, standing just to the left of the centre with Raven, Keon and Krath. They were all wearing some sort of archaic tunic and trousers, with short cloaks. Fian was in white and the rest of them in bluish grey. Since I was dressed as Helena, I guessed that Fian was in costume as the mysterious Paul.

'Cue Jarra,' said Caius.

Lights blazed on me, and white flakes started drifting down from the ceiling. I held out my hand to catch one and it melted on my skin. They really did have a snow machine up there.

I started pacing slowly towards the platform, and my nerves hit a crescendo of blind panic as I saw all the faces turning to look at me.

'Fian's group are to the left of the platform,' said Caius's voice. 'Jarra's group arrive on the platform and take up similar positions on the right. You should all face the audience at this point.'

My personal snowstorm widened as I reached the platform. I moved to my place with paranoid care, terrified of tripping over my dress. I'd been expecting Drago to appear at this point, but it was his father who took the centre of the stage, carrying a partially unrolled parchment scroll. Was that genuine ancient parchment, or . . .?

'Everyone turn to face Dragon,' said Caius.

We followed his instructions and I saw Fian looking at me, his eyes dropping to study the low neckline of my dress. He really was a shockingly badly-behaved Deltan!

'Fian Andrej Eklund, adopted son presumptive of the Tell clan,' said Dragon, 'do you consent to bind yourself in betrothal to Jarra Tellona Morrath, daughter of the Tell clan?'

Fian reluctantly tore his eyes away from my neckline to look at him. 'Does the clan approve this?'

'The clan approves this and has registered consent,' said Dragon Tell Dramis.

'Then I accept the wisdom of the clan and bind myself in betrothal to Jarra Tellona Morrath.'

Fian stepped forward and placed his hand on the scroll. I felt a true nardle. That scroll wasn't just fake, it was a lookup in disguise, and Fian was giving his handprint for Earth Registry.

Fian stepped back to his place and it was my turn. After watching Fian do this, I barely needed the guidance of Caius speaking in my ear.

'Jarra Tellona Morrath, daughter of the Tell clan, do you consent to bind yourself in betrothal to Fian Andrej Eklund, adopted son presumptive of the Tell clan?' asked Dragon Tell Dramis.

'Does the clan approve this?' I asked.

'The clan approves this and has registered consent,' said Dragon Tell Dramis.

'Then I accept the wisdom of the clan and bind myself in betrothal to Fian Andrej Eklund.'

I placed my hand on the scroll, it displayed the acknowledgement from Earth Registry, then Raven, Krath, Keon, Dalmora, Amalie and Issette all gave handprints to register as witnesses. When they were all back in their places, drumbeats sounded, and Dragon Tell Dramis stepped forward to speak.

'Let it be heard in the halls that noble Fian Andrej Eklund and noble born Jarra Tellona Morrath are betrothed under the laws of Zeus and of Beta sector.'

I heard him repeat it twice more, then we did the bow to the Fifty routine and I could relax. The whole thing had been surprisingly painless for a Betan betrothal ceremony.

It was then I saw Drago had taken his father's place and

was smiling out at the audience. 'The formal part of the ceremony, including the legalities specified in the reunification treaty of Artemis, is now complete. This is the point where we all relax and share with you some centuries old Betan betrothal traditions. Sadly, the size of the audience means we can't have everyone throwing flower petals or dancing, but please join in when the singing starts.'

Betan betrothal traditions? We hadn't finished? What exactly . . .?

Drago held out both arms towards the audience in a welcoming gesture. 'You are guests in our hall on a joyful day. Celebrate with us, for out of the chill of winter comes spring, with the promise of new life and new beginnings.'

Fian took a pace towards me. 'I come out of winter and see you, and there is spring around me.'

Oh no. This was obviously going to be chaos soppy and sentimental. Was it really traditional, or had the evil Psych Division been helping with the script? Caius's voice was nervously nagging in my ear, so I made myself step forward and say it.

'I come out of winter and see you, and there is spring around me.'

The snow, which had been gradually covering the platform with a crunchy white layer, suddenly stopped. Something pink was falling now. Flower petals.

'I offer you my love, my life, my honour, and my future,' said Fian.

He had an earnest look on his face, which made the scripted words sound truly personal. I had a nardle emotional moment as I heard him say them, but then the horrible truth hit me. I was going to have to say this too!

I hesitated, and saw Fian's earnest expression change to amusement. Caius's voice was prompting me with the words. I opened my mouth and closed it again.

Drago grinned. 'We know you're a little shy about these things, Jarra, so we ordered plenty of flower petals. You can take all the time you need.'

'Psych Division reports all the chat webs just went crazy,' said Caius in my ear. 'People love seeing Jarra's vulnerable emotional moments. They're saying this is even better than the bit in the clan vid where . . .'

I groaned, then saw Fian's face and completely forgot our audience. 'Stop laughing at me!'

'I can't help it,' said Fian.

'Would some wine help you relax, Jarra?' asked Drago. 'You'll be sharing a goblet of wine with Fian later, but we could . . .'

I scowled at him. 'I don't need wine, I just . . .'

A movement caught my eye, as a tiny hovering vid bee furtively sneaked round to get a better view of my face. I gave it a look of pure horror, remembering exactly how many people were watching us, and there was a burst of laughter in the hall.

I groaned again, and Issette elbowed me painfully in the ribs. 'Say your line, Jarra,' she whispered, 'or I'll tell everyone what happened at the Year Day party when we turned sixteen.'

Issette has a very penetrating whisper. Another burst of laughter from the audience showed most of them had over-heard her threat, and I was perfectly sure the vid feed would have picked it up as well. I obviously had to force myself to do this, or things would get even more embarrassing.

I faced Fian and took a deep breath. 'I offer you my love, my life, my honour, and my future.'

'I will come to you when spring turns to summer,' he said.

'I will come to you when spring turns to summer,' I repeated, and the flower petals were replaced by some golden feathery things that I didn't recognize.

'Our future will be . . .'

Dragon Tell Dramis's voice brutally interrupted Fian. 'I deeply regret we have to stop these celebrations. The Tell clan has received a court order from Delta sector declaring this betrothal illegal.'

21

An hour later, I was sitting in a meeting room with Fian, General Torrek, Colonel Leveque, and Colonel Stone.

'Unfortunately, Legal Division confirm the court order makes a valid legal argument,' said Leveque. 'Apparently, Earth does not belong to any sector, and is therefore excluded from cross-sector reciprocal agreements on recognition of marriage and other relationship contracts. That means Fian, as a citizen of Delta sector, cannot legally enter into a relationship contract while on Earth.'

'I can't believe this,' said Fian.

'I can,' I said, bitterly. 'It's perfectly typical of the whole attitude to the Handicapped that the people making these laws forgot Earth wasn't part of a sector.'

The door opened and Drago came in.

General Torrek waved at an empty chair. 'What's the situation like out there?'

Drago pulled a face of despair and sat down. 'People are furious of course. The younger members of the Military clans are in hall 2. We've put a General from the Ray clan in with them, to make sure they don't try to steal some fighters and attack Delta sector. Everyone else from Beta sector is having an angry conference in hall 1.'

'Are people angry with your clan for making Jarra a member?' asked General Torrek.

Drago shook his head. 'This isn't about Jarra being Handicapped any longer. The court order was sent to us *after* the Fifty had formally witnessed the betrothal. That makes it a direct insult to the banners of Beta sector, so everyone's united against it.'

'I bet my father's behind that court order,' said Fian.

'The court order was obtained by a Deltan legal firm, but not one on Hercules,' said Colonel Leveque. 'There's no evidence your father has even contacted them.'

'My father's more than bright enough to contact them without leaving evidence,' said Fian.

'The immediate problem isn't who was behind the court order, but how we respond to it.' General Torrek looked at Leveque. 'What are our options?'

'This centuries-old legal loophole in civilian law only prevents the betrothal being registered on Earth,' said Leveque. 'Jarra obviously can't travel to another planet to register it, but we may be able to use Military regulations to resolve the problem. Planet First teams opening up new colony worlds work under strict quarantine restrictions, so a special clause in Military regulations allows officers entering into a relationship contract on a Military base to register it in a sector of their choice. Legal Division are checking the exact wording of . . .'

His lookup chimed, and he glanced down at it for a moment. 'Legal Division advise that as clan members Jarra and Fian automatically have Betan citizenship, and there's no possible legal argument against two Betan officers using Military regulations to register their Twoing contract in Beta sector.'

General Torrek glanced at Colonel Stone. 'It's the base commanding officer's responsibility to do the registration.'

'Yes, sir.' Stone worked on her forearm lookup for a moment and then smiled at me and Fian. 'Congratulations and mutual joy on . . .'

Her lookup interrupted her by chiming. Stone frowned at it. 'The registration just got bounced back. It's been rejected because Jarra isn't listed as a Military officer.'

'What?' I shook my head. 'But . . .'

'I'll ask Recruitment what the chaos is wrong.' Stone worked on her lookup again, and then turned to look at General Torrek. 'Sir, Recruitment say they received a court order removing Commander Tell Morrath's Military status on the grounds she's below the minimum Military recruitment age of 18.'

'That's an unfortunate development,' said Colonel Leveque. 'I wonder how the Deltan legal firm found out Jarra is only 17.'

'But I'm 18,' I said.

General Torrek groaned. 'I'm sorry Jarra. I'd no idea you only being 17 would affect your betrothal. Hospital Earth regards you as 18, and Beta sector allows betrothal contracts for people as young as 16.'

I stared at him in disbelief. 'For chaos sake, I was 18 last Year Day!'

'There are several methods used to calculate age,' said Leveque. 'Alpha and Beta sectors measure from the individual's actual date of birth using the interstellar standard Green Time of Earth Europe. For historic reasons, Military regulations use the same age system as Alpha sector.'

I had a hideous moment of understanding. My actual date of birth was 1 August 2771. Today was 25 June 2789, so . . . 'I thought everyone just counted Year Days now. Earth does.'

'Gamma, Delta and Epsilon sectors do as well,' said Stone.

'I don't understand,' said Fian. 'If Jarra is 18 under the Year Day system we use in Delta sector, then she must have a personal age of 18 as well.'

'There is one key difference between the counting of Year Days on Earth and in Gamma, Delta, and Epsilon sectors,' said Leveque. 'Earth counts the first Year Day.'

Fian gave me a startled look before turning back to Leveque and speaking rapidly. 'I was born on Hercules in December 2770. The first Year Day doesn't count, so I was a 1-year-old on 1 January 2772. That meant I became 18 on 1 January 2789.'

'Precisely,' said Leveque. 'Jarra was born on 1 August 2771. Earth does count the first Year Day, so she became a 1-year-old on 1 January 2772. By Earth law, she was 18 on 1 January 2789, but according to the rules of Gamma, Delta and Epsilon sectors she won't be 18 until next Year Day. Military regulations will regard Jarra as being 18 on 1 August of this year.'

'Why does Earth do it that way?' asked Fian. 'It's ridiculous. You'd be saying babies born just before Year Day were a year old. No, wait . . .' He gave an angry shake of his head. 'They must do it that way so they can get all the kids out of the residences and off their hands a year earlier. I know Earth has trouble finding enough staff for the residences, but . . . That's really sick.'

He looked round the table. 'When did you find out about this, and why didn't you tell us?'

'Jarra was recruited at high speed under the Alien Contact procedures,' said General Torrek. 'Those only checked she was flagged as adult. I should have known Jarra's birth date myself, but after her grandmother died I was . . . absent for several years. I only discovered Jarra's age when you two were actually inside the tunnel leading to the alien device.'

He sighed. 'The biometrics on Jarra's suit had been

210

registering extremely high stress levels. Our Medical team leader checked Jarra's records, looking for a reason for the stress. She noticed her date of birth, and contacted me with the information. I was in a difficult position. I could hardly order Jarra out of there, but I did warn you both of potential danger and offer to replace you.'

'I was aware of the situation somewhat earlier,' said Leveque. 'I found both Jarra and Fian sufficiently intriguing that I studied the details of their records the day after they arrived on the base. I was unsure if Riak was deliberately ignoring the issue of Jarra's age. I wasn't going to raise it myself, because she'd already proved useful. Frankly, I'd have recruited a day old baby if it could assist the Alien Contact programme.'

'I knew months ago,' said Drago. 'Jarra was the Honour Child for her grandmother. When she first asked for details of her parents, Military Support saw her record was flagged as 18 and adult, so they assumed it was time to hold the Honour Ceremony. The clan got the shock of their lives when they were sent the vid coverage of the ceremony a year earlier than they thought was possible. Raising objections about Jarra's age at that point would have been shockingly disrespectful to both her and her grandmother's memory, so clan council ruled we should regard Jarra as 18. When she was called in by the Alien Contact programme . . .'

Drago shrugged. 'I thought Jarra would be furious if I told the Military she was only 17 and got her excluded from the Alien Contact programme, so I kept quiet.'

I shook my head. 'You mean everyone knew I was only 17. Everyone except Fian and me!'

'I didn't know either,' said Stone. 'I only found out when Recruitment told me.' She frowned at her husband and pointedly addressed him using his rank. 'Perhaps Colonel Leveque will explain why I wasn't informed earlier.'

'You are in command of this base, sir,' said Leveque. 'However, Commander Tell Morrath is currently assigned to the research effort which is under my command.'

'I'm also deputy commanding officer of the Alien Contact programme,' said Stone, 'and therefore your chain of command.'

'It's not customary to keep the deputy commanding officer informed of routine administrational issues, sir,' said Leveque.

Stone abandoned Military formality and looked up at the ceiling in despair. 'Why did I ever marry him?'

I was angry and frustrated about my personal situation, but I was also burningly aware there were much bigger issues at stake here. 'Whatever the arguments about my age and the betrothal, we've succeeded in setting the precedent about Handicapped kids joining Betan clans. What about the plan to use the betrothal ceremony to generate public support for new worlds for the Handicapped?'

'Lucius Augustus Gordianus will love the idea of having a world in Beta sector where his grandson can live,' said Drago. 'We can count on him talking the August alliance into supporting the change to the Planet First selection criteria. The Fabian alliance will oppose it, but faced with a split between August and Fabian, the rest of the reactionary faction will either vote with August or abstain. Even if the vote in Parliament of Planets fails, we should be able to get Beta sector to request a specialist planet.'

'Things aren't actually that bad then,' I said. 'In just over a month, I'll be Military again, and we'll be able to use Military regulations to register the betrothal. No one in Beta sector can blame Fian and me for just having a Twoing contract until then.'

I didn't like the number of significant glances being exchanged. Drago broke the news to me. 'I'm afraid the court order applies to your Twoing contract as well.'

'What! Our Twoing contract is cancelled too?'

'I'm tired of this,' said General Torrek. 'I'll solve the whole problem by using Alien Contact powers to override the minimum Military recruitment age.'

'With respect, sir, I strongly advise against that,' said Leveque. 'There is a 93 per cent probability the Isolationist Party would challenge your decision. Not only are a high proportion of their members prejudiced against the Handicapped, but they're eager to do everything possible to disrupt the Alien Contact programme. They could accuse you of misusing the powers under your command because of your personal involvement with the Tell clan.'

The look on General Torrek's face at that point would have frightened most officers into shutting up, but Colonel Leveque was a brave man who wore the Thetis medal so he just carried on talking.

'We can't claim it's vital for Jarra to be Military at this particular moment rather than on 1 August. We've established the alien probe is not an immediate threat, and we haven't found the alien home world yet. The situation could escalate into you being forced to resign your position as commanding officer of the Alien Contact programme.'

'We can't risk that,' I said.

'Agreed,' said Stone. 'Both the Military and the public have great confidence in General Torrek. When we find the alien home world, we'll need every bit of that confidence, because the Isolationist Party will be doing their best to spread public panic. They don't just want to block any contact with the alien civilization, but to stop us finding out anything about it.'

'So we can't even have a Twoing contract, let alone a betrothal, for several weeks.' Fian shook his head. 'Nuke that!'

General Torrek carefully failed to notice the swearing. 'Legal Division will work on finding a solution.'

213

'Our alliance legal team will be working on it too,' said Drago.

'And what do we do while we wait for them to find an answer?' asked Fian. 'I'm still Military, so can Jarra stay at Zulu base with me?'

'Partners are normally only allowed in Military accommodation when there's a Twoing, marriage, or betrothal contract, but . . .' General Torrek turned to Leveque. 'Can we waive that requirement?'

'I'd strenuously recommend that both Fian and Jarra return to their class,' said Leveque. 'The Military providing a venue for the betrothal was perfectly justifiable, both for security reasons and since Military bases regularly host Betan Military clan ceremonies, but events are now escalating rapidly politically. The Military must be seen to immediately distance themselves from this to avoid compromising our political neutrality.'

General Torrek frowned. 'But what about the safety issues?'

'That's an additional reason for Jarra and Fian to return to their class,' said Leveque. 'We still have an unknown enemy agent here at Zulu base, so they'll be much safer at the inaccessible location of the California Rift under the protection of Captain Raven and our trusted security team.'

'Unless we let someone wander in carrying another bomb,' said Stone pointedly.

Leveque's eyes flickered towards her for a second, but his voice stayed perfectly calm. 'I'll ensure that all portal access and deliveries have to be personally authorized by Major Rayne Tar Cameron, and any visiting maintenance staff are escorted by a Military Security officer.'

General Torrek nodded. 'Rayne never makes mistakes. Very well, Jarra and Fian will return to their class while we work on identifying the enemy agent.'

'On which subject,' said Leveque, 'I'm eager to hear the full details of Jarra's encounter with an aircraft carrying an incendiary weapon.'

'So am I,' said Fian.

I groaned.

22

The group of seven of us walked towards the portal with Raven in the lead. 'I knew it was a bad idea to let you go off on your own like that,' said Fian, 'and I was right. You could have been burned to death!'

The bigots hadn't just succeeded in throwing me out of the Alien Contact programme this time, but out of the Military as well. I was in no mood to suffer one of Fian's lectures. 'If I hadn't been a nardle going through that animal control barrier, I'd have had no trouble at all.'

'You don't know that, and the fact is . . .'

Fian broke off his sentence because Raven was walking through the portal, followed by Dalmora, Amalie and Krath. We hurried through after them, stepping out into the familiar drab greyness of the portal room at our California Rift dig site dome. As Playdon appeared behind us, Fian started talking again.

'The fact is . . .'

'For chaos sake, stop arguing you two!' said Amalie.

Fian gave me a frustrated look. 'We'll discuss this later.'

I winced.

We headed to the dome hall, and walked straight into

another argument. The rest of the class were all in there, most of them sitting in chairs lined up to face the wall vid. Steen and Petra were standing in front of the blank screen, aggressively facing each other.

'Everyone back home is chaos impressed that I'm friends with people as famous as Fian and Jarra,' said Steen. 'Our local newzie channel interviewed me, and now Gamma Sector News wants to interview me as well. I'm not letting you mess this up for me.'

'Having them back here could put us all in danger,' said Petra. 'I'm entitled to . . .'

'I wish to consult the whole class about exactly that point,' Playdon interrupted her.

People hastily turned to look at him, then at Fian and me. I could see them all take in the fact Fian was in uniform while I was wearing civilian clothes.

Playdon led our group up to the front of the room. 'The bombing made it clear there is a risk in having Jarra and Fian in the class. If you're unwilling to accept that risk, Cassandra 2 have offered to have Jarra and Fian live in their dome and work with them.'

'If that happens,' added Amalie, 'Dalmora, Krath and I have decided to move with Jarra and Fian . . . and not because they're famous.' She glared at Steen.

I gave her a startled look. 'You don't have to . . .'

Krath interrupted me. 'Team 1 stays together.'

Lolmack stood up. 'Lolia and I want Jarra and Fian back with the class.'

'You would!' said Petra.

Akram got to his feet. 'The bombing didn't scare me. It just made me angry.'

Sudi moved to stand next to him. 'If we're unwilling to take risks, we shouldn't be working on dig sites.'

Petra looked at Laik. 'You agree with me, don't you?'

Laik shook his head.

'But you were furious about Jarra lying to us and pretending she was a norm.'

'I changed my mind the second I saw that man throw skunk juice at her.' Laik pointedly stood up. 'Now I've seen the way people treat the Handicapped, I can't blame Jarra for pretending she was a norm.'

Petra turned to Hinata. 'What about you?'

Hinata sighed and stood up. 'I vote to have them back.'

'But you're always saying Jarra irritates you.'

'Jarra's giggle irritates me sometimes,' said Hinata, 'but she's my classmate. I'm on her side. You seem to be on the side of the people who threw skunk juice at her and blew up our dome.'

'Telling a few harmless jokes doesn't mean I'm on their side,' said Petra.

'All my life I've heard people insulting the Handicapped.' Dalmora had the shiny-eyed look that meant she was getting all romantic and emotional. 'Everyone claimed they were just telling harmless jokes, so I didn't protest. This year I've learned how those insults damaged lives and encouraged people to think they had a right to attack the Handicapped. Now I feel guilty about all the times I listened and did nothing. When you see evil, you have to make a stand against it.'

One by one the rest of the class stood up.

'But the danger!' Petra wailed.

'We all know you aren't really worried about the danger, Petra,' said Steen. 'It's just an excuse to carry on your stupid vendetta against Jarra. I bet you wish the bombing had killed her.'

'No, I don't.' Petra seemed to hesitate for a moment, then gave Playdon a defiant look. 'I don't believe in cruelty to animals, I just don't think humans should marry them!'

'That remark is completely unacceptable!' said Playdon. 'You've already been given a final red warning for abuse of fellow students, Petra, I therefore . . .'

Petra raised her hand to stop him. 'Don't bother throwing me off the course. I'm leaving. I hate Earth. It killed my boyfriend!'

She turned back to the watching class. 'I know the rest of you don't believe I really cared about Joth, but I did. He wasn't my first choice of boyfriend, and I wasn't his first choice of girlfriend, but most people have the relationship that's within their reach rather than the one of their dreams. We had a fight, but every couple in this room has had fights, even our precious star-crossed lovers!'

I exchanged embarrassed glances with Fian. Yes, we'd had plenty of fights. Everything from major arguments, to trivial squabbles over which vid programme to watch.

'On any other world, Joth and I would have been friends again the next day,' said Petra, 'but Joth did something silly and Earth killed him. I was a fool to study history in the first place. I only chose it because I thought . . .'

Petra suddenly swung round to face me. 'You keep whining for sympathy, Jarra. Telling everyone how 92 per cent of parents abandon their Handicapped babies. You've never spared a second to think what it's like for people on the other side of that situation.'

'I didn't to start with,' I said, 'but I've learned a lot. Abandoning me wasn't easy for my family.'

'You're still talking about yourself,' said Petra. 'I'm talking about me. I'm talking about my mother dumping my father and me to go to Earth with a throwback baby. I thought that studying history, suffering being on Earth, I'd at least . . .'

She broke off and struggled for a moment before she could speak again. 'But no. I've been on Earth for six months now, and my mother still hasn't suggested us meeting. When she does bother to send me a message, she just talks about my ape sister, her new husband, his throwback kid, and the new baby they're expecting. It's like I don't exist any longer.'

I stared at her, shocked by her words. Petra had been in the same situation as my brother, Jaxon. He'd won his battle to stop his mother going to Earth and lived with guilt, but Petra had lost and lived with anger. 'Your mother could be scared of saying the wrong thing, Petra. She's probably waiting for you to suggest a meeting.'

'Well, that's never going to happen,' said Petra. 'I'm going home to Asgard, where I can forget about my mother, my stinking ape sister, and this whole nuking planet. I'm packing and leaving right away.'

She stalked out of the hall and Playdon hurried after her. As the door closed behind them, there was a babble of excited conversation from the rest of the class. Dalmora, Amalie and Krath joined in with it, but I stood there in silence. If I'd known about Petra's sister earlier, would it have made a difference, or . . .?

'Is something wrong, Jarra?' Fian asked.

'I'm just very tired and a bit stunned.' I looked across at where Steen was noisily celebrating Petra's defeat. 'I should be thanking the class for wanting us back, it's totally zan of them, but that seems heartless when it's made Petra leave.'

'I'm pleased she's going,' said Raven. 'Life will be much easier for everyone.'

'Yes, but . . .' I sighed. 'It was easier when I didn't understand Petra, just hated her.'

Fian pulled a sympathetic face. 'Everyone else seems fully occupied gossiping, so let's take our bags to our room and unpack.'

We headed out of the door, with Raven dutifully trailing after us as always. We left him on guard in the corridor and went into our room. Fian immediately started unpacking, but I sat on the bed and stared gloomily down at my Military forearm lookup. I'd been allowed to keep it for security reasons, but it was designed to attach to a Military uniform or impact suit, so it kept slipping around on my civilian sleeve.

I sighed and sent a message to my history teacher, thanking him and explaining the Military would be replacing the borrowed equipment I'd lost in the fire. I sent another message of thanks to the kids at Home E161/8822, and then Fian and I stayed up until midnight watching the newzie channels. Drago had said that Beta sector would unite against the court order because it insulted the Fifty, but I was still grazzed to hear a Beta Veritas presenter declaring support for our betrothal. He even kept pointedly referring to me as Commander *Tell* Morrath. Amaz!

Eventually, Fian and I went to bed. When we turned out the glows, things got . . . awkward.

'I'm sorry,' I said.

Fian turned the glows back on and sat on the edge of the bed. 'There's no need to apologize. It's not your fault our Twoing contract has been cancelled. One of the first conversations we ever had was about Issette's relationship with Keon, and how you're a nice contract girl. I accept there are boundaries you don't want to cross without a Twoing contract.'

I sat up as well. 'It's silly when we've been together for months, but . . .'

'I'm having some problems as well,' said Fian. 'You haven't reached your personal eighteenth birthday yet. Back home on Hercules, some things that are legal with a Year Day age of 17 are still socially . . . Well, a personal age of 18 is regarded as important in certain areas.'

It was pretty obvious what he meant. I buried my head

221

in my hands. My Military status and rank had been suspended because I was 17. Playdon had told me I mustn't go outside the dig site dome until he'd got official instructions from University Asgard about how to deal with having a 17-year-old on his course. Now Fian was admitting to being uncomfortable about the idea of tumbling me because I was only 17.

Since I'd been an 18-year-old adult for six months now, I was finding it pretty nuking frustrating to be treated like a kid again. At this rate, they'd send me back to Next Step!

I'd tried, and failed, to ignore my own qualms about the Twoing contract situation. Ignoring Fian's feelings wasn't an option. 'I know you said you wouldn't let anyone put a wall between us, but . . .'

'I agree, but we keep remembering this is only for a few weeks. Once you've reached your personal birthday, you'll be Military again and we can sort out the contract situation.' Fian sighed. 'This is all my fault.'

'What? Why?'

'Because I kept avoiding any discussion of ages. I was the youngest in my class at school, born only just before Year Day, and I was teased a lot. I knew you could be nearly a year older than me, so I kept extremely quiet about the whole thing. Ironic really. Even seeing you with your friends from Next Step, I never guessed you were all only 17. Cathan was a bit childish, but . . .'

We got dressed. Fian was obviously trying not to look at me. I was trying not to look at him. This situation stank far worse than being covered in skunk juice.

I'd forgotten Raven was sleeping in the corridor. When we opened the door, he was out of his sleep sack and brandishing a gun with startling speed.

'We're moving a wall,' said Fian.

Raven instantly nodded and put his gun away. He

222

obviously realized why we were moving a wall, and knew we wouldn't welcome any discussion of the subject. 'I'll help.'

We tried to be quiet moving the furniture, but every sound seems a lot louder in the middle of the night. Amalie, Dalmora and Krath had the closest rooms, so they were the first to come and see what was happening, but the rest of the class soon followed them, dressed in a motley collection of robes and sleep suits.

Once Krath had established we were moving furniture into the corridor so we could put the wall back between our rooms, he started offering Fian some helpful advice. 'I'm sure you can persuade Jarra not to be such a prude about tumbling you. She usually gives in if you're stubborn enough.'

Fian hadn't been in a good mood to start with, and he'd just dropped a wall on his foot. He left Raven in charge of the wall, strode out into the corridor, and glared at Krath. 'What goes on between Jarra and me is none of your business!'

'But . . .'

Lolmack stepped forward, looming menacingly over Krath. 'Clanless one, show due respect to the nobility of Zeus or I will give you a lesson in manners!'

'I believe I give the lessons here, Lolmack,' said a calm voice. 'Please back away from Krath.'

People moved aside to let Playdon through. Typically, he'd got fully dressed before coming to investigate the reason for the thumping noises and loud conversation.

'Back away,' repeated Playdon.

Lolmack ignored him and looked at me. 'Noble born?'

'Ignore Krath,' I said. 'He's just being an idiot as usual.'

Lolmack instantly bowed and took a step backwards.

'If we were on my home planet, Miranda,' said Amalie,

223

'we'd send Fian and Krath out to the shed storage dome and let Fian beat some common sense into the nardle.'

'We aren't in Epsilon sector,' said Playdon. 'This course is run by University Asgard, and monitored under the Gamma sector moral code. I remind Krath that members of this class are from a huge variety of cultural backgrounds. It's completely unacceptable for any of them to be subjected to comment on their chosen personal relationship boundaries.'

He paused. 'I must also point out the rules on freedom, equality and respect mean it isn't appropriate to bow to a fellow student. I'll have to research the exact implication of addressing someone as noble born before I can decide if it's acceptable or not, but I very much appreciated Raven requesting no one should bother using his formal titles.'

I hastily responded to the heavy hint in Playdon's words. 'Fian and I would rather not bother with formalities either. Lolmack, you and Lolia don't need to bow to me or to Fian. You defended me when that man threw skunk juice at me, and . . . It's not just Fidelis. You're our friends.'

I saw the glow of pride in Lolmack's face. 'In that case . . . Thank you, Jarra. You honour us.'

Playdon looked round at the watching class. 'If they wish, Dalmora and Amalie can stay and help Raven, Jarra, and Fian. The rest of you go back to bed, except for Krath. I want to have a discussion with him about respect.'

The class reluctantly accepted the entertainment was over for the night and drifted back to their rooms. An apprehensive Krath was led off into the hall by Playdon, while Dalmora and Amalie joined the wall moving effort.

'I think Playdon's telepathic,' I said, as I watched Amalie expertly deal with the tricky job of locking the wall into place. 'Even when he's off in his room, he always appears when there's trouble.'

Raven laughed. 'Telepathic? You know this dome is a standard Military training dome?'

'Yes,' I said.

'Well, all Military domes have a monitoring system to automatically check a whole range of conditions in the dome. Playdon's obviously doing the same thing my Military Academy lecturers did, getting the monitoring system to send a message to his lookup if sound levels get too high.'

We clueless ones, who'd gone a whole six months without figuring this out, exchanged glances acknowledging the fact we were total nardles, then started dragging furniture back into my room.

'What made you decide to join the Military, Raven?' asked Fian.

Raven shrugged. 'There are only two possible careers for an Adonis Knight, politics and the Military. After completing the trials of Adonis, I took the Adonis Knight oath. "Knights shall demonstrate nobility, honour, grace, valour and perfection in all virtues, and be champions of justice."'

He pulled a face of self-mockery as he quoted the words of the oath. 'Politics involves a lot of compromises. I'd seen my uncle making bargains with people he didn't like, to support things he didn't approve of, in exchange for them voting for things he wanted. That didn't seem to fit with the oath I'd taken, so I joined the Military. I expect that sounds naive and idealistic, but . . .'

'I think it's wonderful that you take the oath seriously,' said Dalmora.

Raven blushed. 'Thank you.'

When all the furniture was back in place, Fian turned to me. 'I suppose I'd better go now.'

I pulled an unhappy face and nodded. Fian, Raven, and Dalmora went out of the door, while Amalie paused to make a last check on the newly moved wall.

'You know, Dalmora and Raven would make an ideal couple,' I said.

Amalie laughed. 'There are three major problems with that, Jarra. Firstly, Dalmora has a crush on Playdon. Secondly, there's a huge social divide between an Adonis Knight and a girl from Danae. Thirdly, Dalmora is far too young to have a serious relationship.'

'No she isn't. Dalmora is 18, exactly the same as we . . . you are.'

'But they're Alphans, Jarra.' Amalie sighed. 'Dalmora has the same problem I do, but in reverse. I'm one of the first generation born on Miranda. With far more male than female colonists arriving on frontier worlds, there's a lot of social pressure on girls to marry young and have big families. One of the reasons I decided to go to university was to escape that pressure. I love and admire my mother, but I don't want to marry at 18 and have eleven children the way she did.'

Eleven children! I'd been vaguely aware that Amalie had several brothers and sisters, but . . .

'Things are exactly the opposite for Dalmora,' continued Amalie. 'On her world, you don't start having relationships until you've graduated from university. Dalmora's been having a very hard time on this course. If she was studying with University Danae, all the girls would be in the same situation, giggling in corners about which boys they'd like to be formally introduced to one day, but here . . . Dalmora's not just in a class where couples are pairing off, she's got you two legendary star-crossed lovers right in front of her nose.'

'I hadn't known about . . .' I broke off my sentence. 'Anyway, if Dalmora and Raven did decide they liked each other, I think it would be nardle to let anything stop them from being happy together.'

Amalie gave a despairing shake of her head. 'If you think

226

it's nardle to let cultural values interfere with a relationship, why did we just put a wall back?'

She didn't wait for me to try to think of a good answer to that, just headed out of the room.

I sighed, changed back into my sleep suit, and sat down on my single bed feeling deeply depressed. I tried to focus on the good things. I'd joined my clan, the grandson of Lucius Augustus Gordianus would join the wealthy, powerful, and prestigious clan August, and Lolette would join a disreputable plebeian clan cluster that made sex vids. Other Handicapped kids would have the chance to join their Betan clans in future, and Beta sector would probably request a specialist planet for the Handicapped.

Those were all utterly zan things, but they didn't change the fact I was sitting in a room alone. What should have been our first night as a betrothed couple had ended up with Fian and me on opposite sides of a flexiplas wall.

I wondered what Petra would do now, and if there was any hope of Raven and Dalmora ever getting together. The more I learned about Alphans, the more they confused me. In different ways, Dalmora and Raven both fitted the dignified aristocratic Alphan stereotype, but then there was Rono. He was from Cassandra in Alpha sector, but he'd laugh if anyone described him as either dignified or aristocratic.

My lookup chimed softly for an incoming call. I answered it, and Fian's face appeared.

'I was thinking,' he said. 'We can't share a room, but would a holo be all right?'

'I'm not sure what you . . .'

'Like this.' The image juddered wildly as he lay back on his bed, and then stabilized showing him lying on his side and smiling at me.

'Oh.' I lay back on my bed and set my lookup to project Fian's holo image next to me.

'I thought we could leave the channel open during the night,' he said. 'I know you'll say it's silly and sentimental, but I'm finding this difficult. I'd had other plans for tonight.'

'No, it's . . . It's a good idea. Very good.'

I turned out the glows and lay watching the holo image of Fian until I fell asleep.

23

It was oddly embarrassing meeting the real Fian at breakfast after spending the night with his holo image. I hoped Fian wouldn't mention the holo image thing because it had meant a lot to me. Dalmora and Amalie wouldn't say anything tactless, but Krath . . .

When Raven and the rest of team 1 had joined us at the table, Krath spoke. 'I apologize for my shockingly disrespectful comments. My regrettable conduct won't be repeated.'

'How long did Playdon spend training you to recite that?' asked Fian.

'It felt like twenty years,' said Krath.

Both my lookup and Fian's chimed to signal incoming mail. Over at the next table, two more lookups chimed, and Lolia and Lolmack stood up.

I read my message. 'Our clan is making a statement.'

Fian turned on the wall vid at the end of the hall and set it to Beta Sector Daily. It showed an image of a massive crowd gathered in front of the steps of the Parthenon.

'Look at the banners at the top of the steps!' Lolmack hurried forward and pointed at them. 'Unbelievable! The

Military alliance and August alliance banners haven't been united since . . . They're coming out!'

The image on the screen zoomed in as two toga-clad figures came out of the huge doors and stood in front of the twin banners.

'That's General Dragon Tell Dramis and Lucius Augustus Gordianus,' I said.

Lucius Augustus Gordianus spoke in the ringing tones of a practised public speaker. 'I am not here to tell anyone of the events yesterday, because you know them. I am not here to explain the offence, for you understand it. I am not here to ask what you feel, because I share your outrage. The banners of Beta sector have been challenged by outlanders!'

He paused before speaking in a quieter voice. 'Remember the years after Exodus. Remember how close civilization came to total collapse. Fidelis, our mutual loyalty and sacrifice, saved Beta sector and all humanity. Fidelis remains the united heart of Beta sector.'

His voice started rising in volume again. 'We would not abandon Fidelis when the revisionists demanded conformity with other sectors. We declared the Second Roman Empire and stood alone. When that empire ended with the reunification treaty of Artemis, other sectors swore to respect our customs and honour our betrothal and marriage contracts, but now they have broken the treaty of Artemis, insulted our banners, and challenged Fidelis!'

He raised both arms above his head. 'I call the clans to remember their oaths as Betans. Loyalty to those we love.'

'Fidelis!' The crowd shouted the word.

'Loyalty to family and clan.'

'Fidelis!' The crowd answered him, and I heard Lolmack and Lolia shouting the word along with them.

'Loyalty to Zeus and Beta sector.'

I found myself joining in the massed shout of the crowd. 'Fidelis!'

Raven's voice murmured from beside me. 'Deity aid us!'

After that emotional crescendo, Lucius Augustus Gordianus abruptly changed to a perfectly normal conversational voice. 'I summon the Senate to meet in emergency session. To demonstrate respect for the Fifty, we must draft a reciprocal agreement on relationship contracts between Beta sector and Earth, which will recognize not just future contracts but also apply retrospectively.'

It was a weird anti-climax to such a passionate speech. Beta Sector Daily went back to its studio, where two people started babbling away in incomprehensibly strong Betan dialect, openly defying all the rules about newzie channels only using standard Language. Playdon turned down the sound, and Lolia and Lolmack went off into a corner to keep listening to it on their lookups.

Fian shook his head. 'What's the point of that? Jarra will be 18 and Military again long before Beta sector finishes passing their legislation.'

'This isn't about your betrothal any longer,' said Raven, grimly. 'This is about whether Beta sector declares the Third Roman Empire.'

'What?' I stared at him. 'You can't be serious.'

'I'm perfectly serious,' said Raven. 'Adonis Knights start learning politics in their cradle. The recognition of Betan betrothal contracts and triad marriages was a key clause in the reunification treaty of Artemis. Lucius Augustus Gordianus just pointed out yesterday's court order broke that clause, and demonstrated he only had to say the word to be proclaimed emperor. Then he spelt out exactly what other sectors had to do to stop that happening. Make the same legislation changes as Beta sector, not just to uphold

231

the treaty of Artemis, but as a declaration of support for Betan culture and respect for the Fifty. If they don't . . .'

Raven grimaced. 'If they don't do it, then humanity is divided again, which could mean the sort of full-scale war we haven't had since the days of pre-history when everyone lived on Earth. The united banners of the Military and August alliances send a terrifying message. I've been part of a planetary peacekeeping force keeping two factions of arguing civilians apart, but the idea of war between the sectors . . . Going into combat against the Betan Military clans. My own friends!'

I shared Raven's nightmare for a moment, picturing Fian and myself caught in the middle of cross-sector war. We were Military officers, raised on one side of the divide and members of a clan on the other. I couldn't leave Earth, and that would surely have to remain neutral territory for the sake of the Handicapped babies born on either side, but Fian . . .

'How could something as simple as joining my clan cause so much trouble?' I wailed.

'It didn't,' said Raven. 'When the Second Roman Empire ended, the reunification treaty of Artemis was supposed to be a new beginning, but the divisions between Beta and the other sectors never healed. Tension and mutual suspicion have been building for over a century. If the Tell clan ceremony hadn't triggered this, something else would.'

I thought of Playdon's lectures about the early twentieth century. The First World War hadn't really been caused by the assassination of one man, but by the explosive political situation.

'The other sectors don't even try to understand Betans,' said Lolmack. 'When we came to Earth with our baby, the Hospital Earth staff didn't believe we really wanted to keep Lolette. We were Betan, and we'd been part of a triad marriage, so they thought we just wanted an excuse to try and seduce them.'

'We didn't help things though,' said Lolia. 'We got angry, so we acted like the caricature Betans they expected. We did the same when we first joined this class, to make everyone stay away from us and help keep Lolette's existence a secret.'

'It wasn't our fault,' said Lolmack. 'If the outlanders hadn't judged Beta sector purely by its sex vids, then we'd never have done it.'

'It was partly our fault,' said Lolia. 'They judged Beta sector by its sex vids, which show nothing of the real Betan culture, but our clan *makes* those vids!'

Lolmack frowned. 'You have a point.'

'The newzie channels in every sector have been discussing the Tell clan ceremony for days now,' said Playdon. 'People in other sectors are finally starting to understand the Betan clan system and the importance of the Fifty. The politicians will surely do what Beta sector want.'

He paused. 'I'm not sure if we should go and excavate some pre-history ruins, or stay here watching modern history happen on the wall vid. This year has been the most . . .'

He broke off as a couple of chimes from lookups were followed by a yell of protest, and gave a slight shake of his head. 'Now what?'

Sudi and Akram were on their feet, facing each other. 'How could you do this to me?' demanded Akram.

'Read the full message,' said Sudi. 'I didn't cancel our contract. Earth Registry did!'

She turned to face Playdon. 'Earth Registry says that court order doesn't just mean Jarra and Fian's Twoing and betrothal contracts are illegal, but every relationship contract involving someone who isn't a citizen of Earth. They're cancelling all of them!'

'Something like this must be on . . .' Playdon set the wall vid to show Earth Rolling News.

'Contracts taken out on Earth between two citizens of Earth remain valid,' said a presenter. 'We repeat: Earth Registry regrets yesterday's court order invalidates every Twoing contract or marriage involving a sector citizen that was registered on Earth.'

Four couples in our class had been Twoing, including Fian and me, and all those contracts had been registered on Earth. Twin chimes from behind me meant another couple were getting their bad news. Lolia and Lolmack had been married on Artemis in Beta sector, so they were safe.

'I'm so sorry,' I said.

'It's not your fault. It's the fault of that nuking Deltan law firm!' said Akram in a savage voice. 'I know that word isn't allowed under the Gamma sector moral code, but right now . . .'

'I accept this is an extremely distressing situation,' said Playdon. 'I'm definitely not risking taking people in a state of high emotion to work on the dig site. We'll . . .'

He broke off as his lookup chimed. He glanced at it, his face twisted in pain, and he changed the wall vid to Delta Sector Vision.

'. . . ironically, what was intended as an attack on betrothals between norm and Handicapped is mostly affecting norm couples. Contracts between norm and Handicapped usually involve a norm with Earth citizenship. Either a norm child born on Earth to Handicapped parents, or a norm parent who has accompanied a Handicapped child to Earth and been given automatic citizenship under the Hospital Earth assisted relocation plan.'

Coverage swapped from the studio setting to a presenter standing in some sort of public building. 'The number of people affected by this is far higher than you might expect.

Large numbers of history and medical students have spent time on Earth, and a Twoing contract taken out years ago can have huge implications right now.'

The image panned out to show two women standing next to him. 'Perhaps you could explain your situation for our viewers.'

'We're both citizens of Delta sector,' said one woman. 'We met when we were medical students and we registered our first Twoing contract on Earth.'

'We've been married for twenty-three years,' said the other. 'Now we get a mail message saying our first Twoing contract was invalid. That means we don't have the prior Twoing contracts legally required to marry in Delta sector, so our marriage is invalid. If I get my hands on those lawyers . . .'

'What are you doing about this?' asked the presenter.

'We've petitioned our planetary representatives of course,' said the first woman. 'Beta sector is working on legislation to fix this situation, and Delta sector needs it too, but we aren't waiting around months for the politicians to act. Epsilon sector allows instant marriages without prior Twoing contracts, so we're going there to get married again.'

The couple headed off past big red information signs about off-world portal charges.

'I hope they don't have problems in Epsilon sector,' said Amalie. 'Some people there are prejudiced against two women marrying.'

'They are?' asked Krath. 'Why?'

'Think about it, nardle. Epsilon has far more single men than women. Marriages between two men, or triad marriages between two men and one woman are encouraged, but . . .'

The presenter started talking again. 'This couple have the chance to go to Epsilon and marry again. Many don't. Widows, widowers, and even the heirs of deceased couples are receiving mail messages. An act of hatred against one couple's mixed relationship is . . .'

I missed the rest of the sentence as I hurried out of the hall, scrubbed my arm across my face to get rid of the wetness round my eyes, and tapped urgently at my lookup. I was doing the same thing I'd always done as a child, making an emergency call to my ProMum to ask her to fix the mess I'd created.

'Jarra?' Fian's voice spoke softly. 'Are you all right?'

I looked up and saw both Fian and Raven had followed me. 'No, I'm not. I could have gone to University Earth, but I joined this class to get my revenge on the hated exos. I've done that. Oh yes, I've really done that. Did you see Playdon's expression when his lookup chimed?'

'What?'

I spelled it out for him. 'The news presenter said widows and widowers are getting messages too. Playdon is a widower. He and his wife worked on Earth dig sites, and she was killed here at the California Rift. You can bet that either their marriage, or one of their Twoing contracts, was registered on Earth.'

'Oh nuke!' Fian gave a startled look in the direction of the hall door. 'That must . . .'

Candace answered my call. 'Jarra, what's the . . .?'

I didn't wait for her to finish the question. 'We have to stop Registry doing this. I don't want them hurting all these people just because my betrothal contract was cancelled. I'll be Military again soon, and Fian and I can sort things out.'

Candace shook her head. 'You can't stop this, Jarra. When the bigots attacked your relationship with Fian, it was an attack on all the Handicapped, saying we weren't fit to associate with norms. The Handicapped people working in Earth Registry are telling the sectors they won't accept that. They're saying that prejudice is wrong, and the Handicapped and norms should be treated equally. You agree with that message, don't you?'

'Yes, but why do they have to send it by hurting innocent people?'

'Because this is the first chance the Handicapped have ever had to make a protest that anyone hears,' said Candace. 'For centuries, we've been dumped on Earth and ignored. You can't stop Earth Registry doing this, neither can I, and I wouldn't if I could. I have three norm children, the youngest only a year older than you.'

I was shocked to hear her talking openly about her family. Even more shocked by the raw emotion in her voice as she continued.

'Our lives are ruled by statistics, Jarra. 90 per cent of babies born to a Handicapped couple are norms. When they grow up, they go to off-world universities to study. They're scared of the prejudice, so they hide the fact their parents are Handicapped. They graduate and get jobs, lead double lives, hide their background from friends, partners and employers, but it's a terrible strain. Gradually they stop coming to Earth for visits, and there's longer and longer between calls. Eventually 83 per cent of them break off contact entirely.'

Candace was crying now. 'I'm sorry about hurting your norm friends, Jarra, but we have to take this chance. It may help me keep contact with my children. It may mean I'll meet my grandchildren one day.'

She ended the call and I stood there staring blankly at my lookup. 'Candace is right, I can see she's right, but doing this to Playdon, to all those people . . . I don't know what side I'm on any longer.'

Raven took a step forward. 'Your professional mother is perfectly right, Jarra. If things are ever going to change, it has to be now. When people saw you on the newzies . . .'

He pulled an apologetic face. 'Please don't hate me for this, but I'd always assumed the Handicapped were different from norms. We were taught at school that the only difference was a faulty immune system, but all the jokes people make about the smell, the stupidity, and the ugliness . . . Well, that had a bigger impact than one science lesson.'

He paused. 'I was on a base in Gamma sector when the news broke about the alien probe arriving at Earth. There were three hundred of us packed into a hall watching the vid coverage. We saw you, startlingly young for the job you were doing, with a name that told us you were descended from Tellon Blaze, then . . .'

He shook his head. 'Then some bigoted civilian called you an ape, and we realized you were Handicapped. I think we were as stunned by that as by the news of the alien probe. That moment changed my image of the Handicapped from a slow-witted semi-human to a glowing girl. People in every sector had that same, eye-opening experience, Jarra. You're their image of the Handicapped now and . . .'

He broke off because Rono was striding down the corridor towards us. I caught my breath as I saw a white regrowth fluid patch on Rono's forehead, conspicuous against his dark skin. Fian and I exchanged anxious glances, and followed him into the hall.

'Every relationship on Cassandra 2 just got hit, including my own marriage to Keren,' said Rono. 'We're going to Epsilon to get married again. Given the state my people are in, we're taking the whole team with us. I'm afraid safety protocols mean you can't work on the dig site while we're away.'

'That doesn't matter,' said Playdon. 'I just got a message from the Dig Site Federation. So many people are rushing off world that all dig sites are closing for two days.' He hesitated for a moment. 'Your head? An accident?'

'No, I'm just getting rid of that old scar. I don't want the sight of it bothering Keren when he's this upset.'

Playdon nodded. 'I understand. I've got some students in the same position as you. They'll only need to get to Alpha sector to reregister their Twoing contracts, but Earth Rolling News reports there's chaos in all the Earth Off-worlds. Can you take them through Earth America Off-world to Alpha sector with your team?'

Rono nodded. 'They've got exactly three minutes to pack anything they want to take. My team are deeply distressed. They need to be doing something constructive, even if it's only standing in a queue.'

Six figures sprinted for the door. They knew Rono by now. If he said he was leaving in three minutes, he meant it.

There was a short silence then Krath spoke. 'Amalie, can we go with them? We won't be able to register a Twoing contract on Earth now, so . . .'

'If anyone else is coming, they only have two minutes to pack,' said Rono.

'We don't need luggage,' said Amalie. 'We just need us.'

I gave her a startled look. 'You're really going to Two with Krath? Surely Epsilon sector is full of men who are more . . . more everything.'

Amalie laughed at me. 'You think I'd want to Two with someone intelligent, sensible and mature?'

I nodded.

'But that would be like going to live in Alpha sector where everything has already been built. Krath's the human equivalent of a frontier world.'

Krath frowned at her. 'What? Why?'

Amalie gave him a casual slap on the back of the head. 'Because the raw material is there, but it'll take huge amounts of work to improve you. I can't resist the challenge.'

I stared at her in bewilderment. 'So you like Krath because of all the things that are wrong with him?'

'Exactly.' Amalie grinned at me.

Rono turned to Playdon. 'Dannel, I'm really sorry there's no way you can . . .'

Playdon shook his head. 'No court order can change the fact Cadee was my wife. A marriage is far more than just legal clauses.'

Six breathless figures tumbled back into the hall and looked expectantly at Rono. He glanced at their hover bags.

'We'll go back to my dome to pick up my team, and then portal to America Off-world. It's going to be mayhem there, so you'd better carry your bags instead of letting them chase after you.'

Rono patted Playdon on the shoulder and went out of the door. Eight figures hurried after him, and the hall suddenly seemed very quiet.

24

Playdon didn't want to give lectures when eight of the class were away. We could have spent the day by the pool, but instead everyone sat in the hall watching the newzies. In mid-afternoon, a man in shiny clothes gave a statement on behalf of the Delta Sector Parliament. He had the anxious expression of someone who'd taken a long hard look at the amount of Delta sector that bordered on Beta sector, and was desperate to calm down an explosive situation.

'The Delta Sector Parliament wishes to express its disapproval of the recent intervention by a few individuals in a Betan betrothal ceremony. The people of Delta sector understand and share the feelings of outrage in Beta sector at such disrespect for its traditions and culture. The Delta Sector Parliament is meeting in emergency session to rectify the unfortunate omission in current legislation.'

'Zan!' said Fian.

Raven still looked worried. 'Everything depends on Lucius now, because he's got Beta sector in the palm of his hand. If he's a reasonable man he'll accept that response from Delta sector, but his ancestors were emperors of the Second Roman

Empire. He may have ambitions to join them in wearing imperial purple.'

'Lucius Augustus Gordianus is a good man,' I said. 'He gambled his political career to help his Handicapped grandson.'

Fian nodded. 'I don't believe my father would let the Military alliance support a bid for personal power.'

'What's your father got to do with it?' asked Raven.

'Dragon Tell Dramis is my adoptive father,' said Fian.

'Oh yes.' Raven nodded. 'That must mean Drago's your brother.'

Fian groaned. 'That's a terrible thought, but yes. The sickeningly handsome Drago Tell Dramis is my brother.'

I saw the image of Lucius Augustus Gordianus appear on the wall vid. 'Shhh!'

'Beta sector welcomes the support of Delta sector,' he said. 'There has been a wall between us and other sectors for far too long. Let us hope this signals the start of a new era of mutual understanding.'

Raven made a noise of relief that was somewhere between a sigh and a sob. 'Thank chaos!'

After that, something even more incredible happened. Delta Sector Vision showed an interviewer talking with some of the Handicapped! Pre-recorded of course, because a live link to Earth would have meant the audience being constantly bored by delays as questions and answers were relayed through the series of comms portals between Earth in the centre of Alpha sector, and Isis in Delta sector.

'Award committees won't consider my work because I can't travel off world to collect an award in person,' said a professor from University Earth.

'And I have to pretend I live in Alpha sector and use an off-world agent to sell my paintings,' said an artist. 'People wouldn't buy them if they knew they'd been painted by an ape.'

242

'Don't you prefer to describe yourself as Handicapped?' asked the interviewer.

'No I don't,' said the artist. 'It may be the official polite term, but I think it's just as insulting as ape.'

When the recorded interview ended, Dalmora gave me a worried look. 'Would you rather we didn't use the word Handicapped, Jarra?'

I shrugged. 'The real problem isn't the words people use, but the sneer in their voice when they say them.'

I still didn't like Earth Registry's tactics, but they'd achieved something in one day that no one else had managed in centuries. Handicapped voices were finally being heard on other worlds.

It was almost midnight when the class's Twoing couples arrived back, led by Amalie and Krath.

'Congratulations and mutual joy on your Twoing contract,' I said.

Krath shook his head. 'There's a lot less mutual joy than you might think. Amalie's still refusing to share a room with me.'

Amalie reached out a hand and hit him on the back of his head.

'The Cassandra 2 team members kept making jokes about the things that happen around Jarra,' continued Krath. 'Crashing spacecraft, alien artefacts, and social revolutions! Rono says he's surprised Lecturer Playdon doesn't have to spend every other week in a rejuvenation tank to recover from the strain of having her in his class.'

Playdon came over to join us. 'I'm hoping to struggle on until my first scheduled rejuvenation cycle next year. Have Cassandra 2 gone on to Epsilon sector?'

Amalie nodded. 'They'll probably be there by now. When we arrived at Alpha Sector Interchange 4, things were quite peaceful. The real problem was getting off Earth.'

'I don't understand why that was so difficult,' said Krath. 'Earth gets masses of people off world quickly whenever Solar Watch warns an incoming solar storm is going to bring down the portal network.'

I kept carefully quiet. I was sure the staff of Earth's Off-worlds could have locked open more portals and got everyone to Alpha sector a lot faster, but they'd wanted to maximize the delays to get publicity.

'At one point,' added Krath, 'the queues stopped moving entirely for nearly an hour while thousands and thousands of kids came pouring through. I've no idea why.'

I laughed. 'That was the Earth America kiddie commute coming home at the end of their school day. The normal born kids of Handicapped parents go to orientation schools on Alphan worlds. It's supposed to help them join "real society" when they grow up.'

'I suggest you all get some sleep now,' said Playdon. 'The dig site will still be closed tomorrow, but there'll probably be more exciting events to watch on the newzies.'

Everyone dutifully headed off to bed. Fian and I walked together to the door of my room, and exchanged an awkwardly self-conscious kiss, aware that Raven was, as always, on guard nearby.

'Goodnight, Jarra,' said Fian.

'Goodnight,' I said.

He looked as if he didn't want to go. I didn't want him to go. He went.

The next morning, we all ate breakfast while watching Earth Rolling News show a series of vid clips. Sometime during the night, there'd been announcements from both Gamma and Epsilon sectors that they were rushing through legislation, and Lucius Augustus Gordianus had made another speech in response. Then a presenter started explaining Kappa sector didn't have a problem. Its fledgling colony worlds were still running under the Colony Ten charter, which specifically recognized relationships from any of the worlds of humanity.

'I hope no one can argue about Earth being one of the worlds of humanity,' I said.

'So that just leaves Alpha sector then,' said Krath.

Playdon started giving lectures after that, but it was obvious from the way he kept checking his lookup that he was keeping an eye on the news feed from one of the newzie channels. He suddenly stopped in mid-sentence, and turned on the wall vid to show Alpha and Omega channel. An excited announcer was talking.

'The Adonis Knights are to deliver a petition for justice to the Alpha Sector Parliament. This is the first time this century that . . .'

We all turned to stare at Raven. He looked dreadfully embarrassed.

'I couldn't say anything until the public announcement, but Colonel Leveque is letting me portal to Adonis for a few hours to join the procession.'

The usual team of four Military Security officers arrived a few minutes later, to take over bodyguard duty while Raven was away. We had a couple more hours of lectures, ate lunch, and then sat watching the vid coverage on Alpha and Omega newzie channel.

'Can anyone see Raven?' asked Krath, as the vid image slowly panned along the procession of ornately clad figures with their scarlet and gold cloaks.

'The trial knights, the ones who've completed the trials of Adonis, will be leading the way,' said Dalmora. 'Look, they're going through the Arch of Remembrance into the Courtyards of Memory now.'

The vid image changed to show the leading figures in the procession passing under a huge ceremonial archway.

'I still can't . . . Oh, there's Raven!' yelled Krath. 'Third row from the front.'

'Do you think the woman walking next to Raven is his mother?' asked Amalie. 'She's about the right age and she looks a bit like him.'

'Amaz.' Dalmora's eyes were rigidly fixed on the wall vid. 'Just amaz.'

The knights solemnly presented their petition to Aadi Quilla Amarion, First Speaker of Alpha sector, and marched off again. Alpha and Omega returned to the studio presenter, and Playdon turned off the sound. Dalmora gave a soft regretful sigh. I was sure she'd be replaying the coverage of the procession the second she was alone in her room.

My lookup chimed with three forwarded messages from the Dig Site Federation. The first was a message from University Asgard referring the issue of my age to the Dig Site Federation. The second was the Dig Site Federation's aggressive reply, saying Jarra Tell Morrath was a legally adult citizen of Earth and had far more right to work on Earth's dig sites than any off-worlder. The third was a grovelling apology from University Asgard, explaining their question had been a mere administrative formality, with no offence intended towards Jarra Tell Morrath, to Earth, or to Beta sector.

I showed them to Fian and he laughed. 'After what happened over our betrothal contract, I think University Asgard were worried the Dig Site Federation would throw every off-world team off the dig sites.'

'University Asgard is obviously scared to death of you, Jarra,' said Krath. 'I bet you could pass this course without doing any more work.'

'I bet she couldn't,' said Lecturer Playdon.

A few minutes later, Raven entered the hall and nodded at the four Military Security officers. They headed off, and Raven came to join us.

'We watched the procession,' Dalmora told him. 'Living history. Truly fascinate!'

'It was a . . .'

Fian jumped to his feet, knocking over his chair in his haste. He hurried across to the wall vid, and turned up the volume. A presenter stood in front of an image of the flag of humanity.

'General Marshal Renton Mai, commander-in-chief of the Military, has just requested Parliament of Planets to approve a change to Planet First selection criteria. This would allow the Military to select at least one colony world in each sector with a higher level of solar activity than the current allowable range. Scientists advise such a world would be subject to the same solar storms and portal outages as Earth, but it would also be compatible with the Handicapped immune system.'

25

'Drag net to clear the small rubble please,' I said, and hovered away from the nearby building to give the heavy lifts space to work. I hadn't got my hover belt set to a high enough height, so I caught my foot on a big piece of concraz and felt like a nardle. I hoped no one had noticed, but the background note on my comms changed to that of a private channel and I heard Playdon's voice.

'You've been making a few careless errors today, Jarra.'

I groaned and replied on the private channel. 'Sorry, sir. I've been a bit distracted. Fian and I have been waiting over a month to sort out our betrothal. It'll be my birthday tomorrow, I'll be 18 and Military again, and . . .'

Playdon's voice sounded amused. 'I understand, Jarra, but you can't afford to be careless on a dig site. You don't want to have an accident and spend your birthday in hospital, so I think you'd better just sit and watch for the rest of the morning.'

The background note on the comms changed again as Playdon spoke on the team circuit. 'Team 1 finish your drag net, then team 4 will take over.'

I gave my tag gun and hover belt to Steen, went across

to sit with Raven on one of the bench seats of the nearest transport sled, and unsealed my impact suit hood. I spent a moment enjoying the wind cooling my face. Blizz!

Fian came to join us, opening his own hood with a sigh of relief, and I tapped my lookup to check my mail.

'Issette is starting her two weeks practical experience in a Hospital Earth America casualty unit. She says if anyone throws skunk juice at me again, I mustn't go to her unit.'

Fian and Raven laughed.

'And Keon says the holo caterpillars in his latest test turned blue.'

'I suppose that's a test on the signals from the alien sphere,' said Fian. 'Is blue good or bad? Do you think they're finally getting somewhere?'

'I've given up hope of them ever getting anywhere with that light sculpture,' I said gloomily. 'Anything happening on the newzie channels?'

Fian tapped his lookup. 'Everyone's still arguing about how big a problem it would be to have more worlds with portal outages. Some politician in Gamma sector made a speech, saying the needs of the many must outweigh the needs of the few. Lucius Augustus Gordianus replied, saying humanity has chosen twelve hundred colony worlds for the convenience of the many, and can now afford to select a handful for the survival of the few.'

He paused for a moment. 'Ah, the latest winner of the Physics Nobel has joined in the argument. She says if humanity keeps expanding, we'll reach the point where it's impossible to relay the portal signals of Handicapped babies directly from the frontier to Earth. We'll have to do this eventually, so we should do it now.'

Amalie, Krath and Dalmora arrived, and sat on the next bench facing us. 'Still no news from Alpha sector?' asked Krath.

Fian shook his head.

Krath sighed. 'The Adonis Knights dressing up in their fancy outfits didn't achieve much, did it?'

'Krath!' Amalie frowned at him, and gave a pointed look in Raven's direction.

'Sorry,' said Krath.

'Give the Alpha Sector Parliament time,' said Dalmora.

'They've already had a whole month,' said Krath. 'Other sectors only needed a day.'

Raven laughed. 'But Alpha sector isn't like the others. Many of the planets were settled directly from different regions of Earth, and their cultures still vary hugely, so it's always a struggle to get the planetary representatives to agree on anything. There's an old joke that the Alpha Sector Parliament once voted on whether two plus two equalled four. The motion passed with 755 in favour, 648 against, and 200 abstentions.'

I grinned. 'Lucius Augustus Gordianus had a meeting with Aadi Quilla Amarion, and seems to be fairly happy about whatever's going on.'

'Lucius may be happy, but Rono certainly isn't,' said Krath.

I giggled. The whole class had been by the pool yesterday when Rono was watching an Alphan newzie channel on his lookup and totally lost his temper. By the time Playdon managed to shut him up, we'd all learned some very creative Cassandrian swear words.

'You can't blame him for being frustrated,' said Fian. 'He and Keren have got remarried, but they want their original marriage reinstated.'

I sighed. I was still feeling horribly guilty about everyone's marriages and Twoing contracts being cancelled.

'The Planet First amendment must surely pass,' said Amalie. 'Four sectors are on our side now.'

I shook my head. 'The sectors are changing their

250

relationship legislation to conform with the treaty of Artemis. It doesn't mean they'll support the Planet First amendment as well.'

'And it's a very different sort of vote,' said Fian. 'Anything to do with the Military has to be agreed by full Parliament of Planets. Even if a sector is generally in favour, some of its planetary representatives are bound to vote against, and the Alphan vote is always vital because they have so many representatives.'

'It's unfair that Alpha and Beta sectors have far more planetary representatives than Gamma, Delta and Epsilon,' said Krath. 'Each sector has about two hundred planets, so they should all have the same number of planetary representatives.'

'Do you really think it would be fairer for every world to just have one planetary representative, whatever its population?' asked Dalmora. 'Should the huge population of a world like Adonis only have the same voice as the ten thousand citizens of a frontier world that's newly out of Colony Ten?'

'Well . . .' Krath pulled a face. 'No, but the system does mean the older sectors get to decide everything, and . . .'

He was interrupted by my lookup chiming. Everyone gave it a startled look. When we were on the dig site, we kept our lookups set to only chime for emergency messages.

'What's happened now?' asked Krath.

'I don't know yet.' I anxiously checked the display. 'It's Maeth!'

'Who?' asked Krath.

'A friend from Next Step.' I stabbed my lookup with a finger to accept the call, and saw it display Maeth's face. She looked as if she'd been crying. What the chaos had happened?

'Jarra,' she said, 'I . . . You know when we were 14, I got information about my parents, but never contacted them.'

251

'Yes.' Of the nine of us who'd gone through Nursery, Home and Next Step together, seven had taken up their option to get information about their birth parents at age 14. Maeth was the only one who'd done that, but not actually tried contacting her parents afterwards. She'd never told me why.

'My parents were from Beta sector,' said Maeth. 'All I knew about Betans was they made sex vids, so I couldn't face . . . There's been a lot about Beta sector on the newzies lately. It wasn't what I'd imagined, so I decided to contact my parents and . . . Jarra, they're coming to Earth to see me!'

I was grazzed. 'Maeth, that's totally zan!'

'They want me to join their clan, like you joined the Tell clan.' Maeth gave a tense, shaky laugh. 'I don't know if . . . My clan won't make sex vids, will they?'

'It's unlikely,' I said. 'What's their clan prefix? The bit in the middle of their names?'

'Ston.'

I tapped my lookup, requesting information on the Ston clan. 'You've no need to worry, Maeth,' I said. 'They're a very respectable clan of the middle rank. They manufacture medical equipment.'

'So that's all right then.' Maeth covered her face with her hands. She was crying again.

The image on the lookup screen swung wildly for a second, and then Ross's face appeared. 'Jarra, they're talking about betrothals and adopting me into the clan. There won't be any legal problems, will there?'

'There shouldn't be since you're both citizens of Earth,' I said. 'Would you be happy about getting adopted?'

'I can cope with it so long as we're not on the newzies.' He glanced off to one side, obviously looking at Maeth. 'I'd better go. Thanks, Jarra.'

The lookup screen went blank. I gave a little shake of my head.

Fian laughed. 'There's no need to look so shocked, Jarra. A lot of Betan clans are welcoming their Handicapped children as members now.'

'I know,' I said. 'It's nardle of me not to realize that one of my own friends might . . .'

'This is Dig Site Command,' said a voice on the comms broadcast channel that could be heard by everyone working on the California Rift. 'We have five hours warning of an incoming solar storm. Solar Watch predicts Earth portal network will be in lockdown for approximately twelve hours. California Rift Dig Site is evacuating. I repeat: California Rift Dig Site is evacuating.'

'Working teams retrieve your sensor spikes and pack up,' said Playdon on team circuit. He came over to sit on our transport sled.

'Evacuating the dig site means what exactly?' asked Krath.

'Evacuating means evacuating,' said Playdon. 'If dig teams stayed on the Land Raft when a solar storm shut down the Earth portal network, they'd have no way to escape an earthquake.'

'Where will we evacuate to, sir?' asked Raven. 'There are security issues to consider.'

'Dig Site Command usually arranges accommodation on another dig site, or at a University Earth America campus,' said Playdon, 'but I'm happy to take the class anywhere the Military suggest. It'll only be for a day.'

'I'll call Colonel Leveque,' said Raven.

He made his call, and laughed. 'Colonel Leveque says the established protocol is for Jarra to pick somewhere to hide.'

Amalie giggled. 'We'll probably end up in Zoo America South. Jarra took us there earlier in the year.'

'I'd prefer somewhere more inaccessible than a zoo,' said Raven.

'If you want somewhere inaccessible,' I said, 'I know the perfect place.'

'Where?' asked Krath.

I grinned at him. 'You'll find out when we get there.'

Fian shook his head. 'It'll be somewhere with cheese fluffle.'

'Let's get the sleds moving now,' said Playdon. 'When we're back at the dome, I'll give you exactly one hour to get out of your impact suits, shower, and pack a few things.'

It took only a few minutes to drive back to the dome, and then there was a rush for the showers. Fian and I were among the first to finish packing our bags and arrive in the hall. Playdon checked off our names against the list on his lookup.

'I hope there's some privacy wherever we're going,' said Fian. 'Given what day it is tomorrow . . .'

I felt myself blush.

When the rest of the class had arrived, Playdon turned to look at me. 'Jarra, do you need to make any special arrangements before we portal?'

'I've already called Colonel Leveque and . . . and someone else,' I said. 'I just need to enter the portal code now.'

'Lead the way then,' said Playdon.

I was startled to find the whole of the Cassandra 2 team waiting in the corridor by the portal room. Rono grinned at me. 'My team would hate to miss anything exciting, so we'd like to join the mystery trip. If there's room for us of course.'

I smiled. 'There's plenty of space where we're going.'

I went up to the portal, entered a code, went through, and hurriedly turned so I could watch the others arriving and enjoy seeing their puzzled expressions. Playdon was the last to appear. He glanced round the huge room, and frowned at the glass wall ahead.

'It's pitch dark outside, so we must have changed continent. Where are we, Jarra?'

My smile widened. 'Welcome to the main viewing gallery of Roof of the World. We're in the Himalaya mountain range in Earth Asia, at the top of the highest mountain on Earth. It's called Chomolungma, or Everest.'

26

Everyone moved towards the glass wall of the vast room and looked out.

'Is the white out there snow?' asked Rono. 'It's winter here?'

'It's always snowy and lethally cold this high up whatever the season,' I said. 'You can't see much at the moment, but we'll have an incredible view at dawn.'

'Is it safe here?' asked Playdon. 'Once the Earth portal network goes into lockdown . . .'

'Roof of the World is built in Earth's most hostile environment,' I said. 'Oxygen levels in the air are far lower than normal, and the extreme cold can kill an unprotected person in minutes. It's called the Death Zone.'

Playdon looked extremely unhappy, but I grinned and continued. 'Our visitors can, however, enjoy their visit in perfect safety. Roof of the World is built in three interconnected sections, each with its own independent environmental control system providing heat and air. It has two viewing galleries and a range of hospitality suites, which provide an unforgettable venue for wedding and other parties. To guarantee your safety, Roof of the World is anchored deep into the mountainside, has twenty portals, and its own emergency medical facilities.'

'You sound like a tour guide,' said Fian. 'I suppose you came here on a school trip.'

I laughed. 'Schools don't come to Roof of the World. The admission charges are far too high. If I sound like a tour guide, it's because I *was* a tour guide here. We had to do two lots of work experience at school. The first was the compulsory two weeks in a Hospital Earth Nursery. We could choose what to do for the second, so I came here.'

I glanced round at everyone. 'Roof of the World evacuates the second there's a solar storm warning, so we're the only people up here. They've given us a free run of the whole place, including the refreshments, in exchange for the right to mention our visit in their publicity.'

Krath laughed. 'I can imagine it. Come to Roof of the World, where the famous Jarra Tell Morrath and Fian Eklund took refuge from assassins during a solar storm!'

I giggled. 'It's nearly three o'clock in the morning here, Earth Asia time. Roof of the World portals are in amber safety mode now, so they won't allow anyone else to portal in, and the Earth portal network will be going into lockdown just before dawn. I suggest everyone comes back to the main viewing gallery to watch the sunrise. It's a sight you mustn't miss.'

'No one can portal in,' said Raven, 'but I'd better check no one is already here in hiding.' He headed out of the door waving his hand sensor.

'Before anyone else goes wandering around,' said Playdon, 'I want to make it perfectly clear that no one sets foot outside.'

'Don't worry, they can't,' I said. 'Roof of the World Investment had an epic battle with Hospital Earth to get permission to build this place. They had to change the design a dozen times, and triple their budget, before they were finally allowed to fly in freight portals and start building. The safety systems are unbelievable. It takes a special code, palm prints from three authorized maintenance staff, and a remote confirmation, before you can open an external door.'

'Possibly,' said Playdon, 'but I don't want anyone even trying. I also don't want anyone getting drunk, powered, damaging anything, or leaving a mess behind, and that particularly includes you, Rono!'

Rono laughed. 'The dreadful thing is that Playdon was already like this as a student. Stephan, do you remember the time when we were on our Foundation course, and borrowed a mobile dome?'

'I just felt you should have asked the lecturer's permission before taking a dig site mobile dome,' said Playdon. 'How would you feel if one of your students stole a mobile dome to camp out at a music festival?'

Rono grinned. 'It was a *historical* music festival, Dannel, and I don't have any students. Not since a stuffy inspector turned up seven years ago, filed a scathingly bad report about my behaviour, and University Cassandra decided I wasn't suited to holding a teaching position.'

The rest of Cassandra 2 burst out laughing.

'Everything I said in that report was perfectly true,' said Keren.

That was how Keren and Rono had first met? I exchanged grazzed looks with Fian.

Krath went across to the refreshments area. 'We can't get drunk. The wine is locked up in cabinets.'

'That's extremely good news,' said Playdon.

We spent the next few hours exploring, raiding the refreshments, and lounging around on luxurious cushioned couches. As dawn approached, everybody drifted back into the main viewing gallery. The last few stragglers had just arrived when there was a chime from Playdon's lookup. He glanced down at it.

'Earth portal network is going into lockdown.'

The faces around me showed instinctive fear. These people were all norms. They'd grown up secure in the knowledge that a functioning portal was always somewhere nearby, and any help they needed was just one step away through it. When one of their worlds had a freak solar storm that took out the portals for a couple of hours, it was a terrifying event remembered for decades afterwards.

Everyone turned to look at the portal. I'd grown up on Earth, with its regular solar storms, but even I felt a shadow of nerves as the portal lights started flashing green. The lockdown sequence continued on to amber and then red. We were on top of the highest mountain on Earth, and there was no way to leave.

'It's nearly dawn,' I said in a deliberately brisk voice. 'I'll dim the glows so we get the best effect.'

Everyone found good seats and settled down to watch the sunrise. First there was a bright glowing line in the distance, which made everything else suddenly seem a lot darker, then the sun rose above the horizon and the light flooded out towards us like a wave rolling over a beach. As dawn shift tour guide, I'd seen this a dozen times before, so I didn't watch the sunrise, I watched the look on Fian's face instead. I smiled at his dazed expression and the way he caught his breath.

'Amaz,' said Dalmora, in a broken thread of a voice. 'Just amaz.'

'I'm right, aren't I,' said Fian. 'Those fluffy things, way, way down there, really are clouds?'

'Yes,' I said.

There was total silence for quite a while. Even Krath was too grazzed to babble pointlessly when looking down on a seemingly endless vision of clouds and jagged mountain tops, white areas of snow contrasting with the harsh black of rock.

'Thank you for bringing us here, Jarra,' said Rono. 'I've visited a lot of worlds, but never seen anything like this.'

'Of course not,' I said. 'Planet First choose nice tame worlds for you, and pick the kindest and blandest of their continents for you to live on. This is no carefully vetted colony world, this is Earth!'

'This place is unique,' said Lolmack. 'We're looking for a venue for our daughter's clan presentation ceremony and this . . .'

'This is by far the best we've seen,' said Lolia, 'and when we tell the clan that Jarra herself brought us here . . .'

I frowned. 'You can hire any of the hospitality suites, or even the smaller viewing gallery, for private parties, but the prices are shocking.'

Lolmack tapped at his lookup for a moment. 'Not a problem. We'll hire the viewing gallery of course. Our clan's involvement in the sex vid industry keeps us at the lowest social status, Jarra, but it also makes us extremely wealthy.'

I'd always had the impression that Lolia and Lolmack had plenty of credits, but I hadn't known they were that rich. 'Well, if the price isn't an issue, you can't do better than Roof of the World.'

My lookup chimed and I automatically glanced down at it. 'General Torrek!'

I answered the call and saw his face smiling at me. 'Happy Birthday, Jarra. I'm delighted to inform you that your Military rank has been reinstated.'

'It has? I'm not 18 until tomorrow, sir.'

'Military regulations use interstellar standard Green Time, so it *is* tomorrow.'

Of course it was. I'd been thinking in Earth America time still, and it was 19:00 hours there, but it was five hours later in Earth Europe, home of Green Time. I gave a startled laugh.

'Your betrothal has been registered on Zeus under Military regulations section 14, subsection 3.9,' continued General Torrek. 'Congratulations and mutual joy to you both. You can expect to receive orders to return to Zulu base within the next few days.'

'Thank you, sir,' Fian and I chorused.

The General ended the call, and Fian turned to Raven. 'No one can possibly get up here to murder me or Jarra, so you can stop trailing round after us for a while.'

'I suppose that's true. I'll just do one last check of the area.' Raven headed out of the door, waving his hand sensor again.

'Actually,' I said, 'records say some people did manage to climb this mountain back in the days before impact suits or portals.'

Fian shook his head. 'I don't believe that.'

Playdon tapped away at his lookup for a moment. 'Jarra's right. I've found a list of people who climbed this mountain.'

'Data corruption,' said Rono. 'Must be.'

'Whether it's true or not,' said Fian, 'no one is to say a word about it to Raven. I've been finding things really frustrating lately, and I'm desperate for some privacy.'

Rono laughed and gave us a suggestive wink. 'I think we've all noticed and understood your frustration, Fian.'

I blushed, and was grateful that Raven reappeared at this point.

'Everything seems secure,' he said, 'so I'm declaring myself off duty until the portal network comes back.'

Fian grabbed my hand. 'Zan! Jarra, let's find a . . .'

He broke off and groaned as every lookup in the room chimed at once. 'Now what?'

I stared at my message. 'Hospital Earth wants everyone to watch Earth Rolling News.'

Playdon frowned. 'The top of the highest mountain on Earth could be a very bad place to be if this turns out to be another solar super storm.'

'We've got radiation shielding,' I said. 'I told you the safety systems were unbelievable.'

'Never mind radiation shielding, do we have a wall vid?' asked Krath.

'Of course we have a wall vid.' I hit the switch that made the covers slide open to show a massive wall vid, and set it to Earth Rolling News. A close-up of a man's face appeared.

'Lucius Augustus Gordianus again!' Fian shook his head. 'Does the man never stop talking? I know he's on our side, but . . .'

Lucius Augustus Gordianus obviously wasn't in a studio, because there was a shadowy tree and a glimpse of dark night sky behind him.

'The debate on the issue of selecting worlds for the Handicapped still continues,' he said. 'People question the safety of a colony world that has solar storms and portal outages in the same way as Earth, and yet Earth was our first world. Earth was the world where humanity lived for hundreds of thousands of years. Earth was the world where ancient Rome and Greece flourished.'

He paused. 'A world with portal outages will cause additional problems for the Planet First teams, but the Military are prepared to face them. For those of us who are civilians, the situation is much simpler. We have the freedom not to go to such a world when there are many others to choose from. We have the freedom to go to such a world but leave if a solar storm is forecast. We have the freedom to stay on it during a solar storm, and discover it's really no great problem to be without a portal for a few hours.'

He smiled. 'A solar storm has just hit Earth, and its portal network has entered a twelve hour lockdown. There was five hours warning of this event, which was ample time for those who wished to portal away from Earth. It was also ample time to portal here. I am speaking to you by live link from the Spirit of Man monument in Earth Europe.'

The vid image panned out to show two vast, floodlit figures against the black sky, probably the only landmark on Earth that even off-worlders would recognize.

'You have to admit he's good at this,' said Rono. 'Coming to Earth to make a speech during a solar storm was a brilliant move.'

After giving his audience a moment to take in the view, Lucius Augustus Gordianus started speaking again. 'I was not the only person to portal to Earth before the solar storm arrived. Here with me is Aadi Quilla Amarion, First Speaker of Alpha sector, who has an announcement to make.'

The First Speaker of Alpha sector was here on Earth! What the nuke was happening? I took a step forward, staring at the screen as a woman with close-cropped silver hair stepped into view of the vid bees. She adjusted the folds of her flowing dark blue robe, and gave a formal nod of her head.

'Thank you, Lucius Augustus Gordianus.' She paused dramatically, while I waited in agonized suspense. 'While other sectors responded rapidly to recent events, the Alpha Sector Parliament has been criticized for making no announcement. We could not do so until a decision had been reached, and that decision required much debate and consultation. The Alpha Sector Parliament held a vote eleven hours ago.'

She paused again and the vid image zoomed in closer, focusing on her face. It was hard to judge the age of Lucius Augustus Gordianus, I could only guess it as about seventy, but this woman had skin that was delicately lined despite rejuvenation treatments so she must be approaching her hundredth.

'Other sectors are passing reciprocal relationship agreements with Earth that will contain retrospective clauses to validate past contracts,' she said. 'Alpha sector has chosen not to do this.'

'Chaos take you!' Rono shouted the words. 'You can't leave people's marriages broken and . . .'

'Quiet, Rono,' said Playdon. 'The Aadi of Alpha sector wouldn't come to Earth just to say that.'

'The issue of marriages and other contracts is only one aspect of a much larger problem, and should be dealt with as such,' said Quilla Amarion. 'Alpha sector chooses not to patch a broken vessel, but to make it whole. The Alpha Sector Parliament has voted to offer membership to a new planet. Earth has always been in the physical centre of Alpha sector; it is now invited to be part of it politically.'

The shock of that made me miss a couple of minutes. When I came out of my daze, the Aadi of Alpha sector had been replaced by the president of the board of Hospital Earth.

'. . . procedure begins with the citizens of Earth voting on whether to accept the invitation. Should that vote be in favour then Earth will join Alpha sector at midnight on 15 November. Elections for Earth planetary representatives will follow, and Hospital Earth will begin a transition process, involving handing over planetary government and dividing its remaining functions between a purely medical Hospital Earth and a new Novak-Nadal Syndrome Care Foundation.'

'Novak-Nadal syndrome?' asked Amalie in a puzzled voice.

'When the first colonists portalled from Earth to Adonis, two of them died because they were Handicapped,' said Raven. 'The first names carved on the walls of the Courtyards of Memory are Ernst Novak and Esperenza Nadal.'

'That's a good idea,' said Dalmora. 'It was horribly

unfeeling to call people Handicapped. Do you think Novak-Nadal syndrome is better, Jarra?'

I didn't reply because my head was still whirling. Earth would join Alpha sector on 15 November. That was Wallam-Crane Day. The Handicapped had never celebrated the public holiday that marked the birth of the inventor of the portal, but they would celebrate on 15 November 2789!

'Will Earth's citizens vote in favour of Earth joining Alpha sector?' asked Krath.

I gave him a look of sheer disbelief. 'Of course we will. This offer . . . They're finally admitting we're human!'

I remembered the Adonis Knights marching to deliver their petition for justice. Everyone had assumed they were asking for Alpha sector to pass the relationship legislation, but they'd been asking for far more than that.

I turned to look at Raven. 'You did this.'

He had a strange smile on his face. 'No, Jarra. I talked to a few people, Dalmora's father talked to some people as well, and Lucius Augustus Gordianus has been talking endlessly to everyone. It's been wonderful being part of this, helping to set right something that was wrong, but it was you that really did this.'

I shook my head. 'That's . . . That's just nardle.'

'No, it isn't,' said Raven. 'Lucius Augustus Gordianus was fighting for his grandson, but he wouldn't have risked his career and his clan's social status without the clan of Tellon Blaze leading the way. Dalmora's father could use his fame to talk to influential people, but they only listened because they'd seen Jarra Tell Morrath on the vids. I convinced the Adonis Knights to march, but they weren't doing it for some anonymous citizens of Earth; they marched for a glowing girl.'

Everyone was looking at me. I couldn't manage to speak, and their faces were oddly blurry.

I felt an arm go round me, and heard Fian's voice. 'Jarra needs some space for a while.'

He tugged me out of the room, along a corridor, and guided me through a door. 'Is there a way to lock this?'

I looked blankly at the door for a moment, a memory stirred, and I tapped a code into the controls.

'Good,' said Fian.

I turned round and saw we were in one of the small hospitality suites, decorated in a pale blue and white to blend with the view from the glass wall. I dived through a side door into a bathroom and bathed my face in cool water. When I came out again a few minutes later, Fian was sitting on one of the huge curved couches by the window. I went to sit next to him.

'I made a real idiot of myself back there.'

He shook his head. 'I don't think so.'

'Fian, I just burst into tears in front of Playdon, our class, the whole of Cassandra 2, and an Adonis Knight!'

He gave a low, gentle laugh, put his arm round me, and pulled me against him. 'Jarra, you're allowed a little emotion at a time like this.'

'I've just realized how stupid I've been,' I said.

He looked into my eyes. 'Exactly how have you been stupid?'

'For tactical reasons, the General Marshal wanted other worlds for the Handicapped. The two most heavily populated sectors are Alpha and Beta. Their planetary representatives can easily win a vote against the other three sectors combined. Correct?'

Fian nodded.

'So, the Military knew they had to get Alpha and Beta on our side,' I said. 'I was conveniently part of the Tell clan, so they could start a chain of events in Beta sector with the help of the Betan Military clans. Alpha sector was a bigger problem. Dalmora was my friend, and her father was famous, but he didn't have much political influence.'

I laughed. 'I'm a nardle, an utter nardle. When Colonel Leveque said he'd chosen Raven to be our bodyguard because it would be impossible to bribe an Adonis Knight, I believed him, but his real reason was because an Adonis Knight has direct access to the political heart of Alpha sector.'

Fian gave a little shake of his head. 'The Military are supposed to be politically neutral. They wouldn't dare to order an Adonis Knight to use his influence, but . . . You're right, Jarra. Leveque chose Raven to be our bodyguard, hoping he wouldn't just fight for us physically, but get drawn into fighting for us politically as well. I can just imagine Leveque calculating the probability of success, and the numbers getting higher when he spotted Raven was a romantic trying to live up to the Adonis Knight oath. Just remember the words of that oath.'

'"Knights shall demonstrate nobility, honour, grace, valour and perfection in all virtues, and be champions of justice,"' I quoted.

'Exactly,' said Fian. 'Did you see Raven's face back there? He was looking for a cause to champion, and he found you. His glowing girl. His image of the Handicapped. You represented a group who weren't just suffering from prejudice, but blatant injustices like researchers experimenting on you.'

I remembered Raven's anger when he heard Hospital Earth let its wards be used as test subjects. 'Yes, Raven found his cause to fight for. He's happy now because he's proved whatever he needed to prove to himself.' I sighed. 'It's nardle the way people keep seeing me as symbolizing the Handicapped. We aren't all the same. People never are.'

'Well, I don't see you as a symbol, Jarra. I see you as a person who's amazing, but real, and flawed, and human, and loving, and betrothed to me. I've been waiting weeks for this moment.' Fian looked across at the refreshment area. 'Krath's right, the wine is all in locked cabinets. Would an ex tour guide know how to get into those?'

'The security system forces them to change the codes every week, but they just alternate between Edmund Hillary and Tenzing Norgay. I thought Playdon would prefer me not to tell Krath.'

Fian went over to the wine cabinet, and came back with a bottle and glasses. 'Pity there isn't a table.'

I laughed. 'Furniture command couch extend table.'

A table slid out from the wide, cushioned arm of the couch.

'I've spent too much time in primitive dig site domes,' said Fian. 'I never thought to try voice commands.'

He poured out the wine, and handed one of the glasses to me. 'Fidelis, Jarra.'

'Fidelis, Fian.'

We sipped the wine. I was Military again, Earth was to join Alpha sector, and Fian and I were together on the Roof of the World. What moment could be better than this?

'I will come to you when spring turns to summer,' said Fian.

'I will come to you when spring turns to summer,' I repeated.

'And our future will be golden.'

He leaned towards me and kissed me. I got a bit powered after that, but I was powered from being with Fian again, not from the wine.

27

Earth was out of portal lockdown and my body was back in the real world, sitting on a grey flexiplas chair in the grey flexiplas hall of our dig site dome, but my head was still reliving amaz moments on the Roof of the World. Aadi Quilla Amarion saying that Alpha sector was offering membership to Earth. Fian's urgent kisses, and his hands drifting down to . . .

An elbow jabbed me painfully in the ribs. I turned to give Amalie a reproachful look, before discovering Playdon and the whole class were laughing at me.

'Now I've finally got everyone's attention,' said Playdon, 'I'd like to explain our schedule for the next few days. Cassandra 2 are planning to focus their efforts for the next week on a manufacturing centre near the west side of the Land Raft. We'll be working on a nearby block of buildings that were used for housing and . . .'

He broke off as three lookups chimed simultaneously. One of them was mine. I tapped it, read a message that cleared my head of daydreams, and scrambled to my feet.

'I'm sorry, sir,' I said. 'Fian, Raven and I have orders to portal to Zulu base with all possible speed.'

Playdon sighed but nodded, and I went out of the hall with Fian and Raven a step behind me. Once we were through the door, we started running. The Military phrase 'with all possible speed' meant exactly that. What the chaos was going on?

Raven entered the portal code we'd been sent and stepped through ahead of us. Fian and I followed, and found ourselves in one of the base reception areas. I was grazzed to find not just the usual four Military Security officers waiting for us, but Colonel Leveque as well.

'We're heading straight to Alien Contact Operations Centre,' he said.

Alien Contact Operations Centre! I'd somehow managed to forget the aliens. No, not exactly forget, I'd just had a lot of other things to think about lately.

A base internal portal was only a few steps away, with the portal already active. Within seconds, we were walking through a door into a vast room. I looked round, awed, at the amount of people, desks, equipment, vid screens, and then lost interest in everything but one person. Colonel Nia Stone was sitting at what was obviously the command desk, and she wore a white sash over her uniform jacket.

That white sash meant something desperately important. I fished urgently for memories of vids I'd seen about the Military. A General wore a white jacket, and the General Marshal wore entirely white. A white sash meant . . .?

I got my answer from memories of ent vids about Tellon Blaze. He'd been given field promotions all the way up to Colonel during the Thetis chaos year, and the images of him near the end of it had him wearing a white sash. The Military couldn't give him a field promotion to General, but the white sash showed he was acting in a position that would normally be held by a General.

Nia Stone's white sash must mean she was acting

commanding officer of the Alien Contact programme! Why? What had happened to General Torrek?

Stone's chair swivelled to face me, and she smiled. 'Congratulations, Jarra. You've found the alien home world.'

I stared at her in bewilderment, and she laughed and nodded at Colonel Leveque.

'To be more exact,' he said, 'you've given us a map that should help us find the alien home world. You suggested we should look for a repeating data stream in the alien probe's light sculpture, which would be our Rosetta stone, our key to beginning translation. Yesterday, our researchers finally managed to disentangle the first level data streams of the light sculpture. They didn't find one repeating data stream, they found two.'

He paused. 'One of those appears to be exactly what you predicted, a simple sequence that matches the test sequences we used to reach the signalling device, though there's extra data at the end we don't understand. The other confused us because it was in a series of distinct sections. We've now worked out that those sections were strands that formed a simple static light sculpture themselves.'

He moved across to what was obviously his desk, and tapped a control. A light sculpture appeared in the centre of the room, showing a star with its attendant planets.

'This can't be a scale model,' said Colonel Leveque. 'The ratio of interplanetary distances to planetary diameters makes that impossible. It does, however, appear to give us the relative sizes of each planet and their moons. We're now running checks against every star system in our stellar survey records looking for possible matches. We hope to rapidly eliminate the possibility of the alien home world being in humanity's space, and searching new uncharted sectors will go a lot faster now that we've a clear idea what we're looking for.'

'General Torrek will be extremely happy to hear that when

he returns from his rejuvenation treatment,' said Colonel Stone.

I relaxed. I should have guessed General Torrek was away for a rejuvenation treatment. He was eighty years old, so he'd need them every three months, and there'd been a long period of panic after the alien probe arrived. He was bound to be due, if not overdue, a treatment.

Colonel Stone waved her arm, indicating that Fian and I should go over to some spare seats and sit down. Raven took up an inconspicuous position against a nearby wall.

There was a soft musical chime, and Colonel Leveque leaned forward to study the grid display inlaid into the top of his desk. 'A potential match in Alpha sector. Almost certainly a false alarm since we've already double-checked that star system.'

Colonel Stone glanced at a man in a Commander's uniform who was sitting at a desk to her left. 'Send a team to triple-check it just to be on the safe side.'

'Yes, sir,' he said.

There was a quiet spell, followed by another two possible star systems being found in quick succession. The one in Gamma sector was ruled out. It contained one of our inhabited worlds, so had already been extremely thoroughly checked. Colonel Stone ordered an extra check on the one in Beta sector.

Once that excitement was over, there was another, longer wait. I entertained myself by playing a game of guess the alien home world, pulled up information on Sol system on my lookup, and did a bit of mental comparison between that and the light sculpture image of the alien star system. There were three tiny planets nearest the star, then four great big things, followed by two more tiny ones.

I felt the fact the aliens had visited Earth suggested conditions here weren't wildly different from their own home world. I stared at the planets shown in the light sculpture. The gravity on the giant planets would be scary, and too far from the star would be incredibly cold, which left the three inner planets. Number three was too small, its gravity would be only half that of Earth. The alien home world was probably number one or number two.

There was another chime. 'We have a potential match in Zeta sector,' said Colonel Leveque.

His voice sounded as lazy as ever, but the atmosphere in the room instantly changed to tense expectancy. Everyone expected matches in the other sectors to be false alarms, because Planet First teams had covered those star systems already, but Zeta sector was different. Stellar survey was still in progress there, and Planet First assessments to choose potential colony worlds were only just beginning. A match in Zeta sector could be the real thing.

'This system is a close match,' said Leveque. 'We only have the basic outline stellar survey from a mapping probe bouncing through. That will be followed by . . .'

He broke off and started a new sentence. 'Unfortunately, a Planet First probe entered this star system five days ago.'

'Is the probe still in passive mode?' asked Colonel Stone.

'The last routine contact with it was four hours ago,' said Leveque. 'It had completed passive monitoring phase without detecting any sign of intelligent alien life, and had just started broadcasting standard mathematical and other greets.'

'Chaos!' Colonel Stone snapped out the word. 'The probe's still at the star system threshold then?'

'Correct,' said Leveque. 'It has a further five days of greets scheduled before it starts moving into the star system. Its next routine contact is in eight hours time.'

'Contact the probe now,' said Stone. 'If everything is quiet there, then cut the broadcast. I don't want to stir anything up before the General gets back.'

Leveque worked at his desk for a moment, and the light sculpture of the alien star system abruptly vanished and was replaced by a weird jigsaw of different holo images. One was obviously the matching star system, but there was a lot of multi-coloured stuff and bursts of numbers that didn't mean anything to me.

I saw Leveque's right hand stab at his desk, and the holo image of the star system reappeared. It shifted in size, so only a vastly magnified section of the outer edge of the system was visible. A white dot appeared.

'The white dot,' said Leveque, 'marks the position of our probe at the edge of the star system.'

A second dot appeared. This one was red.

'The red dot,' said Leveque, 'is an object moving on a course that will intercept our probe in fourteen hours seventeen minutes time. The chance of this being a natural object randomly on this course is vanishingly small.'

There was silence for a full minute before Colonel Stone spoke. 'We currently have the option to use remote destruct on our probe before intercept.' She looked slowly round the room. 'You seem to have views on that, Commander Tell Morrath.'

'I'd advise against it, sir,' I said. 'If someone comes to your door, sticks their hand on the door plate, and then runs away, it leaves a bad impression. If they come again, you start off by being suspicious.'

She gave a nod. 'Anyone have an argument in favour of remote destruct?'

No one responded. Stone nodded again and tapped at her lookup. I gave a startled look at the holo head that instantly appeared above her command desk. The General Marshal!

'Sir,' said Stone, 'I assume you've been following the situation on the command feed.'

He nodded. 'You've had my undivided attention since you found a matching system in Zeta sector.'

'Using remote destruct on our probe at this point could have negative implications for a future approach. I therefore recommend against it, sir.'

'I confirm your decision, Colonel,' said the General Marshal. 'It is unfortunate that General Torrek is currently unavailable, but I have every confidence in you and your staff.'

'Thank you, sir,' said Stone.

The holo of the General Marshal vanished, and Stone looked down at her desk for a few seconds before she lifted her head and spoke again.

'We are now committed to first contact in fourteen hours thirteen minutes.'

28

'It's a lot of work,' said Keon.

I glared at him. 'If you say that one more time, I'll not only make the rest of your life extremely painful, but I'll make sure Issette does too!'

Keon considered my threat for a moment, and his tone of voice changed from lazy to businesslike. 'There's no need to get pushy, Jarra. We've already modified some light sculpture emitters to fit on to probes, because it was obvious we might need them. We can program those emitters to display either a light sculpture of the test sequences, or one of the alien star system, but the light sculpture of Sol system is more difficult.'

I decided he wasn't messing about any longer. 'What's the problem with Sol system? You must have all the information.'

'We need to create an entire new light sculpture using the same range of colours as the alien one,' said Keon. 'Some creatures on Earth can see ultraviolet light, which humans can't. The alien light sculpture shows the aliens can see ultraviolet too, but not some colours we can see. We had to adjust their light sculpture so we could see it properly, and we'll have to change ours to suit their eyes.'

Keon's unfortunate research assistants had been silently watching us, probably wondering if Keon was going to be arrested again. At this point, they did some urgent nodding.

'I accept we need to do this properly,' I said. 'How long will it take?'

Keon shrugged. 'Three or four days for the light sculpture of Sol system. You can have the others in less than two hours.'

'Thanks, Keon.'

I headed back to the Operations Centre. Stone and Leveque were having a conversation at the command desk, but broke off to look at me.

'I've sorted out Keon, sirs,' I said. 'We can have probes displaying light sculptures of the alien system and the test sequences in two hours. Making a new light sculpture of Sol system in colours the aliens can see will take about four days.'

Stone nodded. 'We'll use drop portals to send light sculpture probes in to join the original one. The test sequences are enough to show the aliens we're invited guests. We can tell them exactly where we came from later. We don't even know whether they sent spheres to star systems other than Earth.'

'Threat team's current theory is the aliens sent out an unmanned, automated ship, sir,' said Leveque. 'This would leave artefacts and spheres in systems it considered had potential for intelligent life. It passed through Beta sector thousands of years ago, entered Alpha sector, reached Earth, and is currently continuing on its course, probably somewhere around the border between Alpha and Gamma sector. It's highly probable it has left spheres in multiple systems by now.'

'But we haven't actually found the ship itself or any spheres in other star systems,' said Stone.

'Any spheres would be inactive, sir, and probably deliberately hidden among asteroids, waiting for a transmission from an alien artefact. The ship itself is probably travelling through the vast empty space between two star systems. We know the ship's starting point and course now, so we have a much better chance of finding it.'

Stone nodded. 'So our assumption is the alien ship left more than one invitation to visit on its route. We must be the first response they've had to those invitations.'

'We can be reasonably confident that this particular ship would only have encountered advanced intelligent life on Earth, sir,' said Leveque. 'However there's a probability of 83 per cent that having made the necessary initial economic investment, the aliens would launch multiple ships rather than just one. A ship heading in a different direction, through areas of space uncharted by us, may have found something.'

'You're saying we may not be the first to visit,' said Stone. 'We may even be about to encounter more than one alien race.'

She raised her eyes to the ceiling for a second. 'One lot of aliens is quite enough.' There was a slight pause before she spoke again in a decisive voice. 'Until we have evidence otherwise, we assume we are encountering only one alien race. They gave us a map to find their star system, so we assume they wanted us to visit and wish to be friends with us. They sent a sphere to Earth thousands of years ago, so their technology is probably far more advanced than our own by now. That means we definitely wish to be friends with them.'

'Sir,' said Fian, 'their technology is probably far more advanced than ours, and it's possible they have conventional portals they use to travel around their own world, but they clearly don't have the drop portals needed for interstellar travel. If they did, they'd have used a drop portal to come and meet our probe.'

Stone nodded. 'We'll proceed on the assumption that the

aliens don't have portal technology. They're limited to travelling between star systems conventionally, which requires huge amounts of time and resources. If that's the case, we have a single vital strategic advantage that keeps our worlds safe from a significant alien attack.'

She heavily emphasized her next words. 'Our first priority, at all times and at any cost, must be to make sure we don't give the aliens any clues to portal technology.'

All around the room, intent faces and nods showed everyone understood.

'What portal technology is on board our probe?' asked Stone.

'It's a standard Planet First approach probe, sir,' said Colonel Leveque. 'They start at the extreme edge of a star system, spiral inwards collecting information, and eventually burn up in the sun. Since they're designed to be used once and discarded, they contain the minimum possible equipment, and what they do have is mainly sensors and a basic manoeuvring capability. A survey ship fires a drop portal and sends the probe through it, so the probe itself contains no drop portal technology. It does contain a minimal comms portal reception ring, so Planet First teams can communicate with it, but it cannot initiate a comms portal itself.'

Stone briefly raised her eyes to the ceiling again. 'Why did I marry him? Can someone translate that into Language for me?'

'Transmitting portals do all the work, sir,' said Fian. 'The probe contains a reception only comms portal, which isn't much more than a small metal ring. Nobody could learn anything from that.'

'Thank you, Major,' said Stone. 'That means we don't need to worry about our probes, but we must prevent any of our ships falling into alien hands. Major Tar Cameron, what's the progress on our Zeta sector field base?'

Rayne Tar Cameron turned her chair to face Colonel Stone. 'Sir, we've identified two planets with optimal gravity in star systems neighbouring the one containing the alien home world. One world is very similar to the planet Academy before the terraforming experiments. Totally lifeless, and the atmosphere has too little oxygen to be breathable. The other is a potential colony world candidate, with a breathable atmosphere and extensive native plant and animal life.'

Stone nodded. 'We'll use the lifeless planet. The original Planet First teams chose Academy for their Alpha sector headquarters for good reasons. A lifeless world had no threats from the local ecology, and was an ideal place to set up quarantine areas. The same logic applies here. I'm not risking taking aliens or their technology to any of our inhabited worlds, so we'll need quarantine areas.'

Rayne Tar Cameron tapped at her desk. 'Commander Tell Dramis's team are flying in now to assemble freight portals, sir. Those should be calibrated and functioning within two hours. We have other personnel and equipment standing by, so we should have a skeleton field base built and operational five hours before contact.'

'What's the comms portal relay lag on transmissions to and from our probe?' asked Stone.

'Five point seven seconds, sir,' said Leveque.

'Something happens out in . . .' Stone broke off her sentence. 'We need a name for the alien planet. Suggestions?'

I waited, but no one said anything. I hesitantly spoke. 'I don't think Fortuna has been used yet, sir.'

Rayne Tar Cameron tapped at her desk. 'Fortuna is not listed as a current planet name. Fortuna was the Roman goddess of fortune or luck, so is consistent with the naming conventions for inhabited worlds.'

'Commander Tell Morrath, you believe it's fortunate we've found an intelligent alien race?' asked Colonel Leveque.

'Sir, you never knew whether the luck Fortuna gave would be good or bad.'

Stone nodded. 'The alien world will be provisionally known as Fortuna. Our Zeta sector field base world will be called Gateway.'

I was grazzed. I'd named a planet. Only temporarily of course. Eventually, we'd learn the aliens' own name for their world.

'If something happens in Fortuna system,' continued Stone, 'it's five point seven seconds before I know about it. I make a decision, give a command, and it's another five point seven seconds before our probe responds. That's unacceptable during a first contact situation. Even a simple conversation with Commander Tell Dramis is going to be a constant struggle with comms portal relay lag.'

She paused for a second. 'We'll move the Alien Contact Operations Centre core functionality to Gateway base at contact minus three hours.'

'Yes, sir,' said Rayne Tar Cameron.

I bit my lip. Alien Contact Operations Centre was moving to Zeta sector, and I was Handicapped so I couldn't go with them. I knew Colonel Stone was making the right decision, but . . .

Humanity was about to make contact with an alien civilization. This was going to be the most significant moment in history, but I was being left behind.

29

'You could go to Gateway base, Fian,' I said. 'Just because I'm stuck on Earth, there's no reason you . . .'

We were sitting on the luxuriously large couch in our apartment at Zulu base. Fian grabbed a cushion from beside him and threw it at me. 'Say that one more time and I'll strangle you. They've only got a skeleton field base on Gateway, not many people can go there, and they don't need a clueless history student like me getting in their way.'

'You aren't clueless.'

'Yes, I am. We're talking about a field base on a world with an unbreathable atmosphere, Jarra. They'd have to assign someone to constantly nursemaid me, because I don't even know what alarms sound if there's a dome breach.'

'Oh.' I frowned. 'Yes, I suppose . . .'

'Command may have gone to Gateway, but the Command Support and Research teams are still here. The secure command feed coming in from Gateway base has to include all the details for them, so we won't miss anything that's happening. Not that much *is* happening.'

He turned back to our wall vid. One of the group of three Military probes we now had at the edge of Fortuna system was facing an alien sphere. Neither of them were doing anything. They hadn't done anything for the last ten minutes.

Fian sighed. 'This isn't much of a conversation.'

'It's hard to have a proper conversation when the only words . . . light signals . . . we understand are numbers and a few scientific terms,' I said. 'In theory, we should have learned their language properly before contacting them, but since the current estimates are that will take a century . . .'

'Ninety-eight years, one month, and three days,' said Fian, in a solemn imitation of Colonel Leveque's voice.

I giggled.

'I know we've only got a very limited vocabulary,' Fian continued, 'but we've been trying to talk for six hours now and we haven't actually communicated anything yet.'

'Yes we have,' I said. 'We've communicated that we aren't shooting at them, and they aren't shooting at us. That's pretty important.'

'True,' said Fian, 'but . . .'

'Time to eat.' Raven came over from the food dispenser, holding a plate in each hand.

'Furniture command table get over here to position two,' I said.

There was a low table parked by the wall. It obediently slid towards the couch, and Raven put the plates down on it.

Fian looked at my plate and sighed. 'Raven, I wish you'd stop feeding Jarra cheese fluffle.'

I grabbed my plate of cheese fluffle and held on to it defensively. 'You may not like cheese fluffle, Fian, but I do!'

Raven brought drinks and his own meal across to the table, and was just sitting down on a chair opposite us when there was a chime from the apartment door. He jumped up again and went to check the door controls. 'It's Captain Marston with a hover trolley full of our luggage.'

Raven checked the hover trolley with sensors for several

minutes before he allowed Marston to bring it inside the apartment. Fian and I searched through the mountain of hover bags to find their two controlling key fobs and clicked them. There was a minor scuffle as the two sets of hover bags came to life, fought their way off the trolley, and organized themselves into two separate groups that bounced gently in midair next to us. Raven grabbed the sole remaining bag, which belonged to him.

'Thank you,' I said.

'My pleasure, sir,' said Captain Marston in an extremely unpleased voice.

He and his hover trolley vanished off down the corridor, and Raven closed the apartment door.

Fian looked at the hover bags and pulled a face. 'We just asked Playdon and Dalmora to pack a few things, not everything we owned.'

'I think Playdon's guessed about the alien home world and is prepared for us to be away for ages,' I said.

Fian nodded. 'The way we suddenly dashed off was a bit suspicious. I hope Krath isn't loudly discussing it with everyone.'

'I'm sure Playdon will shut him up if necessary.' I checked my lookup. 'I knew it!'

'What?' asked Fian.

'Playdon's started sending us vids of his lectures,' I said.

'He's sending them to me too,' said Raven.

Fian and I laughed, clicked the key fobs, led our processions of luggage off to the bedroom, and left them there to be unpacked later. When we returned to the living room and checked the wall vid, the Military probe was running the light sculpture that represented the test sequences. All three of us could instantly recognize that by now.

Fian sighed. 'I see they're starting from the beginning for the sixth time.'

284

I piled up the dirty dishes and took them over to the cleanser slot of the food processor.

'Now we're back on a Military base, you should let me clear up the dishes, Jarra,' said Raven.

'I thought the Military happily swapped between acting formally and informally,' I said. 'We're being informal here.'

'I know,' said Raven, 'but even when things are informal, you wouldn't expect General Torrek to clear away dirty plates.'

'Of course not, but there's a big difference between a Commander and a General.'

'Well, there's a big difference between a Captain and a Commander too,' said Raven.

'Captain Marston didn't seem impressed by me being a Commander,' I said. 'He was openly sulking about being kept waiting.'

Raven shrugged. 'Qwin Marston's in a foul mood because Rayne Tar Cameron's broken their betrothal and dumped him. He's been thrown out of the Tar clan, and he'll be transferred to another base as soon as General Torrek's back to authorize it.'

Fian had been frowning at the wall vid, but now he joined in the conversation. 'I can see why Qwin Marston couldn't stay in the Tar clan, but it seems unfair that he gets transferred as well. That's because he's the lower rank?'

'The Military are both a professional organization and a family,' said Raven, 'and combining the two sometimes gets complicated. Official policy is to arrange assignments that keep couples together, but also to split them up when relationships go sour. Who moves isn't to do with rank as much as how easy someone is to replace. Qwin Marston is just a supply clerk. He was only assigned to this base because of his betrothal to Rayne, so there's no question about who gets transferred now.'

'What would General Torrek do if Colonel Stone and Colonel Leveque split up?' asked Fian.

'Throw a fit,' said Raven. 'The Alien Contact programme can't afford to lose either of them, so he'd probably order them to have counselling. The same thing would happen if you two split up. The General Marshal has said he approves of your relationship.'

I frowned. 'The Military can't order people to have psychological counselling.'

Raven grinned. 'You could try telling the General Marshal that, but . . .'

'We're definitely not splitting up then,' said Fian. 'Jarra would do anything to avoid psychologists.'

I pulled a rude face at him, and turned back to the wall vid to see what was happening. The Military probe had run the light sculpture of the test sequences, including the very complicated flickering section at the end that seemed to be nothing to do with the tests and no one had managed to translate yet. The alien sphere had responded with the same thing. The Military probe had displayed the light sculpture of the alien system. The alien sphere had responded with the same light sculpture, but with the second planet and its moon flashing brightly, obviously indicating that was the alien home world.

The alien sphere was now continuing with a complex light display. It looked like exactly the same one it had played the previous five times. Nobody had the faintest idea what it meant, apart from the fact it included a couple of numbers.

The alien light display ended, and the Military probe started a new light sequence. I recognized the patterns for two, followed by four, but got muddled after that. I glanced at Fian, who was better at deciphering the patterns than I was. 'What are we saying this time?'

'We're just counting up even numbers,' said Fian. 'I bet

we stop at sixteen, and the alien sphere just sits there and does nothing. Again.'

We waited. He was right.

'Talking to aliens was never going to be easy,' I said.

Fian sighed. 'I know, but basic mathematics should work.'

He changed the wall vid from the command feed to Colonel Leveque's science feed. I didn't even try to understand that, just waited quietly while Fian frowned at it for several minutes.

'There's something wrong,' he said at last. 'The sphere in Earth orbit is 4.71 metres in diameter. So is this one. They're also the same colour, and unfolded in exactly the same way to start displaying their light sculptures. The way they manoeuvre matches perfectly as well. As far as we can tell, they're identical.'

'What's wrong with that?' I asked.

'They shouldn't be,' said Fian. 'Think about it, Jarra. Our dating techniques give wildly varying results on the alien artefact we found in Earth Africa, but we know the tunnel the artefact was found in was at least three thousand years old. The sphere here should be far more advanced than the one in Earth orbit.'

I thought for a minute. 'When we dig up a stasis box in one of Earth's ruined cities, and find an old data chip inside, we have to use a converter to read it. The aliens could be using an old style sphere to talk to us, because it has to be able to recognize and display the old signal sequences.'

'That's possible,' said Fian. 'Now tell me why their sphere gives the same response every time we try and talk to it, and ignores anything new, even the simplest mathematical sequence.'

I couldn't. I groaned, and put the grim truth into words. 'You think the alien civilization has fallen?'

He nodded. 'It's happened over and over again in our own

287

history. We build up civilizations and they fall. Remember how close humanity was to going back to barbarism after Exodus century.'

'We answered their invitation, but we came too late.' I shook my head. 'That's . . .'

'I know,' said Fian.

I forced away my emotion and tried to be practical. 'One of their ancient spheres is talking to us, but it isn't getting any new instructions from them. That probably means the aliens are confined to their own planet these days, and don't have communications technology any longer.'

I turned to Raven. 'We need to talk to Colonel Stone. She's in Zeta sector so . . .?'

'Major Tar Cameron is still here,' said Raven. 'Call her and ask her to set up a secure link with Gateway base.'

I did that and Rayne Tar Cameron replied in a briskly efficient voice. 'Yes, sir. We'll route the link to the wall vid in your quarters.'

It was ten minutes before we saw Colonel Stone and Colonel Leveque looking out at us from the wall vid. They were in a tiny room, sitting on the same sort of grey flexiplas chairs that we had in our dig site dome. Brightly coloured crates were stacked against one wall. Most of them were labelled with incomprehensible jumbles of letters and numbers, but the black lettering on the heap of red crates just said 'OXYGEN'.

'You have a habit of throwing drastic things at us, Jarra,' said Colonel Stone, 'so I thought we'd better take this call in a side room. What have you thought of this time?'

'It's not my idea, sir. It's Fian's. He'll explain.'

There was a twelve-second pause while my words went through the comms portal relays to Zeta sector, and Colonel Stone's reply was sent back. 'Go ahead Fian.'

It was strange watching the faces on the wall vid react to

Fian's explanation with that delay. It underlined exactly why Colonel Stone needed to be in Zeta sector right now rather than on Earth. Finally, Fian stopped talking. Twelve seconds later, Colonel Stone spoke.

'If you're right, this is wonderful news. We need to confirm it as soon as possible, so we'll set up a drop portal to send a probe to take a look at Fortuna itself.' She glanced at Leveque. 'Risk assessment?'

'Minimal if the probe arrives at a reasonable distance from Fortuna and instantly displays the light sculpture of the test sequences,' he said.

Stone nodded. 'Thank you Fian, Jarra.'

The wall vid went blank. There was a short silence before Fian spoke. 'That was a bit of a brutal reaction.'

I sighed. 'I know, but we're reacting like history students, grieving for a fallen civilization and lost knowledge. Colonel Stone's not a historian; she's the acting commander of the Alien Contact programme. If the alien civilization has fallen, then they can't harm us. If I was sitting in her command chair, knowing the survival of the human race could depend on my decisions, then I'd feel nothing but relief too.'

'You're right,' said Fian. 'The collapse must have happened thousands of years ago. The aliens obviously lost space travel entirely, but it's surprising they haven't regained it by now.'

'If it was thousands of years ago, they could have rebuilt their civilization and had it collapse several times since then,' I said. 'Humanity had one major collapse after colonizing too many new worlds in Exodus century, spent a century rebuilding, and then the chimera of Thetis caused more problems.'

A thought suddenly nagged at me. A ridiculous idea, but worrying enough that I had to prove it wrong. The alien ship had passed through Beta sector on its way to Earth, and Thetis had been in Beta sector. I used my lookup to project a holo of the three concentric spheres of humanity's space, and added a bright line running from Fortuna in Zeta sector, to Earth at the centre of the holo.

'What are you doing?' asked Fian.

I didn't explain, just told my lookup to add the dot that marked the position of Thetis. That was supposed to prove me wrong, so I could stop worrying, but it did the opposite. Thetis was on the edge of Beta sector that bordered on Zeta sector, directly positioned on the bright line of the alien ship's course.

'Oh nuke!' I stared at my holo, had a sudden moment of relief as I saw the flaw in my logic, and then felt sick as I realized I'd had it backwards. The real answer was . . . 'Oh nuking hell!'

30

I was vaguely aware of Fian frowning at me, and Raven looking utterly shocked at my swearing. I couldn't make myself explain to them. I just cancelled the holo image, and called Major Rayne Tar Cameron.

'Get me Colonel Stone again,' I said. 'Tell her it's extremely urgent.'

A couple of minutes later, Colonel Stone and Colonel Leveque were back, looking at me from the wall vid. 'You've some extra information for me?' asked Colonel Stone. 'The comms portal relay lag gets really annoying, so just go ahead and say it.'

'I've got a theory, sir, but . . .' I took a deep breath. 'I know this will sound unreasonable, but I can't risk saying this in a call, and I can't leave Earth, so I need you and Colonel Leveque to come back here.'

I had to wait twelve seconds to see her startled face, and another couple of seconds for her to speak. 'This is a secure link, Jarra. Only my most trusted officers could possibly eavesdrop on it.'

'I appreciate that, sir,' I said, miserably. 'We still can't risk it.'

After another anxious wait, I saw her nod. 'Given your past record, Jarra, I trust your judgement. Colonel Leveque and I will come and join you at the meeting room in the Alien Contact Operations Centre at Zulu base. That has every possible security defence against eavesdroppers.'

I opened my mouth to say thank you, but she'd already ended the call.

Fian stared at me. 'Jarra, you've just ordered the acting commanding officer of the Alien Contact programme to come to Earth to talk to you.'

'Yes, I have.' I stood up.

'This is something really bad then.' He stood up as well.

'Yes, it is.'

Raven led the way out of the door, the three of us portalled to the Alien Contact Operations Centre, and walked through its deserted expanse to a side room. Raven checked no assassins were waiting inside the room, then turned to go out of the door again, but I called him back.

'Take a seat, Raven.'

He frowned but sat down at the circular table with us. Only minutes later, Colonel Stone and Colonel Leveque entered the room and sat down as well.

Leveque raised an eyebrow as he saw Raven sitting at the table. 'Should Captain Raven be hearing this?'

'Major Eklund and Captain Raven saw me looking at a holo, sir,' I said. 'Judging from Major Eklund's expression, he's just worked out what that holo meant, and Captain Raven will soon, so . . .'

Leveque nodded. He worked briefly on a bank of controls set into the table, before putting a small flashing pyramid in the centre of it. 'This room is now as secure as possible.'

Colonel Stone looked at me. 'What is so bad that I had to come to Earth to hear it, Commander?'

I couldn't make myself say it, so I showed them instead. The holo of humanity's space. The line marking the course of the alien ship from Fortuna to Earth. I added a red dot and said one word. 'Thetis.'

I heard a gasp from Raven. Leveque frowned, leaned forward in his chair to study the holo in the middle of the table, and then looked at me.

'You think the alien ship visited Thetis? Some chimera got aboard and were carried back to the alien home world, which is why the alien civilization has collapsed?' He shook his head. 'The chimera can survive incredible lengths of time in their hibernation phase, but the flaw in your theory is we know the ship continued to Earth. It would have brought the chimera to us, not to the alien world.'

Leveque had duplicated the first half of my own logic, but not the second. I moistened my lips. 'Sir, I thought of that too, but the real answer is worse.'

'Worse?' asked Stone in a hard, brittle voice.

'I think the chimera caused the collapse of the alien civilization, sir, but the alien ship didn't carry them from Thetis to the alien home world. It was the other way round. The chimera didn't evolve on Thetis, but on a world in Zeta sector.'

I waited for Stone to say something, but she didn't, so I carried on. 'The first ships the aliens built were probably quite simple, and just visited one planet in a neighbouring star system before returning home. One of those ships took the chimera back to Fortuna. The aliens were sending out far more advanced ships by then. Ships designed to travel through star system after star system looking for signs of intelligent life. The chimera caused the collapse of the alien civilization, but not until after a ship had been sent out in the direction of Earth.'

I paused. 'There were chimera hidden aboard that ship.

293

The ship's automated systems detected possible intelligent life on Thetis and stopped there. I hope it was wrong about the intelligent life, because the chimera infested Thetis and wiped out every other living creature on it. Humanity was lucky, because if the chimera had reached Earth . . .'

There was a long silence before Stone spoke. 'This is currently just a theory with no supporting evidence.'

'There is no actual evidence, sir, but the position of Thetis directly between Fortuna and Earth is highly suggestive,' said Leveque.

There was another silence before Stone spoke again. 'If this theory is true then the chimera are not extinct. They still exist on their world of origin, and may have taken over Fortuna as well.'

'They could have hidden aboard more than one alien ship,' added Leveque. 'In which case, they may have reached other worlds in the same way as they reached Thetis.'

Stone stood up. 'I'm going back to Gateway. I want to confirm the alien civilization has collapsed before I face telling the General Marshal the chimera are loose again.'

An hour later, Fian, Raven and I were watching our apartment wall vid again. It was showing the view from a probe approaching the planet Fortuna. The probe was busily playing the light sculpture of the test sequences, in case it met any actual aliens, but I felt there was little chance of that happening now.

The probe passed a group of silent, dead spheres floating in space. A couple showed flickers of activity, but there was nothing as functional as the one that had headed out to the edge of Fortuna system to meet us. Perhaps it was the one lone, sad survivor of its kind.

'Why is the sphere orbiting Earth still working?' I asked. 'Pure luck?'

'It hasn't been operating for as long as these,' said Fian. 'It wouldn't be activated until the ship carrying it reached Sol system.'

The view on the wall vid zoomed in on the planet ahead. The magnified image showed a mass of bright white lines, zigzagging randomly across the planet. Between the lines was a faint, opaque glow.

'What the chaos is that?' I asked.

'No idea.' Fian set the wall vid to give us the sound feed from the Alien Contact Operations Centre at Gateway base.

'. . . sort of planetary defence shield,' said Colonel Leveque's voice. 'The power beams are linking a network of satellites in orbit around Fortuna.'

'It's like a flicker force field then,' I said, 'but around a whole planet.'

Leveque was talking again. 'Some satellites are inactive or missing, leaving gaps in the defences.'

The image was magnified even further, and we could see one of the holes he was talking about.

'We could drop portal a probe straight into the planet's atmosphere,' said Colonel Stone, 'but a probe suddenly appearing from nowhere would be unnerving for any aliens down there. Can we send a probe through one of those holes?'

'Yes, sir,' said Leveque. 'It wouldn't survive atmospheric entry, but we could send it into a low orbit inside the defence shield.'

The probe moved in past Fortuna's single large moon, and I saw a sudden bright flash. 'Chaos! What's that?'

'What's that?' Colonel Stone echoed my words.

There was a column of light reaching up from Fortuna's moon, formed of swirling ribbons of red, green and blue coloured light. It looked exactly the same as the signal Fian and I had sent to the alien sphere in Earth orbit.

'There is a high probability this is intended to attract our attention to something on the surface of Fortuna's moon,' said Leveque.

'This signal is automated?' asked Stone.

'Almost certainly, sir,' said Leveque. 'It's probably responding to the probe's light sculpture.'

There was a short pause before Stone spoke again. 'Send the probe in to do a low fly past. I want to see what's on that moon.'

A barren, rocky landscape sped by on the wall vid. I could only get a fleeting glimpse of what was at the base of the column of light, but the moving image was quickly replaced by a magnified still picture. There was a sculpture down there, not a light sculpture but a physical one, seemingly carved out of the actual rock of the moon's surface. A globe covered in lines.

'How big is that?' asked Stone.

'On the same scale as the Spirit of Man monument, sir,' said Leveque. 'Sensors indicate the globe is hollow.'

'Surely that sculpture is of the planetary defence shield,' said Stone. 'The aliens are telling us there's something inside it that will turn off the defences and let us in?'

'I would concur with that assessment, sir,' said Leveque.

Stone raised her eyes to the ceiling. 'Would it kill him to just say yes?' She didn't wait for an answer, just continued speaking. 'If there's a similar artefact down there to the one in Earth Africa, then we'll need to send in a real person not a probe. I assume Commander Tell Dramis has already volunteered.'

'His message came in one minute fifteen seconds after the light column appeared,' said Leveque.

'Marriage has slowed him down,' said Stone. 'Tell him he'll have to wait a while. I want to take a look at Fortuna itself before I risk sending one of my officers to that moon.'

The probe changed course again, heading for Fortuna's defence shield. While it was on its way, Raven got a tray of food from the dispensers, but none of us did more than half-heartedly nibble at it. None of us had mentioned the chimera since the meeting with Stone and Leveque, Raven had barely said a word, but I knew we were all remembering the horror vids we'd seen set in Thetis chaos year. I was desperately hoping that the probe would find something, anything, to show I was wrong. I would gladly, joyfully, have Colonel Stone think me a complete nardle for scaring her over shadows.

As the probe went through the gap in Fortuna's planetary defence shield, its images broke up into interference for a few seconds, before showing a clear picture again. That suddenly zoomed in to show the planet surface in detail.

'Oh nuke!' said Fian.

The magnified view reminded me of seeing New York Main dig site from the air. Endless ruins stretched as far as you could see. How big was each of those ruins? The size of an ancient house, a skyscraper, or even bigger? Before I could work it out, the screen went black and swapped to showing the Alien Contact Operations Centre at Gateway Base. Colonel Stone was sitting at the command desk. She frowned.

'I thought the probe had made it safely through the planetary defence shield. Did we lose contact?'

It was a moment before Leveque replied. 'It was through the shield, sir, and manoeuvring to enter orbit. It was destroyed by an attack from the planet surface.'

Stone's frown deepened. 'Was that an automated response, or are the aliens actively shooting at us?' She waited for a reply, and grew restless when she didn't get one. 'Colonel?'

'One moment, sir,' said Leveque. There was a long wait before he spoke again. 'The response was definitely automated, sir. Evidence from our probe indicates there is no life on the planet surface.'

'Chaos!' Stone shook her head. 'You're perfectly sure there's no telemetry error?'

'That's unlikely in the extreme,' said Leveque.

'We can try sending probes in through other gaps,' said Stone. 'We may find life at other places on the planet.'

Leveque shook his head. 'To clarify the situation, sir, I'm saying there is absolutely no life of any kind on Fortuna. Not even single-celled organisms. The sterility of the planet at the point examined by our probe has to be an indication of a global extinction event.'

Stone's eyes rolled towards the ceiling for a second in urgent appeal before she spoke in a voice of strained patience. 'You're saying it's totally dead down there, and that can't happen unless everything is dead everywhere on the planet? Something happened that killed everything on that world?'

'Yes, sir,' said Leveque.

Stone ordered in two more probes to make sure there was no error. Those were both destroyed less than a minute after going through the shield, but their readings confirmed there was nothing living on the planet, not even bacteria.

After that, she decided to drop portal probes straight into Fortuna's atmosphere. It's impossible to form a drop portal dust ring at the surface of a planet, but the probes arrived as close to the ground as possible. They were all destroyed within seconds. There was nothing living on the planet, but the automated surface defences were still functioning perfectly.

Finally, Colonel Stone tapped at her lookup, and the holo

head of the General Marshal appeared above her command desk.

'Sir,' said Stone, 'I respectfully request you join me at Military Base 79 Zulu for a command meeting with Colonel Leveque, Commander Tell Morrath, Commander Tell Dramis, and Major Eklund.'

31

I could see why Renton Mai was commander-in-chief of the Military. His face barely reacted as Colonel Stone explained the theory about the chimera, and his voice was perfectly calm as he spoke.

'Let me check I fully understand this. It's possible the true home world of the chimera is in Zeta sector?'

'Yes, sir,' said Stone.

'The chimera infiltrated an alien ship and reached Fortuna. They then moved on to Thetis, and possibly other worlds as well, in other alien ships.'

'Yes, sir,' repeated Stone.

'Something has destroyed all life on Fortuna. Was that a deliberate act by the aliens when they found they were losing to the chimera?'

'It seems highly probable, sir,' said Leveque. 'The extinction event may not have reached Fortuna's moon, so that should still be regarded as suspect.'

The General Marshal sat in silence for a long minute, before finally speaking again. 'Chimera will still exist on their world of origin, and on an unknown number of other worlds as well. How do we find those worlds?'

'The chimera world of origin will be in a star system neighbouring Fortuna system,' said Leveque. 'It will have a breathable atmosphere and what initially appears to be a wide variety of animal life. Colonel Stone showed excellent judgement in choosing to use the lifeless world, Gateway, for our field base, because there is a 72 per cent probability that the other world we considered is actually the chimera planet of origin.'

I pictured what would have happened if the Military had set up the field base on a world infested with chimera, and felt sick.

'Finding the other worlds is virtually impossible,' continued Leveque. 'Alien ships may have travelled in any direction, stopping at an unknown number of planets, and could have reached anywhere in a volume of space as large as twenty sectors by now. Our only real hope is to find records on Fortuna that tell us the courses of the ships they sent out. We could then find and stop the ships, and check the star systems directly on their routes.'

'I hope we're just chasing shadows here,' said the General Marshal, 'but I have to treat any possibility of the chimera still surviving with the utmost seriousness. Any Planet First team landing on a new planet could be walking into a death trap. We could even have the same problems as on Thetis, with chimera breaching portal quarantine to reach existing inhabited worlds. I'll order Planet First to abandon Zeta sector and . . .'

He frowned for a second. 'Would Sigma sector be the furthest of the unsettled frontier sectors from the danger zone?'

'Yes, sir,' said Leveque.

'Then Planet First will move their efforts to find new colony worlds to Sigma sector. When people learn we've discovered the alien home world in Zeta, they'll assume that's the reason for the change.'

The General Marshal ran his fingers through his hair in the first visible sign of stress I'd seen. 'For the time being, information about this theory is to be kept strictly to the people in this room. The merest whisper of the chimera potentially surviving would cause public panic.'

He glanced at the other person who'd just learned about this theory. Drago was looking understandably dazed. I could imagine what he was feeling right now. We'd all grown up watching horror vids, shuddering at the nightmare chimera and deeply grateful that they were extinct. The thought that they might not be was scaring the chaos out of me, and Drago . . . Drago had volunteered to make the landing on Fortuna's moon.

The General Marshal asked the question that must be torturing Drago. 'How high is the risk of finding living chimera on Fortuna's moon?'

'Fortuna's moon has minimal atmosphere,' said Leveque. 'Even chimera, with their incredible adaptability, couldn't survive thousands of years in near total vacuum. The only place on Fortuna's moon where there may still be living chimera is actually inside the sculpture. Our sensors show that's definitely hollow, but something is blocking them from giving us details of the interior.'

He paused for a second. 'I'd estimate the risk at not more than 10 per cent.'

The expression on Drago's face flickered for a second as he heard that. There was a one in ten risk that he was going to be the first human being in a quarter of a millennium to face a chimera.

'In the days of Thetis, the chimera infiltrated our worlds before we had any clue what we were dealing with,' continued Leveque. 'We have chimera detectors in ships, and bio filters on portals now. We have to be prepared to deal with the situation if an alarm goes off, and remember the lessons of Thetis. The chimera constantly adapt in the face of danger.'

'Please wait outside while I discuss this with Commander Tell Dramis,' said the General Marshal.

The rest of us stood up and went out into the huge, echoing emptiness of the Alien Contact Operations Centre. The General Marshal's bodyguards glanced at us, saw the expression on Colonel Stone's face, and hastily adopted the rigid posture of impersonal, incurious guards.

Stone and Leveque went to the command desk and started working, probably looking up details on the chimera. I couldn't face that right now, so I went over to stand by the far wall. Fian and Raven followed me, and Fian gave a wary look at the General Marshal's bodyguards before speaking in a low voice.

'Why is the General Marshal talking to Drago alone?'

'He's giving Drago the chance to change his mind about volunteering,' I said.

'No one could blame Drago if he does change his mind,' said Fian. 'Do you think he will?'

I gave an angry shake of my head. 'Drago can't. He knows if the clan of Tellon Blaze are too scared to face this, then no one else will.'

Fian pulled a face. 'That's a chaos lot of pressure. Can he tell his wife?'

'No. Marlise is his deputy, she'll know he's going to Fortuna's moon, but . . .' I grimaced. 'It's probably better that way. Would you want to know if . . .?'

'Yes!' Fian's voice was savage. 'Yes, I would! Drago will obviously be wearing an impact suit, but . . .'

He let the words trail off, but my mind finished the sentence for him. There was a limit to the protection given by an impact suit, and chimera had needle sharp teeth and claws.

We waited in silence for a few more minutes, then Stone's lookup chimed and everyone went back inside the meeting room and sat down. Drago was giving an amaz impersonation of someone who was completely relaxed; only the clenched fingers of his right hand showed what he was really feeling.

'We'll proceed as planned with investigating the beacon on Fortuna's moon,' said the General Marshal. 'Commander Tell Dramis will carry both weapons and flares.'

I frowned. Using flares to flood an area with glaring light would leave chimera partially blinded and with no shadows to hide in, but it would also make everyone watching guess exactly what was going on. Or maybe not. Given everyone believed the chimera had been extinct for over a quarter of a millennium . . .

'I want the command feed running with a five minute delay during this investigation,' continued the General Marshal. 'Should chimera be detected, the command feed must be cut while the situation is assessed. I don't want hundreds of civilians in the Research area seeing live chimera and going screaming in panic to the newzies.'

'I'll route the command feed through my own work station, sir,' said Leveque.

After a few more minutes of discussion, Stone, Leveque and Drago headed off to portal back to Zeta sector. The General Marshal and his bodyguards went with them. I didn't know if they were going to Zeta sector as well, or returning to Academy, and I didn't care. I was fully occupied with drowning in guilt.

We headed back to our apartment. Fian and I sat on the couch, while Raven set the wall vid to show the command feed. The image of Fortuna's moon appeared, and my feelings exploded in four bitter words.

'It should be me.'

'What?' asked Fian.

'I was the one who thought of the chimera. I belong to the Tell clan. It should be me going to that moon, but Drago has to do my job for me because I'm Handicapped.'

'That isn't true, Jarra,' said Raven. 'Even if you didn't suffer from Novak-Nadal syndrome, Colonel Stone would still send Drago to do this. He's not just a far more experienced officer, he's been through alien warfare training, and that includes holo simulations of combats with chimera.'

I shook my head. 'The worst thing is I know I couldn't do it. The mere thought of going to that moon, knowing any shadow could hide a chimera, makes me freeze with terror. I'm a horrible person, because part of me is worried sick about Drago, but another part is gibbering to itself in gratitude that I can't go myself.'

'It's only human to feel that way, Jarra,' said Fian.

It was a surprisingly short period of time before Drago's ship was ready to drop portal from Gateway to Fortuna's moon. He was flying one of the survey craft used by Planet First teams on new worlds. They carried whole battalions of sensors, and were designed to crash land safely in extreme conditions and protect their occupants from any and all hazards until rescue arrived. Even a chimera would have a tough time ripping its way through a survey ship hull.

Two probes were in position near Fortuna's moon. The command feed showed their images of the drop portal dust ring appearing, and Drago's ship coming through. After that, it swapped to show the view from the ship itself, as it circled slowly above the beacon and the massive sculpture.

'Sensors show no life on the surface of the moon,' said Colonel Leveque's voice. 'We're still getting little detail on the interior of the sculpture.'

'I want a few more circuits before we try a landing,' said Colonel Stone.

She kept Drago flying circuits for another ten or fifteen minutes, while Leveque tried different sensor settings in an attempt to get more information on what was inside the sculpture. Finally, Stone sighed.

'We obviously won't learn anything more until we try a landing. I'm tempted to go out there and make the landing myself.'

It might have been my imagination, but Leveque's voice sounded a bit sharper than usual as he replied. 'Your command position precludes you from such a course of action, sir.'

'I'm perfectly aware of that!' Stone snapped back. 'All right,' she continued in a more normal voice. 'Commander Tell Dramis, you may proceed with the landing in your own time. Please take all possible precautions.'

'Yes, sir,' said Drago.

The survey craft instantly dived straight at the ground and landed next to the giant sculpture. I thought I heard a groan from Colonel Stone, but I was on Drago's side. Why stretch out the suspense when he'd already flown circuits until he was giddy?

'Kindly allow us time to check the ground level sensor readings before you go outside, Commander,' said Leveque.

'Yes, sir.' Drago's tense impatience was obvious in his voice, so there was a ripple of background laughter from the Command staff, who had no idea what was really going on here.

I turned to watch Fian working on his forearm lookup. Several blocks of incomprehensible symbols and images appeared in midair.

'It seems fine to me, but I'm no expert.' Fian tapped his lookup and the floating images vanished.

'Drago's going outside!' said Raven.

The image on the wall vid had changed to show the view from one of the vid bees hovering in midair inside the survey ship. I watched Drago open the door, step outside, and activate a hover belt that kept him floating just above the ground. The vid bees chased after him, giving us a view of a landscape of scattered reddish rocks and dust. The giant sculpture ahead of Drago had a reddish hint as well.

Drago had an equipment net on his back, which held flares and some other things I didn't recognize. His left hand held a small sensor, that I knew would be checking for the distinctive body chemistry of a chimera. His right hand held something large with a shape that screamed it was a weapon. He headed towards the sculpture, slowly at first with constant checks of the sensor in his hand, then suddenly picking up speed. I guessed he was talking to Leveque and Stone on a private comms channel.

Now we could see the beacon of light was being transmitted from the top of a large black cube, positioned pointedly next to an arched opening in the side of the rock sculpture. Drago turned off his hover belt and walked into the opening.

There was an almost inaudible murmur from Raven. 'I swear I'll never watch another horror vid.'

The vid image swung wildly for a moment, as the vid bees jostled for position and followed Drago into a tunnel. He had a light strapped to his left arm, and the vid bees seemed to have their own lights as well. I was watching nervously for flickering, almost invisible movements in the shadows, but could see nothing.

'Curious,' said Leveque. 'Sensors show no doors or barriers ahead.'

I frowned. I'd been too busy worrying about the chimera

to think about doors, but there should surely be some in this tunnel.

Drago walked on, and his pool of light suddenly widened as he entered the hollow centre of the sculpture. He stopped, checked the sensor he was carrying, took a flare from the net on his back and tossed it into the darkness ahead.

Light blazed, blinding the vid bees. Before they could adjust to it, the image on the wall vid abruptly cut out. I jumped to my feet, staring pointlessly at the blank screen. 'Oh nuke, nuke, nuke!'

'There can't be chimera. There can't possibly be chimera.' Fian was talking rapidly to himself. 'There were no doors in the tunnel, there's no atmosphere in there, the chimera couldn't have survived.'

'They adapt their bodies to their environment,' said Raven. 'Could they somehow . . .?'

He broke off as the image on the wall vid cut in again. I saw Drago standing in a large cavern, totally featureless apart from a black pedestal at the centre. There were no dark shapes frozen by the light, no creatures of nightmare. I heard a soft sob of relief, and realized it had come from me.

'You were right about the chimera then, Jarra,' said Raven in a harsh voice.

I turned to look at him in bewilderment. 'What? There aren't any chimera there. Leveque must have cut the command feed by mistake.'

'Leveque doesn't make mistakes,' said Raven. 'He cut the command feed because there were the remains of a long dead chimera. Drago's standing on it. You see the scattering of grey fragments on the rock floor?'

I took a step closer to the wall vid. 'That's . . .?'

'Yes,' said Raven. 'Drago's shot at it, blown it to tiny pieces, but that's the remains of a chimera.'

I went back to the couch, sat down, and Fian put his arm

308

round me. If there was a dead chimera on Fortuna's moon, it meant there'd be living ones on at least one world, perhaps several.

The image on the wall vid showed Drago walking up to the pedestal. A glowing circle appeared on its side, showing it still had power.

'I just have to put my hand on the circle then?' said Drago. 'I was expecting doors, tests, something. It doesn't make sense to create a huge planetary defence system, and then allow anyone to walk in and shut it down.'

'Alien logic may not match our own, but this is definitely a curious approach,' said Leveque's voice.

'Shall I try it, sir?' asked Drago.

'Go ahead, Commander,' said Stone.

The wall vid was showing two images now, one of Drago placing his hand on the circle, and the other an image of Fortuna from a probe out in space. Nothing happened for a few minutes, then part of the circle glowed brighter, but there was no change to the glittering lines of the defence shield around Fortuna.

'How long do I keep my hand on this circle?' asked Drago. 'I'm starting to feel rejected.'

'Only one small section of the circle is glowing,' said Leveque. 'On Earth, the signal was sent by both Commander Tell Morrath and Major Eklund.'

'So we may need both a man and a woman there?' asked Stone. 'Send Major Weldon to join Commander Tell Dramis.'

There was a nerve-wracking wait before Marlise landed a fighter next to Drago's survey ship, entered the tunnel, and joined him at the pedestal.

'I'll count us down,' said Drago. 'Three, two, one, now!'

Drago and Marlise both put a hand on the circle. A few minutes later, part of it glowed exactly as before.

'This is getting annoying,' said Drago. 'If we can't shut down the planetary defence system . . .'

He didn't finish the sentence. Everyone listening knew that we needed to shut down the defence system to be able to explore the alien planet. Everyone listening knew that we could gain incredible amounts of knowledge from the ruins of an alien civilization. Only seven people knew that we desperately needed some very specific knowledge about the ships the aliens had sent out.

'Is the pedestal broken?' asked Stone.

'It's at least partially functional, sir,' said Leveque. 'Part of the circle is glowing and . . .' He paused for a moment. 'Commander Tell Dramis, exactly what is your genetic relationship to Commander Tell Morrath?'

I felt a stab of blind panic at the mention of my name, even before my conscious mind worked out what Leveque was thinking.

'We have two great-grandparents in common,' said Drago.

'Which explains why you were able to light part of the circle,' said Leveque. 'The reason there are no doors or tests to prevent anyone reaching that pedestal, is because it performs some sort of genetic scan and will only respond to selected people.'

I daren't look at Fian or Raven. My mind was facing total disaster.

'I don't see how the pedestal in Zeta sector could know who activated the artefact on Earth,' said Colonel Stone. 'The aliens don't appear to have had portal technology, so how could a message have reached it this fast?'

'It knows because we told it.' Leveque's voice was unusually grim. 'Our probe played the light sculpture of the test sequences, and the beacon responded to attract our attention. Unfortunately, the light sculpture of the test sequences includes a very complex end section. We didn't understand what that section was about. Now we do. The end section is the genetic information of the people who triggered the artefact on Earth.'

'But why?' asked Stone. 'If they don't have portal technology, how could they expect us to travel here fast enough for the same people to activate this pedestal?'

'It's possible the aliens expected us to take the time to fully translate their message and follow some special instructions that would have avoided this problem,' said Leveque, 'but I suspect the answer is much simpler. The aliens reproduced asexually, and they assumed other intelligent species would too.'

'What?' asked Stone.

'Only one parent was involved in reproduction, so their offspring were exact genetic copies of them. Asexual reproduction is most common in plants but in rare cases it happens in animals too.'

'So they didn't expect the same person to activate this pedestal, they expected one of their descendants to do it.' Stone paused for a moment. 'Major Weldon, please touch the circle again. By yourself this time.'

I stared down at my trembling hands. The pedestal in Zeta sector needed both me and Fian to activate it, but I was Handicapped and couldn't leave Earth. Even worse, this situation was entirely my own fault. I'd dared to help send that signal to the alien probe instead of letting a normal born human do it alone. I'd stood there afterwards, celebrating doing something good, but I'd actually done something terrible.

The sheer magnitude of the disaster slowly sank in. People saw me as representing the Handicapped. When this news went public . . .

I pictured what would happen then, and shuddered. People would blame me for blocking humanity from reaching

Fortuna, and there'd be a huge backlash against me and everyone I represented. When they found out about the chimera as well, learned I'd stopped us finding out where the other alien ships had gone . . .

I felt Fian's hand take mine, but I didn't trust myself to look at him. I just kept numbly watching the wall vid. The circle didn't respond to Marlise at all. Of course it wouldn't. She wasn't related to either me or Fian. When she stepped away from the pedestal, Colonel Stone asked the key question.

'What are the chances of the pedestal accepting Major Eklund without Commander Tell Morrath?'

'50 per cent,' said Leveque.

The Military lookup on Fian's forearm chimed a moment later. I knew what the message would say. He'd just been ordered to go to Fortuna's moon.

Fian let go of my hand and stood up. 'Everything will be all right, Jarra. The pedestal will work for me.'

I watched him change into his impact suit and go off, escorted by the usual four Military Security officers since Raven was staying with me. Fian had to try of course, but I already knew the pedestal wouldn't respond to him alone. When I was born, the odds were a thousand to one against me being Handicapped, but I'd still lost. I was going to lose this gamble too.

There was only one thing I could possibly do. I tapped my lookup and Rayne Tar Cameron answered me. It was obviously no surprise to her that I wanted to speak to Colonel Stone. Judging from the compassionate look on her face, she knew exactly what I was going to say as well.

It was only a moment before Colonel Stone's face appeared on my lookup. I took a deep breath. 'Sir, I volunteer to portal to Fortuna's moon.'

I knew it would be twelve seconds before she could reply.

I was mentally counting those seconds, when I heard Raven's lookup chime and turned to see him pointing his gun at me.

'I'm really sorry about this, Jarra, but you're under arrest.'

32

My Military lookup had been remotely disabled, so I wasn't sure of the exact time, but I must have been locked in my cell for nearly four days when Colonel Leveque finally appeared at the other side of the metal bars. I'd burned through my initial blind anger by then, and was feeling a weird, icily calm despair.

I rolled off the bed and went to stand facing him. 'The pedestal obviously didn't work for Fian or you'd have let me out ages ago.'

Colonel Leveque shook his head. 'Regrettably, Major Eklund only succeeded in lighting precisely half the circle.'

'But why keep me in a prison cell? You don't have to force me to portal to Fortuna's moon. I've already volunteered!'

'That's precisely why I've been keeping you in a prison cell, Commander,' said Leveque. 'Some worlds are compatible with the Handicapped immune system, but unfortunately Fortuna is not one of them. When I realized the problem with the pedestal, I estimated a 97 per cent probability you would volunteer to commit suicide. Since ordering you not to do it might result in you making creative plans to make the attempt without permission, I preferred to keep you safely behind bars while we investigated all possible options for dealing with this situation.'

'There is only one option. You set up a portal right next to that pedestal. You have Fian waiting there with his hand on it. I go through the portal and put my hand on it too.'

'The attempt would certainly fail. We've been using Commander Tell Dramis, Major Eklund, your brother, and your sister, to make a series of tests.'

'You've dragged Jaxon and Gemelle into this?'

'Since they're both Military officers, it was the logical next step. Although no combination of your relatives could actually activate the pedestal, they helped gather considerable information about it. That information included the fact you'd need to keep your hand on the pedestal for three minutes six seconds while it performs a scan.'

I sat back down on the bed and tugged at my hair with both hands. 'It might still work even if I . . . die in the middle.'

Leveque shook his head. 'Major Eklund was unable to affect the pedestal at all while unconscious.'

Unconscious? They must have drugged Fian and . . . I dismissed that thought. 'Even if it can't work, I still need to try. You won't be able to hide this situation for long, and when people find out . . . The Planet First vote will fail. Alpha sector will change its mind about having Earth as a member. Prejudice against the Handicapped will be worse than ever before, and it's all my fault!'

'You are possibly taking an overly negative view of the situation, Commander,' said Leveque.

'No, I'm not. The Military were using me as a symbol of the Handicapped, using me to change things, but when people know how badly I messed things up by sending that signal to the alien probe . . . If they know I tried to fix it, then it might limit the damage.'

'I'm sure that Lucius Augustus Gordianus could make some very stirring speeches about you martyring yourself in a hopeless attempt to activate the pedestal on Fortuna's moon,' said Leveque. 'That might help the Handicapped situation, however my overriding priority is the safety of all humanity. We don't need heroic self sacrifice here, we need access to Fortuna and the information we may find there about the chimera's whereabouts.'

He'd been standing on the other side of the bars, but now he tugged across a chair and sat down facing me. 'We can bypass the Fortuna outer defence shield by drop portalling low into the atmosphere, but the surface defences are incredibly efficient. After two hundred and seven attempts, we still haven't managed to land a probe on the planet surface. We must shut down those defences.'

I didn't bother saying anything. Shutting down the defences meant me putting my hand on that pedestal. I'd volunteered to do that. Leveque was refusing to let me. There weren't any other options.

'We've considered cloning you,' said Leveque.

I stared at him. 'Cloning human beings is against the protection of humanity laws!'

Leveque shrugged. 'The Alien Contact programme can override those laws. However, records of previous experiments indicate your genetically identical clone would also be Handicapped.'

'What? Someone tried cloning the Handicapped? I've never heard about that. When did it happen? Why?'

'That information is classified.' He paused for a moment. 'Our only remaining course of action is to attempt to use an individually tailored web to artificially control your immune system. Although highly dangerous, this does have a significant chance of success.'

'This is the same cure you told me about before? I thought you said the risk was suicidal.'

'General Torrek was concerned you might wish to try the cure,' said Leveque, 'so he ordered me to exaggerate the dangers. For the average person, the chance of success is 51 per cent. In your case, it rises to 68 per cent.'

'Why do I get a better chance? I'm not complaining, but . . .'

'At age 14, you had the right to make one attempt to portal off world. You had the excellent forethought to take up that option. Very few of the Handicapped do this, so Hospital Earth researchers are always present to study the event.'

I remembered the number of medical staff who'd been present that day. 'They were studying me? I thought they were doctors!'

'They were,' said Leveque. 'They were giving you every possible care, while also performing extensive scans of your immune system before, during, and after the attempt. Hospital Earth has also taken every opportunity to perform follow up scans during your routine medical checks and emergency medical treatment for dig site accidents. This means they have extremely detailed data on the operation of your immune system over the last four years.'

I'd always felt that doctors were obsessive about scanning me. My friends had just laughed and said I was imagining things, but apparently I hadn't been. 'What does this cure involve?'

'The first stage is a modified channelrhodopsin therapy which . . .'

I lifted a hand to stop him. 'If I'm going to understand this, you'll need to explain it simply.'

317

Leveque started his explanation again. 'The first stage is an injection of special cells that can be switched on or off using pulses of light. These will seek out and attach themselves to all areas of your immune system. A variation of this technique was once widely used in medical treatments before being replaced by regrowth techniques.'

I held up my hand again. 'I think I understand so far, but you're still being very technical.'

'The second stage is whole body surgery to implant a web under your skin,' continued Leveque. 'This web will send the light signals round your body to control your immune system. Again, an implanted web that will regenerate in the event of injury was an established method of medical treatment centuries ago, although it was used for a very different purpose.'

I wrinkled my nose. 'Whole body surgery must mean tank time.'

'Correct,' said Leveque. 'Surgery would be followed by two days in a regrowth tank to heal your body. After that, comes stage three, which is the critical point when the natural controls of your immune system are shut down and the artificial controls of the web take over. Unfortunately, shutting down your natural immune system is irreversible.'

'So if the web doesn't work, I'll die?'

Leveque nodded. 'There is a 32 per cent chance that stage three will cause you to suffer total immune system failure and a rapid death. However, if the transition to the artificial controls is successful, the web will control your immune system perfectly whether you're on Earth or any other planet.'

There was a one in three chance I'd die, but that was much better than the certain death I'd been expecting. 'I obviously have to do this, I've no choice, but I've a few more questions. Will this involve overriding the protection of humanity laws?'

'I assure you, Commander, medical treatment to give you a normally functioning immune system is perfectly legal under the protection of humanity laws.'

It would be legal, but . . . 'If this doesn't kill me, what will I look like afterwards? Will this web show?'

'Hospital Earth's doctors will do their best not to adversely affect your appearance, but functionality must override aesthetics.'

I was tempted to copy Colonel Stone, look up at the ceiling, and ask why Leveque couldn't just talk ordinary Language instead of including lots of fancy words. 'You're saying I'll look different. How different?'

'The effect should be small.'

The question I was really trying to ask was if I'd still be human, but I couldn't make myself say those words. I tried to forget that issue. 'What will you do if I die? Clone me?'

'If you suffer brain death before we stabilize your immune system, and your existing body is viable afterwards, then we would regrow your brain tissue. If your existing body was not viable, we would clone you, but in that case the clone would need to undergo the web implantation process.'

'A clone would have a one in three chance of dying too,' I said.

'Our chance of the web implantation being successful would be improved due to the knowledge gained during the first attempt,' said Leveque. 'Unfortunately, there is a significant probability that either your own body with a regrown brain, or a clone, would be unable to activate the pedestal. Our tests lead us to believe it requires not only identical genes but similar brain patterns.'

'What? Why?'

'It seemed strange that an intelligent alien race would have reproduced asexually because it has evolutionary disadvantages. Those disadvantages may have been outweighed by some form of genetic memory.'

I looked at him blankly.

'The alien offspring weren't just identical genetic copies of their parent, they also inherited some memories and brain patterns.' Leveque paused to check I understood that before continuing. 'Either your clone, or your own body with a regrown brain, would be missing your current memories and personality. This would cause significant changes to brain activity.'

That meant it wouldn't be me any longer. Everything that made me a person would be gone. Despite that, I couldn't help thinking . . . 'If you do have to use cloning and put them through this as well, can you do that before you . . . first wake them up?'

'Of course, Commander. As a Threat specialist, I'm trained to supply information dispassionately, to avoid my personal emotions influencing my commanding officer's decisions. That can mean I appear cold and indifferent in public, but I assure you that I have perfectly normal human feelings and compassion. I find the current situation extremely distressing.'

He let the carefully controlled mask of his face slip for a second, showing an expression of pure pain. I'd never really understood the reasons for the traditional emotionless act of Threat specialists. Now I did. The knowledge that this situation was hurting Leveque only made things worse.

'How soon will I have the operation, sir?' I asked.

Leveque went across to a panel at the side of the room, and did something that made a section of bars slide aside. 'The doctors are ready to proceed with the stage 1 injection immediately. It will take effect within forty-eight hours, by which time they should have finished creating the web to match your individual requirements.'

I walked out of my prison cell. 'I'd like to visit Lecturer

Playdon before the operation and warn him what's happening. His wife was killed four years ago, so he's got the personal experience to help Fian if this goes badly.'

'Lecturer Playdon has taken the Security Oath,' said Leveque, 'so there's no problem with that so long as you don't mention the chimera.'

'I'd like to visit Candace too, but I'd better not. She knows me far too well. She could tell if I lied, and if I told her even part of the truth . . .'

I pictured how Candace would react to the news I'd volunteered for something that had a one in three chance of killing me, and winced. It wasn't even as simple as that. Chaos, I could have coped with a one in three chance of dying, but the idea of some replacement me wearing my face, taking over my life, was . . .

'While there is no medical urgency,' said Leveque, 'it would be beneficial if the web is implanted within the next ninety-one hours.'

'Why? What happens in ninety-one hours time?'

'General Torrek will be decanted from his rejuvenation tank,' said Colonel Leveque. 'He will be extremely unhappy with recent developments.'

'General Torrek won't blame you for this.'

Colonel Leveque shook his head. 'General Torrek is normally a patient and understanding man, but he's going to react strongly to the news that a girl he regards as his granddaughter is undergoing a procedure that has a 32 per cent chance of killing her. I confidently expect his first action after resuming command of Alien Contact will be to demote myself and Colonel Stone to the rank of Lieutenant.'

33

Fian can be incredibly stubborn. I knew he wanted to be stubborn about this, argue against me doing it, but he just accepted my decision. I don't think I could have done that if I was in his place, but Fian is totally zan and a much better person than I will ever be.

So Fian held my hand while some doctors gave me the stage 1 injection and waved scanners at me. After that, Raven appeared, and the three of us portalled to our class dome on the California Land Raft to visit Lecturer Playdon.

Raven was grimly silent, and the expression on his face told me he was suffering his own personal hell over what was happening. He wasn't just our bodyguard, he was our friend, and given he'd been the one who arrested me . . .

'You mustn't blame yourself, Raven,' I said.

'I put you in that prison cell.'

'Which stopped me killing myself in a hopeless attempt to activate the pedestal.' I tried to sound cheerful and optimistic. 'There's every chance this cure will work.'

We headed out of the portal room and walked down the corridor towards the hall. It was early evening, so I expected the whole class to be there, but it was deserted.

'Where is everyone?' asked Fian. 'They surely can't still be out on the dig site. Playdon's a slave driver sometimes, but . . .'

I frowned as I saw something burgundy red and silver on the hall floor, and stooped to pick it up. 'Why is one of Dalmora's scarves lying . . .?'

I broke off and exchanged startled looks with Fian. He'd obviously had the same thought as me, because he led the way out of the hall and opened the nearest room door. All the storage spaces were open and empty.

'They've packed and evacuated!' he said.

'But why?' asked Raven.

'There must have been a quake warning.' I turned to head back to the portal. 'We've got to get out of here. I don't understand why . . .'

I broke off my sentence because a figure in a sealed Military impact suit was coming out of the portal room. The glowing name and rank markings on the front of the suit said that it was Major Rayne Tar Cameron, but she wasn't that tall. Something was horribly wrong here.

If that fact was obvious to me, it was even more obvious to Raven. By the time I was reaching for my gun, Raven already had his aimed and was firing, or trying to fire. The gun did nothing. He gave it a single angry shake and shouted.

'Guns are disabled. Run! Nuke it, run!'

Fian and I turned and ran for the dome exit at the far end of the corridor. Fian operated the door controls, while I glanced behind us for Raven. I'd expected him to be following us, but he'd stopped, turned, and was launching himself at the advancing anonymous person in the impact suit. He'd know there was no chance he could injure them when they were protected by the suit, but he was buying us time to get the door open.

It was then that I saw the blinding line of light appear

from something in the intruder's right hand. A laser cutter! It was pointless yelling warnings. Raven must have seen the laser when he told us to run. That was why an Adonis Knight had used the nuke word.

Raven sent the intruder flying against the corridor wall. I saw the material in the flailing left arm trigger, freezing it at a ludicrous angle, but the flexiplas wall wasn't hard enough to trigger a whole impact suit. The laser cutter in the right hand swung round and went straight through Raven just above the waist.

Raven didn't even cry out, just toppled apart in two, hideously gory, separate pieces. I forced my eyes away, saw the dome door was opening, grabbed Fian's hand and ran. Raven had given his life to buy us precious seconds. We couldn't waste them.

We sprinted down the path past the swimming pool. I was on the edge of tears, but fought them back. I had to be practical now, or Fian and I would soon be dead too. I let go of Fian's hand so I could check my gun, and saw the red light warning it was disabled. I tried to use the lookup on my left forearm to send an emergency call, but that was dead too. They'd both been remotely disabled. Nuke it, what was going on here?

I desperately tried to think, to plan. Fian and I didn't have impact suits. The intruder chasing us did. There was a good side to that. Impact suits wouldn't protect us against a laser cutter, and we could run faster without them.

If I had a tag gun, I could fire tags at our pursuer, keep triggering their impact suit so we could grab the laser cutter. There were tag guns in the store rooms of both our dome and that of Cassandra 2, but we'd have to go back past the laser cutter to reach them. Nuke that!

'We're running out of path,' said Fian. 'We'll have to go into the ruins.'

'Chaos! I suppose we've no other choice, but we'll have to stay between the safety lines or we'll get killed by concraz blocks falling on our heads. That means we'll be easy targets for a gun.'

'If whoever is in that suit had a gun,' said Fian, 'they'd surely have shot at us by now.'

We ran out of the park and along Gap 15, careful to keep safely in the centre and away from the buildings. I took another glance over my shoulder, saw the Military impact suit was well behind us now, and slowed to a safer speed. We couldn't afford a fall or a trip because an injury would kill both of us. I wouldn't leave Fian and I knew he'd never leave me.

Fian was looking behind us too. 'They're still chasing us. Where's Raven?'

I realized Fian had been concentrating on opening the dome door. He hadn't looked behind us, and there'd been no scream to tell him what had happened.

'Raven's dead,' I said. 'Whoever is in that suit has a laser cutter.'

Fian made the sound of someone trying not to be sick. I'd be sick myself when I had time. If I had time.

'I didn't see . . .' Fian looked over his shoulder again. 'I still can't see a laser beam.'

'They're obviously not stupid enough to run along with it turned on.' I looked back at the figure myself. 'They aren't very fast. An impact suit always slows you down, but it looks like they aren't used to wearing one.'

'Who do you think is inside the suit?' Fian asked. 'It's not Rayne Tar Cameron, because the shape looks like a man.'

'It's not Rayne in the suit, but if she's involved then it would explain how our guns and lookups got disabled, and why we didn't get a mail from Playdon about the class evacuating. You know how paranoid he is about safety. He'd have sent us a mail message to warn us not to come back here.'

'You're right. Rayne's the Command Support team leader. She's got the authority to remotely disable guns and lookups. She's filtering our mail messages. She's authorizing portal access to . . .' Fian broke off his sentence as the ground suddenly rocked under our feet, and the buildings on either side of us rained heavy lumps of concraz.

I gave a laugh of pure despair. This was utter nightmare.

The instant the ground stabilized, we started moving again, but a glance over my shoulder told me the figure behind us was moving as well. 'I think it's Qwin Marston in that suit,' I said. 'He's a supply clerk, so he wouldn't have a gun, but he could get access to a laser cutter.'

'That would explain why he's slow in an impact suit,' said Fian. 'Supply clerks wouldn't wear them very often. It's a good job he didn't think of bringing a hover belt or we'd be in real trouble.'

'You don't think we're in real trouble already?' I asked.

'At least we know help is coming,' said Fian. 'Raven's implant will have sent a signal to SECOP when he died.'

I'd forgotten about that. I did some hasty mental calculations. 'Military Security must be on their way, but they can't possibly catch us up before we reach the edge of the island.'

We jogged on in silence for a few minutes. We were running out of time. When we reached the edge of the island, we'd be trapped.

'Qwin Marston doesn't know this place,' I said. 'We do. It's our only advantage, so we have to use it.'

'Hiding inside the buildings would be far too dangerous,' said Fian.

I had a truly mad idea. 'Playdon brought the class down Gap 15 to show us the view from the edge of the Land Raft. Remember seeing all the birds? Qwin doesn't know about them. We'll collect a few rocks as we go along. When we get to the edge of the island, we wait for Qwin to get close and then throw rocks at nests.'

'The birds will mob all of us,' said Fian. 'Qwin's got a suit to protect him, but we haven't.'

'Exactly,' I said. 'Those beaks and claws are nasty. They'll hurt us, they won't hurt Qwin, but they will keep triggering the material of his impact suit. If his right arm locks up, we may get a chance to grab the laser cutter.'

Fian groaned. 'That's a fast way to lose a hand, but . . . At least it's a chance, and losing a hand wouldn't be fatal if we made a tourniquet with something.'

We ran on. The edge of our Land Raft island was in sight now, so I paused to grab a few rocks.

'Why?' Fian loaded up with rocks as well. 'Why would Rayne help him do this? She always seemed such a perfect Military officer.'

'Plenty of people who've never even met me want to kill me. Why shouldn't Rayne want to kill me too? I always had the impression she didn't approve of us being recruited.'

'It's a bit of a leap from not approving to committing murder,' said Fian.

We were getting close to the crumbling remains of the wall that guarded the edge of the Land Raft island. I looked up at the buildings, looking for nests on windowsills, then turned to face our attacker. There was a flash of light as he triggered the laser beam. He must have seen us gathering rocks, but he'd naturally expect us to throw them at him.

I waited until he was less than thirty paces away, then whirled round and started hurling rocks at the windows of the nearest building. Fian was throwing rocks too. For a couple of seconds there was no reaction, and I was panicking because the beam of the laser cutter was too close and we'd nowhere left to run, then a dark shape suddenly plummeted down at us, followed by another, and then a whole flock of smaller birds.

The first bird went for me, hitting me far harder than I'd expected, gouging the side of my head painfully with its claws. I staggered, used my hands to protect my face, and peered through my fingers to watch our attacker. He could have reached me and killed me then, but he made the mistake of stopping. Perhaps he wasn't sure whether to go for me, or for where Fian was battling with the second large bird.

Whatever the reason, he hesitated, and the smaller birds started mobbing him. He lashed out blindly with the laser cutter, and I risked a brief glance upwards. At least a dozen large birds had been circling high above in the thermals, and were now joining the attack, their height translating into speed as they dived at us.

I saw the leading bird hit Fian, knocking him to the ground, and took a desperate gamble, dropping to the ground myself and curling into a defensive ball. My hope was most of the birds would go for the only remaining upright figure, conspicuously holding the dazzlingly bright line of the active laser cutter.

I was lucky, most of them did, and I saw the right arm of our attacker's impact suit lock up. It was the moment I'd hoped for, our chance to grab his weapon, but Fian and I each had three or four birds attacking us. I tried to get back to my feet, but the weight of the birds and the stabbing beaks kept me down. Blood was running down my face into my eyes.

Fian had somehow got to his feet, but our attacker had worked out what we were trying to do now. His right arm was still frozen, but he could move his legs, and he backed away from Fian, getting dangerously close to the buildings. If he was fool enough to use the treacherous buildings to shelter from the birds, then falling rubble might solve our problem by burying both him and his laser cutter.

I finally managed to stand up. The figure in the Military blue impact suit was flailing the white laser beam at the birds, and gradually getting closer to the buildings. My hopes were growing, but then a block of concraz fell from above. The figure glanced at it and moved further away from the buildings. Nuke it, he'd realized their dangers. We'd have to go for the laser cutter after all.

Claws suddenly dug deep into my right arm, and huge wings beat against my head. I had to fight off the bird before I could see or move again. Our attacker was heading towards Fian now, brandishing the laser cutter. I tried to run towards them, but the ground shook under my feet and I fell. Chaos take the idiots who'd built San Angeles across an earthquake fault line!

When I got up again, I saw the earth tremor had sent the birds flying upwards. Fian was cornered now, trapped against the edge of the island, caught between lethal laser and lethal drop. I couldn't possibly reach him in time to help, and I'd run out of rocks. I grabbed my useless gun to try throwing it, and was shocked to see its green light glowing.

'Tell Morrath confirmed,' said the gun. 'Active power 3. Single . . .'

I didn't pause to wonder how or why it was working now, just turned off the safety and fired. I saw the figure in the impact suit topple forwards, the active laser still in his hand. Its glowing beam was heading straight for Fian!

I screamed a warning, but Fian was already diving to one side. The laser beam skimmed terrifyingly close to his blond hair, cutting through the wall behind him instead of his head.

The wall had already been crumbling before the laser cut through it. Now a whole section of it broke away, falling over the sheer drop at the edge of the island, and an impact suit clad figure tumbled after it.

I ran towards the edge, terrified Fian had fallen too, but he was scrabbling his way clear on hands and knees. I thrust my gun back in its holster, pulled him to his feet, and hugged him. We were safe!

Then the ground shook, reminding me we weren't safe at all. There was still the minor problem of the earthquake. We had to reach the dig site domes and portal out of here.

Fian and I turned to run back towards the centre of the island, but there was a sudden huge jolt that sent us tumbling sideways, grabbing at the ground with our hands to stop us rolling into the buildings that were shedding concraz blocks.

I waited for the ground to steady and right itself, but it didn't. 'Nuke it!' I yelled at Fian above the screaming sound of metal reinforcement wires snapping. 'The island's legs are giving way.'

His reply was drowned out by a sound like a clap of thunder. Drop portal! It was followed by a roaring sound growing deafeningly loud, and I lifted my head to see an aircraft flying insanely low and fast between the tilting buildings, heading straight for me.

I instinctively covered my head as it went over, and then skidded round to look after it. The pilot must have engaged maximum reverse thrusters in a stomach-churning manoeuvre, because it came to a standstill for a moment, hovering just above the ground. Two figures in Military blue impact suits jumped from it, and the aircraft soared off into the air again.

The two figures staggered as they landed, then started running towards Fian and me. For a moment, I stayed there on my hands and knees like a nardle, just watching them come, then I came to my senses, grabbed my gun, and aimed it at them.

'Jarra, it's me, Drago,' said one of the figures.

'You're lying,' I said. 'Drago would be flying the aircraft.'

He unsealed the front of his impact suit hood and tugged it down, showing tangled black hair and an outrageously handsome face. 'Marlise is flying the aircraft.'

I'd hardly noticed my wounds from the attacking birds before, but now they suddenly started hurting like chaos, and I couldn't seem to think properly. 'Marlise wouldn't fly like a lunatic.'

'Of course she would, and she does.' Drago laughed. 'Why do you think I fell in love with her? If it helps convince you I'm me, I could take my clothes off, but we really need to get out of here before this crazy place falls apart.'

It really was him. Only Drago Tell Dramis would joke about stripping in the middle of an earthquake. I put my gun in its holster. 'Sorry, Drago.'

'You naturally weren't sure who to trust,' said Drago. 'Let me put this harness on you.'

He put straps round my waist and over my shoulders. I glanced across at Fian, and saw he was wearing a harness too.

'What's this for?' I asked.

'You don't have suits, so we're getting tagged out in tandem.' He grinned at me. 'Hug me, cousin!'

The ground picked this moment to start shaking again, so I didn't argue, just hugged him. Drago clipped my harness onto his suit, put one arm round me, and spoke to thin air. 'Marlise, we're ready to leave.'

'Coming in,' Marlise's voice responded.

I stood there, hugging Drago and feeling embarrassed, then the island gave another huge lurch and I quit being embarrassed in favour of being scared stiff. A moment later, there was the roar of an aircraft overhead, and a beam locked on to the tag point of Drago's suit and yanked him upwards,

331

taking me along with him. I twisted my head round, urgently looking for Fian, and saw another aircraft with a beam that dangled two more figures. I gave a small sobbing sound of relief.

'Is Lorin still down there?' Drago shouted over the wind and aircraft noise. 'He's disabled his impact suit telemetry so we can't use it to track him.'

'What?' I screamed back. 'Who's Lorin?'

'The man attacking you. Captain Lorin.'

'He's probably dead. I shot him and he fell off the edge of the island. My gun had been disabled, so I don't know why it started working again.'

'Your guns started working again because Military Security turned them back on.'

'Oh I see.' I remembered where I'd heard the name Lorin. 'Captain Lorin was Rayne Tar Cameron's deputy, wasn't he? I thought it was Qwin Marston in the suit. Stupid of me.'

'Qwin Marston was involved as well. The Marius clan paid him and Lorin to try and stop you joining our clan. Marston's under arrest for murdering Rayne Tar Cameron. He'd somehow found out her command codes. We think she caught Marston using them to authorize Lorin to portal here, so he killed her.'

'Oh.' My numb brain tried to take that in. The flawless Rayne Tar Cameron had finally made a mistake. She'd believed Qwin Marston loved her, when he only wanted a transfer to Zulu base and access to her command codes. 'But what was the point in killing me and Fian now? I've already joined my clan.'

'Marston and Lorin were also militant Isolationists,' shouted Drago. 'They knew only you and Fian could shut down the alien defences and give us access to Fortuna, and they wanted to stop human culture being polluted by alien influences.'

I bit my lip. When I decided to gatecrash a class of norms at the start of this year, I'd had no idea it would end like this. I'd just killed a man, and Major Rayne Tar Cameron and His Excellency Captain Draven Fedorov Seti Raven, Knight of Adonis had sacrificed their lives for me. For chaos sake, Rayne hadn't even liked me!

I brushed mingled tears and blood from my eyes, and watched the teetering, crippled wreck of the Land Raft island recede into the distance, as the lift beam carried Drago and me to safety.

34

When we arrived back at Zulu base, Fian and I went to our apartment to endure the agonizing wait before I had my surgery. I was scared to death, not just of this cure failing, but also of it succeeding. If it worked, I'd have to live the rest of my life with an artificial web controlling my immune system.

All my life, I'd hated what fate had done to me, and desperately wanted two things. To be able to travel to the stars, and to prove I was as human as the norms. Society was finally accepting the Handicapped as being truly human rather than throwbacks, but after this operation I wouldn't be either norm or Handicapped. I'd have the stars I always wanted, but would I really be human?

I didn't want to go through with this operation, but I had to. There was too much at stake for me to refuse, and anyway I quite literally had no choice. If I changed my mind, said I wouldn't go through with this . . .

General Torrek would be back in command of the Alien Contact programme soon. He'd cared deeply for my grandmother. I was her Honour Child, born to carry her name, and he cared about me too. He'd never use Alien Contact emergency powers to order the doctors to do the operation without my consent, he'd resign from his post as commanding officer instead, but then Colonel Stone would have to do it and find it hard to live with herself afterwards.

I didn't want to put either of them through that, so I had to survive the torture of the waiting hours and go through this voluntarily. Fian wasn't saying anything about how he felt, but I could see by the look in his eyes that this was even harder for him than for me. I tried to fill the time with practical things that would help him if events went badly.

Military officers are supposed to record a farewell message to be sent to friends and family in the event of their death in action. This seemed a good time to record mine. I'm not sure how much sense it made, there was so much I couldn't explain because of security restrictions, but at least it meant Fian wouldn't have to contact everyone and tell them himself.

I sent the recording off to the section of Military Support that's officially called Life Events, and unofficially Death Events, because that's what they really deal with. Then I sent Fian off into another room for a few minutes, while I made another recording that was just for him.

'This is for Major Fian Andrej Eklund, so anyone else should stop watching right now.' I waited a few seconds before speaking again. 'Fian, I'm really bad at emotional stuff, so there are things I've never really said. I can't say them even now, because I don't know how to put them into words. I'm better at showing I care with physical actions, so . . . Remember every hug. Remember every night. Remember the way we'd watch our favourite nardle vid series and have fun acting out the scenes. I love you, and we may not have had long together, but every minute was totally, totally zan!'

I hesitated. If I was a truly good person like Candace, or Dalmora, I'd say something else now. Something about how I hoped Fian would find someone else one day, and be happy with them. I'm not a good person though. I didn't want Fian to be happy with someone else, even my own clone. I wanted him to be happy with me.

I wasn't giving up on us yet. I was going to fight for my life, and if I did live . . . Fian had been stubborn enough to still care about me when he found out I was Handicapped. Maybe he'd be stubborn enough to still care about me when I was . . . whatever I ended up being.

So I just ended the message, tagged it as being private for Fian, and sent that off to Life Events as well. Then I called Fian back into the room. 'You remember I had one call from my parents before they were killed?'

He nodded. 'Back on New York Dig Site.'

'All I remember of it is a huge emotional blur, but I recorded the call. I think I'm finally ready to watch that recording.'

'You want me to see this too?'

I nodded. 'We're past the stage where I shut you out of things.'

We sat on the couch, Fian put his arm round me, and I played the recording on our wall vid in split screen. One side showed a man and woman in Military uniform. The other showed a girl in a black impact suit, her hood tugged down, her hair tangled round a tear-stained face, her expression flickering between passionate anger and delight.

'It was a difficult situation when you were born,' said the woman with the hair that was like mine but longer. 'You were portalled to a Hospital Earth Infant Crash unit. I was still having medical treatment on a Military base in Kappa sector. Your father . . .'

'I was on assignment as an emergency replacement

commanding officer for a Planet First team,' said the man with the face that was a darker skinned, male version of my own. 'They were in deep trouble, they'd already lost one commanding officer, and I couldn't walk out on them.'

Part of me was caught up in the emotions I'd felt back then, but another part was catching details I'd missed when the call happened. I knew so much more about the Military now than I had back then. The insignia my parents wore showed they were both Colonels. They would normally have been together when I was born, but my father had been sent on emergency assignment. If a Planet First team had lost their commanding officer, then they must indeed have been in deep, deep trouble. No, my father couldn't just walk out on them.

'Hospital Earth rules said at least one parent had to go to live on Earth, or you'd be raised as their ward,' said my mother. 'When I suggested moving to Earth, your sister, Gemelle, was just shocked, but your brother . . . Jaxon said he'd rather kill himself, and I was afraid he really meant it.'

I remembered Jaxon breaking down with guilt at the betrothal ceremony. He'd described what happened when I was born as him throwing childish tantrums, but it had actually been worse than that.

'I didn't know what to do,' my mother continued. 'No one else could go in our place, because Hospital Earth said it had to be a genetic parent. We took legal advice, but we were told Hospital Earth made the laws on Earth so . . .'

The end of the call was the only bit I'd remembered clearly. I was crying as I listened to it again.

'In theory, we're on this assignment for at least another three months,' said my mother, 'but things are getting messy on this planet so we may have to pull out. If we do, then perhaps you'll let us visit you on Earth.'

Things hadn't just got messy on that planet in distant Kappa sector, they'd ended in a disaster that killed both my parents. I felt a stab of pain as the recording ended, not for the loss of childhood dreams of fantasy parents and happy endings, but for the death of two real and humanly imperfect people. My parents had abandoned their newborn baby, and that wasn't the right thing to do, but sometimes things are such a mess that you can't do what's right, you can only do the best you can.

'What now?' asked Fian.

'I've got a book to write. This cure may . . . mess up my memory. If it does, I'll want to know what happened and why I had to do this. There isn't time to write a proper book, but I can at least record myself telling the story.' I paused and chose my next words carefully. 'Perhaps one of us can tidy it up later and add the ending.'

Fian gave the promise I needed, without saying the words I didn't want to hear. 'Yes, one of us will definitely do that.'

So we spent hours hugging, while I talked into my lookup, and Fian interrupted me when I forgot something important. Sometimes we both laughed at silly little things, like Raven charging in on us playing *Stalea of the Jungle* games, and me arriving at the betrothal ceremony clutching a carton of cheese fluffle.

When Fian and I finished recording the story, we spent the remaining hours lying awake in each other's arms, because neither of us wanted to waste time sleeping. Finally, Military Security escorted us to the Medical Centre, and a doctor took me off into a featureless white room and asked me to lie down on a bed.

'One last thing,' I said. 'If I make it through this, I want to be the first person to see what I look like afterwards. No one should visit me before then. I don't mean doctors, I mean other people.'

'I understand what you mean, Commander.' The doctor sprayed something into my neck that sent me into nothingness.

35

There was agonizing pain crushing my chest and radiating down my arms. For years, I'd been determined that when I was 14 I'd take up my option to try portalling off world. Everyone told me I was a fool to do it, because Hospital Earth didn't make mistakes about diagnosing people as Handicapped. Issette and all my friends told me, Candace told me, the Principal of my Next Step told me, my teachers told me, even my nuking ProDad insisted on meeting me and going on record that he'd told me.

They all told me, and I insisted on doing it anyway, but I hadn't thought it would hurt this much. Why weren't the doctors sending me back to Earth? Were they going to let me die here?

I tried to open my eyes, tried to yell at them to send me back to Earth, but the pain was paralysing me. There was a jumble of voices that seemed a long way away. I couldn't work out what they were saying, but then one of them shouted above the rest.

'None of this is working. She's entering brain death. Get her back in the tank!'

Tank? Regrowth tank? My brain fought off the pain long

enough to work out what was happening. I was 18, not 14. Sending me back to Earth wouldn't save me, because I was already on Earth. I was dying.

I didn't want to die alone in a tank. I wanted Fian! I tried to say that but I couldn't move my mouth. The pain reached a crescendo of pure agony, then abruptly stopped and the world went away.

36

Someone was calling my name, which meant I was back out of the tank. I instinctively tensed, ready for the crushing pain to start again, but it didn't.

'Commander Tell Morrath, can you hear me?' That was Colonel Leveque's voice.

'Yes, sir.' I opened my eyes and saw him looking down at me. I was alive, things didn't hurt, and I recognized Colonel Leveque. I was still me!

'Please remain lying perfectly still,' said Leveque.

My jubilation turned to alarm. 'What's wrong? Why do I have to lie still, and why are you here instead of a doctor?'

'You have to lie still because your implanted web is still in primary initialization mode, Commander. We're under time pressure, so I'm here to brief you on recent developments while primary initialization completes.'

That did nothing to help the sick feeling in my stomach. What was going on here? I furtively tried wriggling fingers and toes, and was relieved that everything seemed to be there and working and humanly warm.

'We encountered some problems with the artificial control of your immune system,' said Leveque.

'I remember being put back in the tank.'

He nodded. 'Your immune system wasn't responding to the signals from the web. You went into brain death, so the doctors put your body back in the tank while they worked on a solution to the problem.'

'Brain death? I have brain damage?'

'Full brain function has been restored by significant regrowth of brain tissue,' said Leveque.

'They can't have regrown my brain. That affects memories and . . .' I spent a second scanning through memories of Nursery, Home, Next Step, and the events of this year. Nursery was a little hazy of course, but the rest of it was definitely still there.

'Your memories and personality had already been recorded by technology developed by Cioni's Apprentices, and were restored after the brain regrowth,' said Leveque. 'The use of this technology was forbidden under the protection of humanity laws after the Persephone incident, so it's preferable the issue of brain damage does not become public knowledge.'

'Persephone! How could the Military use the Persephone technology?'

'We were assisted by Cioni's Apprentices,' said Leveque. 'Again, it's preferable this should not become public knowledge.'

'What! The Apprentices still exist? How did they get involved?'

'You were in a tank for far longer than expected, Commander,' said Leveque.

'Longer than expected? How much longer?' Had I been in that tank for years, decades even? I thought of Fian getting older, giving up hope, finding someone else. He might have a wife and kids by now, and . . .

'Today is 10 November 2789,' said Leveque.

343

Not years then, just three months. I relaxed for a brief second before I thought of a new reason to panic. 'Three months! That means the Planet First vote has already happened! What did . . .?'

'Please let me brief you on events in the order they happened,' said Leveque. 'The Military had to inform Joint Sector High Congress Committee of the discovery of the alien home world. They were also told about the planetary defence system, and the problems activating the pedestal. On your first day in the tank, one of the Alpha sector committee members gave that information to the newzies. She was deeply prejudiced against those born with Novak-Nadal syndrome, and hoped to prevent Earth from joining Alpha sector.'

I groaned. 'So everyone knows I messed up. The Planet First vote must have failed and . . . Sorry, carry on.'

'There was a storm of angry debate on the newzies, so the General Marshal obtained Major Eklund's consent to give a full statement on your medical situation. When people heard the risks you were taking, public opinion swung back in your favour. There was also an unexpected development. Major Eklund's father contacted him offering the help of Cioni's Apprentices. Apparently, Major Eklund had never been told of his father's membership, because the Apprentices felt his preference for history over science made him an undesirable recruit.'

'Fian's father is . . . Well, that explains a lot, but why the chaos would he want to help me?'

'The Apprentices are dedicated to the advancement of science, and therefore eager for humanity to gain access to the alien technology. They wished to safeguard your memories and personality so you could successfully activate the pedestal.'

Now I understood. Fian's father didn't care about me, but he did care about science.

'After the web failed, and you were returned to the tank, the mood of Parliament of Planets was unclear,' continued Leveque. 'Lucius Augustus Gordianus opted to delay the Planet First vote to the last day of the current session of Parliament.'

'What date is that?' I asked.

Leveque frowned. 'Your memory of that is missing?'

'I never knew it. I've never been interested in off-world politics.'

'The fifth Parliament session of the year always ends the day before Wallam-Crane Day,' said Leveque.

'So the vote is in four days time, on 14 November,' I muttered to myself.

'The doctors are now attempting to solve the web control issue, by a combination of recalibrating the web and increasing the intensity of the light pulses.' Leveque glanced at a small object in his hand. 'Primary initialization is now complete and the web is entering the stabilization phase. That will take between one and five hours. If stabilization successfully completes, then your immune system problems will be permanently cured. Unfortunately, there is a significant chance of failure. I estimate a probability of . . .'

I interrupted him. 'I don't want to know the probability. Just tell me what happens if it isn't successful. I die?'

'If the web fails to stabilize, then control of your immune system will begin to slowly degrade over several hours. You would be returned to a tank while doctors work on a new solution.'

I'd be back in a tank again. Even if they eventually found a new solution, it might fail as well. I had visions of a nightmare future, where I went through this over and over again. That wouldn't be living, that would be . . .

I forced that thought aside. There were much more

important things at stake than my life, and Leveque was telling me these things for an obvious reason. 'So we may only have a few hours for me to get to Fortuna's moon and activate the pedestal. I have to go there right away.'

'That would be highly desirable,' said Leveque.

'Do the newzies know what's happening?'

He nodded. 'The General Marshal felt it was best to keep them fully informed.'

'But they don't know the chimera aren't extinct?'

'We've managed to keep that knowledge restricted to heads of sector and a small number of Military personnel. The General Marshal would like us to have access to the alien home world before making an announcement. It may,' Leveque added drily, 'cause considerable public anxiety.'

'Can I move yet?'

He nodded. 'You can move freely now. I must warn you, however, that your appearance has been affected far more than expected.'

'I'd rather guessed that. Is there a mirror somewhere?'

Leveque gestured at the corner of the room. I swung my legs over the side of the bed, stood up, faced the mirror, and gasped. I didn't look monstrous, but I did look shockingly different. The lights of the web were constantly flickering under my skin. I could even see them through my hair.

I rolled up the white sleeves of the hospital sleep suit I was wearing, and stroked my shimmering arms with my shimmering hands. My skin felt perfectly smooth and normal to the touch, it just looked . . .

At the start of this year, I'd joined a class of norms, told them a lot of lies, and convinced them I was normal too. There'd been no visible sign I was Handicapped, but now . . . No one would ever mistake me for a human being again.

'Major Eklund and a number of other visitors are waiting outside,' said Leveque.

'Fian hasn't seen me looking like . . . He hasn't seen me since I went into the tank?'

'No. You made your wishes quite clear on that point.'

There were a Military impact suit and a skintight hanging on the wall. I lifted them down. 'I'll suit up before I see people.'

'Your regrown skin couldn't fully harden while in a tank, so you'll find it uncomfortable putting on the suit,' said Leveque. 'I'll call a doctor to give you pain medication.'

I shook my head. 'I hate taking meds.'

'I'll wait outside then.' Leveque went out of the room.

I stripped off my sleep suit and put on my skintight without any problems, but getting into the impact suit was a struggle, my skin protesting at the harsh touch of the fabric. When I finally had the suit on, I pulled the hood up and sealed it, checked that the suit display with my name and rank was set correctly, and then stood still for a moment. The sharp stinging pain from my skin gradually eased down to a nagging soreness, and I gave a sigh of relief.

I went to the door, opened it, and walked into a large open area. I had a blurred impression of a lot of people sitting on chairs, but I was only really aware of the one standing up facing me.

'I knew it,' said Fian. 'I knew you'd come out here with your hood up and sealed.'

His voice was a mixture of exasperation and amusement. His long blond hair was tangled, as if he'd been running his hands through it. His face was strained, tired, and somehow older than before. I wasn't surprised. If I'd been waiting for three endless months to find out if Fian would live or die, if I finally had him back but knew it might only be for a few hours, I'd be a complete wreck.

'You don't need to hide yourself from me,' he said. 'I don't care what you look like, so long as I don't lose you. If it was the other way round, if I looked different, would you want to dump me?'

I shook my head. I'd first been attracted to Fian because he looked like Arrack San Domex, the vid star I had a crush on, but I'd stayed attracted to him because of all the things that made him so uniquely special. His intelligence. His stubbornness. His love of history. The way he could be grimly serious, and the way he could make me laugh. After all we'd been through together, what he looked like didn't matter so long as he was Fian.

'Of course I wouldn't,' I said, 'but the first priority is to sort out the pedestal. We can deal with personal stuff afterwards if . . . . if there's time.'

'There's going to be time,' said Fian. 'The changes to the web will work, they have to because I can't go through all that again, and I want your Military Oath that you won't hide your face from me after we've dealt with the pedestal.'

This was so typical of Fian that I had to giggle. 'Major Fian Andrej Eklund, you have my Military Oath that I won't hide from you.'

Keon Tanaka's voice spoke in typically lazy tones, reminding me that Fian and I had an audience. 'Jarra claimed she didn't order Fian around, but I didn't believe her. I certainly didn't believe he gave her orders. Amaz! I'd think it was someone else in that suit, but no one could fake the distinctive Jarra giggle.'

There was a ripple of laughter at his words. I took a hasty look round, and was startled by the number of familiar faces. Keon was sitting with Issette and Candace. Dalmora, Amalie and Krath were with Playdon. Colonel Leveque was sitting on one side of General Torrek, and a female

Commander I didn't recognize was on the other. Beyond her were the Medical team leader, Colonel Stone, Drago and . . .

'Oh nuking hell!' I stared blankly at the figure sitting next to Drago.

'Bad, bad Jarra!' Issette sounded truly appalled at my shocking language.

'Sorry, but . . .' The world seemed to whirl round me in a giddying fashion.

Fian's hand shot out to catch my arm and steady me. 'Colonel Leveque didn't tell you Raven was alive? I didn't know myself for several days. The doctors had to wait to see if there was brain damage.'

How could Raven be alive? For chaos sake, I'd seen the man cut in half! And that, I suddenly realized, was exactly the reason Leveque hadn't said anything about it. I'd seen Raven cut in half, so I'd have asked a lot of questions he didn't want to answer. Questions about why Raven hadn't been legally brain dead before the rescue team reached him. The Military had broken a lot of laws to keep me alive, which was perfectly legal because my survival was vital for the Alien Contact programme. They must have broken laws to save Raven as well, and that wasn't legal at all.

The important thing was that Raven was alive. The reality of that finally sank in, I stopped worrying about how it could be true, and just celebrated the fact that it was.

'I'm so glad you made it, Raven. I thought . . . Thank you. You saved both our lives.'

Raven's worried expression changed to a smile. 'I was just doing my job, Jarra.'

I turned to Colonel Stone. 'I see you didn't get demoted, sir.'

'I was strongly tempted to demote both Colonel Stone

and Colonel Leveque,' said General Torrek, 'but Fian talked me out of it.' He turned to the stranger next to him. 'Psych are ready?'

'Yes, sir. Media interest is at fever pitch. I'll join my team now. We'll play your pre-recorded announcement, then open the live link to the newzies.' She headed off down a corridor.

The woman was obviously a team leader from the evil Psych Division. I groaned at her mention of a live link to the newzies.

'My team's already on standby,' said Drago. 'The three of us just need to suit up and we can all head to the launch area.'

Drago, Fian and Raven reached under their chairs, produced impact suits, and started taking off their uniforms to reveal they were already wearing their Military skintights underneath. Playdon, Dalmora, Amalie and Krath were used to seeing people wearing just skintights, but I saw Candace hastily turn her head to gaze at the nearest wall. Issette was pretending to look at the wall as well, but I could see her sneaking furtive looks at Drago. Keon was watching her, appearing amused rather than angry.

I made a mental note to tease Issette about this later, and tell her she was a bad, bad Issette. If there was a later.

'Why are we going to the launch area, Drago?' I asked. 'Aren't we portalling to Gateway base?'

Drago paused for a moment before putting on his suit, unconsciously giving Issette the chance for some more furtive admiration. 'Isolationist agents attempted to infiltrate Portal Network Administration. Their plan was to stop you and Fian from reaching Fortuna's moon by sabotaging your portal signal as you portalled to Gateway base.'

'Sabotaging our portal signals!' I felt sick. I'd once seen a horror vid where someone tried to portal during a solar storm. The storm messed up the creation of the portal signal by the transmitting portal, so what arrived at the other end was just a twisted, dying lump of flesh.

'Military Security arrested the people involved, but we're playing safe by taking you all the way by ship,' said Drago. 'The Orbital Ship Portal Network is run by the Military and far more secure than the civilian portal networks, so we'll use that to travel between Adonis and Gateway systems.'

'Psych Division felt this method of travel would also provide more entertainment for the newzies,' added Colonel Leveque.

Drago, Fian and Raven finished putting on their suits, though they left their hoods down for now. Everyone else was on their feet too, apparently coming along to see us off. I'd stopped Leveque from telling me the probability of the web failing to stabilize, but it was obvious everyone else knew, and the look on Candace's face told me it was uncomfortably high.

We had a five-minute walk to reach the launch area, where several vid bees were hovering in midair, waiting for us. I stared past them, counting the array of fighters parked in front of a giant portal. Fifteen of them. At the centre of their formation was a survey ship, like the one Drago had landed on Fortuna's moon.

'The survey ship can take all four of us,' said Drago.

We stopped at the edge of the launch area, and Leveque attached something to the left shoulder of my suit. I looked down and saw a metal disk flashing amber.

'A steady green light will indicate the web stabilization phase has successfully completed,' said Leveque. 'A flashing red light indicates immune system control is degrading and you require medical attention as soon as possible.'

He stepped back. Drago, Fian, Raven and I walked on

towards the survey ship, with the vid bees chasing after us. I forgot about the flashing disk on my shoulder, as all my worries were drowned out by awed excitement. After a lifetime of frustration, I was finally going to the stars!

37

Drago opened the door of the survey ship. 'Marlise has run the pre-flights for us.' He gestured at the two front seats. 'Jarra, you're flying us. Fian will be your co-pilot.'

'I'm flying?' I shook my head in disbelief.

Drago laughed. 'You're finally leaving Earth, Jarra. I think you should do it in style.'

'I'd love to fly, but . . . Shouldn't you be co-pilot? I've never done anything like this so I'll need help.'

He laughed again. 'Fian's a qualified fighter pilot and can give you all the help you need.'

'He is? How totally, totally zan!' I turned to stare at Fian and saw him blush. 'But how did . . .?'

'The Military were worried Isolationist agents might try to destroy the alien sphere in Earth orbit,' he said, 'so Drago's team were ordered back here to help guard it. Drago and Marlise saw I was going crazy sitting around worrying about you. I'd already had some flying lessons from you, so they decided to finish teaching me to fly to keep me busy.'

'But you have to do an awful lot more than learn to fly to qualify as a fighter pilot, and you've only had three months.'

Fian shrugged. 'Sleeping only took up eight hours a day. Watching Playdon's lecture vids and eating meals occupied another four. That left six hours a day flying time and six hours in flight simulators. You can learn an awful lot in three months when you've got sixteen fighter pilots taking turns to teach you.'

I opened my mouth, about to eagerly say that Fian would have to give me fighter pilot lessons, but closed it again. I couldn't plan my future beyond the next couple of hours.

'Of course, I'm still useless compared to Drago and Marlise,' added Fian.

'Everyone is useless compared to Marlise,' said Drago. 'In our first flight simulator duel, she shot me to pieces in three minutes and seventeen seconds, and I fell hopelessly in love.'

I climbed into the pilot's seat, Fian sat beside me, and Drago and Raven took the two seats behind us. They pulled up their hoods and sealed their suits. I tapped the door control and it obediently closed, shutting out the nosy vid bees.

Fian pointed at the control panel. 'Jarra, hit the flashing light on your right to signal you're ready to launch.'

I touched the control, the light went solid green, and I heard a female voice on my suit broadcast channel.

'Zulu base to Earth Flight, your portal to Earth orbit is established and you are clear to launch.'

Earth Flight! I gave a startled laugh. They'd designated us Earth Flight, like the historic first drop portal flight to Adonis. That had to be Psych Division's idea.

The first bank of black fighters lifted smoothly off the ground. The centre one, with the silver flashes that showed it belonged to Marlise, led the way through the portal, followed by the fighter on its right and then the one on its left. The second bank of fighters rose into the air and followed them, and then it was our turn.

I engaged hovers and our ship lifted into the air. A survey ship was much wider than a fighter, so I took it slowly, literally holding my breath as we flew through the portal. I was prepared to see the blackness of space, and the heart-grabbing beauty of Earth from orbit, but I wasn't expecting the dazzling light sculpture ahead of me, or the vast wing of a solar array overshadowing me to my left.

'Engage thrusters and move clear of the portal, Jarra,' Fian's voice gently reminded me. 'Our wingmen need to be able to follow us through.'

I hastily engaged the thrusters and flew to join the group of fighters to my right. 'Sorry,' I said. 'I'm a nardle. I should have realized we were going through one of the portals they use to send fighters up to guard the alien sphere, so we'd arrive near that and the Earth Africa solar array.'

He laughed. 'It's an amaz view, isn't it?'

'It's totally zan!'

I didn't know which way to look first. There was Earth, blue mixed with the white swirls of cloud. There were the wings of the solar array, each one only paper thick but reaching out a vast distance. There were the constantly changing patterns and colours of the alien sphere's light sculpture.

'We need to move well clear of the array before we drop portal,' said Drago.

The fighters had all arrived and formed a neat formation around me. Marlise's fighter led the way and I followed along with the others. Fian leaned across for a second, checking something on the bank of controls on my right.

'Zulu base to Earth Flight,' said the voice on broadcast channel, 'you are clear of hazards and free to drop portal to Adonis.' She paused for a second and spoke with an odd emphasis. 'Zulu base to Earth Flight, are you ready for this?'

I giggled as I realized she was quoting the words from the original Earth Flight.

'Answer her, Jarra,' said Drago.

I briefly opened broadcast channel to give the answer Major Kerr had given. 'Earth Flight to Zulu base. I've been ready for this all my life. Let's do it.'

'Earth Flight, starburst ready for drop portal.' Drago spoke on the comms channel that pilots called ship to ship.

The formation of fighters instantly broke, scattering outwards. Ships only risked drop portalling in tight formation in emergencies.

'Drop portal countdown is set to ten seconds,' said Drago. 'Call it for us on broadcast channel, Jarra.'

I'd never done this, even in a simulator, so I turned my comms off for a second to ask a nardle question. 'The drop portal control is the red button on the right?'

'Yes,' said Drago. 'You've never portalled further than between continents, Jarra, so you won't know there's a momentary dizzy sensation on interstellar distances. That's perfectly normal so don't worry about it.'

Drago was both wrong and right. I'd portalled to an Alpha sector world once when I was 14, but I hadn't noticed any dizzy sensation, only blinding pain.

I spoke on broadcast channel. 'Earth Flight, prepare to initiate drop portal sequence on my mark. Mark!'

I hit the red button, and an automated voice started counting down. As it reached zero, a dust ring appeared ahead, moving towards our ship at high speed. It engulfed us and there was a split second of disorientation, then I saw the blue and white planet had moved position and its continents had changed shape.

'This is Adonis Orbital Traffic Control welcoming Earth Flight,' said a deep male voice on the broadcast channel. 'It's night here on the inhabited continent of Adonis, but we've got our lights on for you, and we hope you still think it looks like a beautiful world.'

I recognized another quote from that long ago flight. I laughed, looked down at night on Adonis, and saw something odd was happening. The swathes of lights were blinking on and off. It took me a moment to work out the population of Adonis had been watching our arrival on their equivalent of Earth Rolling News, and it had organized them to turn their lights off and on in unison. Nearly half a millennium ago, the original Earth Flight had left the Handicapped behind, but now Adonis was welcoming one of us.

'Earth Flight to Adonis Orbital Traffic Control,' I said on broadcast channel, trying to keep my voice from shaking and failing miserably. 'I can see your lights saying welcome, and it's truly the most beautiful sight I've ever seen.'

'Adonis Orbital Traffic Control to Earth Flight. We're glad to hear that, Commander Tell Morrath. Transmitting your flight path to Orbital Interchange 1 now. Your orbital portal is already pre-empted and established to take you through to Gateway.'

A flashing line appeared on my screens, but I didn't have to worry about it. The fighters had formed their formation around us again, Marlise was leading the way, and I just had to follow as we flew above the inhabited continent of Adonis, chasing the brightness of dawn.

I saw the orbital interchange ahead of us, and magnified the view on my screen to get a closer look at the six great portals floating in space. Five of them had red flashing lights around their perimeter, while one had lights that were solid green. I was confused by that, and by the fact it was deserted. There should be a cloud of ships around an orbital interchange like this, all waiting for their outgoing portal slot.

'Where is everyone else?' I asked.

'Adonis Orbital Traffic Control has cleared all traffic from Orbital Interchange 1 while we go through,' said Drago.

I was utterly grazzed. Few worlds had enough ships visiting

them to justify having even one orbital portal, let alone a full orbital interchange that could handle the vast cross-sector distances. Adonis was the closest inhabited world to Earth, right at the heart of humanity's space. Most cross-sector ship journeys were routed through its two famous orbital interchanges, but they'd dedicated one of them solely to sending Fian and me through to Zeta sector!

'Adonis Orbital Traffic Control to Earth Flight.' The male voice on broadcast channel was sharp with tension. 'We have a ship leaving Orbital Interchange 2 on an intercept course to you. They are not responding to calls and should be considered hostile.'

Hostile! My joyful mood was shattered. The lights of Adonis had welcomed us, but we had enemies too. What should I . . .?

General Torrek's voice spoke on broadcast channel. 'Alien Contact Command to Earth Flight. Confirming you are authorized to use deadly force.'

'Earth Flight acknowledging deadly force.' Drago said on broadcast channel, then swapped to talk on ship to ship. 'Fian, take the controls. Marlise, what are you seeing incoming?'

'Looks like an old style survey 6,' said Marlise. 'Those won't carry weapons, but . . .'

'Fire ship!' Drago and Marlise said the words in unison.

What was a fire ship? I glanced at Fian, saw he had co-pilot controls active, and locked off my own.

'She'll be set for proximity activation in the hope we're fool enough to attack her,' said Drago. 'Stay back and form wall ready for incoming missiles. Silver wing take first wave, then green, blue, red, yellow. Fian, remember the missile evasion simulations.'

The fighters moved to form their defensive wall between us and the incoming ship, and there was a full minute of silence. I didn't dare to say a word, just watched the dot on the main screen. It would intercept us just before we reached the portals.

'Fire ship confirmed,' said Marlise. 'She's on autopilot, packed full of missiles. There goes the hatch!'

The single white dot of the ship exploded into a whole cluster. The ship had dumped its missiles and they'd activated.

'Incoming seven and twelve,' said Marlise. 'Silver on seven.'

'Green on twelve,' said a male voice.

'Blue on seven. Red and yellow on twelve,' said Drago.

The fighters were streaking off to intercept the missiles. Our ship was alone now, still on course for the portal. I could do nothing except watch the two incoming waves of dots on the screen and listen to the babble of voices on ship to ship.

'If anyone knows what those missiles are, then I'd be really happy to know.' Drago waited a moment. 'Positively ecstatic to know. Oh, come on, somebody must have visual by now.'

'If it helps at all, they're plain pink,' said Marlise.

'Pink?' Drago made a choking noise. 'What missiles are pink?'

'Someone obviously painted them to hide the identification markings,' said Marlise. 'Engaging now. Fox ten!'

'Fox ten!' Multiple voices echoed her.

The dots of missiles started vanishing from the screen until there were only two left. Those two were still heading straight for us, with the fighters chasing after them. They couldn't possibly catch them in time.

'They're acting like Siren class missiles,' said Drago. 'Fian, try bounce two and roll on my mark. Mark!'

The view through the window ahead changed rapidly from showing the portal to showing a view of Adonis, and then random sets of stars span past at sickening speed. I glimpsed what I thought was a missile going past, and then heard two voices shouting.

'Fox ten!'

The last two dots of missiles vanished from the screen.

'All clear,' said Marlise.

'That's it?' Drago asked. 'I was expecting worse. Back in formation everyone. Nice work.'

'Jarra, you can take the controls again now,' said Fian.

The danger was over, fighters were reappearing all around us, and we were approaching the orbital interchange. I took some deep breaths to try and calm down, then unlocked my pilot controls.

Drago spoke on broadcast channel. 'Earth Flight to Alien Contact Command. Situation secure.'

'Alien Contact Command to Earth Flight,' said General Torrek's voice. 'The vid bees at Orbital Interchange 1 gave us an excellent view of the combat. Good job everyone. I'm considering recommending you for promotion, Commander Tell Dramis.'

'Not again,' said Drago. 'Please, not again.'

I joined in the laughter on ship to ship channel, and then Fian's voice brought me back to reality. 'Jarra, you aren't used to manoeuvring in space, so take your time and be very, very gentle with the thrusters as you go through the portal.'

I imagined colliding with the portal and physically shuddered. The portal I'd flown through at Zulu base was just designed to send ships up into Earth orbit, but would still be terrifyingly expensive. An interstellar distance orbital portal must cost a fortune, and a cross-sector distance one . . .

The first half of the fighters flew casually through the portal and I crept through after them. This time the feeling of disorientation was much stronger, presumably because we'd travelled further, but I fought it off and remembered to follow the fighter ahead of me and leave the portal area clear for the others to come through.

'Well done, Jarra,' said Drago on ship to ship.

'There's no need to sound so relieved, Drago,' said Marlise. 'You're the only person here who's ever collided with a portal.'

There was the sound of laughter, and Drago groaned. 'My lateral thrusters were out, and I couldn't exactly take it slowly given I'd got a whole pack of giant flying lizards chasing me.'

'That's another thing,' said Marlise. 'You were supposed to bring back a specimen for the scientists, but the idea was that it would be dead.'

I wasn't laughing at the jokes, because I was too busy looking at the third planet I'd seen from space within a few minutes. Gateway wasn't blue and white like Earth and Adonis and all the other colony worlds of humanity. This was a barren, waterless world with an unbreathable atmosphere.

Drago spoke on the broadcast channel. 'Earth Flight to Gateway base. Requesting clearance for drop portal to Fortuna's moon.'

'Gateway base to Earth Flight. You are confirmed clear of hazards and free to drop portal.'

I was startled to recognize Colonel Stone's voice. How could she be here in Zeta sector when she'd been waving goodbye to us on Earth? I'd no sooner thought the question than I realized I was a nardle. Stone had had plenty of time to walk to a portal and use a pre-empt to step through it to Gateway base.

General Torrek and Colonel Leveque would probably be in the Gateway Alien Contact Command Centre as well, ready for when Fian and I activated the pedestal. *If* we activated the pedestal. If it ignored us, we were going to look chaos silly in front of the whole of humanity.

Drago spoke on ship to ship again. 'Everyone change to the second stored drop portal settings.'

Fian leaned towards me and whispered. 'The control to the right of the red button.'

I tapped the control and saw the new settings appear.

'Jarra, your drop portal is set to take us to directly above the sculpture,' said Drago. 'The fighters will come through at higher altitude and fly circuits to guard us. There'll be no atmosphere and low gravity. If you bounce when you engage hovers for landing, don't worry, we've all done it.'

He paused for a second. 'Everyone, starburst ready for drop portal, then Jarra will call it on broadcast.'

I waited for the fighters to scatter, then spoke on broadcast channel. 'Earth Flight, prepare to initiate drop portal sequence on my mark. Mark!'

I hit the red button, and the automated voice started counting down as before. When it reached three seconds, Colonel Stone spoke on broadcast channel in a self-conscious voice. 'Earth Flight, take us to Fortuna!'

The dust ring appeared, enfolded us, and then we were flying above a bleak landscape of reddish rock. I saw the huge sculpture was directly below us, and didn't bother to look up for the fighters, just concentrated on the thrusters and picking a landing site.

'Wish me luck,' I said on ship to ship.

I made one turn to lose height, a second turn to line myself up correctly, and then landed. The newzies were bound to be showing images from the fighters, or from the vid bees on the surface of the moon. I was deeply thankful that I didn't bounce, at least not much.

'Earth Flight to Gateway base,' I said, 'we've landed on Fortuna's moon.'

Fian laughed. 'I'd try saying that on broadcast channel instead of ship to ship.'

I giggled, and said it again on broadcast channel.

'Everyone double-check your suits are properly sealed before we vent ship air,' said Drago. 'We shouldn't be outside for long, but it's stupid to take risks with your air supply so we'll each carry six oxygen booster cells.'

He passed round packs of oxygen booster cells, and I attached mine to my impact suit. I was feeling oddly breathless, but that was nothing to do with my air supply. I was about to step out onto the surface of Fortuna's moon!

Warning lights flashed red to say that ship's air was disabled, and Drago and Raven moved to the doorway. Fian and I tried to follow them, and collided with each other.

'Careful in the low gravity,' said Drago. 'Please don't try and see how high you can jump. Gravity is a lot lower here but you still have momentum and . . .' He broke off and groaned. 'I'm sounding exactly like the pedantic Military Academy lecturer who took my class on our first Environment H training trip. I don't want to spoil your fun, but there are vid bees out there that will be watching our every move.'

'We'll try not to look utter nardles on all the newzie channels,' said Fian.

'What's Environment H training?' I asked.

'Hostile environments,' said Drago. 'Basically, it's how not to kill yourself in them.'

He opened the door, jumped lightly through it, and Raven followed him. Fian and I took things more slowly, dropping gently down on to the ground. I gave it a furtive kick with one foot, found there was just a thin layer of dust over rock, then lifted my head and gasped. The planet Fortuna filled the sky overhead, its surface hidden behind a misty whiteness, and zigzagged by the bright lines of its defence shield.

Drago and Raven set off at a carefully controlled walk towards the tunnel entrance. Fian and I followed them in a rather less dignified fashion, and half a dozen floating vid bees appeared to chase alongside us. I was in a crazy exuberant mood, as if I was powered on something, and had to fight the temptation to skip or jump along.

There were a series of glows lighting the tunnel, and a lot more in the central cavern, as well as several piles of boxes and equipment. Of course, people would have been working here for months while I was in a tank. I was looking ahead at the pedestal, when I heard something crunch under my feet. I glanced down to see tiny grey fragments. I was walking on the dry, broken remains of chimera!

Drago gestured at the pedestal. 'I really hope you do better with it than I did.'

So did I. Oh, so did I! Fian and I walked up to the pedestal. I wondered if we should call the Alien Contact Command Centre before trying this, but it seemed pointless when they were watching us with the vid bees. I remembered how we'd done this before on Earth, and opened my mouth to speak, but Fian said it first.

'We're in this together.'

I giggled. 'Always.'

We linked hands, I did the countdown, and we reached out to touch the circle. There was an agonizingly long wait, and then a column of light flashed up from the top of the pedestal. The one on Earth had been ribbons of red, green and blue, but this was just flickering pulses of pure white.

Fian and I instantly turned and hurried back through the tunnel, forgetting all about trying to walk in a dignified manner in the low gravity. When we were outside, we gazed upwards at what everyone watching the newzies must have already seen. The bright lines of the defence shield around Fortuna had vanished, and the white mist was clearing to reveal the planet surface below.

'We have three probes in Fortuna's atmosphere,' said

364

Leveque's voice on broadcast channel, 'and the surface defences have not attacked them.'

'Look!' said Fian.

'I'm already looking,' I said.

'Not the planet, Jarra. Look at your shoulder!'

I peered down at the metal disk on my shoulder, and saw the light was a steady green. The way to Fortuna was open, and I was going to live!

38

After Fian and I were in contact with the alien technology on Earth, we spent ages in quarantine. This time the Military had already been analyzing the alien technology for months, and knew there weren't any hidden hazards, so we just had to have our suits sprayed with decontaminant fluid.

Less than three hours after sending the signal, Raven, Fian and I followed Drago through a portal, and arrived in a small, stone-walled room. The others opened their impact suit hoods and tugged them down. I didn't. I saw Fian glance at me, but he didn't say anything.

'Zeus has a roughly twenty-five hour day,' said Drago. 'It's just past midnight here. The clan would have stayed up to welcome you home, but I thought you'd be tired and prefer some privacy tonight.'

I nodded.

He gestured at the walls. 'You can tell by the stonework we're in the original building. Your rooms are in the much newer garden wing, but I thought you'd like a quick glance at the clan hall before going there.'

We followed him out into a corridor, through a wide doorway, and into a staggeringly large hall. I stopped and stared round it, utterly grazzed. When a grateful Beta sector built a clan hall for Tellon Blaze, they'd done it in style.

'This is genuine stone?' I asked.

Drago laughed. 'It's genuine.'

Once I got over the sheer size of it, and the height of the arched ceiling, I could take in a few details. The flaming torches lighting the room. The portrait of Tellon Blaze, looking much younger and far more human than in the official vid images. The ancient banners. The incongruous sight of a battered flag with an image of Earth. The . . .

'Oh nuke! Surely that isn't real?' I pointed at the chimera crouching in an alcove.

'That's only a flexiplas fake,' said Drago.

I relaxed and saw Raven take his hand away from his gun.

'The real one is locked in the cellar,' Drago added casually. 'Tellon Blaze had cut it in pieces when he killed it, then it was stuck back together and stuffed, so it was very, very dead, but he still had it imbedded in a solid piece of glass. Partly to avoid any idiot deciding to take cell samples and genetically salvage the chimera to study them.'

Fian gave a shocked laugh. 'The real chimera's in the cellar!'

'You'll be glad to know we only use this hall for formal occasions,' said Drago. 'There's another, far less intimidating, dining hall.'

He turned and led the way back into the corridor, along it, and through an archway. 'This is the garden wing. Still stone of course, but slightly paler.'

We walked along another corridor, turned right, and stopped outside a door. 'Jarra and Fian, this is your room,' said Drago. 'Your bags are already in there waiting for you. Goodnight.'

We said goodnight as well, went inside, and Fian closed

the door behind us. 'If Raven insists on sleeping outside our door here, then he'll be pretty cold on the paving stones.'

I forced out a laugh at his joke, but I was horribly nervous. The two of us were finally alone, and there was something I had to say. 'Fian, we need to talk.'

'You only say those words when you think you're facing total disaster,' said Fian. 'You're alive, Jarra. We've shut down the alien defence shield. There is no disaster.'

I shook my head. 'Leveque told me about your father contacting you. I don't know exactly what the doctors and the Apprentices did to save me, but it must have cut whole swathes through the protection of humanity laws. I know how strongly you feel about those laws.'

Fian pulled a face. 'Yes, the protection of humanity laws are important, but with so much at stake for humanity . . .'

He stopped and ran his fingers through his long blond hair. 'No, I have to be honest with you. I discovered there's a chaos big difference between debating ethics in theory and facing harsh reality. Your life was at stake, Jarra. I was perfectly happy to nuke the protection of humanity laws into cinders if it would save you.'

I wanted to hug him, but we were still in our impact suits, and . . . 'There's my artificial web as well. Every time you look at me, you'll be reminded of it. That's bound to start worrying you.'

'It won't.'

'How can you be sure?'

'I can be sure because I've been through this already with Raven. After they'd tried and failed to get your artificial immune system working, I was in total despair. The way the doctors dodged answering my questions . . . When I heard Raven was going to be all right, I had some hope again. If he could make it, there was a chance for you as well.'

Fian paused. 'Raven should have been brain dead when the rescue team reached him, but he wasn't because of his implant. That didn't just send for help, it did some things to delay brain damage. That's technically against the protection of humanity laws, but those laws were made by civilians living nice safe lives.'

He shook his head. 'It's the Military who do all the dangerous jobs. Every Remembrance Day, they list the names of the people who've lost their lives giving new worlds to humanity. For the civilians, those are the names of strangers, but for the Military they're relatives, friends, people they love. The Military are a family, and they aren't going to just sit around and let members of that family die unnecessarily. Sometimes there's nothing they can do, your parents were beyond any help, but . . .'

Fian shrugged. 'The Military take the view that things aren't always black and white, there are grey areas too, things that can do good as well as harm. The Military keep it quiet, but they regularly cross the line into the grey areas to save lives. I agree with them doing that. Raven's implant doesn't bother me, I'm deeply glad he has it, because it means my friend is alive instead of dead. Don't you feel like that?'

'Of course.'

'And I feel exactly the same way about your web.' Fian paused. 'I think it's time for you to show me your face, Jarra.'

I reached up to unseal my hood, but pulled my hand away at the last minute. 'I do look very . . . different now.'

'I don't care what you look like, Jarra. I care about the person you are.'

'Yes, but . . .' I indulged myself with a last delaying action. 'My hair will be a mess. I need to shower and change.'

'Your hair will be a mess.' Fian repeated, and startled me

369

by bursting out laughing. 'Jarra, how many times have I seen you work yourself to death on a dig site, and then happily yank down the hood of your impact suit? You've never, ever, worried about your hair being a mess.'

I looked round at our room. It wasn't ostentatiously grand like the clan hall, just a quietly comfortable bedroom. The only sign this belonged to the Tell clan, was a painting on the wall showing a formation of fighters. 'Have we got a bathroom?'

'We've got two bathrooms, so we can both shower and change.' Fian went across to the hover bags in the corner of the room, opened mine, grabbed a sleep suit and tossed it towards me. 'You've got fifteen minutes. If you're still hiding in there after that, I'll break down the door.'

I hugged my sleep suit against my chest. 'You can't smash up a Tell clan guest room!'

'Watch me do it,' said Fian.

The Cassandrian skunk meant it. I retreated into a bathroom, and carefully peeled off my impact suit and skintight. My skin instantly felt a lot less sore, and it felt even better after I'd showered on hot jet and then on dry cycle. Finally, I put on the sleep suit and checked myself in the mirror. The sleep suit seemed very skimpy, showing far too much glimmering skin.

I could hide in here for another five minutes, but it was better to get it over with. I took a deep breath, opened the door, and went out.

Fian was already in the bedroom, wearing a sleep suit himself. He'd been frowning at the painting on the wall, but he span rapidly round to look at me. 'Nuking hell!'

His words would have scared me if I hadn't recognized the expression on his face, and known exactly what it meant. He stood there for a moment as his mouth slowly widened into a grin.

370

'Jarra, are the . . . the flickering lights under the sleep suit too?'

My fears and my panic had vanished like a chimera running from sunlight. I grinned back at him and nodded.

'I really think,' said Fian in a solemn voice, 'I should get this terrible experience over with all at once. Show me the rest of you.'

I giggled, and slowly peeled off my sleep suit while he stood there staring at me.

'You're completely crazy,' he said. 'I'd love you whatever you looked like, but . . . don't you realize you're even more beautiful than before?'

'All my life, I've heard the jokes on the vids about the Handicapped being ugly. Even knowing I was no different from norms, it still had an effect. I really am different now. People will look at me and see . . .'

'They'll see you're stunningly lovely.' Fian took my arm and tugged me across to a mirror. 'Look at yourself, Jarra!'

When Dalmora dressed in her finest clothes, with her face made up and her hair adorned with lights, she looked like a dazzling vid star. I'd had a wistful moment once, watching her and knowing I would never, ever look like that, but the girl in the mirror . . . Her skin shimmered in a myriad intricate patterns, as mesmerizing as the light sculpture displayed by the alien probe.

I gave a shaky laugh. 'The doctors of Hospital Earth promised they'd do their best for me, and they did. I may not be normal or ordinary, but . . .'

'You never were ordinary, Jarra. If anyone doesn't like the way you look now, it's because there's something wrong with them, not you.' Fian paused. 'Can we turn the lights off?'

I nodded.

'Room command lights off,' said Fian.

The room went totally dark, except for the flickering lights under my skin.

'Nuking hell.' Fian repeated the words in an awed voice.

The shining girl in the mirror looked indescribably lovely now. I saw a shadowy figure step up to her and kiss her, and then I was too occupied with reality to spend time thinking about reflections.

39

It was 14 November 2789, the day of the Planet First vote. Fian, Raven and I had stayed on Zeus for a couple of days. I'd explored the Tell clan hall, and wandered its gardens and surrounding countryside, stunned to see some familiar plants and birds of Earth casually mingling with the native wildlife of Zeus. I'd met a bewildering number of my relatives. I'd spent a disturbingly emotional hour laying flowers at the memorial to Major Rayne Tar Cameron. I'd even visited my mother's clan hall, and joined in their celebrations of a distant cousin's triad marriage.

Somewhere in the middle of all that, I'd finally dared to look at the Tell clan family tree, which included Tellon Blaze's ancestry back to before Exodus century. I'd been startled by the details of my grandmother's marriage, and even more shocked when I saw the names of some of my ancestors.

Last night I'd hardly slept, worrying about the Planet First vote. Now we'd portalled back to Earth, and I was standing outside the hall door of a Berlin Main Dig Site accommodation dome, being a coward about opening a door and facing my own classmates.

'It'll be fine,' said Fian. 'The Military statement said your appearance had been significantly affected, and the newzies have been speculating about it for days. The class will probably be expecting something dreadful, but you look amaz.'

Raven nodded. 'You're beautiful, Jarra.'

'She's literally a glowing girl,' said Fian, giving a teasing look at Raven.

I took a deep breath and forced myself to open the hall door and go inside. The class were sitting at tables, eating breakfast and talking noisily, but there was a sudden silence as everyone turned to stare at me. I had a mad urge to run and hide, but then a voice spoke.

'Amaz! Jarra, are the lights everywhere, even your . . .' Krath's words ended in a yelp of protest as Amalie hit him.

I giggled. 'Mind your own business.'

Playdon came forward, obviously struggling not to stare at me himself. 'Krath, please remember that intrusive personal questions display a lack of respect that breaches the Gamma sector moral code. Jarra, Fian, and Raven, welcome back to the class.'

'Jarra,' said Dalmora, 'you look totally, totally zan. We'd no idea . . .'

There was another long silence, with everyone looking at me, and I felt myself grow hot with embarrassment. Fian is an amaz tag support, and stepped in to rescue me.

'Can we put on the wall vid to watch the final debate before the Planet First vote, sir?'

'Of course.'

Playdon turned on the wall vid, and set it to show Earth Rolling News. A couple of presenters were pointlessly explaining what their listeners must already know, that today's vote in Parliament of Planets would decide whether there were new planets for the Handicapped or they would remain confined to Earth.

Suddenly the presenters vanished, replaced by the live

link feed from the Parliament of Planets session on Concordia. It was early afternoon there, the vast hall was filled with people, and the symbol of humanity on the wall was glowing amber to show a vote was in progress.

'They're already voting?' I shook my head. 'They weren't scheduled to go to the vote for at least another two hours. What's going on?'

The rest of the class abandoned their breakfasts and came to stand around us, alternating between watching the wall vid and watching me.

Raven checked his lookup. 'Lucius Augustus Gordianus proposed the amendment. Desper Valden made the speech of opposition. The moderator called for a show of hands in the hall, ruled the final debating period unnecessary, and directed Parliament to move to an immediate formal vote.'

I still didn't understand. 'I wish I'd paid more attention to politics. Why would the moderator do that? What does it mean?'

'It means opinion in the hall seemed decisive, so the moderator felt further debate couldn't change the result,' said Raven.

Was that a good or bad sign? I'd soon find out because the symbol of humanity had just turned red to show the voting period was over. As the automated voice of the voting system started speaking, I felt Fian's arm go round me and leant gratefully against him.

'Amendment 2789/1 of the Planet First Charter,' said the voice. '4462 of 4490 planetary representatives cast their vote. Votes in favour 3570. Votes against 892. Amendment 2789/1 of the Planet First Charter has been carried.'

The last few words were drowned out by cheers and applause from the rest of the class, while I just stood there like a nardle. The Handicapped would have their planets, and that was . . . I buried my face in my hands for a second.

Fian guided me to a seat at a table, and Raven, Dalmora, Krath and Amalie came to sit with us.

Dalmora smiled at me. 'There was no need to worry, Jarra. The vote was bound to pass. The whole of humanity saw the live vid coverage of the missile attack at Adonis, so there's widespread public anger against both the Isolationist Party and those prejudiced against Novak-Nadal syndrome sufferers.'

Raven was staring at his lookup. 'The sector vote break-down . . . Every Beta sector representative voted in favour. That's incredible!'

'That's Fidelis, the united heart of Beta sector.' Fian turned to me. 'You must eat something now, Jarra. You've been so nervous about this vote that you haven't eaten in twenty-four hours.'

I shook my head. My stomach was still churning with the aftermath of tension. 'I'm really not hungry.'

Fian reached under the table for a moment, straightened back up, and plonked something in front of me. 'Eat!'

I blinked at the label on the yellow carton in front of me. 'Is that really cheese fluffle?'

Fian grinned. 'By now I'm used to you starving yourself when you're worried about something. I came prepared.'

I ripped open the carton, there was the glorious smell of cheese fluffle, and I grabbed the spoon and ate a mouthful. Blizz! Pure blizz! I didn't know if Fian had smuggled the carton in here himself, or if Raven had helped him, but either way . . .

'Fian Andrej Eklund,' I said, 'you are totally zan!'

He laughed. 'I know I am.'

I stuffed myself with cheese fluffle until I reached the bottom of the carton, then leant back in my chair while Dalmora and Raven talked politics. Krath joined in with some nardle remarks, but Amalie was silent.

We'd won the Planet First vote! I drifted off into a daydream of a future with new worlds for the Handicapped. It wouldn't happen overnight, but in five or ten years time those worlds would be moving into Colony Ten phase, with the first colonists going to live there.

I could picture my friends, Maeth and Ross, among those first colonists. Issette would never want to live anywhere other than Earth, but she might visit another world for a holiday. Candace would love to see the birds and flowers of another planet. Cathan would only go so he could complain about all the things that hadn't been built yet.

The scraping of chairs brought me back to the present. Playdon was standing in front of the wall vid, waiting to start talking to us. I guiltily hurried to help the others finish stacking the tables away and lining up chairs. Everyone sat down, and Playdon began speaking.

'Tomorrow won't just be Wallam-Crane day, but a historic occasion for Earth, so all Earth dig sites have begun a three day closure for the celebrations.'

There was a loud cheer from team 5 on the back row, which Playdon ignored. 'I remind everyone that I need your degree course applications by the end of today, so I can process and submit them by the day after tomorrow. Two weeks ago, I sent each of you individual reports with your predicted grades for both the theoretical and practical sides of this course, highlighting any areas of concern that you should work on.'

'You can't have sent one to Jarra,' said Krath. 'She was in a tank and . . .' He turned to look at me. 'Playdon didn't?'

I grinned. 'Yes, he did. It said I'd already been issued with the highest practical grade for the course, but had missed a large number of theory lectures which I'd need to view before Year End if I wished to improve my predicted theory grade to the one he would expect from a student of my ability.'

The class burst out laughing. Playdon waited for them to calm down, and started talking again. 'I've also sent everyone details of the various history degree courses being run next year by University Asgard. I understand Lolia and Lolmack won't be continuing to do a full history degree course.'

'No,' said Lolmack. 'We only joined this course because we needed an excuse for being on Earth. Now our daughter isn't just openly acknowledged, but a clan member, we no longer need to pretend to be interested in history.'

'We have learned some very useful things from our course though,' added Lolia hastily.

'I wish you and your daughter the very best for the future.' Playdon returned to addressing the whole class. 'Some of the rest of you won't be submitting degree course applications either, since they're choosing a different option. At the start of next year, the Military will be sending archaeological teams including both civilians and Military officers to the alien home world, Fortuna. I've been invited to lead one of those teams.'

There was a startled reaction from those members of the class who hadn't been told about this.

'I've spoken in confidence to some members of the class to offer them the chance to join my team,' continued Playdon. 'Our work on Fortuna will be accredited by University Asgard, and should lead to a new degree in xeno-archaeology, but it will obviously involve unknown hazards. I asked all those considering places on the team to think deeply about both the commitment and the risks involved. If any of those people wish to apply to one of the standard University Asgard history courses instead, then please just remain seated. Those of you who wish to go to Fortuna, please stand.'

There was a shuffling of chairs and a scattering of people stood. No one would be surprised that Fian, Raven, and I were standing, but there were startled glances at a couple of the others. I was only interested in the fact the whole of team 1 were on their feet.

Playdon's eyes went round the standing figures as if he was checking them off against a mental list. 'Thank you, please sit down again now. I . . .'

He broke off because there was the sound of voices out in the corridor. I twisted round in my seat, saw the hall door open, and Rono lead in the Cassandra 2 team.

'Playdon, the teams on Fortuna will be working in pairs, the same way as on the California Land Raft. Would you . . .' Rono's voice trailed off, and he stared at me. 'Chaos take it, Jarra!'

'I think our teams pairing up would be an excellent idea,' said Playdon, 'but please stop staring at Jarra. You shouldn't embarrass my students.'

'Sorry.' Rono shook his head. 'I just wasn't expecting anything so . . .'

Keren folded his arms and frowned at him. 'Should I be getting jealous?'

Rono gave one of his huge laughs. 'Oh no. Jarra's very decorative now, but she still scares me to death.'

'You're all coming to Fortuna then?' I asked.

Stephan grinned at me. 'Chaos yes! We aren't civilians, we're xenoarchaeologists!'

I laughed.

'We've been there for the crashing spacecraft, alien arte-facts, and social revolutions,' said Rono. 'We aren't going to miss the alien planet.'

Playdon started discussing the Fortuna arrangements with the Cassandra 2 team, so I took my chance to speak to Dalmora, Amalie and Krath. 'I don't want anyone to feel forced to go to Fortuna just because they've been on the same class dig team as Fian and me.'

Dalmora had her idealistic, shiny-eyed look as she answered me. 'It's an amazing opportunity, Jarra. The chance to join the first excavation of an alien civilization! I hope to make vids of our work. Obviously, we'd need permission from Military Security before any of those vids could be shown, but . . .'

I couldn't argue with Dalmora's decision. Playdon had chosen to accept a unique professional opportunity that gave him the chance to continue the work he loved away from ruins that held too many memories of his dead wife. Dalmora was making a career decision too in her own romantic way. Working together on Fortuna, perhaps she and Raven might . . .

I abandoned that thought and looked at Amalie. She was the one who really worried me. 'Amalie, you were so determined to get your degree and return home to teach at University Miranda. We may end up with a degree, but it will be in xenoarchaeology. Will that still let you do what you want?'

She shrugged. 'What I want doesn't matter anymore.'

'Of course it matters!'

Amalie sighed. 'No it doesn't, Jarra. There's a new plaque on the Spirit of Man monument, listing everyone who helped contact the alien probe.'

'Yes, I've seen it on the newzies, but I don't understand why . . .'

'Our class went to the unveiling,' said Amalie. 'At the top, the plaque lists the Military officers. Below that the civilians from Earth, then those from Alpha, Beta, Gamma, Delta, and Epsilon. Mine is the last name on the list, and the only name from Epsilon. When Krath and I visited my family last month, I was shocked by the way people . . .'

Her face twisted as if she was trying not to cry. 'I'm famous, Jarra. Not just on my home planet, but on every world in Epsilon sector. We're a low population frontier sector. Only a handful of our first generation of children are studying history or in the Military, so I'm the only one with the chance to do this. I represented Epsilon during the contact with the alien sphere, and I have to join the Fortuna teams so Epsilon remains part of some of the biggest events in human history.'

I pulled a face and nodded. After being the symbol of the Handicapped and of Earth, I understood the pressure Amalie was feeling.

'Jarra, I'm feeling horribly guilty about the grades,' Amalie continued.

'What? Why?'

'Playdon's message to me said I'm top of the class, but I know that's only because you were in a tank for months. It isn't fair.'

I was startled. When I first joined this course, I'd been obsessed with being the top of the class, proving I was better at everything than my norm classmates, but that seemed so trivial now.

'Amalie, I came to this class with a big advantage over everyone else and especially you. I was an Earth girl who'd studied history and worked on the dig sites for years. You'd had patchy schooling in Epsilon sector, and you'd never even set foot on a dig site. You've caught up with the theory, you were tag leader for team 1 for months while I was away, and you've more than earned your place at the top of the class.'

'But . . .'

I shook my head. 'There's no need for you to feel bad about it, because I think it's wonderful.'

I finally turned to Krath, and he immediately started

chatting. 'I think going to Fortuna is a great chance. We'll be civilian advisers, so we won't just get our degrees without paying fees, the Military will actually be paying us! How much do they pay civilian advisers, Jarra?'

I shook my head. 'I've no idea.'

'It probably won't be as much as a Commander or a Major,' said Krath. 'How much does a Commander get?'

'I've no idea about that either,' I said. 'I've been a civilian on a Military scholarship, then a Major, then a Commander, then a civilian, then a Commander again, then on reduced pay in Military prison, and then a Commander again. Military Payroll is still desperately trying to sort it out.'

'In prison?' Dalmora sounded shocked.

I noticed Raven's embarrassed face, and wished I hadn't mentioned Military prison. Fortunately, Krath was staying firmly on the subject of money. 'Fian must know what he gets paid.'

Fian grinned at him. 'Fian does know, but Fian isn't going to tell you.'

'But . . .' Krath's lookup chimed and he broke off. 'It's my nuking dad, messaging me about an interview.'

'He surely can't still be hoping that Jarra and I will appear on his nardle vid channel,' said Fian.

'No,' said Krath. 'This time he wants to interview *me*!'

40

It was Wallam-Crane day 2789, and I was at the Earth Olympic Arena in Earth Europe for a medal ceremony. I'd taken part in one here before, when I was awarded the Artemis medal, and this ceremony had the same massive audience and hovering vid bees. Even the layout in the arena was identical; the podium in the centre, with the Military seated on one side of it and the civilians on the other.

Some things were different though. Fian and I were wearing uniforms and sitting with the Military, there were security fields guarding the arena, and the General Marshal himself stood at the podium to award the special commemorative medal for all those who'd played a part in contacting the alien sphere and in finding Fortuna.

The other thing that was different this time was the darkness outside the lights of the arena. The ceremony was being held late in the evening, because it was timed to finish just before midnight Green Time, when Earth would officially join Alpha sector.

Fian and I were the first to be called up for the Fortuna medal. The spotlights hit us as we stood, and we walked to the podium with a storm cloud of hovering vid bees surrounding us. I could see the huge arena screens showing close-ups of our faces, and knew the images would be echoed across every newzie channel in every sector.

I wondered what the news presenters were saying about how I looked, and deliberately tilted my head back to let them get a good view. Fian and I were happy with it, and if anyone else didn't like it then they could nuke off.

The General Marshal gave us our medals, showing the red, green and blue twisted ribbons of light that had signalled the alien probe and led us to Fortuna's moon. We saluted and turned, but it was two long minutes before the wall of vid bees would part to let us through and back to our seats.

Everyone else was going up to get their medals now, so I settled back in my chair to enjoy spotting familiar faces among the crowd. General Torrek, Colonel Stone, Colonel Leveque, Drago and Marlise among the Military. Civilian advisers were next, including Keon of course. It was too dark to see the figures in the audience, but I knew Issette would be out there going totally wild with excitement.

The ordinary civilians followed, including the dig teams who'd helped find the artefact. I applauded like crazy for the little group of Playdon, Dalmora, Amalie and Krath, and then again as Rono led up Cassandra 2.

After that, it was time for some individuals to get special medals. I knew Fian and I were getting something, but Fian wasn't very interested in medals and I didn't care what they gave me. I already had the golden sunburst of the Artemis on my shoulder, and no other medal could ever matter much compared to that. I was far more interested in the medals being awarded to General Riak Torrek, to Mason Leveque, to Nia Stone, and, with the arena flags dipped in salute, to the absent, murdered, Rayne Tar Cameron.

I knew Fian and I were next when the arena screens started showing the familiar vid sequence of us sending the signal to the alien sphere. That was followed by another sequence of the Fortuna defence shield shutting down. When that finished, there was an expectant hush around the arena.

'The Pallas Athena,' said the General Marshal. 'Commander Jarra Tell Morrath and Major Fian Eklund.'

The what? I heard a startled gasp from Fian, which confused me even more. I'd never heard of the Pallas Athena medal, so how would Fian know about it?

We stood up again and went up to the podium. I got the new medal pinned to my shoulder, squinted down at it, but couldn't see it well enough to get any clues. I couldn't investigate further, because it was time to salute, and then Fian headed back to the seats by himself and the General Marshal stepped down from the podium.

A sick feeling of nerves hit me, but I clenched my fists and forced myself to step up to the empty podium. There is a medal that has its own traditions. It's always presented last at any medal ceremony, and there are some very special rules about who should present it.

I waited for the audience to quieten down, before saying two words that brought everyone in the arena to their feet. 'The Artemis.'

I had mixed feelings at this moment. Raven would get the Artemis, but not today. Because of the classified nature of many of their assignments, Military Security officers weren't presented with their medals until they left active duty.

I was sad that Raven wouldn't get the Artemis today, but glad that someone else would. Around me, the arena screens showed the vid coverage from months ago that had been classified code black until this moment. I heard shocked gasps from the audience as they saw the alien sphere fire its meteor defence and accidentally catch Drago's fighter. That was drowned out by the magnified voices of General

Torrek taking the base to war status and giving the kill order, and then Drago desperately shouting.

'Incoming fighters stay back, stay back! Remain at the portals. Do not engage! Do not engage!'

The sequence finished with Drago's battered fighter coming through the portal to crash land back at base. I finally said the name that everyone was waiting for.

'Commander Drago Tell Dramis.'

Drago came forward, looking oddly surprised. Only the General Marshal, General Torrek, Fian, myself, and a stray Captain in charge of the vid sequences officially knew about this in advance, but Drago should have guessed it would happen when he wasn't called up for an individual medal earlier. The fact the chimera weren't extinct was still a closely guarded secret, so publicly Drago was getting the Artemis for stopping us destroying the alien sphere, but he'd also gone down to Fortuna's moon knowing the chimera might be there waiting for him.

Well, Drago should have guessed this would happen, but he obviously hadn't. There was a dazed look in his eyes, and his air of boundless self-confidence was missing for once. I smiled as I pinned the medal to his shoulder, and whispered in his ear.

'You deserve this far more than I did. I couldn't have landed on that moon.'

He shook his head. 'And I couldn't have faced that operation. No one can say you haven't earned the Artemis by now, Jarra.'

We both turned to salute the General Marshal and the ranks of the Military, they returned the salute, and the ceremony was over. Drago and I went back to our seats, and everyone in the arena and in the audience relaxed, but no one was leaving. The arena screens were black now, just showing the time counting down slowly to midnight.

I remembered the medal mystery, turned to Fian, and saw he was still looking as grazzed as Drago had been earlier. 'Fian, what's the Pallas Athena?'

He stared at me. 'You don't know?'

I shook my head. 'My grandmother had a lot of medals, but not that one.'

'Last year, there was a major discovery by two researchers at University Mextli who were working in the same area as my father. It really put his nose out of joint when they won the Nobel. One of the two researchers was Military, so he didn't actually get the Nobel. Military officers are awarded the Pallas Athena medal instead.'

I blinked, and squinted down at the new medal on my shoulder. 'You mean that's the Military version of the . . . But . . . Why?'

'The Pallas Athena is for an outstanding contribution to human knowledge. I suppose the General Marshal felt that getting an alien probe to communicate with us, and gaining access to a ruined alien civilization, counts as that. You certainly earned it. I'm not so sure about me, but I'm not complaining.'

He paused and gave a shaky laugh. 'My father's in the audience.'

I glanced across at the nearest bank of the audience. Somewhere among the shadowy figures were our friends, Fian's mother, Candace, my history teacher, the man who'd taught me to fly, and the two kids from Home E161/8822. I hadn't known Fian's father was there too. 'You gave him an arena ticket? You're friends with him again?'

Fian shook his head. 'Leveque gave him the ticket, not me. My father admitted he arranged for that Deltan law firm to get the court orders, and he only helped us later because the Apprentices wanted access to the alien world. We still disagree on just about everything, even the protection of humanity laws. I think there should be some flexibility about them, but my father still thinks they should be completely ignored.'

He paused. 'I wonder what he thought when he saw me get the Pallas Athena. I hope he remembered all the times he told me studying history was a betrayal of our family tradition, and I was a disappointing failure who . . .'

He broke off because spotlights had flashed on, showing figures walking out into the arena. The members of the main board of Hospital Earth led the way, followed by Aadi Quilla Amarion, First Speaker of Alpha sector, and her honour guard of four Adonis Knights in full scarlet and gold regalia.

They took their positions in the centre of the arena, and the ground beneath them moved upwards so they stood on a raised stage. The Aadi of Alpha sector stepped forward, holding something long and slender that shone silver in the spotlights.

'The symbolic torch of Alpha sector represents our guardianship of the flame of human civilization. Centuries have passed since it was last presented to a new world.'

She paused. 'I am here today not to *give* that torch, but to *return* it to the world that lit the flame, to the birthplace of civilization, to the home of humanity, to Earth.'

The president of the board of Hospital Earth stepped forward to join her, and there was a hostile murmur from the crowd around the arena. He waited for the crowd to quieten down before he spoke.

'Today the role of Hospital Earth changes, as Earth becomes part of Alpha sector and gains representation in Parliament of Planets. It is no longer appropriate for me to act on behalf of Earth. The symbol of Alpha sector should be handed to a citizen of this planet.'

He turned to face me. 'The symbol of Alpha sector will

be received by someone who is not just *an* Earth girl, but *the* Earth girl. Jarra Tell Morrath.'

Spotlights shone on me as I sat there, frozen with shock. The crowd were applauding madly, but I literally couldn't move. Fian had to stand up, tug me to my feet, and push me towards the stage. I could see my own grazzed face looking at me from the arena screens, as one of the Adonis Knights came to meet me. It was a second before I recognized the resplendent figure with the ceremonial sword at his hip.

'Please take off your jacket, Jarra,' Raven whispered.

I was confused for a moment, then understood. I was representing Earth here, not the Military. I slipped off my jacket, revealing my sleeveless tunic, and Raven shepherded me up onto the stage, where I joined the Aadi of Alpha sector in a blaze of light. The arena screens were showing the countdown to midnight. There were only a few seconds to go now, and suddenly the crowd was yelling as if it was a Year Day party.

'Ten! Nine! Eight!'

Aadi Quilla Amarion lifted her arm to hold the silver torch high above her head. The crowd were still chanting numbers as a flame leapt up from the torch. The spotlights went dark, and now the arena screens all showed giant close-ups of that flame.

'Three! Two! One!'

The crowd shouted the last numbers, and the Aadi lowered the torch and held it towards me. I took it with nervous fingers, terrified I'd wreck the historic moment by dropping it. There were deafening cheers as I held the torch up in one hand. Earth was part of Alpha sector now!

I saw my image on the arena screens, and realized the real reason I'd been asked to do this wearing a sleeveless tunic. The screens only showed my head and upstretched arm, and in the pitch-dark arena those shone almost as brightly as the torch I was holding.

The screens held that image for a full minute, then fireworks shot upwards, filling the sky above the arena with a glorious rain of blue and silver, the colours of Earth seen from space. Fian came out of the darkness to put his arm round me, and we looked up at the sky as the fireworks above us were echoed by more displays in the distance.

For the past day, the Transits of every continent had been stretched to capacity as most of the population of Earth portalled to Earth Europe to be in the Green Time zone at midnight. There were crowds gathered in every shopping square, public place, and on the hillsides around the Spirit of Man monument. This was the biggest celebration Earth had ever known.

I felt the warmth of Fian's laughter against my cheek. On Year Day 2790, the two of us would leave Earth to help search the ruins of the alien world, seeking the answers humanity needed. I could escape from the newzies and the people who wanted to kill me, stop acting the Military officer, and return to being what I'd always been at heart. An archaeologist.

I'd dreamed of the stars, and now I was going to them, but I would be back one day. I'd return to the glowing ruins of Eden, the dark caverns of Ark, the breathtaking views of the Roof of the World, and the mad defiance of the California Land Raft. Earth was no longer my prison, but Earth would always be my home.

My name is Jarra Tell Morrath, and you only have to look at me to know I am *the* Earth girl.